MICHAEL MOORCOCK'S

THE ROADS BETWEEN THE WORLDS

THE ROADS BETWEEN THE WORLDS

BY MICHAEL MOORCOCK

Published by:

White Wolf Inc.
780 Park North Blvd. Suite 100
Clarkston, Georgia 30021
www.white-wolf.com

Cover Artwork by BROM
Three-Dimensional Jacket Background by Henry Gordon Higginbotham
Art Direction by Richard Thomas
Interior and Jacket Design by Michael Scott Cohen

C O N T E N T S

INTRODUCTION

Dear Reader,

In a relatively long career I've produced very little work in the science fiction genre. After discovering Alfred Bester's two extraordinary classics, which remain more original and innovative than almost anything produced these days and which were written in the mid-1950s, I found that most modern sf held very little interest for me. Bester's *The Stars My Destination* (called *Tiger! Tiger!* in England) and *The Demolished Man*, together with the best work of Fritz Leiber and Philip K. Dick and the anti-authoritarian parables of Kornbluth or Pohl, were the standards by which I judged the genre and pretty much everything in it fell short of them, at least until I began reading the work of J.G. Ballard and Brian W. Aldiss in E.J. Carnell's magazines NEW WORLDS, SCIENCE FANTASY and SF ADVENTURES and the banned early novels of William Burroughs, published in Paris by Olympia Press, which showed the real possibilities of the form. Unlike most readers of sf, I had no honeymoon in space. I found most hard sf, with the exception of Asimov's best, silly.

It was at this point that I was offered the editorship of NEW WORLDS, when Carnell retired, and I decided to encourage the kind of thing I had enjoyed in Bester, Dick and Leiber, together with the more experimental work being produced by Aldiss, Ballard, myself and an increasing number of writers like John Sladek, Thomas M. Disch, Samuel R. Delany, Norman Spinrad, James Sallis, Langdon Jones, Barrington Bayley, M. John Harrison, Harlan Ellison, Pamela Zoline, John Clute and others who had grown frustrated by the restrictions of a form which had ceased to produce the sharp, socially questioning stories of GALAXY in her heyday and increasingly revealed a natural affinity for the monumental orthodoxy its proponents, like Robert Heinlein, claimed to question and attack.

The irony was that in pursuing this somewhat uncommercial policy, I had to keep the magazine going. Increasingly, both to spread the budget (I rarely got paid for my own contributions) and to pay the costs, I found myself writing work which was pretty solidly in the pulp tradition! This is, I should add, a tradition from which I continue to derive inspiration and from which I take considerable pleasure to this day. But it was a little at odds with the riot of experiment going on in the magazine's pages, where writers like Ballard, Aldiss and Disch were busily rejecting every convention associated with pulp sf and developing a literary language which was to have an enormous effect, especially on fiction in English.

One of the other reasons for writing serials like *The Shores of Death* or *The Wrecks of Time* was to make a bridge between the obsessions of the sf "New Wave" (never our own term for ourselves) and the older sf traditions. I felt I had to offer the readers something a little easier than much of the work I was publishing with rather more enthusiasm than I published my own!

There is a traditional wisdom that I somehow emerged, a wondering naïf, from the pulp world to develop my work into the literary forms it takes today. The fact is my first novel was a realistic novel, owing something to Kerouac, set in the Soho underworld then familiar to me, while my second, published many years after it was first written, was an allegory. The first novel only existed, I believe, in a single manuscript and was eaten by rats some years ago in a Ladbroke Grove cellar. The second was *The Golden Barge*. Only later would I try my hand at sf. The first of these stories, written as a serial for Carnell's SCIENCE FICTION ADVENTURES, was *The Sundered Worlds* (published in *Von Bek*) and the second, written as a serial for Carnell's NEW WORLDS, was *The Winds of Limbo*. Unfortunately for me, Carnell was winding down the inventory when it seemed the magazine was not going to survive his retirement, and it was never published there. It appeared a year or two later as a paperback. I was still learning how to write fiction and decided, in my enthusiasm for Disraeli's *Coningsby*, to learn by imitation.

Unsurprisingly, there's little of *Coningsby* left in *The Winds of Limbo*, save for a few similarities of plot and theme, but it helped me understand what I had to do to write a political novel. I was working for the British Liberal Party at the time, writing speeches, pamphlets and policy documents, and the daily business of politics was inevitably interesting to me (I also learned why party politics was not a suitable career for me). What I have discovered in these early stories, is a similarity of theme and character. It seems to me that both Manny Bloom and Doctor Faustaff are versions of Joseph Kiss from *Mother London* and certain enduring themes and conflicts (inevitably those between "Law" — or Reason — and "Chaos" — or Romance) are discernible — the beginnings of the dialogue between Law and Chaos, Skepticism and Faith, between those contradictions which exist in all of us (and which I believe should be embraced rather than suppressed).

The idea of a multiplicity of space-time continua, each describing its own orbit and occasionally intersecting with others, which I introduced as "the multiverse" in *The Sundered Worlds*, was further explored in *The Wrecks of Time*. This novel also touched on themes obsessing a number of the NEW WORLDS writers in those days, especially Jones and Ballard. That Entropic Future, that wasteland of lost dreams filled the modern romantic soul with the same profound feelings which had celebrated the Gothic past a century or so earlier. Shelley's savage mountains had been replaced by Ballard's hallucinatory beaches, but the perceptions had a lot in common. Ruins still had their old appeal, but now we could describe entire worlds of ruins, for we had grown up in such worlds and they were absolutely, relentlessly real. My first memories are of exploding rockets and aerial dog-fights, of the London Blitz (as in *Mother London*). Ballard had survived a childhood in the Japanese camps (as in *Empire of The Sun*). A teenager, Aldiss had served in the jungles of Malaya (as in *A Soldier Erect*). Between us, we had known a lot of terror, a lot of ruins and a lot of blasted landscapes. They were complex symbols for us. The worlds we described were not exaggerated. They were versions of what we had seen. We turned to science fiction as the medium best suited for our particular understanding of our own world. We were neither playing games nor indulging ourselves in subtle escapism. We were trying to describe what had happened to us.

A literature attempting to realize such ambitions can sometimes seem raw, crude and, of course, vulgar, profoundly unfamiliar to ordinary middle class people whose culture is designed to resist and deny unpleasant information and which rewards lies while penalizing truth, but it almost always has a vitality which those works it influences lack. A similar phenomenon might be perceived in the work of sophisticated writers like Hammett, Chandler and Cain, who had turned the pulp urban adventure story into an extremely effective literary form a generation or two earlier. Just as BLACK MASK had attracted them, so GALAXY attracted Bester or Ballard. For my own part, and being rather younger than the others, I looked to the somewhat wilder delights of PLANET STORIES which had made the science fantasy story its own and it is this enthusiasm, I suspect, which most characterizes these stories. I always found it hard to accept the rationalist parameters of conventional, and in my interpretation, insanely conservative pulp sf, whose concerns were so successfully parodied a few years ago in Norman Spinrad's *The Iron Dream* (the sf novel Adolf Hitler might have written).

This conflict between an image chiefly used as a symbol and one used as a piece of stage machinery designed to suspend disbelief, is probably evident in all these stories, but less, I would guess, in the last one, which was where I gained sufficient confidence to use the rationalist apparatus developed predominantly by US pulp writers in the 30s, and by the minor successors of H.G. Wells in England. In most of my sf thereafter, and in common with other NEW WORLDS writers, I emphasized the symbolic function of the image, making it work thematically *as narrative*, as I did a year or two later with *Behold The Man*, which was interpreted one way in the literary reviews and another in the sf reviews. Neither notices were, in the main, unsympathetic, but the sf critics saw the story primarily as a tabu-breaking development of the time travel story, while the literary press understood the time travel element to be no more than a means of exploring the story's theme. I have never had trouble with conflicting interpretations of my work. Once the story is published, it belongs to the reader.

Nowadays good sf critics, unlike their petrified literary counterparts, are able to bring a far wider range of understanding and experience to almost any work of fiction. Most sf critics are also easily distinguished from their general literary counterparts because they condescend to what is poorly imagined, stale or too simple-minded, rather than castigate or ignore that which is vital, immediate, complex and original. I am afraid that the stories here would not come up to their present standards. They were written quickly and the first draft sent to a copy-editor, the proofs sent to a proof-reader. Between the pages leaving my typewriter and publication there was generally no point where I was able to read the stories. I have, with John Davey's help, made the few revisions necessary for inclusion here, but have otherwise had the sense not to begin tinkering with them. Whatever vitality they possess has not been refined to extinction.

These novels owe much to writers like Leigh Brackett and Charles Harness, whose metaphysical science fantasies were published so boisterously in PLANET STORIES and STARTLING STORIES. I dedicate them to all aspiring writers and offer them the two most important lessons I learned from Alfie Bester and William Shakespeare: Never worry about seeming vulgar. And never be too proud to steal a decent plot.

Yours,
Michael Moorcock
Lost Pines,
Texas.
December 1995

RENARK VON BEK, *Count of the Rim, removed the spent shells from his Purdy and regarded the angelic corpse at his feet with a certain distant pity. It was unrealistic to offer the creatures mercy, but he loathed killing them. And they were always so surprised. These days, von Bek loaded nothing but angel shot. Anything else he could handle with his Webley .45, a little bit of nerve and experience.*

He lifted his eyes to observe the surrounding flames.

It had been an impossible age since he had first become the thing he was, a wanderer across the multiverse, walking the moonbeam roads between the worlds. He had known so many worlds, so many identities, each a minute variant of the other. He had profound experience of the truth that time and space were not linear but a field and the field proliferated constantly, each fresh wave producing such minuscule variations in billions of realities that to the inexperienced traveler it was impossible to tell one plane of the multiverse from another. It was only when you learned to traverse the moonbeams, which crossed and recrossed those billions of scales in such a way as to create short-cuts from one plane-cluster to another, that you became a true walker of the roads between the worlds, carrying a million routes or more in your head, voyaging to versions of reality far removed from your own.

Renark von Bek was the acknowledged master of guide-sensers, the first choice of any who required help to travel the multiverse. Because so much of the multiverse existed inside his head, he sought to forget what he could in habits founded in tradition, even orthodoxy. Others of his kind considered the Purdy elephant gun an affectation, but it worked for him and he was comfortable with it. His rather conservative costume of a 19th century big-game hunter had earned him the nickname, amongst those familiar with his references, of "Allan Quatermain", the famous Victorian hunter and explorer who discovered King Solomon's Mines and was an influential negotiator for Disraeli's "African Purchase" of 1880. He was best remembered, these days, as the model for Sir Winston Churchill, the hero of the popular boys' series during the 1930s and 1940s.

Von Bek resheathed his wonderful gun and looked for a way

out of the firmament. Unless he thought quickly, he was facing at least a thousand years of boredom. He remembered his earliest encounter with the multiverse, when his path had crossed with that of Doctor Faustaff, the portly Don Juan, who had driven his Cadillac into the heart of a singular plot to recreate Earth's archetype and sought, in that story, a route through the corrupted scales of a billion deliquescent planes. He was running out of chances. He regarded the odds with cultivated defiance. He intended to beat them. Doctor Faustaff, and those close versions of him existing elsewhere about the multiverse, was someone for whom he felt a special fondness. Of course, von Bek himself had been a very different person, in those days, when they had first met...

THE WRECKS OF TIME

For Jimmy Ballard

When all the world dissolves,
And every creature shall be purified,
All place shall be hell that is not heaven.
— Christopher Marlowe, *Doctor Faustus*

P R O L O G U E

There they lay, outside of space and time, each hanging in its separate limbo, each a planet called Earth. Fifteen globes, fifteen lumps of matter sharing a name. Once they might have looked the same, too, but now they were very different. One was comprised almost solely of desert and ocean with a few forests of gigantic, distorted trees growing in the northern hemisphere; another seemed to be in perpetual twilight, a planet of dark obsidian; yet another was a honeycomb of multicoloured crystal and another had a single continent that was a ring of land around a vast lagoon. The wrecks of Time, abandoned and dying, each with a decreasing number of human inhabitants for the most part unaware of the doom overhanging their worlds. These worlds existed in a kind of subspacial *well* created in furtherance of a series of drastic experiments...

CHAPTER ONE

THE GREAT AMERICAN DESERT

In Doctor Faustaff's code-book this world was designated as Earth 3. The doctor steered his flame-red Cadillac convertible along the silted highway that crossed the diamond-dry desert, holding the wheel carefully, like the captain of a schooner negotiating a treacherous series of sandbanks.

The desert stretched on all sides, vast and lonely, harsh and desolate beneath the intense glare of the sun swelling at its zenith in the metallic blue sky. On this alternate Earth there was little but desert and ocean, the one a flat continuation of the other.

The doctor hummed a song to himself as he drove, his bulk sprawling across both front seats. Sunlight glinted off the beads of sweat on his shiny red face, caught the lenses of his polaroid glasses and brightened those parts of the Cadillac not yet dulled by the desert dust. The engine roared like a beast and Doctor Faustaff chanted mindlessly to its rhythm.

He was dressed in an Hawaiian shirt and gold beach-shorts, a pair of battered sneakers on his feet and a baseball cap tilted on his head. He weighed at least two hundred and eighty pounds and was a good six and a half feet tall. A big man. Though he drove with care his body was completely relaxed and his mind was at rest. He was as at home in this environment as he was in more than a dozen others. The ecology of this Earth could not, of course, support human life. It did not. Doctor Faustaff and his teams supported human life here and on all but two of the other alternates. It was a big responsibility. The doctor carried it with a certain equanimity.

The capital of Greater America, Los Angeles, was two hours behind him and he was heading for San Francisco where he had his headquarters on this alternate Earth. He would be there the next day and planned to stop at a motel he knew en route, spend the night there, and continue in the morning.

Peering ahead of him Faustaff suddenly saw what appeared to be a human figure standing by the side of the highway. As he drove closer he saw that it was a girl dressed only in a swimsuit, waving at him as he approached. He slowed down. The girl was a pretty redhead, her hair long and straight, her nose fairly sharp and freckled. Her mouth was large and pleasant.

Faustaff stopped the car beside the girl.

"What's the trouble?"

"Truck driver was giving me a lift to 'Frisco. He dumped me when I wouldn't go and play amongst the cactus with him." Her voice was soft and a trifle ironic.

"Didn't he realize you could have died before someone else came along?"

"He might have liked that. He was very upset."

"You'd better get in." Most young women attracted Faustaff and the redhead particularly appealed to him. As she squeezed into the passenger seat beside him he began to breathe a little more heavily than usual. Her face seemed to assume a more serious expression as he glanced at her but she said nothing.

"My name's Nancy Hunt," she said. "I'm from L.A. You?"

"Doctor Faustaff, I live in 'Frisco."

"A doctor — you don't look like a doctor — a businessman more, I guess, but even then — a painter, maybe."

"Well, I'm sorry to say I'm a physicist — a physicist of all work you could say." He grinned at her and she grinned back, her eyes warming. Like most women she was already attracted by Faustaff's powerful appeal. Faustaff accepted this as normal and had never bothered to work out why he should be so successful in love. It might be his unquestioning enjoyment of love-making and general liking for women. A kindly nature and an uncomplicated appreciation for all the bodily pleasures, a character that demanded no sustenance from others, these were probably the bases for Faustaff's success with women. Whether eating, boozing, smoking, love-making, talking, inventing, helping people or giving pleasure in general, Faustaff did it with such spontaneity, such relaxation, that he could not fail to be attractive to most people.

"What are you going to 'Frisco for, Nancy?" he asked.

"Oh, I just felt like traveling. I was with this swimming party, I got sick of it, I walked out on to the street and saw this truck coming. I thumbed it and asked the driver where he was going. He said 'Frisco — so I decided to go to 'Frisco."

Faustaff chuckled. "Impulsive. I like that."

"My boyfriend calls me moody, not impulsive," she smiled.

"Your boyfriend?"

"Well, my ex-boyfriend as from this morning I suppose. He woke up, sat up in bed and said 'Unless you marry me, Nancy, I'm going now'. I didn't want to marry him and told him so. He went." She laughed. "He was a nice guy."

The highway wound on through the barren world and Faustaff and Nancy talked until naturally they moved closer together and Faustaff put his arm around the girl and hugged her and a little later kissed her.

By late afternoon they were both relaxed and content to enjoy one another's company silently.

The convertible sped on, thudding tyres and pumping pistons, vibrating chassis, stink and all, sand slashing against the windscreen and the big yellow sun in the hot blue above. The vast, gleaming desert stretched for hundreds of miles in all directions, its only landmarks the few filling stations and motels along the rare highways, the occasional mesa and clumps of cactus. Only the City of Angels, in the exact centre of the desert, lay inland. All other cities, like San Francisco, New Orleans, Saint Louis, Santa Fe, Jacksonville, Houston and Phoenix, lay on the coast. A visitor from another Earth would not have recognized the continental outline.

Doctor Faustaff chanted wordlessly to himself as he drove, avoiding the occasional crater in the highway, or the places where sand had banked up heavily.

His chant and his peace were interrupted by a buzzing from the dashboard. He glanced at the girl and made a decision with a slight shrug of his shoulders. He reached inside the glove compartment and flicked a hidden switch there. A voice, urgent and yet controlled, began to come from the radio.

"'Frisco calling Doctor F. 'Frisco calling Doctor F."

"Doctor F. receiving," said Faustaff watching the road ahead and easing off a little on the accelerator. Nancy frowned.

"What's that?" she asked.

"Just a private radio — keep in touch with my headquarters this way."

"Crazy," she said.

"Doctor F. receiving you," he said deliberately. "Suggest you consider Condition C." Faustaff warned his base that he had someone with him.

"Understood. Two things. A U.M. situation is anticipated imminent on E-15, Grid areas 33, 34, 41, 42, 49 and 50. Representatives on E-15 have asked for help. Would suggest you use I-effect to contact."

"It's that bad?"

"From what they said, it's that bad."

"Okay. Will do so as soon as possible. You said *two* things."

"We found a tunnel — or traces of one. Not one of ours. A D-squader we think. He's somewhere in your area, anyway. Thought we'd warn you."

Faustaff wondered suddenly if he'd been conned and he looked at Nancy again.

"Thanks," he said to the radio. "I'm arriving in 'Frisco tomorrow. Keep me informed of any emergency."

"Okay, doctor. Cutting out."

Faustaff put his hand into the glove compartment again and flicked the switch off.

"Phew!" grinned Nancy. "If that was a sample of the kind of talk you physicists go in for I'm glad I only had to learn Esperanto at school."

Faustaff knew that he should feel suspicious of her but couldn't believe that she was a threat.

His 'Frisco office did not use the radio unless it was important. They had told him that an Unstable Matter Situation was imminent on the fifteenth and last alternate Earth. An Unstable Matter Situation could mean the total break-up of a planet. Normally, representatives of his team there could cope with a U.M.S. If they had asked for help it meant things were very bad. Later Faustaff would have to leave the girl somewhere and use the machine that lay in the trunk of his car — a machine called an invoker, which could summon one of Faustaff's representatives through the subspacial levels so that Faustaff could talk with him directly and find out exactly what was happening on Earth Fifteen. The other piece of information concerned his enemies, the mysterious D-squad who were, Faustaff believed, actually responsible for creating the U.M. Situations wherever they arose. At least one of the D-squad was already on this Earth and could be after him. That was why he knew he should suspect Nancy Hunt and be cautious. Her appearance on the highway *was* mysterious, after all, although he was still inclined to believe her story.

She grinned at him again and reached into his shirt pocket to get cigarettes and his lighter, putting a cigarette between his lips and cupping the flame of the lighter so that he was forced to bend his large head towards it.

As evening came and the sun began to set the sky awash with colours, a motel-hoarding showed up. The sign read :

LA PLEJ BON AN MOTELON
Nagejo — Muziko — Amuzoj

A little later they could just make out the buildings of the motel and another sign.

"PLUV ATA MORGAU"
Bonvolu esti kun ni

Faustaff read Esperanto fluently enough. It was the official language, though few people spoke it in everyday life. The signs offered him the best motel, swimming, music and amusements. It had humorously been called *The Rain Tomorrow* and invited him to join the host.

Several more hoardings later they turned off the road into the car park. There were only two other cars there under the shade of the awning. One was a black Ford Thunderbird, the other was a white English M.G. A pretty girl in a frilly ballerina skirt that was obviously part of her uniform, a peaked cap on her head, strode towards them as they got stiffly out of the car.

Faustaff winked at her, his body dwarfing her. He put his sunglasses in his pocket and wiped his forehead with a yellow handkerchief.

"Any cabins?" he asked.

"Sure," smiled the girl, glancing quickly from Faustaff to Nancy. "How many?"

"One double or two singles," he said. "It doesn't matter."

"Not sure we've got a bed to take you, mister," she said.

"I curl up small," Faustaff grinned. "Don't worry about it. I've got some valuables in my car — if I close the roof and lock it will they be safe enough?"

"The only thieves in these parts are the coyotes," she said, "though they'll be learning to drive soon when they find that cars are all that's left to steal."

"Business bad?"

"Was it ever good?"

"There are quite a few motels between here and 'Frisco," Nancy said, linking her arm in Faustaff's. "How do they survive?"

"Government grants mainly," she replied. "There've got to be filling stations and motels through the Great American Outback, haven't there? Otherwise how would anyone get to Los Angeles?"

"Plane?" the redhead suggested.

"I guess so," said the girl. "But the highways and motels were here before the airlines, so I guess they just developed. Anyway some people actually *like* crossing the desert by car."

Faustaff got back into the car and operated the hood control. It hummed and extended itself, covering the automobile. Faustaff locked it and got out again. He locked the doors. He unlocked the trunk, flipped a switch on a piece of equipment, relocked it. He put his arm around the redhead and said: "Right, let's get some food."

The girl in the cap and the skirt led the way to the main building. Behind it were about twelve cabins.

There was one other customer in the restaurant. He sat near the window, looking out at the desert. A big full moon was rising.

Faustaff and the redhead sat down at the counter and looked at the menu. It offered steak or hamburger and a variety of standard trimmings. The girl who'd first greeted them came through a door at the back and said: "What'll it be?"

"You do all the work around here?" asked Nancy.

"Mostly. My husband runs the gas pumps and does the heavy chores. There isn't much to do except maintain the place."

"I guess so," said Nancy. "I'll have a jumbo steak, rare with fries and salad."

"I'll have the same, but four portions," said Faustaff. "Then three of your Rainbow Sodas and six cups of coffee with cream."

"We should have more customers like you," the girl said without raising an eyebrow. She looked at Nancy. "Want anything to follow, honey?"

The redhead grinned. "I'll have vanilla icecream and coffee with cream."

"Go and sit down. It'll be ten minutes."

They crossed to a window table. For the first time Faustaff saw the face of the other customer. He was pale, with his close-cropped black hair growing in a widow's peak, a neat, thin black beard and moustache, his features ascetic, his lips pursed as he stared at the moon. He turned suddenly and glanced at Faustaff, gave a slight inclination of the head and looked back at the moon. His eyes had been bright, black and sardonic.

A little while later the girl came with the order on a big tray. "Your other steaks are in that dish," she said as she set it on the table. "And your trimmings are in those two smaller dishes. Okay?"

"Fine," Faustaff nodded.

The girl put all the contents of the tray on to the table and then stood back. She hesitated and then looked at the other customer.

"Anything else you want — er — Herr Kloset... sir...?"

"Klosterheim," he said smiling at her. Although his expression was perfectly amiable, there was still a touch of the sardonic gleam Faustaff had seen earlier. It seemed to faze the girl. She just grunted and hurried back to the counter.

Klosterheim nodded again at Faustaff and Nancy.

"I am a visitor to your country I am afraid," he said. "I should have invented some sort of pseudonym that could be more easily pronounced."

Faustaff had his mouth full of steak and couldn't respond at once, but Nancy said politely: "Oh, and where are you from, Mr...?"

"Klosterheim," he laughed. "Well, my present home is in Sweden."

"Over here on business or holiday?" Faustaff asked carefully. Klosterheim was lying.

"A little of both. This desert is magnificent isn't it?"

"Hot, though," giggled the redhead. "I bet you're not used to this where you come from."

"Sweden does have quite warm summers," Klosterheim replied.

Faustaff looked at Klosterheim warily. There was very little caution in the doctor's make-up, but the little there was now told him not to be forthcoming with Klosterheim.

"Which way are you heading?" asked the girl. "L.A. or 'Frisco?"

"Los Angeles. I have some business in the capital."

Los Angeles — or more particularly Hollywood, where the presidential Bright House and the Temple of Government were situated — was the capital of the Greater American Confederacy.

Faustaff helped himself to his second and third steaks. "You must be one of those people we were talking about earlier," he said, "who prefer to drive than go by plane."

"I am not fond of flying," Klosterheim agreed. "And that is no way to see a country, is it?"

"Certainly isn't," agreed the redhead, "if you like this sort of scenery."

"I am very fond of it," Klosterheim smiled. He got up and bowed slightly to them both. "Now, please excuse me. I will have an early night tonight, I think."

"Goodnight," said Faustaff with his mouth half-full. Once again Klosterheim had that secret look in his black eyes. Once again he turned quickly. He left the restaurant with a nod to the girl who was still behind the counter, fixing Faustaff's sodas.

When he had gone the girl came over and stood by their table.

"What you make of him?" she asked Faustaff.

Faustaff laughed. The crockery shook. "He's certainly got a talent for drawing attention to himself," he said. "I guess he's one of those people who go in for making themselves seem mysterious to others."

"No kidding," the girl agreed enthusiastically. "If you mean what I think you mean, I'm with you. He certainly gives me the creeps."

"Which way did he drive in from?" Faustaff asked.

"Didn't notice. He gave an L.A. hotel as his address. So maybe he came from L.A."

Nancy shook her head. "No — that's where he's going. He told us."

Faustaff shrugged and laughed again. "If I read him right this is what he wants — people talking about him, wondering about him. I've met guys like him before. Forget it."

Later the girl showed them to their cabin. In it was a large double bed.

"It's bigger than our standard beds," she said. "Just made for you, you might say."

"That's kind of you," Faustaff smiled.

"Sleep well," she said. "Goodnight."

"Goodnight."

The redhead was eager to get to bed as soon as the girl had left. Faustaff hugged her, kissed her and then stood back for a moment, taking a small, green velvet skull cap from his shorts' pocket and fitting it on his head before undressing.

"You're crazy, Fusty," giggled the redhead, sitting on the bed and shaking with amusement. "I'll never make you out."

"Honey, you never will," he said, as he stripped off his clothes and flipped out the light.

Three hours later he was awakened by a tight sensation round his head and a tiny, soundless vibration.

He sat upright, pushing back the covers, and getting as gently as possible out of bed so as not to disturb the girl.

The invoker was ready. He had better lug it out into the desert as soon as possible.

C H A P T E R T W O

M E N I N T - S H I R T S

Doctor Faustaff hurried from the cabin, carrying his huge naked bulk with extraordinary grace and speed towards the car park and his Cadillac.

The invoker was ready. It was a fairly compact piece of machinery with handles for moving it. He heaved it from the Cadillac's trunk and began hauling it out of the car park, away from the motel and into the desert.

Ten minutes later he squatted beneath the moon, fiddling with the invoker's controls. He set dials and pressed buttons. A white light blinked and went out, a red light blinked, a green light blinked, then the machine seemed still again. Doctor Faustaff stood back.

Half-seen traceries of light now seemed to spring from the invoker and weave geometric patterns against the darkness. At length a figure began to materialize amongst them, ghostly at first but steadily becoming more solid. Soon a man stood there.

He was dressed in a coverall and his head was bandaged. He was unshaven and gaunt. He fingered the disc, strapped wrist-watch fashion to his arm, and said nothing.

"George?"

"Hello, doctor. Where are we? — I got the call. Can you make it fast? — we need everybody at the base." George Forbes spoke tonelessly, unlike his normal self.

"You really are in trouble there. Give me the picture."

"Our main base was attacked by a D-squad. They used their disruptors as well as more conventional weapons, helicopters flying in low. We missed them until they were close. We fought back, but the bastards did their usual hit and run attack and were in and out again in five minutes — leaving us with five men alive out of twenty-three, wrecked equipment and a damaged adjustor. While we were licking our wounds they must have gone on to create a U.M.S.

We're trying to fight it with a malfunctioning adjustor — but it's a losing battle. Four others just won't be enough. We'll get caught in the U.M.S. ourselves if we're not careful — then you can write off E-15. We need a new adjustor and a full replacement team."

"I'll do my best," Faustaff promised. "But we've no spare adjustors — you know how long one takes to build. We'll have to risk shipping one from somewhere else — E-1 is the safest, I guess."

"Thanks, doctor. We've given up hope — we don't think you can do anything for us. But if you can do anything…" Forbes rubbed his face. He seemed so exhausted that he didn't really know where he was or what he was saying. "I'd better get back. Okay?"

"Okay," said Faustaff.

Forbes tapped the disc on his wrist and began to dematerialize as the E-15 invoker tugged him back through the subspacial levels.

Faustaff knew he had to get to 'Frisco quickly. He would have to travel tonight. He began to haul the invoker back towards the motel.

When he was quite close to the car park he saw a figure in silhouette near his Cadillac.

The figure seemed to be trying to open the car door. Faustaff bellowed: "What d'you think you're trying to do, buster?" He let go of the invoker and strode towards the figure.

As Faustaff approached the figure straightened and whirled round and it wasn't Klosterheim as Faustaff had suspected but a woman, blonde, tanned, with the shapely synthetic curves of a dressmaker's dummy — the kind of curves an older woman bought for herself. This woman seemed young.

She gasped when she saw the fat giant bearing down on her, dressed only in a green velvet skull cap, and she moved away from the car.

"You haven't any clothes on," she said. "You could be arrested if I screamed."

Faustaff laughed and paused. "Who'd arrest me? Why were you trying to get into my car?"

"I guess I thought it was mine."

Faustaff looked at the English M.G. and the Thunderbird. "It's not dark enough to make that kind of mistake," he said. The big yellow moon was high and full. "Which is yours?"

"The Thunderbird," she said.

"So the M.G.'s Klosterheim. I still don't believe you could make a mistake like that — a red Cadillac for a black Thunderbird."

"I haven't broken into your car. I guess I was just peeking inside. I was interested in that equipment you've got in there." She pointed to a small portable computer in the back seat. "You're a scientist aren't you — a doctor or something?"

"Who told you?"

"The owner here."

"Here. I see. What's your name, honey?"

"Maggy White."

"Well, Miss White, keep your nose out of my car in future." Faustaff was not normally so rude, but he was sure she was lying, as Klosterheim had been lying, and his encounter with George Forbes had depressed him. Also he was puzzled by Maggy White's total sexlessness. It was unusual for him to find any woman unattractive — they were always attractive in some way — but he was unmoved by her. Subconsciously he also realized that she was unmoved by him. It made him uncomfortable without realizing quite why.

He watched her flounce on high heels back towards the cabins. He saw her enter one, saw the door close. He went to get his invoker and hauled it into the trunk, locking it carefully.

Then he followed Maggy White towards the cabins. He would have to wake Nancy and get going. The sooner he contacted his team in 'Frisco the better.

Nancy yawned and scratched her scalp as she climbed into the car. Faustaff started the Cadillac up and drove out on to the highway, changed gear and stepped on the accelerator.

"What's the rush, Fusty?" She was still sleepy. He had had to waken her suddenly and also wake the motel owner to pay him.

"An emergency in my 'Frisco office," he said. "Nothing for you to worry about. Sorry I disturbed you. Try and get some sleep as we drive, huh?"

"What happened tonight? You bumped into a girl or something in the car park. What were you doing out there?"

"Got a buzz from the office. Who told you?"

"The owner. He told me while he was filling the tank for you." She smiled. "Apparently you hadn't any clothes on. He thought you were a nut."

"He's probably right."

"I get the idea that the girl and that Klosterheim character are connected — have they anything to do with this emergency of yours?"

"They just might have." Faustaff shivered. He had no clothes but the shirt and shorts he wore and the desert night was cold. "Might just be salvagers, but…" He was musing aloud.

"Salvagers?"

"Oh, just bums — some kind of con-team. I don't know who they are. Wish I did."

Nancy had fallen asleep by the time dawn came. The rising sun turned the desert into an expanse of red sand and heavy black shadows. Tall cactus, their branches extended like the arms of declamatory figures, paraded into the distance; petrified prophets belatedly announcing the doom that had overtaken them.

Faustaff breathed in the cool, dawn smells, feeling sad and isolated suddenly, retiring into himself in the hope that his unconscious might produce some clue to the identities of Herr Klosterheim and Maggy White. He drove very fast, egged on by the knowledge that unless he reached 'Frisco quickly E-15 was finished.

Later Nancy woke up and stretched, blinking in the strong light. The desert shimmered in the heat haze, rolling on for ever in all directions. She accepted the bizarre nature of the continent without question. To her it had always been like this. Faustaff had known it as very different five years before — when a big U.M.S. had only just been checked. That was something he would probably never fully understand — tremendous physical changes took place on a planet, but the inhabitants never seemed to notice. Somehow the U.M. Situations were accompanied by a deep psychological change in the people — similar in some ways, perhaps, to the mass delusions involving flying saucer spottings years before on his own world. But this was total hallucination. The human psyche seemed even more adaptable than the human physique. Possibly it was the only way the people could survive and protect their sanity on the insane planets of subspace. Yet the mass delusion was not always complete, but those who remembered an earlier state of existence were judged insane, of course. Even on a mass level things took time to adapt. What the inhabitants of Greater America didn't realize now, for instance, was that theirs was the only inhabited land mass, apart from one island in the Philippines. They still talked about foreign countries, though they would forget little by little, but the countries were only in their imagination, mysterious and romantic places where nobody actually went. Klosterheim had given himself away immediately he said he was from Sweden, for Faustaff knew that on E-3 a gigantic forest grew in the areas once called Scandinavia, Northern Europe and Southern Russia. Nobody lived there — they had been wiped out in the big U.M.S. which had warped the American continent too. The trees of that area were all grotesquely huge, far bigger than North American redwoods, out of proportion to the land they grew on. And yet these were one of the best results of the partial correction of a U.M.S.

On all the fifteen alternate Earths with which Faustaff was familiar Unstable Matter Situations had manifested themselves and been countered. The result of this was that the worlds were now bizarre travesties of their originals and the further back down the subspacial corridor you went the more unearthly were the alternate Earths. Yet many of the inhabitants survived and that was the important thing. The whole reason for Faustaff's and his team's efforts was to save lives. It was a good reason as far as they were concerned, even though it seemed they were fighting a slow, losing battle against the D-squads.

He was convinced that Klosterheim and Maggy White were representatives of a D-squad and that their presence heralded trouble for himself, if not the whole of his organization. 'Frisco might have some new information for him when he got there. He hoped so. His usual equanimity was threatening to desert him.

'Frisco's towers were at last visible in the distance. The road widened here and cactus plants grew thicker in the desert. Behind 'Frisco was the blue and misty sea, but the only ships in her harbour were coast-going freighters.

The sedate pace of 'Frisco compared to the frenetic mood he had left behind in L.A. made Faustaff feel a little better as he drove through the peaceful old streets that had retained a character that was somehow redolent of an older America, an America that had only really existed in the nostalgic thoughts of the generation which had grown up before the first World War. The streets were crammed with signs lettered in Edwardian style, there was the delicious smell of a thousand delicatessens, the tolling of the trolley cars echoed amongst the grey and yellow buildings, the air was still and warm, people sauntered along the sidewalks or could be seen leaning against bars and counters within the cool interiors of little stores and saloons. Faustaff liked 'Frisco and preferred it to all other cities in Greater America, which was why he had chosen to set up his headquarters here rather than in the capital of L.A. Not that he minded an atmosphere of noise, bustle and neurosis — in fact he rather enjoyed it — but 'Frisco had a greater air of permanence than elsewhere on E-3 so that psychologically at any rate it seemed the best place for his H.Q.

He drove towards North Beach and soon drew up beside a Chinese restaurant with dark-painted windows with gold dragons on them. He turned to the redhead.

"Nancy, how would you like a big Chinese meal and a chance to wash up?"

"Okay. But is this a brush off?" She could see he didn't intend to join her.

"Nope — but there's that urgent business I must attend to. If I don't come in later, go to this address." He took a small notebook from his shirt pocket and scribbled the address of his private apartment. "That's my private place. Make yourself at home." He handed her a key. "And tell them you're a friend of mine in the restaurant."

She seemed too tired to question him any further and nodded, getting out of the car, still in her swimsuit, and walking into the restaurant.

Faustaff went up to the door next to the restaurant and rang the bell.

A man of about thirty, dark-haired, saturnine, wearing a T-shirt, white jeans and black sneakers, opened the door and nodded when he saw Faustaff. There was a large old-fashioned clock-face stenciled on to the front of his T-shirt. It looked like any other gimmick design.

Faustaff said: "I need some help with the equipment in the trunk. Anyone else here?"

"Mahon and Harvey."

"I guess we can get the stuff upstairs between us. Will you tell them?"

The man — whose name was Ken Peppiatt — disappeared and came back shortly with two other men of about the same age and build, though one of them was blond. They were dressed the same, with the clock design on their T-shirts.

Helped by Faustaff they manhandled the electro-invoker and the portable computer through the door and up a narrow stairway. Faustaff closed the door behind them and kept an eye on the young men until they had set the equipment down in a small room on the first floor. The boards were bare and the room had a musty smell. They went up more uncarpeted stairs to the next floor which was laid out like a living room, with old, comfortable furniture untidily crammed into it. There were magazines and empty glasses littered about. The three men in T-shirts flopped into chairs and looked up at Faustaff as he went to an Art Deco cocktail cabinet and poured himself a large glass of bourbon. He spooned ice-cubes into the drink and sipped it as he turned to face them.

"You know the problem they have on E-15."

The three men nodded. Mahon had been the man who had contacted Faustaff the day before.

"I gather you're already arranging for a team to relieve the survivors?"

Harvey said: "They're on their way. But what they really need is an adjustor. We haven't a spare — it'll be dangerous to let one go from another alternate. If a D-squad attacks a world without an adjustor — you can say goodbye to that world."

"E-1 hasn't had an attack yet," Faustaff mused. "We'd better send their adjustor."

"Your decision," said Mahon getting up. "I'll go and contact E-1." He left the room.

"I'll want reports on the situation whenever possible," Faustaff told him as he closed the door. He turned to the two others. "I think I've been in touch with the people who made that tunnel you found."

"What are they — salvagers or D-squaders?" Harvey asked.

"Not sure. They don't seem like salvagers and D-squaders usually only turn up to attack. They don't hang about in motels." Faustaff told about his encounter with the pair.

Peppiatt frowned. "That's not a real name — Klosterheim — I'd swear." Peppiatt was one of their best linguists. He knew the root tongues of all the alternates, and many secondary languages as well. "It doesn't click. Just possibly German, I suppose, but even then…"

"Let's forget about the name for the time being," Faustaff said. "We'd better put a couple of people on to watching them. Two Class H agents ought to be okay. We'd better have recordings, photographs of them, everything we can get for a file. All the usual information — normal whereabouts and so on. Can you fix that, Ken?"

"We've got a lot of Class H agents on retainer. They'll think it's a security job — Class H still believe we're some kind of government outfit. You might as well use half-a-dozen — they're available."

"As many as you think. Just keep tabs on the pair of them." Faustaff mentioned that they were probably in L.A. or 'Frisco judging by what they had said. Their cars shouldn't be hard to trace — he'd taken the numbers as he left the car park that morning.

Faustaff finished his drink and picked up a clip-board of schedules lying on a table. He flipped through them.

"Cargoes seem to be moving smoothly enough," he nodded. "How's the fresh-water situation here?"

"We'll need some more. They're recycling already, of course, but until we get those big sea-water condensers set up we'll have to keep shipping it in from E-6." E-6 was a world that now consisted of virtually nothing but fresh-water oceans.

"Good," Faustaff began to relax. The E-15 problem was still nagging him, though there was little he could do at this stage. Only once before had he experienced a Total Break-up — on the now extinct E-16 — the planet that had taken his father when a U.M.S. got completely out of hand. He didn't like to think of what had happened there happening anywhere else.

"There's a new recruit you might like to talk to yourself," Harvey said. "A geologist from this world. He's at main H.Q. now."

Faustaff frowned. "This will mean a trip to E-1. I guess I'd better see him. I need to go to E-1, anyway. They'll want an explanation about the adjustor for one thing. They'll be nervous, quite rightly."

"They sure will, doctor. I'll keep you in touch if anything breaks with this Klosterheim and the girl."

"Have you got a bed free? I'll get a couple of hours sleep first, I think. No point in working tired."

"Sure. The second on the left upstairs."

Faustaff grunted and went upstairs. Though he could last for days without sleep, it was mainly thanks to his instinct to conserve his energy whenever he had the chance.

He lay down on the battered bed and, after a pang or two of conscience about Nancy, went to sleep.

CHAPTER THREE
CHANGING TIMES

Faustaff slept for almost two hours exactly, got up, washed and shaved and left the house, which was primarily living quarters for a section of his E-3 team.

He walked down towards Chinatown and soon reached a big building that had once been a pleasure house, with a saloon and a dance floor downstairs and private rooms for one night rental upstairs. Outside, the building looked ramshackle and the old paint was dull and peeling. A sign in ornate playbill lettering could still be made out. It read, somewhat unoriginally, *The Golden Gate*. He opened a side door with his key and went in.

The place was still primarily as it had been when closed down by the cops for the final time. Everything that wasn't faded plush seemed tarnished gilt. The big dance hall, with bars at both ends, smelt a little musty, a little damp. Big mirrors still lined the walls behind the bars, but they were fly-specked.

In the middle of the floor a lot of electronic equipment had been set up. Housed in dull metal casings, its function was hard to guess. To an outsider many of the dials and indicators would have been meaningless.

A wide staircase led from tile floor to a gallery above. A man, dressed in standard T-shirt, jeans and sneakers, was standing there now, his hands on the rail, leaning and looking at the doctor below.

Faustaff nodded to the man and began to climb the stairs.

"Hi, Jas."

"Hi, doctor." Jas Hollom grinned. "What's new?"

"Too much. They said you had a new recruit."

"That's right." Jas jerked his thumb at a door behind him. "He's in there. It was the usual thing — a guy getting curious about the paradoxes in the environment. His investigations led him to us. We roped him in."

Faustaff's team made a point of drawing its recruits from people like the man Hollom had described. It was the best way and ensured a high standard of recruits as well as a fair amount of secrecy. The doctor didn't court secrecy for its own sake but didn't approach governments and declare himself simply because his experience warned him that the more officials who knew about him and his organization the more spanners there would be in his organization's works.

Faustaff reached the gallery and moved towards the door Hollom had indicated, but before he entered he nodded towards the equipment below.

"How's the adjustor working. Tested it recently?"

"Adjustor and tunneler both in good shape. Will you be needing the tunneler today?"

"Probably."

"I'll go down and check it. Mahon's in the communications room if you want him."

"I saw him earlier. I'll talk to the recruit."

Faustaff knocked on the door and entered.

The new recruit was a tall, well-built, sandy-haired young man of about twenty-five. He was sitting in a chair reading one of the magazines from the table in the centre. He got up.

"I'm Doctor Faustaff." He held out his hand and the sandy-haired man shook it a little warily.

"I'm Gerry Bowen. I'm a geologist — at the university here."

"You're a geologist. You found a flaw in the plot of the Story of the Rocks, is that it?"

"There's that — but it was the ecology of Greater America — not the geology — that bothered me. I started enquiring, but everybody seems to be in a half-dream when it comes to talking about some subjects. A sort of..."

"Mass hallucination?"

"Yes — what's the explanation?"

"I don't know. You started checking, eh?"

"I did. I found this place — found it was turning out a near-endless stream of goods and supplies of all kinds. That explained what was supporting the country. Then I tried to talk to one of your men, find out more. He told me more. It's still hard to believe."

"About the alternates, you mean?"

"About everything to do with them."

"Well, I'll tell you about it — but I've got to warn you that if we don't get loyalty from you after you've heard the story we do what we always do..."

"That's...?"

"We've got a machine for brainwashing you painlessly — not only wiping your memory clean of what you've learned from us, but getting rid of that bug of curiosity that led you to us. Okay?"

"Okay. What happens now?"

"Well, I thought I'd give you a good illustration that we're not kidding about the subspacial alternate worlds. I'm going its take you to another alternate — my home planet. We call it E-1. It's the youngest of the alternates."

"The youngest? That seems a bit hard to figure."

"Figure it out after you've heard more. There isn't much time. Are you willing to come along?"

"You bet I am!" Bowen was eager. He had an alert mind and Faustaff could tell that in spite of his enthusiasm his intellect was working all the information out, weighing it. That was healthy. It also meant, Faustaff thought, that it wouldn't take long for positive information to convince him.

When Faustaff and Gerry Bowen got down to the ground floor Jas Hollom was working at the largest machine there. A faint vibration could be felt on the floor and some indicators had been activated.

Faustaff stepped forward, checking the indicators. "She's doing fine." He looked at Bowen. "Another couple of minutes and we'll be ready."

Two minutes passed and a thin hum began to come from the machine. Then the air in front of the tunneler seemed full of agitated dust which swirled round and round in a spiral until delicate, shifting colours became visible and the part of the room immediately ahead of the tunneler became shadowy until it disappeared.

"Tunnel's ready," Faustaff said to Bowen. "Let's go."

Bowen followed Faustaff towards the tunnel that the machine had created through subspace.

"How does it *work?*" Bowen asked incredulously.

"Tell you later."

"Just a minute," Hollom said, making an adjustment to the machine. "There — I was sending you to E-12." He laughed. "Okay — *now!*"

Faustaff stepped into the tunnel and grabbed Bowen, pulling him in too. Faustaff propelled himself forward.

The "walls" of the tunnel were grey and hazy, they seemed thin and beyond them was a vacuum more absolute than that of space. Sensing this Bowen shuddered; Faustaff could feel him do it.

It took ninety seconds before, with an itching skin but no other ill-effects, Faustaff stepped out into a room of bare concrete — a store-room in a factory, or a warehouse. Bowen said: "Phew! That was worse than a ghost train."

But for one large piece of equipment that was missing, the equipment in this room was identical to that in the room they'd just left. It was all that occupied the dully-lit room. A steel door opened and a short, fat man in an ordinary lounge suit came in. He took off his glasses, a gesture that conveyed surprise and pleasure, and walked with a light, bouncing step towards Faustaff.

"Doctor! I heard you were coming."

"Hello, Professor May. Nice to see you. This is Gerry Bowen from E-3. He may be coming to work with us."

"Good, good. You'll want the lecture room. Um…" May paused and pursed his lips. "We were a bit worried by E-15 requisitioning our adjustor, you know. We have some more being built, but…"

"It was on my orders. Sorry, professor. E-1 has never had a raid, after all. It was the safest bet."

"Still, a risk. This could be the time they pick. Sorry to gripe, doctor. We realized the emergency was acute. It's odd knowing at the back of your mind that if a U.M.S. occurs we've nothing to fight it with."

"Of course. Now — the lecture room."

"I take it you won't want to be disturbed."

"Only if something bad crops up. I'm expecting news from E-3 and E-15. D-squad trouble on both."

"I heard."

The corridor seemed to Bowen to be situated in a large office block. When they reached the elevator he guessed that that must be what it was — outwardly, anyway.

The building was, in fact, the central headquarters for Faustaff's organization, a multistorey building that stood on one of Haifa's main streets. It was registered as the offices of the Trans-Israel Export Company. If the authorities had ever wondered about it, they hadn't done anything to let Faustaff know. Faustaff's father was a respected figure in Haifa — and his mysterious disappearance something of a legend. Perhaps because of his father's good name, Faustaff wasn't bothered.

The lecture room was appropriately labeled LECTURE ROOM. Inside were several rows of seats facing a small cinema screen. A desk had been placed to one side of the screen and on it was mounted a control console of some kind.

"Take a seat, Mr Bowen," said Professor May as Faustaff walked up to the desk and squeezed his bulk into a chair. May sat down beside Bowen and folded his arms.

"I'm going to be as brief as I can," Faustaff said. "And use a few slides and some V-clips to illustrate what I'm going to say. I'll answer questions, too, of course, but Professor May will have to fill you in on any particular details you want to know. Okay?"

"Okay," said Bowen.

Faustaff touched a stud on the console and the lights dimmed.

"Although it seems that we have been traveling through the subspacial levels for many years," he began, "we have actually only been in contact with them since 1971 — that's twenty-eight years ago. The discovery of the alternate Earths was made by my father when he was working here, in Haifa, at the Haifa Institute of Technology."

A picture came on to the screen — a picture of a tall, rather lugubrious man, almost totally unlike the other Faustaff, his son. He was skinny, with melancholy, overlarge eyes and big hands and feet. He looked like the gormless feed-man for a comedian.

"That's him. He was a nuclear physicist and a pretty good one. He was born in Europe, spent some time in a German concentration camp, went to America and helped on the Bomb. He left America soon after the Hiroshima explosion, traveled around a little, had a job directing an English Nuclear Research Establishment, then got this offer to come to Haifa where they were doing some very interesting work with high-energy neutrinos. This work particularly excited my father. His ambition — kept secret from everyone but my mother and me — was to discover a device which would counter a nuclear explosion — just stop the bomb going off. A fool's dream, really, and he had sense enough to realize it. But he never forgot that that was what he would like to work on if he had the chance. Haifa offered him that chance — or he thought it did. His own work with high energy neutrinos had given him the idea that a safety device, at very least, could be built that would have the effect of exerting a correcting influence on unstable elements by emitting a stream of high energy neutrinos that on contact with the agitated particles would form a uniting link, a kind of shell around the unstable atoms which would, as it were, 'calm them down' and allow them to be dealt with easily and at leisure.

"Some scientists at Haifa Tech had got the same idea and he was offered the job of directing the research.

"He worked for a year and had soon developed a device which was similar to our adjustors in their crudest form. In the meantime my mother died. One day he and several others were testing the machine when they made a mistake in the regulation of the particles emitted by the device. In fiddling with the controls they accidentally created the first 'tunnel'. Naturally they didn't know what it was, but investigation soon brought them the information of the subspacial alternate Earths. Further frenzied research, which paralleled work on the adjustor, the tunneler and the invoker, produced the knowledge of twenty-four alternate Earths to our own! They existed in what my father and his team called 'subspace' — a series of 'layers' that are 'below' our own space, going deeper and deeper. Within a year of their discovery there were only twenty alternates and they had actually witnessed the total extinction of one planet. Before the end of the second year there were only seventeen alternates and they knew, roughly, what was happening.

"Somehow the complete disruption of the planet's atomic structure was being effected. It would start with a small area and gradually spread until the whole planet would expand into gas and those gasses drift away through space leaving no trace of the planet. The small disrupted areas we now call Unstable Matter Locations and are able to deal with. What at first my father thought was some sort of natural phenomenon was later discovered to be the work of human beings — who have machines that create this disruption of matter.

"Although my father's scientific curiosity filled him, he soon became appalled by the fantastic loss of life that destruction of these alternate Earths involved. Whoever was destroying the planets was cold-bloodedly killing off billions of people a year.

"These planets, I'd better add, all had similarities to our own — and your own, Mr Bowen — with roughly similar standards of civilization, roughly similar governmental institutions, roughly similar scientific accomplishments — though all, in some way or another, had come to a dead end — had stagnated. We still don't know why this is."

A picture came on to the screen. It was not a photograph but an artist's impression of a world the same size as Earth, with a moon the same as Earth's. The picture showed a planet that seemed of a universally greyish colour.

"This is E-15 now," Faustaff said. "This is what it looked like ten years ago."

Gerry Bowen saw a predominantly green and blue world. He didn't recognize it. "E-1 still looks like this," Faustaff said.

Faustaff flashed the next picture. A world of green obsidian, shown in close-ups to be misty, twilit, ghastly, with ghoul-like inhabitants.

And this is what E-14 looked like less than ten years ago," came Faustaff's voice.

The picture Bowen saw next was exactly the same as the second picture he'd seen — a predominantly green and blue world with well-marked continental outlines.

"E-13, coming up now," said Faustaff.

A world of blindingly bright crystal in hexagonal structures like a vast honeycomb. Deposits of earth and water had been collected in some of the indentations. Vs showed the inhabitants living hand to mouth existences on the strange world.

"E-13 as it was."

A picture identical to the two others Bowen had already seen.

The pattern was repeated — worlds of grotesque and fantastic jungles, deserts, seas, had all once been like E-1 was now. Only E-2 was similar to E-1.

"E-2 is a world that seemed to stop short, in our terms, just around 1960 and the expansion of the space programmes. You wouldn't know about those, even, since E-3 stopped short, as I remember, just after 1950. This sudden halting of all kinds of progress still mystifies us. As I said, a peculiar change comes over people as well, on the whole. They behave as if they were living in a perpetual dream and a perpetual present. Old books and Vs that show a different state to the one they now know are ignored or treated as jokes. Time, in effect, ceases to exist in any aspect. It all goes together — only a few, like you, Mr Bowen break out. The people are normal in all other respects."

"What's the explanation for the changes of these worlds?" Bowen asked.

"I'm coming to that. When my father and his team first discovered the alternate worlds of subspace they were being wiped out, as I mentioned, rapidly. They found a way of stopping this wholesale destruction by building the adjustors, refinements of the original machines they'd been working on which could control the U.M. Situations where they occurred.

"In order to be ready to control the U.M.S. where and when it manifested itself, my father and his team had to begin getting recruits and had soon built up a large organization — almost as large as the one I now have. Well-equipped teams of men, both physically and mentally alert, had to be stationed on the other alternates — there were fifteen left by then, not fourteen as now.

"Slowly the organization was built up, not without some help from officials in the Israeli government of the time, who also helped to keep the activities of my father and his team fairly secret. The adjustors were built and installed on all the worlds. By means of an adjustor's stabilizing influence they could correct, to some extent, a U.M.S. — their degree of success depending on the stage the U.M.S. had reached before they could get their machine there and get it working. Things are much the same nowadays. Though we can 'calm down' the disrupted matter and bring it back to something approximately its original form, we cannot make it duplicate its original at all perfectly. The deeper back you go through the subspacial levels, the less like the original the planet is and the more U.M. Situations there have been. Thus E-15 is a world of grey ash that settles on it from thousands of volcanoes that have broken through the surface, E-14 is nothing but glassy rock, and E-13 is primarily a crystalline structure these days. E-12 is all jungle and so on. Nearer to E-1 the worlds are more recognizable — particularly E-2, E-3 and E-4. E-4 had it lucky — it stopped progressing just before the First World War. But it mainly consists of the British Isles and Southern and Eastern Europe now — the rest is either wasteland or water."

"So your father founded the organization and you carried it on, is that it?" Bowen asked from the darkness.

"My father died in the Total Break-up of E-16," Faustaff said. "The U.M.S. got out of control — and he didn't get off in time."

"You said the U.M.S. weren't natural — that somebody caused them. Who?"

"We don't know. We call them the D-squad — the Demolition Squad. They make it their business to attack our stations as well as creating U.M. Situations. They've killed many people directly, not just indirectly."

"I must say it's hard to believe that such a complicated organization as yours can exist and do the work it does."

"It has built up over the years. Nothing strange about that. We manage."

"You talk all the time about alternate Earths — but what about the rest of the universe. I remember reading the theory of alternate universes some years ago."

"We're pretty sure that the only alternates are of Earth and the moon in some cases. It's a pity space-flight is not yet sufficiently sophisticated, otherwise we could put the theory to the test. My father reached this conclusion in 1985 when the second manned spaceship reached Mars and 'disappeared'. It was assumed it had gone off course into a meteor storm on its return flight. Actually it turned up on Earth 5 — its crew dead due to the stresses of passing through subspace in a most unorthodox way. This seemed to prove that some distance beyond Earth there are no subspacial alternates. Whether this is a natural phenomenon or an artificial one, I don't know. There's a lot we don't understand."

"You think there is a force at work, apart from you?"

"I do. The D-squad speaks of that. But though we've done some extensive checking up, we haven't found a trace of where they come from — though it must be from somewhere on E-1. Why they should murder planets — and more specifically the inhabitants of those planets — the way they do, I cannot understand. It is inhuman."

"And what is your real reason for doing all this, doctor, risking so much?"

"To preserve human life," said Faustaff.

"That is all."

Faustaff smiled. "That's all."

"So it's your organization against the D-squad, basically."

"Yes." Faustaff paused. "There are also the people we call salvagers. They came from several different alternates — but primarily from E-1, E-2, E-3 and E-4. At different stages they have discovered our organization and found out what it does. Either they have found us out of curiosity, as you did, or stumbled upon us by accident. Over the years they have formed themselves into bands who pass through the subspacial alternates looting what they can and selling it to worlds that need it — using E-1 as their main base, as we do. They are pirates, freebooters using stolen equipment that was originally ours. They are no threat. Some people are irritated by them, that's all."

"There's no chance that they are connected with these D-squads."

"None. For one thing it wouldn't be in their interest to have a planet destroyed."

"I guess not."

"Well, that's the basic set-up. Are you convinced?"

"Convinced and overwhelmed. There are a few details I'd like filled in."

"Perhaps Professor May can help you?"

"Yes."

"You want to join us?"

"Yes."

"Good. Professor May will tell you what you want to know, then put you in touch with someone here who'll show you the ropes. I'll leave you now, if you don't mind."

Faustaff said goodbye to Bowen and May and left the little lecture room.

C H A P T E R F O U R

T H E S A L V A G E R S

Faustaff drove his Cadillac towards the centre of San Francisco where he had his private apartment. The sun was setting and the city looked romantic and peaceful. There wasn't much traffic on the roads and he made good speed.

He parked the car and walked into the old apartment house that stood on a hill giving a good view of the bay.

The decrepit elevator took him up to the top and he was about to let himself in when he realized he'd given his key to Nancy. He rang the bell. He was still wearing the beach shirt and shorts and sneakers he had been wearing the day before when he left Los Angeles. He wanted a shower and a change before anything.

Nancy opened the door. "So you made it," she smiled. "Is the emergency over?"

"The emergency — oh, yes. It's in hand. Forget about it." He laughed and put his arms around her, lifting her up and kissing her.

"I'm hungry," he said. "Is my icebox well-stocked?"

"Very well-stocked," she grinned.

"Well, let's have something to eat and go to bed." He had now forgotten about wanting a shower.

"That seems a good idea," she said.

Later that night the VC started ringing. Faustaff woke up instantly and picked it up. Nancy stirred and muttered but didn't wake.

"Faustaff."

"Mahon. Message from E-15. Things are bad. They've had another visit from the D-squad. They want help."

"They want me, maybe?"

"Well, yes, I think that's about the size of it."

"Are you at H.Q.?"

"Yes."

"I'll be over."

Faustaff put the VC down and got up. Once again he was careful not to disturb Nancy who seemed a good sleeper. He put on a black T-shirt and a pair of dark pants and socks, then laced up his old sneakers.

Soon he was driving the Cadillac towards Chinatown and not much later was in *The Golden Gate*, where Mahon and Hollom were waiting for him.

Hollom was working on the tunneler, his face screwed up in impatience.

Faustaff went behind the bar and reached under it, putting a bottle of bourbon and some glasses on the counter.

"Want a drink?"

Hollom shook his head angrily.

Mahon looked up from where he was intently watching Hollom. "He's having trouble, doctor. Can't seem to drive the tunnel deep enough. Can't reach E-15."

Faustaff nodded. "That's sure proof that a big D-squad is working there. It happened that time on E-6, remember?" He poured himself a large drink and swallowed it down. He didn't interfere with Hollom who knew as much about tunnelers as anyone and would ask for help if he needed it. He leant on the bar, pouring himself another drink and singing one of his favourite old numbers, remembered from when he was a youngster. "Then take me disappearing through the smoke rings of my mind, down the foggy ruins of time, far past the frozen leaves, the haunted, frightened trees, out to the windy beach, far from the twisted reach of crazy sorrow…" It was Dylan's *Mr Tambourine Man*. Faustaff preferred the old stuff, didn't care much for modern popular music which had become too pretentious for his taste.

Hollom said tight-faced: "D'you mind, doctor? I'm trying to concentrate."

"Sorry," said Faustaff shutting up at once. He sighed, trying to remember how long it had taken them to break through to E-6 the last time there had been a heavy block.

Hollom shouted wildly, suddenly: "Quick — quick — quick — I won't hold it long."

The air in front of the tunneler began to become agitated. Faustaff put down his drink and hurried forward.

Soon a tunnel had manifested itself. It shimmered more than usual and seemed very unstable. Faustaff knew that if it broke down he would be alone in the depths of subspace, instantly killed. Though possessing very little fear of death Faustaff did have a strong love of life and didn't enjoy the prospect of having to give up living. In spite of this he stepped swiftly into the subspacial tunnel and was soon moving along past the grey shimmering walls. His journey was the longest he had ever made, taking over two minutes, then he was through.

Peppiatt greeted him. Peppiatt was one of several volunteers who had gone with the replacement team to E-15. Peppiatt looked haggard.

"Glad to see you, doctor. Sorry we couldn't use the invoker — it's busted."

"You are having trouble."

The invoker was a kind of subspacial "grab", working on similar principles to the sister machines, that could be used primarily to pull agents out of U.M.S. trouble-spots, or get them through the dimensions without needing a tunnel. A tunnel was safer since the invoker worked on the principle of forming a kind of shell around a man and propelling it through the layers in order to break them down. Sometimes they resisted and didn't break down. Then a man "invoked" was lost for good.

Faustaff looked around. He was in a large, natural cave. It was dark and the floor was damp, neon lighting sputtering on the walls, filling the cave with lurid light that danced like firelight. Pieces of battered electronic equipment lay everywhere, much of it plainly useless. Two other men were by the far wall working at something that lay on a bench. Cables trailed across the floor. Several more men moved about. They carried laser rifles, their power-packs on their backs. The rifles had been stolen from the U.S. government on E-1 and technicians in Haifa were trying to mass-produce them, but hadn't had much success as yet. Faustaff's men were not normally armed and Faustaff had given no order to fight back at the D-squad. Evidently someone had decided it was necessary. Faustaff didn't like it, but he decided not to question the order now that it had been made. The one thing the doctor ever seemed adamant about was the fact that like physicians their business was to save, not take, life. It was the entire *raison d'être* of the organization, after all.

Faustaff knew that his presence on E-15 wasn't likely to serve any particular practical purpose since the men working here were trained to cope with even the most desperate situation, but gathered that he was needed for the moral support the men might get from thinking about it. Faustaff was not a very introspective man on the whole. In all matters outside of his scientific life he acted more according to his instinct than his reason. "Thinking causes trouble" was a motto he had once expressed in a moment of feeling.

"Where's everyone else?" he asked Peppiatt.

"With the adjustor. Areas 33, 34, 41, 42, 49 and 50 were calmed down for a while, but the D-squad came back. Evidently those areas form the key-spot. We're still trying to get them under control. I'm just going back there, now."

"I'll come along."

Faustaff grinned encouragingly at the men he passed on his way to the exit.

Peppiatt shook his head wonderingly. "Their spirit's better already. I don't know what you do, doctor, but you certainly manage to make people feel good."

Faustaff nodded absently. Peppiatt operated a control beside a big steel door. The door began to slide back into the wall, revealing a bleak expanse of grey ash, a livid sky from which ash fell like rain. There was a stink of sulphur in the air. Faustaff was familiar with the conditions on E-15, where because of the volcanic upheavals almost everywhere on the planet, the people were forced to live in caves such as the one they'd just left. Their lives were fairly comfortable, however, thanks to Faustaff's cargoes brought from more fortunate worlds.

A jeep, already covered by a coating of ash, stood by. Peppiatt got into it and Faustaff climbed into the back seat. Peppiatt started the engine and the jeep began to bounce away across the wasteland of ash. Apart from the sound of the jeep the world was silent. Ash fell and smoke rolled in the distance. Occasionally when the smoke cleared a little the outline of an erupting volcano could be seen.

Faustaff's throat was clogged by the ash carried on the sulphurous air. It was a grey vision of some abandoned hell and infinitely depressing.

Later a square building, half buried in the ash, came in sight.

"That's one of our relay stations, isn't it," Faustaff pointed.

"Yes. It's the nearest our 'copters can get to the main base without having a lot of fuel difficulties. There should be a 'copter waiting."

A few men stood about outside the relay station. They were dressed in protective suits, wearing oxygen masks and heavy, smoked goggles. Faustaff couldn't see a 'copter, just a small hovercraft, a useful vehicle for this type of terrain. But even as they drew up, an engine note could be heard in the air above and soon a helicopter began to come down nearby, its rotors thrumming as it settled in the dust.

Two men ran from the station as the 'copter landed. They were carrying flapping suits, similar to those that all the men here wore. They ran up to the jeep.

"We'll have to wear these, I'm afraid, doctor," Peppiatt said.

Faustaff shrugged. "Well, if we must." He took the suit offered him and began to pull it over his bulk. It was tight. He hated feeling constricted. He slipped mask and goggles over his face. At least breathing and seeing were easier.

Peppiatt led the way through the clogging, soft ash to the helicopter. They climbed in to the passenger seats. The pilot turned his head. "They're coming out with fuel pellets now. Won't be long."

"How are things up at the U.M.S.?" Faustaff asked.

"Pretty bad, I think. There are some salvagers here — we've seen them once — drifting around like buzzards."

"There can't be much for them to salvage here."

"Only spare parts," the pilot said.

"Of course," said Faustaff.

Using stolen or salvaged equipment belonging to Faustaff's organization, the salvagers needed to loot spare parts whenever possible. In the confusion following a major D-squad attack this could be done quite easily. Though they resented the salvagers, Faustaff's team had orders not to use violence against them. The salvagers were apparently prepared to use violence if necessary, thus the going was pretty easy for them.

"Do you know which gang is here?" Faustaff asked as the 'copter was fueled.

"Two gangs working together, I think. Gordon Begg's and Cardinal Orelli's."

Faustaff nodded. He knew both. He had encountered them several times before. Cardinal Orelli was from E-4 and Gordon Begg was from E-2. They were both men whose investigations had led them to discover Faustaff's organization and had worked for it for a while before going "rogue". Most of their gangs were comprised of similar men. Faustaff had a surprisingly few number of deserters and most of those were now salvagers.

The helicopter began to lift into the ash-laden air.

Within half-an-hour Faustaff could see signs of the U.M.S. ahead.

The Unstable Matter Situation was confined in a rough radius of ten miles. Here there was no grey ash, but boiling colour and an ear-shattering, unearthly noise.

Faustaff found it hard to adjust his eyes and ears to the U.M.S. He was familiar with the sight and sound of disrupted, unstable matter, but he never got used to it.

Great spiraling gouts of stuff would twist hundreds of feet into the air and then fall back again. The sounds were almost indescribable, like the roar of a thousand tidal waves, the screech of vast sheets of metal being tortured and twisted, the rumble of gigantic landslides.

Around the perimeter of this terrifying example of nature's death-throes there buzzed land-craft and helicopters. A big adjustor could be seen, trained on the U.M.S., the men and machines completely dwarfed by the swirling fury of the unstable elements.

They were now forced to use the radios in their helmets to speak to one another, and even then words were difficult to make out through the crackles of interference.

The helicopter landed and Faustaff got out, hurrying towards the adjustor.

One of the men near the adjustor was standing watching the instruments, arms folded.

Faustaff tapped him on the shoulder.

"Yes," came a distant voice through the crackle.

"Faustaff — what's the situation like?"

"More or less static, doctor. I'm Haldane."

"From E-2 isn't it?"

"That's right."

"Where are the original E-15 team — or what's left of them?"

"Shipped back to E-1. Thought it best."

"Good. I hear you had another D-squad attack."

"That's right — yesterday. Unusual intensity for them. As you know, they usually attack and run, never risk the chance of getting themselves hurt — but not this time. I'm afraid we killed one of them — died instantly — sorry to have to do it."

Faustaff controlled himself. He hated the idea of dying, particularly of violent death. "Anything I can do here?" he asked.

"Your advice might be needed. Nothing to do at present. We're hoping to calm Area 50 down. We might do it. Ever seen something like this?"

"Only once — on E-16."

Haldane didn't comment, although the implication must have been clear. Another voice came in. It was an urgent voice.

"'Copter 36 to base — U.M.S. spreading from Area 41. Shift adjustor round there — and hurry."

"We need another dozen adjustors," Haldane shouted as he waved a hovering 'copter down to pick up the adjustor with its magnetic grab.

"I know," Faustaff shouted back. "But we can't spare them." He watched as the grab connected with the adjustor and began to lift it up and away towards Area 41. Adjustors were hard to build. It would be folly to take others from more subspacial Earths.

The dilemma was insoluble. Faustaff had to hope that the one adjustor would finally succeed in checking and reversing the U.M.S.

A distorted voice that he eventually recognized as Peppiatt's said: "What do you think, doctor?"

He shook his head. "I don't know. Let's get back to that 'copter and go round the perimeter."

They stumbled back towards the 'copter and climbed in. Peppiatt told the pilot what to do. The 'copter rose into the air and began to circle the U.M.S. Looking it over carefully Faustaff could see that it was still possible to get the U.M.S. under control. He could tell by the colours. While the whole spectrum was represented, as it was now, the elements were still in their natural state at least. When they began to transform the U.M.S. would take on a purple-blue colour. When that happened it would be impossible to do anything.

Faustaff said: "You'd better start getting the native population assembled in one place as soon as possible. We'll have to anticipate evacuation."

"We won't be able to evacuate everyone," Peppiatt warned him.

"I know," Faustaff said tiredly. "We'll just have to do what we can. We'll have to work out the best place to ship them to, as well. Perhaps an uninhabited land area somewhere — where they won't come in contact with the natives of another world. This has never happened before — I'm not sure what a meeting between two different populations would produce and we don't want more trouble than we have." A memory of Klosterheim popped into his mind. "The Scandinavian Forests on E-3 might be okay." Already, tacitly, he was accepting that E-15 was finished. He was half-aware of this but his mind was struggling against the defeatist attitude beginning to fill him.

Suddenly the pilot broke in. "Look!"

About six 'copters in close formation were coming through the ash-rain in the distance. "They're not ours," the pilot said, banking steeply. "I'm going back to the base."

"What are they?" Faustaff asked.

Peppiatt answered. "Probably D-squaders. Might be salvagers."

"D-squaders! Again!" The D-squads rarely attacked more than once after they had started the initial U.M.S.

"I think they're out to destroy E-15," Peppiatt said. "We'll have to defend, you know, doctor. Lots of lives at stake."

Faustaff had never quite been able to make the logical step which excused the taking of life if it saved life. His mind was slightly confused as he nodded and said, with a tight feeling in his chest, "Okay."

The 'copter landed near the adjustor and the pilot got out and spoke to Haldane the chief operator. Haldane came hurrying to where Faustaff and Peppiatt were climbing down. He was fiddling with his helmet. Then his radio blasted on all the frequencies they were using.

"Alert! Alert! All guards to Area 41. D-squad about to attack adjustor."

Within seconds helicopters began to move in towards Area 41 and land, disgorging armed men.

Faustaff felt infinitely depressed as he watched them take up their defensive positions around the adjustor.

Then the D-squad 'copters began to come in.

Faustaff saw black-clad figures, seemingly faceless with black masks completely covering their heads. They had weapons in their hands.

The barely-seen lance of concentrated light from a laser rifle suddenly struck down from one of the leading D-squad 'copters. A man on the ground fell silently.

The guards around the adjustor began to aim a criss-cross lattice of laser rays at the coming 'copters. The 'copters dodged, but one of them exploded.

Like tiny, lethal searchlights the beams struck back and forth. The fact that the D-squads used E-1 equipment for all their attacks indicated to Faustaff that that was their origin. The only device they had which Faustaff and his men didn't have was the Matter Disrupter. Faustaff could make out the 'copter which carried it, flying well behind the others and rather lower.

More of Faustaff's men fell and Faustaff could barely stop himself from weeping. He felt a helpless anger, but it never once occurred to him to strike back at the men who had done the killing.

Another 'copter exploded, another went out of control and flew into the U.M.S. Faustaff saw it become incredibly luminous and then its outline grew, becoming fainter as it grew, until it vanished. Faustaff shuddered. He wasn't enjoying his visit to E-15.

Then he saw several of his guards fall in one place and realized that the attacking D-squad were concentrating their fire. He saw laser beams touch the adjustor, saw metal smoulder and burst into white flame. The helicopters rose and fled away, their mission accomplished.

Faustaff ran towards the adjustor. "Where's Haldane?" he asked one of the guards.

The guard pointed at one of the corpses.

Faustaff cursed and began checking the adjustor's indicator dials. They were completely haywire. The adjustor was still powered and its central core hadn't been struck, but Faustaff could see immediately that it would take too long to repair. Why had the D-squads intensified their attacks so much, risking their lives — indeed, losing their lives — to do so? It wasn't like them. Normally they were strictly hit-and-run men. Faustaff pushed this question from his mind. There were more immediate problems to be solved.

He switched his helmet mike to all frequencies and yelled. "Begin total population assembly immediate. Operate primary evacuation plan. The U.M.S. is going to start spreading any time — and when that happens we won't have much notice before the whole planet breaks up."

The 'copter with the grab began to move down towards the adjustor but Faustaff waved it away. The adjustor was heavy and it would take time to get it back to base. The evacuation of all the men from the area was more important. He told as much to the pilot over his radio.

Against the background of the vast, undulating curtain of disrupted matter, the team worked desperately to get out of the area, Faustaff helping men into 'copters and giving instructions wherever they were needed. There weren't enough 'copters to get everyone out at once. The evacuation would have to be organized in two lifts.

As the last of the 'copters took off, a handful of men, including Faustaff and Peppiatt, were left behind.

Faustaff turned to look at the U.M.S. with despair, noting that the spectrum was slowly toning down. It was the danger signal.

He looked back and saw some land vehicles bumping across the grey wasteland towards them. They didn't look like his organization's jeeps or trucks. As they drew closer he could make out figures sitting in them, dressed in a strange assortment of costumes.

Sitting high in the back of one jeep was a man dressed in red — a red cap on his head, a red smock covering most of his body. He had a small oxygen mask over his nose and mouth, but Faustaff recognized him by his clothes. It was Orelli, leader of one of the biggest teams of salvagers. He had a laser rifle pack on his back, and the rifle across his knees.

Peppiatt's voice came through the crackle of static in his ear piece. "Salvagers. Not wasting much time. They must be after the adjustor."

The remaining guards raised their weapons, but Faustaff shouted: "No firing. The adjustor's no use to us. If they want to risk their lives salvaging it, it's up to them."

Now Faustaff could make out a figure in a jeep just behind Orelli's. An incredibly tall, incredibly thin figure, in a green, belted jacket covered in ash, black trousers and ash-smeared jackboots. He carried a machine-gun. He had a mask but it hung against his chest. His face was like a caricature of a Victorian aristocrat's, with thin, beaklike nose, straggling black moustache and no chin. This was Gordon Begg who had once ranked high in Faustaff's organization.

The jeeps came to a halt close by and Orelli waved blandly to the little group standing near the ruined adjustor.

"Rights of salvage are ours, I think, doctor. I gather that *is* Doctor Faustaff in the bulky suit and helmet. I recognize the distinguished figure." He had to shout this through the noise of the raging U.M.S.

Orelli leapt down from the jeep and approached the group. Begg did likewise, approaching at a loping gait reminiscent of a giraffe. While Orelli was of average height and inclined to plumpness, Begg was almost seven feet tall. He cradled his machine-gun in his left arm and stepped forward, extending his right hand towards Faustaff. Faustaff shook it because it was easier to do that than make a display of refusing.

Begg smiled vaguely and wearily, brushing back dirty, ash-covered hair. Except in extreme cases he normally scorned any kind of protective gear. He was an Englishman in love with the early 19th century mystique of what an

Englishman should do and be, a romantic who had originally opposed Faustaff purely out of boredom inspired by the well-organized routine of Faustaff's organization. Faustaff still liked him, though he felt no liking for Orelli, whose natural deceit had been brought to full flower by his church training on E-4. Even his high intelligence could not counter the rare loathing that Faustaff felt for this man whose character was so preternaturally cruel and treacherous. Faustaff found it bewildering and disturbing.

Orelli's eyes gleamed. He cocked his head to one side, indicating the adjustor.

"We noted the D-squad flying back to its base and gathered you might have an old adjustor you didn't want, doctor. Mind if we look at it?"

Faustaff said nothing and Orelli minced towards the adjustor, inspecting it carefully.

"The core's still intact, I note. Seems mainly a question of ruined circuits. I think we could even repair it if we wanted to — though we haven't much use for an adjustor, of course."

"You'd better take it," Faustaff said grimly. "If you hang around talking you'll be caught by the U.M.S."

Begg nodded slowly. "The doctor's right, Orelli. Let's get our men to work. Hurry up."

The salvagers instructed their men to begin stripping the adjustor of the essential parts they wanted. While Faustaff, Peppiatt and the rest looked on wearily, the salvagers worked.

Begg glanced at Faustaff and then glanced away again. He seemed embarrassed momentarily. Faustaff knew he didn't normally work with Orelli, that Begg despised the ex-cardinal as much as Faustaff did. He assumed that the difficulty of getting a tunnel through to E-15 had caused the two men to join forces for this operation. Begg would have to be very careful that he was not betrayed in some way by Orelli when the usefulness of the partnership was over.

Faustaff turned back to look at the U.M.S. Slowly but surely the spectrum was toning down towards the purple-blue that would indicate it was about to spread in full force.

THE BREAK-UP OF E-15

When the 'copters had returned and taken Faustaff and the rest back to base, leaving the salvagers still picking the bones of the adjustor, Faustaff immediately took charge of the evacuation plans. It was proving difficult, he was informed, to get many of E-15's natives to the central base. Being in ignorance of Faustaff and his team, they were suspicious and reluctant to move. Some were already at the base, gathered from the nearby underground communities. Looking dazed and unable to comprehend where they were and what was happening, they even seemed to be losing touch with their own individual identities. Faustaff was interested to see this, since it gave him additional data on their reactions which might help him understand the queer psychic changes that took place amongst the populations of the inhabitants of subspace. His detached interest in their state didn't stop him from approaching them individually and trying to convince them that they were better off at the centre. He realized he would have to put several sympathetic members of his team in with their group when they were re-located on E-3's gigantic forest areas.

With some difficulty the group had succeeded in putting a tunnel through to E-3. The evacuees were already beginning to be shuttled through.

In dribs and drabs they came in and were escorted through the tunnel. Faustaff felt sorry for them as they moved, for the most part, like automatons. Many of them actually seemed to think they were experiencing a strange dream.

Eventually the last of the evacuees were through and the team began to gather up its equipment.

Peppiatt was in charge of the tunneler and he began to look worried as the subspacial "opening" flickered.

"Can't hold it open much longer, doctor," he said. The last few guards stepped forward into the tunnel. "We're the last," he said with some relief, turning to Faustaff.

"After you," said Faustaff.

Peppiatt left the tunneler's controls and stepped forward. Faustaff thought he heard him scream as the tunnel collapsed. He rushed back to the tunneler and desperately tried to bring the tunnel back to normal. But a combination of the subspacial blocks and the steadily increasing disruption on E-15 made it impossible. Eventually he abandoned the tunneler and checked the invoker-disc on his wrist. There wasn't much hope of that working, either, under these conditions.

It looked as if he was trapped on the doomed world.

Faustaff, as usual, acted instinctively. He rushed from the cavern-chamber and out to where a 'copter still stood. He had had some training in piloting the 'copters. He hoped he could remember enough of it. He forced his huge frame into the seat and started the engine. Soon he had managed to get the 'copter into the air. On the horizon the peculiar purple-blue aurora indicated that there was little time left before the whole planet broke up.

He headed east, to where he had gathered the salvagers had their camp. He could only hope that they hadn't yet left and that their tunnel was still operating. There was a good chance that even if that were the case they would refuse to help him get off the planet.

He could soon see the shimmering, light plastic domes of a temporary camp that must be that of the salvagers. He could see no signs of activity and at first thought that they had left.

He landed and went into the first tent he came to. There were no salvagers there, but there were black-clad corpses. This wasn't the salvagers' camp at all — it was the camp of the D-squad. Yet as far as he could tell the D-squaders were dead for no apparent reason. He wasted time checking one of the corpses. It was still warm. But how had it died?

He ran from the tent and climbed back into the 'copter.

Now he flew even more urgently, until he saw a small convoy of jeeps moving below him. With some relief he realized that they had not yet even reached their base. They seemed to be heading towards a smoking volcano about ten miles away. He guessed that the salvagers had no 'copters on this operation. They were risking a lot in using the comparatively slow-moving turbojeeps. Had they killed the D-squaders? he wondered. If so, it still didn't explain how.

Soon he saw their camp — a collection of small inflated domes which he recognized as being made of the new tougher-than-steel plastic that seemed as flimsy as paper. It was used by the more advanced nations on E-1, mainly for military purposes.

Faustaff landed the 'copter with a bump that half-threw him from his seat. An armed guard, dressed in a heavy greatcoat and a helmet that looked as if it had been looted from some 19th century fire station, moved cautiously towards him.

"Hey — you're Doctor Faustaff. What are you doing here? Where are Begg and Orelli and the others?"

"On their way," Faustaff told the man, who seemed amiable enough. He recognized him as Van Horn, who had once worked for the organization as a cargo control clerk. "How's it going, Van Horn?"

"Not so comfortable as when I worked for you, doctor, but more variety — and more of the good things of life, you know. We do pretty well."

"Good," said Faustaff without irony.

"Situation bad here, is it, doctor?"

"Very bad. Looks like there's going to be a break-up."

"Break-up! Phew! That is bad. Hope we get off soon."

"It'll have to be soon."

"Yes… What are you doing here, doctor? Come to warn us? That's pretty decent." Van Horn knew Faustaff and knew he was capable of doing this.

But Faustaff shook his head. "I've already done that. No — I came to ask for help. My tunneler went wrong. I'm finished unless I can get through your tunnel."

"Sure," Van Horn said with a grin. Like most people he liked Faustaff, even though his gang and Faustaff's organization were somewhat opposed. "Why not? I guess everybody will be pleased to help. For old time's sake, eh?"

"All except Orelli."

"Except him. He's a poison snake, doctor. He's so mean. I'm glad my boss is Begg. Begg's a weird guy, but okay. Orelli's a poison snake, doctor."

"Yes," Faustaff nodded absently, seeing the jeeps approaching through the smoke and falling ash. He could make out Orelli in the leading jeep.

Orelli was the first salvager to encounter Faustaff. He frowned for a second and then smiled blandly. "Doctor Faustaff again. How can we help you?"

The question was rhetorical, but Faustaff answered directly. "By giving me a chance to use your tunnel."

"Our tunnel?" Orelli laughed. "But why? Your father invented tunnelers — and now you come to us, the despised salvagers."

Faustaff bore Orelli's amused malice. He explained how his tunnel had broken down. Orelli's smile grew bigger and bigger as he listened. But he said nothing.

Orelli looked like a cat who'd been handed a mouse to play with. "I'll have to talk this over with my partner, you understand, doctor. Can't make a hasty decision. It could affect our whole lives in one way or another."

"I'm asking you for help, man, that's all!"

"Quite."

Gordon Begg came loping up, looking vaguely astonished to see Faustaff there.

"What are you doing here, doctor?" he asked.

"The doctor is in trouble," Orelli answered for him. "Serious trouble. He wants to use our tunnel to get off E-15."

Begg shrugged. "Why not?"

Orelli pursed his lips. "You are too casual, Gordon. Too casual. 'Why not?' you say. This could be a trap of some kind. We must be careful."

"Doctor Faustaff would not lay *traps*," Begg said. "You are over-suspicious, Orelli."

"Better safe than sorry, Gordon."

"Nonsense. There is no question of the doctor not coming through with us — assuming that we *can* get through."

Faustaff saw Orelli's expression change momentarily to one of open anger and cunning, then the smile returned.

"Very well, Gordon. If you wish to be so reckless." He shrugged and turned away.

Begg asked Faustaff what had happened and Faustaff told him. Begg nodded sympathetically. Originally some sort of British soldier-diplomat on E-2, Begg's manner was gentle and remote and he was still an essentially kindly man, but the romantic mind of a Byron lay behind the mild eyes and courteous manner. Begg saw himself, even if others did not quite see him in the same way, as a freebooter, a wild adventurer, risking his life against the warped and haunted landscapes of the subspacial alternates. Begg lived this dangerous life and no doubt enjoyed it, but his outward appearance was still that of a somewhat vague and benign British diplomat.

Begg led Faustaff to the main tent where his men were already going through the tunnel with their loot.

"The tunnel's to E-11," Begg said. "It seemed no good in trying to get through to E-2 or E-1 under current conditions."

"Perhaps we should have realized that," Faustaff murmured, thinking of Peppiatt dead in subspace. E-11 wasn't a pleasant world, being comprised primarily of high mountains and barren valleys, but he could contact his base on E-11 and soon get back to E-1.

Orelli came into the tent smiling his brotherly love to everyone. "Are we ready?" he asked.

"Just about," said Begg. "The men have to collapse the other tents and get the heavy stuff through."

"I think it might be wise to leave the rest of the jeeps behind," Orelli said. "The doctor's prediction appears to have been accurate."

Begg frowned. "Accurate?"

"Outside," Orelli waved a hand. "Outside. Look outside."

Faustaff and Begg went to the entrance of the tent and looked. A great, troubled expanse of purple-blue radiance filled the horizon, growing rapidly. Its edges touched a blackness more absolute than the blackness of outer space. The grey ash had ceased to fall and the ground close by had lost its original appearance. Instead it was beginning to seethe with colour.

Wordlessly Begg and Faustaff flung themselves back towards the tunneler. Orelli was no longer in the tent. Evidently he hadn't waited for them. The tunnel was beginning to look unsteady, as if about to close. Faustaff followed Begg into it, feeling sick as he remembered Peppiatt's death earlier. The grey walls flickered and threatened to break. He moved on, not walking or propelling himself by any normal means, but drifting near-weightlessly until, with relief, he found himself standing on a rocky mountain slope at night time, a big, full moon above him.

Silhouetted in the darkness, other figures stood around on the mountain side. Faustaff recognized the outlines of Begg and Orelli.

Faustaff felt infinitely depressed. E-15 would soon be nothing more than fast-dissipating gas.

Even the salvagers seemed moved by their experience. They stood around in silence with only their breathing to be heard. In the valley below Faustaff could now make out a few lights, probably those of the salvagers' camps. He was not sure where this camp was in relation to his own base on E-11.

Faustaff saw a couple of men begin to climb down the slope, feeling their way carefully. Others followed and soon the whole party was beginning to pick its way down towards the camp, Faustaff in the rear.

At length they got to the valley and paused. Faustaff could now see that there were two camps — one at either side of the short valley.

Begg put his hand on the doctor's arm. "Come with me, doctor. We'll go to my camp. In the morning I'll take you to your base here."

Orelli gave a mock salute. "*Bon voyage*, doctor." He led his men towards his own camp. "I will see you tomorrow on the matter of spoil-division, Gordon."

"Very well," Begg said.

Begg's camp on E-11 had the same impermanent air as the hastily abandoned one on E-15. Begg took Faustaff to his personal quarters and had a extra bed brought in for him.

They were both exhausted and were soon asleep in spite of the thoughts that must have occupied both their minds.

CHAPTER SIX

KLOSTERHEIM ON A MOUNTAIN

Just after dawn Faustaff was awakened by the sounds of activity in Gordon Begg's camp. Begg was no longer in the tent and Faustaff heard his voice calling orders to his men. It sounded like another panic. Faustaff wondered what this one could be.

He went outside as soon as he could and saw Begg supervising the packing up of tents. A tunneler stood in the open air, and the salvager technicians were working at it.

"You're going through to another world," Faustaff said as he reached Begg. "What's happening?"

"We've had word of good pickings on E-3," Begg said, stroking his moustache and not looking directly at Faustaff. "A small U.M.S. was corrected near Saint Louis — but parts of the city were affected and abandoned. We can just get there before the situation's properly under control."

"Who told you this?"

Begg said: "One of our agents. We have quite good communications equipment, too, you know, doctor."

Faustaff rubbed his jaw. "Any chance of coming through your tunnel with you?"

Begg shook his head. "I think we've done you enough favours now, doctor. We're leaving Orelli's share of the loot behind us. You'll have to make some sort of deal with him. Be careful, though."

Faustaff would be careful. He felt somewhat vulnerable, being left to the doubtful mercies of Orelli, yet he had no intention of pressing Begg to let him through the tunnel to E-3. He watched numbly as the salvagers got their equipment and themselves through the subspacial tunnel and then witnessed the peculiar effect as the tunneler itself was drawn through the tunnel it had created. Within seconds of the tunneler's disappearance, Faustaff was alone amongst the refuse of Gordon Begg's camp.

Begg had left him behind knowing that he ran a fifty percent risk of being killed outright by the malicious Orelli. Perhaps in Begg's mind this was a fair chance. Faustaff didn't stop to wonder about Begg's psychology. Instead he began to walk away from the camp towards the mountains. He had decided to try to make his way to his own base rather than trust Orelli.

By midday Faustaff had sweated his way through two crooked canyons and half-way up a mountain. He slept for an hour before continuing. His intention was to reach the upper slopes of the mountain, which was not ρ articularly hard to climb and there was no snow to impair his progress. Once there, he would be able to get a better idea of where he was and plan his route. He knew that his base lay somewhere to the north-east of where he was, but it could be half-way around the world. Barren, and all-but completely covered by bleak mountain ranges though it might be, this planet was still Earth, with the same approximate size as Earth. Unless his base was fairly close, he couldn't give himself very good odds on his surviving for much more than a week. He still consoled himself that he was better off here than with Orelli and that there was a slim chance of search parties being sent out for him, though probably he was already thought to have been killed. That was the worst part of it. Without being self-important, he was aware that with him dead there was a good chance of his organization losing heart. Though he did little but co-ordinate his various teams and advise where he could, he was an important figure-head. He was more than that — he was the dynamic for the organization. Without him it might easily forget its purpose and turn its attention away from the real reason for its existence, the preservation of human life.

Sweating and exhausted Faustaff at last reached a point less than thirty feet from the mountain peak where he could look out over what seemed to be an infinity of crags. There were none he recognized. He must be several hundred miles from his base.

He sat down on the comparatively gradual slope and tried to reason out his predicament. Before long, he fell asleep.

He awoke in the evening to the sound of a muted cough behind him. Turning, unbelievingly, towards this human sound, he saw with some astonishment the dapper figure of Klosterheim sitting on a rock just above him.

"Good evening, Doctor Faustaff," Klosterheim smiled, his black eyes gleaming with ambiguous humour. "I find this view a trifle boring, don't you?"

Faustaff's depression left him and he laughed at the ludicrousness of this encounter. Klosterheim seemed bewildered for a second.

"Why do you laugh?"

Faustaff continued to laugh, shaking his large head slowly. "Here we are," he said, "with no human habitation to speak of in hundreds of miles…"

"That's so, doctor. But…"

"And you are going to try to pass this meeting off as coincidence. Where are you on your way to now, Herr Klosterheim? Paris? Are you just waiting here while you change planes?"

Klosterheim smiled again. "I suppose not. In fact I had a great deal of difficulty locating you after E-15 was eliminated. I believe E-15 is your term for that particular Earth simulation."

"It is. Simulation, eh? What does that mean?"

"Alternate, if you like."

"You're something to do with the D-squads, aren't you?"

"There is some sort of link between myself and the Demolition squads — an apt term that. Coined by your father wasn't it?"

"I think so. Well, what *is* the link? What are the D-squads? Who do they work for?"

"I didn't take the trouble of visiting this planet just to answer your questions, doctor. You know, you and your father have caused my principals a great deal of trouble. You would never believe how much." Klosterheim smiled. "That is why I am so reluctant to carry out their orders concerning you."

"Who are your 'principals' — what orders?"

"They are very powerful people indeed, doctor. Their orders were for me to kill you or otherwise make you powerless to continue interfering in their plans."

"You seem to approve of the trouble I have caused them," Faustaff said. "You're opposed to them, then? Some sort off double-agent? You're on my side?"

"On the contrary, doctor — your aims and theirs have many similarities. I am opposed to both of you. To them, there is some purpose in all this creation and destruction. To me, there is none. I feel that everything should die slowly, sweetly rotting away…" Klosterheim smiled, more wistfully this time. "But I am a dutiful employee. I must carry out their orders in spite of my own aesthetic fancies…"

Faustaff laughed, once again struck by the comedy of Klosterheim's affectation. "You are in love with death, then?"

Klosterheim seemed to take the question as a statement carrying some sort of censure.

"And you, doctor, are in love with life. Life, what is more, that is imperfect, crude, half-formed. Give me the overwhelming simplicity of death to *that!*"

"Yours seems a somewhat adolescent rejection of the tangle of being alive,"

Faustaff said, half to himself. "You could try to relax a bit — take it more as it comes."

Klosterheim frowned, his assurance leaving him even more, while Faustaff, calm, for some reason, and in fairly good spirits, pondered on what Klosterheim had said.

"I think you are a fool, Doctor Faustaff, a buffoon. I am not the adolescent, believe me. My life-span makes yours seem like the life-span of a mayfly. You are naïve, not I."

"Do you get no enjoyment from being alive, then?"

"My only pleasure comes from experiencing the decay of the universe. It *is* dying, doctor. I have lived long enough to *see* it dying."

"If that is true, does it matter to you or me?" Faustaff asked bemusedly. "Everything dies eventually — but that shouldn't stop us enjoying life while it is there to be enjoyed."

"But it has no purpose!" shouted Klosterheim, standing up. "No purpose! It is all meaningless. Look at you, how you spend your time, fighting a losing battle to preserve this little planet or that — for how long? Why do you do it?"

"It seems worthwhile. Have you no sympathy, then, for the people who are destroyed when a planet breaks up? It's a shame that they shouldn't have the chance to live as long as possible."

"But to what use do they put their stupid lives? They are dull, fuddled, materialistic, narrow — life gives them no real pleasure. The majority do not even appreciate the art that the best of them have produced. They are dead already. Hasn't that occurred to you?"

Faustaff debated this. "Their pleasures are perhaps a little limited, I'd agree. But they do enjoy themselves, most of them. And living is enough in itself. It is not just the pleasures of life that make it worthwhile, you know."

"You talk like one of them. Their amusements are vulgar, their thinking obtuse. They are not worth wasting time for. You are a brilliant man. Your mind is tuned to appreciating things they could never appreciate. Even their misery is mean and limited. Let the simulations die, doctor — let the inhabitants die with them!"

Again Faustaff shook his head in baffled amusement. "I can't follow you, Herr Klosterheim."

"Do you expect their gratitude for this stupid dedication of yours?"

"Of course not. They don't realize what's going on, most of them. I am a little arrogant, I suppose, now that you mention it, to interfere in this way. But I am not a thinking man in most spheres, Herr Klosterheim." He laughed. "You may be right — I am probably something of a buffoon."

Klosterheim seemed to pull himself together, as if Faustaff's admission had restored his assurance.

"Well, then," he said lightly. "Will you agree to let the planets die, as they must?"

"Oh, I'll continue to do what I can, I think. Assuming I don't starve out here, or fall off a mountain. This conversation is a little bit hypothetical when you consider my circumstances, isn't it?" he grinned.

It seemed rather incongruous to Faustaff that at that point Klosterheim should reach into his jacket and take a gun out.

"You puzzle me, I admit," said Klosterheim. "And I should like to watch you caper a little more. But since the moment is convenient and I have tiresome orders to carry out, I think I will kill you now."

Faustaff sighed. "It would probably be better than starving," he admitted, wondering if there was any chance of making a dash at Klosterheim.

CHAPTER SEVEN

CARDINAL ORELLI S CAMP

In a manner that was at once studied and awkward, Klosterheim pointed the gun at Faustaff's head while the doctor tried to think of the best action to take. He could rush Klosterheim or throw himself to one side, risking falling off the mountain ledge. It would be best to rush him.

He probably would not have succeeded if Klosterheim hadn't looked up at the moment he ran forward, crouching to keep as much of his great bulk out of the line of fire as possible. Klosterheim had been distracted by the sound of a helicopter engine above him.

Faustaff knocked Klosterheim's gun to one side and it went off with a bang that echoed around the peaks. He hit Klosterheim in the stomach and the bearded man went down, the gun falling out of his hand.

Faustaff picked up the gun and leveled it at Klosterheim.

Klosterheim frowned and gasped in pain. It was obvious that he expected Faustaff to kill him and a peculiar expression came into his eyes, a kind of introspective fear.

The helicopter was nearer. Faustaff heard it behind him and wondered who the pilot was. The noise of its engine became louder and louder until it deafened him. His clothes were ruffled by the breeze created by its rotors. He began to sidle round Klosterheim, keeping him covered, so he could see the occupant of the helicopter.

There were two. One of them, wearing a smile of infinite cruelty, was the red-robed Cardinal Orelli, his laser rifle pointing casually at Faustaff's stomach. The other was a nondescript pilot in brown overalls and helmet.

Orelli shouted something through the roar of the motor, but Faustaff couldn't hear what he was saying. Klosterheim got up from the ground and looked curiously at Orelli. Momentarily Faustaff felt more closely allied to Klosterheim than to Orelli. Then he realized that both were his enemies and that Klosterheim was much more likely to side with Orelli. Orelli must have come looking specifically for him, Faustaff decided, watching the pilot skillfully bring the helicopter down on the slope a little below him. Orelli's rifle was still pointing at him.

The engine noise died and Orelli climbed from the cockpit to the ground, walking up towards them, the fixed, cruel smile still on his lips.

"We missed you, doctor," he said. "We were expecting you at our camp much earlier. You lost your way, eh?"

Faustaff could see that Orelli had guessed the truth; that he had deliberately chosen to enter the mountains rather than join the malicious ex-clergyman.

"I haven't had the pleasure," said Orelli, turning a warier smile on Klosterheim.

"Klosterheim," said Klosterheim looking quizzical. "And you are…?"

"Cardinal Orelli. Doctor Faustaff calls me a 'salvager'. Where are you from, Mr Klosterheim?"

Klosterheim pursed his lips. "I am something of a wanderer," he said. "Here today, gone tomorrow, you know."

"I see. Well, we can chat at my camp. It is more comfortable there."

Faustaff realized that there was little point to arguing. Orelli kept him and Klosterheim covered a they walked down to the helicopter and climbed in, squeezing into the scarcely adequate back seats. With the gun cradled in his arm so that the snout pointed in their general direction over his shoulder, Orelli settled himself in the seat next to the pilot and closed the door.

The helicopter took to the air again, banked and began to fly back in the direction from which it had come. Faustaff, grateful for his reprieve, though expecting a worse fate, perhaps, from Orelli, who hated him, looked down at the grim mountains that stretched, range upon range, in all directions.

Quite soon he recognized the valley, and Orelli's camp came into sight, the collection of grey dome-tents hard to make out against the scrub of the valley floor.

The helicopter descended a short distance from the camp and landed with a bump. Orelli climbed out and signaled for Klosterheim and Faustaff to go ahead of him. They got down on to the ground and began to walk towards the camp, Orelli humming faintly what sounded like a Gregorian chant. He seemed in good spirits.

At Orelli's signal they bent their heads and entered his tent. It was made of material that permitted them to see outside without being visible themselves. There was a machine in the centre of the tent and Faustaff recognized it. He had also seen, once before, the two bodies that lay beside it.

"You recognize them?" Orelli asked casually, going to a large metal chest in one corner of the tent and producing a bottle and glasses. "A drink? Wine only, I'm afraid."

"Thank you," said Faustaff, but Klosterheim shook his head.

Orelli handed Faustaff a glass filled to the brim with red wine. "St Emilion, 1953 — from Earth Two," he said. "I think you'll find it pleasant."

Faustaff tasted it and nodded.

"Do you recognize them?" Orelli repeated.

"The bodies — they're D-squaders, aren't they?" Faustaff said. "I saw some like them on E-15. And the machine looks like a disrupter. I suppose you have plans to use it in some way, Orelli."

"None as yet, but doubtless I shall have. The D-squaders are not dead, you know. They have been at a constant temperature ever since we found them. We must have passed through that camp of theirs on E-15 shortly before you. The body temperature is low, but not that low. Yet they aren't breathing. Suspended animation?"

"That's nonsense," said Faustaff, finishing his drink. "All the experiments tried in that direction have proved disastrous. Remember the experiments at Malmo in '91 on E-1? Remember the scandal?"

"I would not remember, of course," Orelli pointed out, "since I am not a native of E-1. But I read about it. However, this seems to be suspended animation. They live, and yet they are dead. All our attempts to wake them have been useless. I was hoping that you, doctor, might help."

"How can I help?"

"Perhaps you will know when you have inspected the pair."

As they talked, Klosterheim had bent down and was examining one of the prone D-squaders. The man was of medium height and seemed, through his black overalls, to be a good physical specimen. The thing that was remarkable was that the two prone figures strongly resembled one another, both in features and in size. They had close-cropped, light brown hair, square faces and pale skins that were unblemished but had an unhealthy texture, particularly about the upper face.

Klosterheim pushed back the man's eyelid and Faustaff had an unpleasant shock as a glazed blue eye appeared to stare straight at him. It seemed for a second that the man was actually awake, but unable to move. Klosterheim let the eyelid close again.

He stood up, folding his arms across his chest. "Remarkable," he said. "What do you intend to do with them, Cardinal Orelli?"

"I am undecided. My interest is at present scientific — I wish to learn more about them. They are the first D-squaders we have ever managed to capture, eh, doctor?"

Faustaff nodded. He felt strongly that the D-squaders should have fallen into any hands other than Orelli's. He did not dare consider the uses which Orelli's twisted mind could think of for the disrupter alone. With it he would be able to blackmail whole worlds. Faustaff resolved to destroy the disrupter as soon as he received a reasonable opportunity.

Orelli took his empty glass from his hand and returned to the metal chest, pouring fresh drinks. Faustaff accepted the second glass of wine automatically, although he had not eaten for a long time. Normally he could hold a lot of liquor, but already the wine had gone slightly to his head.

"I think we should return to my headquarters on E-4," Orelli said. "There are better facilities for the necessary research. I hope you will accept my invitation, doctor, and help me in this matter."

"I assume you will kill me if I refuse," Faustaff replied tiredly.

"I should certainly not take it kindly," smiled Orelli, sharklike.

Faustaff said nothing to this. He decided that it was in his interest to return to E-4 with Orelli since once there he would stand a much better chance of contacting his organization once he had escaped.

"And what brought you to this barren world, Mr Klosterheim?" Orelli asked, with apparent heartiness.

"I had word that Doctor Faustaff was here. I wanted to talk to him."

"To talk? It appeared to me that you and the doctor were engaged in some sort of scuffle as I came on the scene. You are friends? I should have thought not."

"The argument was temporarily settled by your appearance, cardinal," said Klosterheim, his eyes matching Orelli's for cynical guile. "We were discussing certain philosophical matters."

"Philosophy? Of what kind? I myself have an interest in metaphysics. Not surprising, I suppose, considering my old calling."

"Oh, we talked of the relative merits of living or dying," Klosterheim said lightly.

"Interesting. I did not know you were philosophically inclined, Doctor Faustaff," Orelli murmured to the doctor. Faustaff shrugged and moved closer to the prone D-squaders until his back was to Klosterheim and Orelli.

He bent and touched the face of one of the D-squaders. It was faintly warm, like plastic at room-temperature. It didn't feel like a human skin at all.

He had become bored with Orelli's and Klosterheim's silly dueling. They evidently enjoyed it sufficiently to carry on with it for some time until Orelli theatrically interrupted Klosterheim in the middle of a statement and apologized that time was running short and he must make preparations for a tunnel to be made through subspace to his headquarters on E-4. As he left the tent a guard entered, covering the two men with his gun. Klosterheim darted Faustaff a sardonic look but Faustaff didn't feel like taking Orelli's place in the game. Although the guard would not let him approach too closely to the disrupter he contented himself with studying it from where he was until Orelli returned to say that a tunnel was ready.

CHAPTER EIGHT

Even more tired and very hungry, Faustaff stepped through the tunnel to find himself in what appeared to be the vault of a church, judging by the Gothic style of the stonework. The stone looked old but freshly cleaned. The air was cold and a trifle damp. Various stacks of the salvagers' field equipment lay around and the room was lighted by a malfunctioning neon tube. Orelli and Klosterheim had already arrived and were murmuring to one another. They stopped as Faustaff came up.

The D-squaders and the disrupter arrived soon after Faustaff, the prone D-squaders carried by Orelli's men. Orelli went ahead of them, opening a door at the far end of the vault and leading the way up worn, stone stairs into the magnificent interior of a large church, alive with sunshine pouring through stained glass. The only obvious change in the interior was the absence of pews. This gave the whole church an impression of being even larger than it was. It was a place that Faustaff could see easily compared to the finest Gothic cathedrals of Britain or France, an inspiring tribute to the creativeness of mankind. The church furniture remained, with a central altar and pulpit, an organ, and small chapels to left and right, indicating that the church had probably been Catholic. The wine was still affecting Faustaff slightly and he let his eyes travel up the columns, carved with fourteenth century saints, animals and plants, until he was looking directly up at the high, vaulted roof, crossed by a series of intricate stone cobwebs, just visible in the cool gloom.

When he looked down again he saw Klosterheim staring at him, a light smile on his lips.

Drunk with the beauty of the church Faustaff waved his hand around at it. "These are the works of those you would have destroyed, Klosterheim," he said, somewhat grandiosely.

Klosterheim shrugged. "I have seen finer work elsewhere. This is pitifully limited architecture by my standards, doctor — clumsy. Wood, stone, steel or glass, it doesn't matter what materials you use, it is always clumsy."

"This doesn't inspire you, then?" Faustaff asked rather incredulously.

Klosterheim laughed. "No. You are naïve, doctor."

Unable to describe the emotions which the church raised in him, Faustaff felt at a loss, wondering to what heights of feeling the architecture with which Klosterheim was familiar would raise him if he ever had the chance to experience it.

"Where is this architecture of yours?" he asked.

"In no place that you are familiar with, doctor." Klosterheim continued to be evasive and Faustaff once again wondered if he could have any connection with the D-squads.

Orelli had been supervising his men. Now he approached them. "What do you think of my headquarters?"

"Very impressive," said Faustaff for want of something better to say. "Is there more?"

"A monastery is attached to the cathedral. Those who live there follow somewhat different disciplines to those followed by the earlier occupants. Shall we go there now? I have a laboratory being prepared."

"I should like to eat before I do anything," Faustaff said. "I hope your cuisine is as excellent as your surroundings.

"If anything it is better," said Orelli. "Of course we shall eat first."

Later the three of them sat in a large room that had once been the abbot's private study. The alcoves were still lined with books, primarily religious works of various kinds; there were reproductions framed on the walls. Most of them showed various versions of *The Temptation of St Anthony* — Bosch, Brueghel, Grunëwald, Schöngauer, Huys, Ernst and Dali were represented, as well as some others whom Faustaff did not recognize.

The food was almost as good as Orelli had boasted and the wine was excellent, from the monastery's cellar. Faustaff pointed at the reproductions. "Your taste, Orelli, or your predecessor's?"

"His and mine, doctor. That is why I left them there. His interest was perhaps a little more obsessive than me. He went mad in the end, I hear. Some thought it possession, others…" he smiled his cruel smile and raised his glass somewhat mockingly to the Bosch — "delirium tremens."

"And what caused the monastery to become deserted — why isn't the cathedral used now?" Faustaff asked.

"Perhaps it will be obvious if I tell you our geographical location on E-4, doctor. We are in the area once occupied by North Western Europe. More precisely we are near where the town of Le Havre once stood, although there is no sign of the town and none of the sea, either, for that matter. Do you remember the U.M.S. that you managed to control in this area, doctor?"

Faustaff was puzzled. He had not yet seen outside the monastery walls and where, logically, windows should look beyond the cathedral or the monastery, they were heavily curtained. He had assumed he was in some rural town. Now he got up and went to the window, pulling back the heavy velvet curtain. It was dark, but the gleam of ice was unmistakable. Beneath the moon, and stretching to the horizon, was a vast plain of ice. Faustaff knew that it extended through Scandinavia, parts of Russia, Germany, Poland, Czechoslovakia and parts of Austria and Hungary, covering, in the other direction, half of Britain as far as Hull.

"But there is ice for hundreds of miles about," he said, turning back to where Orelli sat, sipping his wine and smiling still. "How on earth can this place have got here?"

"It was here already. It has been my headquarters since I discovered it three years ago. Somehow it escaped the U.M.S. and survived. The monks fled before the U.M.S. developed into anything really spectacular. I found it later."

"But I've never heard of anything quite like this," Faustaff said. "A cathedral and a monastery in the middle of a waste of ice. How did it survive?"

Orelli raised his eyes to the ceiling and smirked. "Divine influence, perhaps?"

"A freak, I suppose," Faustaff said sitting down again. "I've seen similar things — but nothing so spectacular."

"It took my fancy," Orelli said. "It is remote, roomy and, since I installed some heating, quite comfortable. It suits me."

Next morning, in Orelli's makeshift laboratory, Faustaff looked at the two now naked D-squaders lying on a bench in front of him. He had decided that either Orelli was playing with him, or else Orelli believed his knowledge to extend to biology. There was very little he could do except what he was doing now, having electroencephalographic tests made on the subjects. It was not expedient to disabuse Orelli altogether, for he was well aware that, if there was no likelihood of his coming up with something, Orelli would probably kill him.

The skins still had the quality of slightly warm plastic. There was no apparent breathing, the limbs were limp and the eyes glazed. When the assistants had placed the electrodes on the heads of the two subjects he went over to the electroencephalograph and studied the charts that began to rustle from the machine. They indicated only a single wave — a constant wave, as if the brain were alive but totally dormant. The test only proved what was already obvious.

Faustaff took a hypodermic and injected a stimulant into the first D-squader. Into the second he injected a depressant.

The electroencephalographic charts were exactly the same as the previous ones.

Faustaff was forced to agree with Orelli's suggestion that the men were in a total state of suspended animation.

The assistants Orelli had assigned to him were expressionless men with as little apparent character as the subjects they were studying. He turned to one of them and asked him to set up the X-ray machine.

The machine was wheeled forward and took a series of X-ray plates of both men. The assistant handed the plates to Faustaff.

A couple of quick glances at the plates were sufficient to show that, though the men on the table seemed to be ordinary human beings, they were not. Their organs were simplified, as was their bone structure.

Faustaff sat down. The implications of the discovery swam through his mind but he felt unable to concentrate on any one of them. These creatures could have come from outer space, they could be a race produced on one of the parallel earths.

Faustaff clung to this last thought. The D-squaders did not function according to any of the normal laws applied to animals. Perhaps they *were* artificial; robots of some kind. Yet the science needed to create such robots would be far more advanced than Earth One's.

Who had created them? Where did they come from? The extra data had only succeeded in making everything more confusing than it had been.

Faustaff lit a cigarette and made himself relax, wondering whether to mention any of this to Orelli. He would discover the truth for himself soon enough anyway.

He got up and asked for surgical instruments. With the aid of the X-ray plates he would be able to carry out some simple surgery on the D-squaders without endangering them. He cut through to the wrist of one of them. No blood flowed from the cut. He took a bone sample and a sample of the flesh and the skin. He tried to reseal the incision with the normal agents, but they refused to take. Finally he had to cover the incisions with ordinary tape.

He took his samples to a microscope, hoping he had enough basic biology to be able to recognize any differences they might have to normal skin, bone and flesh.

The microscope revealed some very essential differences which didn't require any specialized knowledge for him to recognize. The normal cell structure was apparently totally absent. The bone seemed composed of a metal alloy and the flesh of a dead, cellular material that resembled foam plastic, although the cells were much more numerous than on any plastic he was used to.

The only conclusion he could draw from this evidence was that the D-squaders were not living creatures in the true sense and that they were, in fact, robots — artificially created men.

The appearance of the materials that had gone into their construction was not familiar to Faustaff. The alloy and the plastic again indicated a superior technology to his own.

He began to feel perturbed for it was certain that the creatures had not been manufactured on any Earth that he knew. Yet they were capable of traveling through subspace and had obviously been designed for the sole purpose of manipulating the disrupters. That indicated the only strong possibility — that the D-squaders were the creation of some race operating outside subspace and beyond the solar system, from a base in ordinary space-time. The attack, then, probably did not come from a human source, as Faustaff had always believed. This was the reason for his uneasiness. Would it be possible to think out the motives of an unhuman race? It was unlikely. And without an indication of why they were trying to destroy the worlds of subspace, it seemed impossible to invent ways of stopping them for any real length of time.

He came to a decision then. He must destroy the disrupter, at least. It lay in one comer of the laboratory, ready for investigation.

He walked towards it.

At that moment he felt a tingling sensation in his wrist and the room seemed to fade. He felt sick and his head began to ache. He found it impossible to draw air into his lungs. He recognized the sensations.

He was being invoked.

CHAPTER NINE

E - ZERO

Professor May looked relieved. He stood wiping his glasses in the bare concrete room which Faustaff recognized as being in Earth One's headquarters at Haifa.

Faustaff waited for his head to clear before advancing towards May.

"We never thought we'd get you back," said May. "We've been trying for the last day, ever since you disappeared in the break-up of E-15. I heard our adjustor was destroyed."

"I'm sorry," said Faustaff.

May shrugged and replaced his glasses. His pudgy face looked unusually haggard. "That's nothing compared to what's going on. I've got some news for you."

"And I for you." Faustaff reflected that May's invocation had come at exactly the wrong time. But it was no use mentioning it. At least he was back at his own base and could perhaps conceive a plan that would permanently put Orelli out of action.

May walked towards the door. Technicians were disconnecting the big invoker which had been used to pull Faustaff through subspace once they had picked up the signal from the invocation disc on his wrist.

Faustaff followed May out into the corridor. May led the way to the lift. On the fourth floor, they found the man's office.

Several other men were waiting there. Faustaff recognized some of them as heads of Central Headquarters departments and others he knew as communications specialists.

"Have you something to tell us before we begin?" May said, picking up a VC after introductions and greetings. He ordered coffee and replaced the VC.

"It won't take me long to fill you in," Faustaff said. He settled himself into a chair. He told them of Klosterheim's attempt to kill him and how it was plain that Klosterheim knew much more about the worlds of subspace than he had admitted, that he had referred to his "powerful principals" and indicated that the Faustaff organization couldn't stand a big attack — and neither could the worlds of subspace. He then went on to describe Orelli's "specimens" and what he had discovered about them.

The reaction to this wasn't as startled as he had expected. May simply nodded, his lips set tightly.

"This fits in with our discovery, doctor," he said. "We have just contacted a new alternate Earth. Or I should say part of one. It is at this moment being formed."

"An alternate actually being created!" Faustaff was excited now. "Can't we get there — see how it happens. It could tell us a lot…"

"We've tried to get through to E-Zero, as we've called it, but every attempt seems to have been blocked. This Earth isn't being created naturally — there is an intelligence behind it."

Faustaff took this easily. The logical assumption now could only be that some non-human force was at work not only, as was now obvious, destroying worlds, but creating them as well. Somewhere the D-squaders, Klosterheim and Maggy White fitted in — and could probably tell them a lot. All the events of recent days showed that the situation was, from their point of view, worsening. And the odds that faced them were bigger than they had guessed.

Faustaff helped himself to a cup of coffee from the tray that had been brought in.

Professor May seemed impatient. "What can we do, doctor? We are unprepared for the attack, we are certainly ill-equipped to deal with even another big D-squad offensive of the kind you have just experienced on E-15. It is obvious that up to now these forces have been playing with us."

Faustaff nodded and sipped his coffee. "Our first objective must be Orelli's headquarters," he said. He felt sick as he made his next statement. "It must be destroyed — and everything that is in it."

"Destroyed?" May was well acquainted with Faustaff's obsessive views about the sanctity of life.

"There is nothing else we can do. I never thought — I hoped I would never find myself in a situation like this, but we shall just have to follow the line of killing a few for the sake of the many." Even as Faustaff spoke he heard his own voice of a short time ago talking about the dangers of justifying the taking of life under any conditions.

Professor May seemed almost satisfied. "You say he's on E-4. The area would be covered by grid sections 38 and 62 roughly. Do you want to lead the expedition? We shall have to send 'copters and bombs, I suppose."

Faustaff shook his head. "No, I won't go with it. Give them a five-minute warning, though. Give them that, at least. That won't allow them time to set up a tunneler and escape with the disrupter. I told you about the place — it'll be easy to spot, a cathedral."

After Professor May had gone off to arrange the expedition Faustaff sat studying the information that had so far been gathered about Earth Zero. There was very little. Apparently the discovery had been almost accidental. When E-15 was breaking up and it was becoming increasingly difficult to get tunnels between the worlds the technicians on E-1 found data being recorded on their instruments that was unusual. A check had led to contact with E-0. They had sent out probes and had found a planet that was still unstable, at that stage only a sphere consisting of elements still in a state of mutation. Soon after this their probes had been blocked and they had been unable to get anything but faint indications of the existence of the new body. All they really knew was that it was there, but they did not know how it had come there or who was responsible for it. Faustaff wanted to know *why* above everything else.

It was perhaps an unscientific attitude, he reflected as he got up. He had never before had quite such a strong sense of being unable to control a situation he found himself in. There was so little he could do at this stage. Philosophically he decided to give up and go to his house in the outer suburbs of Haifa, get a full night's sleep — the first he would have had in some time — hoping to have some ideas in the morning.

He left the building and walked out into the midday sunshine of the busy modern city. He flagged down a taxi and gave his address. Wearily he listened to the taxi-driver talking about the "crisis" which seemed to have developed in his absence. He couldn't quite follow the details and made no serious attempt to, but it appeared that the East and West were having one of their periodic wrangles, this time over some South East Asian country and Yugoslavia. Since Tito's death Yugoslavia had been considered fair game for both blocs and although the Yugoslavs had steadfastly resisted any attempts at colonialism on the part of both East and West their situation was getting weaker. A revolution — from what appeared to be an essentially small group of fundamentalist Communists — had given the U.S.S.R. and the U.S.A. an excuse for sending in peace-keeping forces. From what the taxi-driver was saying there had already been open fighting between the Russians and the Americans and the Russian and American ambassadors had just withdrawn from the respective countries. Faustaff, used to such periodic events, was not able to feel the same interest in the situation as the taxi-driver. In his opinion the man was unnecessarily excited. The thing would die down eventually. It always had. Faustaff had more important things on his mind.

The taxi drew up outside his house, a small bungalow with a garden full of orange blossom. He paid the driver and walked up the concrete path to the front door. He felt in his pockets for the key, but as usual he had lost it. He reached up to the ledge over the door and found the spare key, unlocked the door, replaced the key and went in. The house was cool and tidy. He rarely used most of the rooms. He walked into his bedroom which was in the same state as he'd left it several weeks before. Clothes lay everywhere, on the floor and the unmade bed. He went to the window and opened it. He picked a towel off the V that faced the foot of his bed and went into the bathroom. He began to shower.

When he returned, naked, to his room, there was a girl sitting on the bed. Her perfect legs were crossed and her perfect hands lay folded in her lap. It was Maggy White, whom Faustaff had encountered at the same time as he had first met Klosterheim in the desert motel on E-3.

"Hello, doctor," she said coolly. "Do you never wear clothes, then?"

Faustaff remembered that the first time he'd met her he had been naked. He grinned and in doing so felt immediately his old relaxed self.

"As rarely as possible," he smiled. "Have you come to try to do me in, too?"

Her humourless smile disturbed him. He wondered if making love to her would produce any real emotion. Her effect on him was far deeper than Klosterheim's. She didn't reply.

"Your friend Klosterheim had a bash at it," he said. "Or have you been in touch with him since then?

"What makes you think Klosterheim is my friend?"

You certainly travel together."

"That doesn't make us friends."

"I suppose not."

Faustaff paused and then said: "What's the latest news concerning the simulations." The last word was one Klosterheim had used. He hoped that he might trick her into giving him more information if he sounded knowledgable.

"Nothing fresh," she said.

Once again Faustaff wondered how a woman so well-endowed on the surface could appear to be so totally sexless.

"Why are you here?" he asked, going to the wardrobe and getting fresh clothes out. He pulled on a pair of jeans, hauling the belt around his huge stomach. He was putting on weight, he thought, the belt could hardly be pulled to the first notch.

"A social visit," she said.

"That's ridiculous. I see that a new Earth is taking shape. Why?"

"Who can explain the secrets of the universe better than yourself, doctor, a scientist?"

"You."

"I know nothing of science."

Out of curiosity Faustaff sat on the bed beside her and stroked her knee. Once again she smiled coolly and her eyes became hooded. She lay back on the bed.

Faustaff lay beside her and stroked her stomach. He noticed that her breathing remained constant even when he stroked her breasts through the cloth of her buttoned-up grey suit. He rolled over and stood up.

"Could you be Mark Two?" he asked. "I dissected a D-squader a while ago. They're robots, you know — or androids, I think the term is."

Perhaps he spotted a flash of anger in her eyes. They certainly widened for a moment and then half-closed again.

"Is that what you are? An android?"

"You could find out if you made love to me."

Faustaff smiled and shook his head. "Sweetheart, you're just not my type."

"I thought any young woman was your type, doctor."

"So did I till I met you."

Her face remained expressionless.

"What are you here for?" he asked. "You didn't come because you felt randy, that's certain."

"I told you — a social visit."

"Orders from your principals. To do what, I wonder."

"To convince you of the silliness of continuing this game you're playing." She shrugged. "Klosterheim was unable to convince you. I might be able to."

"What line are you going to take?"

"A reasonable one. A logical one. Can't you see that you are interfering with something that you will never understand, that you are just a minor irritant to the people who have almost total power over the parallels…"

"The simulations? What do they simulate?"

"You are dull, doctor. They simulate Earth, naturally."

"Then which Earth is it that they simulate. This one?"

"You think yours is any different from the others? They are all simulations. Yours was, until recently, simply the last of many. Do you know how many simulations there have been?"

"I've known of sixteen."

"More than a thousand."

"So you've destroyed nine hundred and eighty-six altogether. I suppose there were people on all of them. You've murdered millions!" Faustaff could not stop himself from feeling shocked by this revelation.

"They owed their lives to us. They were ours to take."

"I can't accept that."

"Turn on the V. Get the news," she said suddenly.

"What for?"

"Turn it on and see."

He went to the set and switched it on. He selected the English-speaking channel for convenience. Some people were being interviewed. They looked grim and their voices were dull with fatalism.

As Faustaff listened he realized that war must have been declared between the East and West. The men were not talking about the possible outcome. They were discussing which areas might survive. The general effect was that they didn't expect anywhere to survive.

Faustaff turned to Maggy White who was smiling again. "Is this it? The nuclear war? I didn't expect it — I thought it was impossible."

"Earth One is doomed, doctor. It's a fact. While you were worrying about the other simulations your own was nearing destruction. You can't blame anyone else for this, doctor. Who caused the death of Earth One...?"

"It must be artificially done. Your people must have..."

"Nonsense. It was built into your society."

"Who built it in?"

"They did, I suppose, but unknowingly. It is not in their interest, I assure you, to have this happen to a planet. They are hoping for a utopia. They are desperately trying to create one."

"Their methods seem crude."

"Perhaps they are — by their standards, but certainly not by yours. You could never comprehend the complicated task they have set themselves."

"Who are they?"

"People. In the long run your ideals and theirs are not so different. Their scheme is vaster, that is all. Human beings must die. It is thought to be unfortunate by many of them. They aren't unsympathetic..."

"Not unsympathetic? They destroy worlds casually, they let this happen — this war — when from all you say they could stop it. I can't have much respect for a race that regards life so cheaply."

"They are a desperate race. They are driven to desperate means."

"Haven't they ever — reflected?"

"Of course, many thousands of your years ago, before the situation worsened. There were debates, arguments, factions created. A great deal of time was lost."

"I see. And if they are so powerful and they want me out of the way, why don't they destroy me as they destroy whole planets? Your statements appear to be inconsistent."

"Not so. It is a very complicated matter to eliminate individuals. It must be done by agents, such as myself. Usually it has been found expedient to destroy the whole planet if too many irritating individuals interfered in their plans."

"Are you going to fill me in — tell me everything about these people. If I'm going to die because of a nuclear war, it shouldn't matter."

"I wouldn't run the risk. You have a large share of pure luck, doctor. I would suffer if I told you more and you escaped."

"How would they punish you?"

"I'm sorry. I've told you enough." She spoke rapidly, for the first time.

"So I'm to die. Then why did you come here to dissuade me if you knew what was going to happen?"

"As I said, you may not die. You are lucky. Can't you simply accept that you are complicating a situation involving matters that are completely above your head? Can't you accept that there is a greater purpose to all this?"

"I can't accept death as a necessary evil, if that's what you mean — or premature death, anyway."

"Your moralizing is naïve — cheap."

"That's what your friend Klosterheim says. But it isn't to me. I'm a simple man, Miss White."

She shrugged. "You will never understand, will you?"

"I don't know what you mean."

"That's what I mean."

"Why didn't you kill me, anyway?" He turned away and began to put on a shirt. The V continued to drone on, the voices becoming hollower and hollower. "You had the opportunity. I didn't know you were in the house."

"Both Klosterheim and myself have a fairly free hand in how we handle problems. I was curious about these worlds, particularly about you. I have never been made love to." She got up and came towards him. "I had heard that you were good at it."

"Only when I enjoy it. It seems odd that these people of yours understand little of human psychology from what I've gathered."

"Do you understand the psychology of a frog in any detail?"

"A frog's psychology is a considerably simpler thing than a person's."

"Not to a creature with a much more complex psychology than a person's."

"I'm tired of this, Miss White. I must get back to my headquarters. You can write me off as an irritant from now on. I don't expect my organization to survive the coming war."

"I expected you to escape to some other simulation. It would give you a respite anyway."

He looked at her curiously. She had sounded almost animated, almost concerned for him.

In a softer tone he said: "Are you suggesting that?"

"If you like."

He frowned, looking into her eyes. For some reason he suddenly felt sympathy for her without knowing why.

"You'd better get going yourself," he said tersely, turning and making for the door.

The streets outside were deserted. This was unusual for the time of day. A bus stopped nearby. He ran to catch it. It would take him close to his headquarters. He was the only person on the bus apart from the driver.

He felt lonely as they drove into Haifa.

CHAPTER TEN

ESCAPE FROM E-1

Faustaff and Professor May watched as men and equipment were hurried through the tunnel which had been made to E-3. The expression on May's face was one of hopelessness. The bombs had already started to drop and the last report they had seen had told them that Britain had been totally destroyed, as had half of Europe.

They had given themselves an hour to evacuate everything and everyone they could. Professor May checked his watch and glanced at Faustaff.

"Time's up, doctor."

Faustaff nodded and followed May into the tunnel. It took a great deal to depress him, but to see the organization he and his father had built up crumbling, forced to abandon its main centre, made him miserable and unable to think clearly.

The trip through the grey tunnel to the familiar gilt and plush dance hall of *The Golden Gate* which was their main transceiving station on E-3, was easily made. When they arrived, the men just stood around, murmuring to one another and glancing at Faustaff; he knew that he was expected to cheer them up. He forced himself out of his mood and smiled.

"We all need a drink," was the only thing he could think of to say as he walked towards the dusty bar. He leaned across it and reached under, finding bottles and glasses and setting them on the counter. The men moved forward and took the glasses he filled for them.

Faustaff hauled himself up so that he was sitting on the bar.

"We're in a pretty desperate situation," he told them. "The enemy — I've hardly any better idea of them than you have — have for some reason decided to launch an all-out attack on the subspacial worlds. It's plain now that all their previous attacks, using the D-squaders, have hardly been serious. We underestimated the opposition, if you like. Frankly my own opinion is that it won't be long before they succeed in breaking up all the subspacial alternates — that's what they want."

"Then there's nothing we can do," Professor May said wearily.

"Only one thing occurs to me," Faustaff said. "We know that the enemy considers these worlds as something to be destroyed. But what about E-Zero? This has just been created — either by them or by someone else like them — and I gather they aren't normally willing to destroy a recently created world. Our only chance is in getting a big tunnel through to E-Zero and setting up our headquarters there. From then on we can evacuate people from these worlds to E-Zero."

"But what if E-Zero can't support so many?" a man said.

"It will have to." Faustaff drained his glass. "As far as I can see our only course of action is to concentrate everything on getting a tunnel through to E-Zero."

Professor May shook his head, staring at the floor.

"I don't see the point," he said. "We're beaten. We're going to die sooner or later with everyone else. Why don't we just give up now?"

Faustaff nodded sympathetically. "I understand — but we've got our responsibilities. We all took those on when we joined the organization."

"That was before we knew the extent of what we'd let ourselves in for," May said sharply.

"Possibly. But what's the point of being fatalistic at this stage? If we're due to be wiped out, we might at least try the only chance we have."

"And what then?" May looked up. He seemed angry now. "A few more days before the enemy decides to destroy E-Zero? Count me out, doctor."

"Very well." Faustaff glanced at the others. "Who feels the same as Professor May?"

More than half of the men there indicated that they shared May's views. At least half of the remainder seemed undecided.

"Very well," he said again. "It's probably best that we sorted this out now. Everyone who is ready to start work can remain here. The rest can leave. Some of you will be familiar with E-3, perhaps you can look after those who aren't."

When May and the others had left, Faustaff spoke to his chief of Communications on E-3, John Mahon, telling him to call in all operatives from the other subspacial alternates and get them working on an attempt to break through to E-Zero.

Class H agents — those who worked for the organization without realizing what it was — were to be paid off. When Faustaff brought up the subject of Class H, Mahon snapped his fingers. "That reminds me," he said. "You remember

I put some Class H men on to checking up on Klosterheim and Maggy White?"

It seemed a long time ago. Faustaff nodded. "I suppose nothing came of it."

"The only information we got indicates that they have a tunneler of their own — or at least some method of traveling through the subspacial levels. Two Class H agents followed them out to L.A. to a cottage they evidently use as their base on E-3. They never came out of that cottage, and a check showed that they weren't there. The agents reported finding a lot of electronic equipment they couldn't recognize."

"It fits with what I found out," Faustaff said. He told Mahon about his encounters with the two. "If only we could get them to give us more information we might stand a better chance of getting a concrete solution to this mess."

Mahon agreed. "It might be worth going out to this cottage of theirs, if we could find the time. What do you think?"

Faustaff debated. "I'm not sure. There's every likelihood that they'd have removed their equipment by now anyway."

"Right," said Mahon. "I'll forget about it. We can't spare anyone now to go out and have a look for us."

Faustaff picked up a tin box. It contained the information gathered about E-Zero. He told Mahon that he was going to his apartment to go through it again and could be contacted there.

He drove his Cadillac through the sunny streets of 'Frisco, his enjoyment of the city's atmosphere now somewhat tainted by his mood of unaccustomed grimness.

It was only as he entered his apartment and saw how tidy the place was that he remembered Nancy Hunt. She wasn't there now. He wondered if she had given him up and left, although the indications were that she was only out temporarily.

He went to his desk and settled down to work, the VC beside him. As he studied the data, he called ideas through to his team at *The Golden Gate*.

Nancy came in around midnight.

"Fusty! Where have you been? You look dreadful. What's been happening?"

"A lot. Can you make me some coffee, Nancy?"

"Sure."

The redhead went straight into the kitchen and came out later with coffee and doughnuts. "Want a sandwich, Fusty? There's Danish salami and liver sausage, rye bread and some potato salad."

"Make me a few," he said. "I'd forgotten I was hungry."

"There must be something important up, then," she said, laying the tray down on a table near him and returning to the kitchen.

Faustaff thought there might be a way of creating a new kind of warp in subspace, something they'd thought of in the past but dismissed since their methods had then been adequate. He called through to *The Golden Gate* and spoke to Mahon about it, telling him to find all the notes that had been made at the time. He realized that it was going to be several days before anything could be worked out properly and more time would be wasted in adapting the tunnelers, but his team was good, if depleted, and if anything could be done, they'd do it.

His brain was beginning to get fuzzy and he realized he would have to relax for a while before continuing. When Nancy came back with the sandwiches he went and sat next to her on the couch, kissed her and ate his way through the food. He sat back feeling better.

"What have you been doing, Nancy?"

"Hanging around, waiting for you. I went to see a V-drama today."

"What was it about?"

"Cowboys. What have *you* been doing, Fusty? I was worried."

"Traveling," he said. "Urgent business, you know."

"You could have called."

"Not from where I was."

"Well, let's go to bed now and make up for all that time wasted."

He felt even more miserable. "I can't," he said. "I've got to go on with what I'm doing. I'm sorry, Nancy."

"What's all this about, Fusty?" She stroked his arm sympathetically. "You're really upset, aren't you? It's not just a business problem."

"Yes, I'm upset. D'you want to hear the whole story?" He realized that he needed Nancy's comforting. There would be no harm now in telling her the whole story. Briefly he outlined the situation.

When he'd finished she looked incredulous. "I believe you," she said. "But I can't — can't take it all in. So we're all going to die, is that it?"

"Unless I can do something about it. Even then, most of us will be destroyed." The VC began to ring. He picked it up. It was Mahon. "Hello, Mahon. What is it?"

"We're checking the new warp theory. It seems to be getting somewhere, but that wasn't why I called. Just thought I'd better tell you that E-14 and E-13 are in Total Break-up. You were right. The enemy's getting busy. What can we do?"

Faustaff sighed. "Assign emergency teams to evacuate as many as possible from the deeper worlds. Evidently the enemy are working systematically. We'll just have to hope we can consolidate on here and E-2 and make a fight of it. Better order all the adjustors brought to E-2 and E-3. We'll spread them out. There might be a chance. We'll have to fight."

"There was one other thing," Mahon said. "I think May organized an expedition to E-4 before you left E-1."

"That's right. They were going to bomb Orelli's headquarters. Were they successful?"

"They couldn't find it. They came back."

"But they must have found it — they couldn't have missed it."

"The only thing they found was a crater in the ice. It could just be that the whole cathedral had vanished — been shifted. You said Klosterheim was with them, they had two D-squaders and a disrupter. It could easily mean that Klosterheim is helping Orelli. He probably knows the potentialities of the disrupter. Or maybe something went wrong and the cathedral was destroyed in some way. The only thing that's certain is that they've vanished."

"I don't think they've destroyed themselves," Faustaff replied. "I think we'll have to watch for them in the near future. The combination of Orelli and Klosterheim is a bad one for us."

"I won't forget. And I'll get the evacuation scheme moving. Any more details for us?"

Faustaff felt guilty. He'd spent too much time talking to Nancy.

"I'll let you know," he said.

"Okay." Mahon put the receiver down.

"Got to get on with it now, Nancy," he said. He told her what he'd heard from Mahon.

He settled himself at his desk and began work again, making notes and equations on the pad beside him. Tomorrow he would have to go back to the centre and use the computers himself.

As he worked, Nancy kept him supplied with coffee and snacks. By eight the next morning he began to feel he was getting somewhere. He assembled his notes, put them in a folder, and was about to say goodbye to Nancy when she said:

"Mind if I come along, Fusty? I wouldn't like to have to hang around here for you again."

"Okay," he said. "Let's go."

As they arrived at *The Golden Gate* they found that the place had a visitor. It was Gordon Begg. He came forward with John Mahon, through a confusion of technicians and machinery that now filled the dance hall.

"Mr Begg wants to see you, doctor," Mahon said. "He's got some news about Orelli, I think."

"We'd better go upstairs, Gordon," Faustaff said. They climbed the staircase to the second floor and entered a small, cluttered room where old furniture had been piled. "This'll have to do," Faustaff said as they sat down where they could. Nancy was still with them. Faustaff didn't feel like asking her to wait anywhere else.

"I must apologize for leaving you behind on E-11." Begg stroked his long moustache, looking even more mournful than usual. "But then I had no conception of what was going on. You know it all, I suppose — the destruction of E-14 and E-13, the war that is destroying E-1?"

"Yes." Faustaff nodded.

"And you know that Orelli has leagued himself with this chap with a funny name...?"

"Klosterheim. I suspected it. Though I'm still unable to think what mutual interest they have. It is in yours and Orelli's for things to remain basically unchanged."

"As salvagers, yes. But Orelli has other schemes. That's why I came to see you. He contacted me this morning, at my base on E-2."

"So he is alive. I thought so."

"This other chap — Klosterheim — was with him. They wanted my help. From what I can gather Klosterheim was working for another group, but he's turned traitor. That was a little obscure. I couldn't quite make out who the other group were. There's a new parallel been formed, I gather..."

"E-Zero, that's right. Did they tell you anything about it?"

"Nothing much. Klosterheim said something about its not having been 'activated' yet, whatever that means. Anyway they have plans for going there and setting up their own government, something like that. Orelli was cautious, he didn't tell me much. He concentrated mainly on telling me that all the other worlds are due to break up soon and nothing will be able to stop this happening, that I might just as well throw in my lot with him and Klosterheim since I had everything to lose and something to gain. I told him that I wasn't interested."

"Why did you do that?"

"Call it a psychological quirk. As you know, doctor, I have never felt any malice towards you and have always been careful never to attack you or any of your men by using violence. I preferred to leave you and work on my own — that's part of the same psychological quirk. But now it looks as if the crunch is coming, I wondered if I could help."

Faustaff was touched by Begg's statement. "I am sure you could. Just the act of offering has helped me, Gordon. I suppose you have no idea how Orelli and Klosterheim intend to get through to E-Zero?"

"Not really. They did refer to E-3 at one point, I think they might have had some equipment here. They certainly boasted of a refined tunneler — Klosterheim seemed to link it with a disrupter that Orelli had captured. They can shift much bigger masses through subspace, I gathered."

"So that's what happened to the cathedral. But where is it now?"

"The cathedral?"

Faustaff explained. Begg said he knew nothing of this.

"I have the feeling," Faustaff said, "that the shifting of the cathedral has no real significance. It would have been done simply to exhibit the power of the new tunneler. But it is difficult to see why Klosterheim has reneged on his own people. I'd better fill you in on this." He repeated all he knew about Klosterheim and Maggy White.

Begg took all the information expressionlessly. "An alien race manipulating human beings from somewhere beyond Earth. It sounds too fantastic, doctor. Yet I'm convinced."

"I think I've been foolish," Faustaff said. "You say they mentioned a base on E-3. We know about it. There might be a chance of finding something after all. Do you want to come and see, Gordon?"

"If you'd like me along."

"I would. Come on."

The three of them left the room. Faustaff enquired about air transport, but there was none available. He did not dare wait on the off-chance of a 'copter coming through and he was not sure enough of himself to requisition one being used for evacuation purposes. He got into his Cadillac and they drove out of San Francisco, heading for Los Angeles.

They looked a strange trio, Faustaff driving, his huge body squeezed into the inadequate seat of the car, Nancy and Begg in the back seats. Begg had insisted on bringing the antiquated machine-gun he always carried. His tall, thin body was held erect, the gun cradled in his arm. He looked like a Victorian nobleman on safari, his eyes staring straight ahead down the long road that stretched into the Great American Desert.

CHAPTER ELEVEN

THE WAY THROUGH

They found the house that had been marked for them on their map by Mahon before they left.

It lay in a quiet Beverly Hills cul-de-sac about fifty yards from the road. A well-kept lawn lay in front and a gravel drive led to the house. They drove up it. Faustaff was too tired to bother about secrecy. They got out of the car and a couple of heaves of Faustaff's body broke the door open. They moved into the hall. It was wide and an open staircase led up from it.

"Mahon said they'd found the equipment in the back room," Faustaff said, leading the way there. He opened the door. Orelli stood there. He was alone, but his rifle was pointing straight at Faustaff's head. His thin lips smiled.

"Doctor Faustaff. We'd missed you."

"Forget the villainous dialogue, Orelli." Faustaff skipped suddenly to one side and rushed at the ex-cardinal who pulled the trigger. A beam went high and pierced the outer wall. Faustaff began to grapple the gun from Orelli who was now snarling.

Orelli plainly hadn't expected such sudden action from Faustaff who was normally loathe to indulge in any sort of violence.

Begg stepped in behind him while Nancy hovered in the doorway. He pushed the muzzle of his machine-gun into Orelli's back and said softly: "I shall have to kill you unless you are sensible, Orelli. Drop your rifle."

"Turncoat!" Orelli said as he dropped the gun. He seemed offended and surprised by Begg's allying himself with Faustaff. "Why have you sided with this fool?"

Begg didn't bother to reply. He tugged the laser rifle's cord from the power pack on Orelli's back and threw the gun across the room.

"Where's Klosterheim and the rest of your men, Orelli?" Faustaff asked.

"We're impatient — we want to know a lot quickly. We're ready to kill you unless you tell us."

"Klosterheim and my men are on the new planet."

"E-Zero? How did you get through when we couldn't?"

"Klosterheim has far greater resources than yours, doctor. You were stupid to offend him. A man with his knowledge is worth cultivating."

"I wasn't interested in cultivating him, I was more interested in stopping him from killing me, if you remember."

Orelli turned to Begg. "And you, Gordon, taking sides against me, a fellow salvager. I am disappointed."

"We have nothing in common, Orelli. Answer the doctor's questions."

Just then Nancy shouted and pointed. Turning, Faustaff saw that the air behind him seemed to glow and the wall beyond became hazy. A tunnel was being formed. Klosterheim must be coming through. He picked up the useless laser rifle and stood watching the tunnel as it shimmered and took shape. It was of a glowing reddish colour, unlike the dull grey of the tunnels he was used to. Out of it stepped Klosterheim, he was unarmed. He smiled, apparently unperturbed, when he saw what had happened.

"What are you trying to do, doctor?" Behind him the tunnel began to fade.

"We're after information primarily, Herr Klosterheim," Faustaff answered, feeling more confident now that it was plain Klosterheim had no more men with him. "Are you going to give it to us here, or must we take you back to our headquarters?"

"What sort of information, Doctor Faustaff?"

"Firstly we want to know how you can get through to E-Zero when we can't."

"Better machines, doctor."

"Who made the machines?"

"My erstwhile principals. I could not tell you how to build one, only how to work one."

"Well, you can show us."

"If you wish." Klosterheim shrugged and went to a machine that was evidently the main console for the rest of the devices in the room. "It is a simple matter of tapping out a set of co-ordinates and setting a switch."

Faustaff decided that Klosterheim was probably telling the truth and he didn't know how the advanced tunneler worked. He would have to get a team down here immediately and have them check it over.

"Can you keep them covered, Gordon?" he said. "I'll call my headquarters and get some people here as soon as possible."

Begg nodded and Faustaff went into the hall where he'd seen the VC.

He got through to the operator and gave her the number he wanted. The

VC rang for some time before someone answered. He asked for Mahon.

At length Mahon came on the line and Faustaff told him what had happened. Mahon promised to send a team up by 'copter right away.

Faustaff was just going back into the room when he heard footsteps on the path outside. He went to the door and there was Maggy White.

"Doctor Faustaff," she nodded, as seemingly unsurprised by his presence as Klosterheim had been. Faustaff began to think that all his recent actions had been anticipated.

"Were you expecting me to be here?" he asked.

"No. Is Klosterheim here?"

"He is."

"Where?"

"In the back room. You'd better join him."

She went ahead of Faustaff, looked at Nancy curiously and then stepped into the room.

"We've got them all now," Faustaff said, feeling much better. "We'll wait for the team to arrive and then we can get down to business. I suppose," he turned to Klosterheim, "you or Miss White wouldn't like to tell us the whole story before they come?"

"I might," Klosterheim said, "particularly since it would now be best if I convinced you to throw in your lot with Cardinal Orelli and myself."

Faustaff glanced at Maggy White. "Do you feel the same as Klosterheim? Are you prepared to tell me more?"

She shook her head. "And I shouldn't believe too much of what he tells you, either, doctor."

Klosterheim glanced at his wrist watch.

"It doesn't matter now," he said, almost cheerfully. "We appear to be on our way."

Suddenly it seemed that the whole house was lifted by a whirlwind and Faustaff thought briefly that Orelli had rightly called him a fool. He should have realized that what could be done with a gigantic cathedral could also be done with a small house.

The sensation of movement was brief, but the scene through the window was very different. Amorphous, it gave the impression of an unfinished painted stage set. Trees and hedges were there, the sky, sunlight, but none of them seemed real.

"Well, you wanted to get here, doctor," smiled Klosterheim, "and here we are. I think you called it E-Zero."

CHAPTER TWELVE

THE PETRIFIED PLACE

Maggy White glowered at Klosterheim who seemed very full of himself at that moment.

"What do you think you're doing?" she said harshly. "This goes against…"

"I don't care," Klosterheim shrugged. "If Faustaff could get away with so much, then so can I — we, if you like." He turned a light-hearted eye on Faustaff who had still not completely recovered from the shock of transition between E-3 and E-Zero.

"Well, doctor," Faustaff heard Klosterheim say. "Are you impressed?"

"I'm curious," said Faustaff slowly.

Orelli began to chuckle and moved towards Faustaff, but was stopped short by Begg's now somewhat nervous gun nudging at him. Begg's expression had become resolute, but he seemed baffled. Nancy looked rather the same.

Orelli said sharply: "Gordon! Put the gun away. That was a silly gesture. We are in the position of power now, no matter how many guns you point at us. You realize that? You must!"

Faustaff pulled himself together. "What if we order you to return us to E-3? We could kill you if you refused."

"I am not so sure you would kill us, doctor," Klosterheim smiled. "And in any case it takes hours to prepare for a transition. We would need technical help too. All our people are at the cathedral." He pointed out of the window to where a spire could be seen over the tops of roofs and trees. The spire seemed unnaturally solid in the peculiarly unreal setting. Part of the impression was gained, Faustaff realized, by the fact that the whole landscape, aside from the spire, looked unused. "Also," Klosterheim continued, "they are expecting us and will come here soon if we do not turn up there."

"We still have you," Begg reminded him. "We can barter your lives for a safe transport back to where we came from."

"You could," Klosterheim admitted. "But what would that gain you? Isn't E-Zero where you wanted to come?" He glanced at Faustaff. "That's true isn't it, doctor?"

Faustaff nodded.

"You will have to be careful here, doctor," Orelli put in. "I am serious. You had better throw in with us. United we stand, eh?"

"I prefer to stay divided, particularly if you fall as well," Faustaff replied dryly.

"This antagonism is unrealistic, doctor. Cut your losses." Klosterheim looked somewhat nervously out of the window. "The potential danger here is great; this is an unactivated simulation — it's delicate. A few wrong moves on your part would, among other things, make it almost impossible to return to any one of the other simulations…"

"Simulations of what?" said Faustaff, still trying to get concrete information from Klosterheim.

"The original…"

"Klosterheim!" Maggy White broke in. "What are you doing? The principals might easily decide to recall us!"

Klosterheim responded coolly. "How will they reach us?" he asked her. "We are the most sophisticated agents they have."

"They can recall you — you know that."

"Not easily — not without some co-operation from me. They will never succeed with the simulations. They have tried too many times and failed too many times. With our knowledge we can resist them — we can become independent — live our own lives. We can leave this world only semi-activated and rule it. There would be nothing to stop us."

Maggy White lunged towards Begg and tried to grab the machine-gun from him. He backed away. Faustaff got hold of the woman, but she already had both hands on the gun. Suddenly the gun went off. It had been set to semi-automatic. A stream of bullets smashed through the window.

"Careful!" shrieked Klosterheim.

As if startled by the firing, Maggy White took her hands away. Orelli had moved towards Begg, but the tall Englishman turned the gun on him again and he stopped.

Klosterheim was staring out of the window.

Faustaff looked in the same direction, and saw that where the bullets had struck the nearest house its walls were falling. One had cracked and was crumbling, but the others fell neatly down, to lie on the ground in one piece. The impression of a stage set was retained — yet the walls, and the revealed interior of the house, which was now falling slowly, were evidently quite solid and real.

Klosterheim turned on Maggy.

"You accuse me — and cause that to happen," he said, pointing out at the wreckage. "I suppose you were going to try to kill me."

"I still intend to."

Klosterheim swung the pointing finger at Faustaff. "There is the one you should kill. One of us should have done it long since."

"I am not so sure now," she said. "He might even be of use to the principals. Not you, though."

"No indeed," smiled Klosterheim, lowering his arm. "You realize what your action might have started?"

She nodded. "And that wouldn't be to your advantage, would it, Klosterheim?"

"It would be to no-one's advantage," Klosterheim said, rubbing his eyes. "And it would be very unpleasant for Faustaff and the others — including you, Orelli, as I've explained."

Orelli smiled to himself. It was a wickedly introspective smile as if he looked into his own soul and was pleased with the evil he found there. He leant against one of the pieces of machinery and folded his arms. "What you told me sounds almost attractive, Klosterheim."

Faustaff became impatient. He felt that he should be taking some sort of action but he could think of nothing to do.

"We'll pay a visit to the cathedral I think," he said on impulse. "Let's get going."

Klosterheim was plainly aware of Faustaff's uncertainty. He did not move as Begg waved the gun towards the door. "Why would the cathedral be better, Doctor Faustaff?" he asked lightly. "After all, there are more of our men there."

"True," Faustaff answered. "But we might just as well go. I've made up my mind, Klosterheim. Move, please." His tone was unusually firm. Hearing it, he was not sure that he liked it. Was he compromising himself too much? he wondered.

Klosterheim shrugged and walked past Begg towards the door. Orelli was already opening it. Maggy White and Nancy followed Begg with Faustaff keeping an eye on Maggy.

They went out into the hall and Orelli pulled the front door wide.

The lawn and gravel path looked only slightly different from what they had left on E-3. Yet there was something hazy about them, something unformed. Faustaff thought that the feeling they aroused was familiar and as they began to walk down the path towards the street he realized that, for all their apparent reality, they had the effect of making him feel as if he were experiencing a particularly naturalistic dream.

The effect was made perfect by the stillness of the air, the complete silence everywhere. Though he could feel the gravel beneath his feet, he made no sound as he walked.

Even when he spoke, his voice seemed so distant that he had the impression its sound carried around the whole planet before it reached his ears.

"Does that street lead to the cathedral?" he asked Klosterheim, pointing to the street at the bottom of the lawn.

Klosterheim's lips were tight. His eyes seemed to express some kind of warning as he turned and nodded at Faustaff.

Orelli appeared more relaxed. He also turned his head while he walked jauntily towards the street. "That's the one, doctor," he said. His voice sounded far away, too, although it was perfectly audible.

Klosterheim looked nervously at his partner. To Faustaff it seemed that Klosterheim was privately wondering if he had made a mistake in joining forces with Orelli. Faustaff had known Orelli much longer than Klosterheim and was well aware that the ex-cardinal was at best a treacherous and neurotic ally, given to moods that seemed to indicate a strong death-wish and which led him and anyone associated with him into unnecessary danger.

Wanting something to happen, something he could at least try to deal with, Faustaff almost welcomed Orelli's mood.

They reached the street. Cars were parked there. They were new and Faustaff recognized them as the latest on E-1. Evidently, whoever created these "simulations" didn't start from scratch.

There was no-one about. E-Zero seemed unpopulated. Nothing lived. Even the trees and plants gave the impression of lifelessness.

Orelli stopped and waved his arms shouting. "They're here, doctor! They must have heard the shots. What are you going to do now?"

Turning a corner came about a dozen of Orelli's brigandly gang, their laser rifles ready in their hands.

Faustaff bellowed: "Stop! We've got Klosterheim and Orelli covered!" He felt a bit self-conscious, then, and looked at Begg, feeling he was better able to take the initiative.

Begg said nothing but he straddled his legs slightly and moved his machine-gun a little. His expression was abnormally stern. Orelli's men stopped.

"What are you going to do now Faustaff?" Orelli repeated.

Faustaff glanced at Begg again but Begg apparently refused to meet his gaze. There was a big hovercar close by. Faustaff contemplated it.

Klosterheim said softly: "It would be unwise to do anything with the automobile. Please doctor, don't use any of the things you find here."

"Why not?" Faustaff asked in the same tone.

"To do so could trigger a sequence of events that would snowball until nobody could control them. I'm speaking the truth. There is a ritual involved — every simulation has its ritual before it becomes completely activated. The gun going off doesn't appear to have had any result — but starting a car could begin the initial awakening..."

"I'll kill him if you come any closer!"

Begg was talking to Orelli's men who had begun to stir. He was pointing the gun directly at Orelli, Klosterheim apparently forgotten. The normally stoical Begg now seemed to be under stress. He must have hated Orelli for a long time, Faustaff reflected. Or perhaps he hated what Orelli represented in himself. It was quite plain to them all that Begg hoped to kill Orelli.

Only Orelli himself seemed relaxed, grinning at Begg. Begg frowned now, sweating. His hands shook.

"Gordon!" Faustaff said desperately. "If you kill him, they'll start shooting."

"I know," Begg replied, and his eyes narrowed.

Behind them Maggy White had started to run up the road, away from Orelli's men. Klosterheim was the only one to turn his head and watch her, his face thoughtful.

Faustaff decided to go to the car. He gripped the door handle. He pressed the button and the door opened. He noticed that the keys were in the ignition. "Keep them covered Gordon," he said as he got into the driving seat. "Come on, Nancy."

Nancy followed him, sitting next to him.

"Gordon!" he called. He started the engine. He realized that he hadn't considered the possibility that the car wouldn't work. The motor began to turn over.

Faustaff called to Begg again and was relieved to see that he was edging towards the car. Nancy opened the back door for him and he slid in. His gun was still pointing directly at Orelli.

Faustaff touched a button. The car rose on its air-cushion and they began to move down the road, slowly at first.

One shot came from a laser rifle. The beam went high.

Faustaff put his foot down, hearing Klosterheim order the men to stop firing.

"Faustaff!" Klosterheim yelled, and although they were now some distance away he could hear him perfectly. "Faustaff — you and your friends will suffer most from this!"

They passed Maggy White on the way, but they didn't stop for her.

CHAPTER THIRTEEN

THE TIME DUMP

As Faustaff drove into downtown Los Angeles he realized that everything was not as normal as he had thought. Much of the area was unfinished, as if work on the "simulation" had been abandoned or interrupted. Houses were intact, stores bore familiar signs — but every so often he would pass something that clashed with the effect.

A tree in a garden, for instance, was recognizable as a Baiera tree with sparse, primitive foliage. The tree had flourished during the Jurassic, up to 180 million years in the past. A block that Faustaff remembered as having once been taken up with a big movie theatre was now a vacant lot. On it were pitched Indian wigwams reminiscent of those that had been used by the Western plains Indians. The whole appearance of the settlement did not give the impression of its having been built as an exhibit. Elsewhere were wooden houses of a style typical of three centuries earlier, a brand new 1908 Model T Ford with gleaming black enamel, brass fittings, and wheel-spokes picked out in red. A store window displayed women's fashions of almost two hundred years before.

Although, in general appearance, the city was the modern Los Angeles of 1999 on E-1, the anachronisms were plentiful and easily noticed standing out in sharp contrast to everything else. They added to Faustaff's impression that he was dreaming. He began to experience vague feelings of fear and he drove the car away very fast, heading towards Hollywood for no other reason than because that was where the highway was leading him.

Nancy Hunt gripped his arm. Evidently close to hysteria herself, she tried to comfort him. "Don't worry, Fusty," she said. "We'll get out of this. I can't even believe it's real."

"It's real enough," he said, relaxing a little. "Or at least the threat is. You just can't — I don't know — get to grips with the place. There's something basically intangible about it — the houses, the street, the scenery — it isn't one thing or another." He addressed Gordon Begg who was still grim-faced, hugging his machine-gun to him, eyes hooded.

"How do you feel, Gordon?"

Begg moved in his seat and looked directly at Faustaff whose head was half-turned towards him. Faustaff saw that there were tears in Begg's eyes.

"Uncomfortable," Begg replied with some effort. "It's not just the scenery — it's me. I can't seem to control my emotions — or my mind. I feel that this world isn't so much unreal as…" he paused. "It's a different quality of reality, perhaps. We are unreal to *it* — we shouldn't be here. Even if we had a right to be here, we shouldn't be behaving as we are. It's our state of mind, if you like. That's what's wrong — our state of mind, not the place."

Faustaff nodded thoughtfully. "But do you think you'd be willing to enter the state of mind you feel this world demands?"

Begg hesitated. Then he said: "No, I don't think so."

"Then I know what you mean," Faustaff went on. "I'm going through the same thing. We've got to try to hang on, Gordon — this world wants us to alter our identities. Do you want to alter your identity?"

"No."

"Do you mean personality?" Nancy asked. "That's the feeling I've got — that at any moment if I relaxed enough I just wouldn't be me any more. It's like dying, almost. A sort of dying. I feel that something of me would be left but it would be — naked…"

Their attempts to express and analyze their fears had not helped. Now the atmosphere in the car was one of terror — they had brought their fears to the surface and they were unable to control them.

The car rushed down the highway, carrying a frightened cargo. Above them, the featureless sky added to their impression that time and space as they knew it no longer existed, that they no longer possessed a fragment of potential influence over their situation.

Faustaff tried to speak again, to suggest that perhaps after all they should turn round and throw themselves on Klosterheim's mercy, that he at least would have an explanation of what was happening to them, that they might accept his suggestion of their combining forces with him until they saw an opportunity of escaping from E-Zero.

The words that came out of his mouth held no meaning for him. The other two did not hear him, it seemed.

Faustaff's large hands shook violently on the steering wheel. He barely resisted the urge to let the car crash.

He drove on a while longer and then, with a feeling of hopelessness, stopped the car suddenly. He leaned over the steering wheel, his face contorted, his mouth gibbering while another part of his mind sought the core of sanity that must still be within him and which might help him resist the identity-sapping influence of E-Zero.

Did he want to resist? The question kept entering his mind. At length, in trying to answer, he recovered partial sanity. Yes, he did — at least, until he understood what he was resisting.

He looked up. There were no houses in the immediate vicinity. There were some seen in the distance behind and ahead of him, but here the highway went across sparse grassland. It looked like a site that had been leveled for development and then left. What caught his eye, however, was the dump.

At first glance it looked like a garbage dump, a huge hill of miscellaneous junk.

Then Faustaff realized that it wasn't junk. All the objects looked new and whole.

On impulse he got out of the car and began to walk towards the vast heap.

As he got closer he could see that it was even bigger than he had first thought. It rose at least a hundred feet above him. He saw a complete Greek Winged Victory in marble; a seventeenth century arquebus, gleaming oak, brass and iron; a large Chinese kite painted with a dragon's head in brilliant primary colours. A Fokker Triplane of the type used in the 1914-18 war lay close to the top, its wood and canvas as new as the day it left its factory. There were wagon wheels and what looked like an Egyptian boat; a throne that might have belonged to a Byzantine Emperor; a big Victorian urn bearing a heavy floral pattern; an Indian elephant howdah; a stuffed Timber Wolf; a sixteenth century arbalest — a crossbow made of steel; a late eighteenth century electric generator; a set of Japanese horse armour on a beautifully carved wooden horse, and a North African drum; a life-sized bronze statue of a Sinhalese woman; a Scandinavian rune stone and a Babylonian obelisk.

All history seemed to have been piled together at random. It was a mountain of treasure, as if some mad museum curator had found a way of up-ending his museum and shaking its contents out on to the ground. Yet the artifacts did not have the look of museum-pieces. Everything looked absolutely new.

Faustaff approached the heap until he stood immediately beneath it. At his feet lay a near-oval shield of wood and leather. It looked as if it belonged to the fourteenth century and the workmanship seemed Italian. It was richly decorated with gold and red paint and its main motif showed an ornate mythical lion; beside it, on its side, was a beautiful clock dating from around 1700. It was of steel and silver filigree and might have been the work of the greatest clockmaker of his time, Thomas Tompion. Few other craftsmen, Faustaff thought abstractedly, could have created such a clock. Quite close to the clock he saw a skull of blue crystal. It could only have been fifteenth century Aztec. Faustaff had seen one like it in the British Museum. Half-covering the crystal skull was a grotesque ceremonial mask that looked as if it came from New Guinea, the features painted to represent a devil.

Faustaff felt overwhelmed by the richness and beauty — and the sheer variety — of the jumble of objects. Somehow it represented an aspect of what he had been fighting for since he had taken over the organization from his father and agreed to try to preserve the worlds of subspace.

He reached down and picked up the heavy Tompion clock, running his fingers over the ornate silver. A key hung by a red cord from the back. He opened the glass door at the front and inserted the key. Smoothly the key turned and he started to wind the clock. Inside a balance wheel began to swing with a muted tick-tock. Faustaff set the hands to twelve o'clock and, holding the clock carefully, put it down.

Although the sense of unreality about his surroundings was still strong, this action had helped him. He squatted in front of the clock and tried to think, his back to the great mound of antiques.

He concentrated his whole attention on the clock as, with an effort, he considered what he knew about E-Zero.

It was fairly obvious that E-Zero was simply the latest "simulation" created by whoever had employed Klosterheim, Maggy White and the D-squaders. It was also almost certain that this simulation was no different from what the other thousand had been like at the same stage. His own world, E-1, must therefore have been created in the same way, its history beginning at the point where E-2's history had become static. That would mean that E-1 had been created in the early sixties, shortly before his own birth, but certainly not before his father's birth — and his father had discovered the alternate worlds in 1971. It was unpleasant to consider that his father, and many of the people he had known and some of whom he still knew, must have been "activated" on a world that had originally been a world like E-Zero. Had the inhabitants of his own world been transported from one subspacial world to another? If so, how had they been conditioned into accepting their new environment? There was no explanation as he wondered again why the inhabitants of all the worlds other than E-1 accepted without question the changes in their society and their geography resulting from a series of Unstable Matter Situations? He had often wondered about it. He had once described them as seeming to live in a perpetual dream and a perpetual present.

The difference on E-Zero was that he felt real enough, but the whole planet seemed to be a dream-world also in a state of static time. For all the bizarre changes that had taken place on the other subspacial worlds, he had never got this impression from them — only from the inhabitants.

Evidently the conditioning that occurred on the drastically altered worlds would be applied more or less in reverse on E-Zero.

He could not consider who had created the alternate Earths. He would have to hope that at some time he would be able to get the answers once and for all, from either Maggy White or Klosterheim. He could not even guess why the worlds had been created and then destroyed. The kind of science necessary for such a task would be far too sophisticated for him to comprehend immediately, even if he never learned its principles.

The creators of the subspacial worlds seemed unable to interfere with them directly. That was why they had created the android D-squaders, obviously — to destroy their work. Klosterheim and Maggy White had made a more recent appearance. Plainly, they were either human or robots of a much more advanced type than the D-squaders and their job was not directly concerned with demolishing the subspacial Earths but with eliminating random factors like himself.

Therefore the creators, whoever and wherever they were, were not able to control their creations completely. The inhabitants of the worlds must have a fair degree of free will, otherwise he and his father would never have been able to set up the organization they had used to preserve and bring relief to the other alternates. The creators, in short, were by no means omnipotent — they were not even omniscient, otherwise they would have acted sooner than they had in sending Klosterheim and Maggy White in to get rid of him. That was encouraging, at least. It was obvious, too, that Klosterheim believed they could be disobeyed, for Klosterheim had plainly reneged on them and was out to oppose them. Whether or not this opposition would succeed Faustaff could not tell since only Klosterheim and Maggy White knew exactly what was opposed. Maggy White was still loyal. Perhaps she had some way of contacting her "principals" and had already warned them of Klosterheim's treachery. Klosterheim hadn't appeared to be worried by this possibility. Could these principals be relying solely on Klosterheim and Maggy White? Why, if that were the case, were they so powerful and at the same time so powerless? Another question he could not yet begin to answer.

Faustaff remembered that he had recently considered temporarily taking Klosterheim up on his offer. Now he rejected the idea. Klosterheim and Orelli had both proved untrustworthy — Klosterheim to his employers, Orelli to him. But Maggy White seemed loyal to her principals and she had once said that Faustaff's ideals and theirs were not so different in the long-term.

Maggy White then, must be found. If he were going to seek anyone's help — and it was evident that he must — then she was the one. There was a strong possibility, of course, that she had now left E-Zero or been captured by Klosterheim.

All that he could hope for now, he thought, would be a chance of contacting the creators. Then at least he would know exactly what he fought. Perhaps Maggy White could be convinced. Hadn't she said to Klosterheim that he, Faustaff, would be of more use to her principals than Klosterheim now? Faustaff had failed to thwart them, but he could still hope to find a way of convincing them of the immorality of their actions.

He had no idea where Maggy had gone. The only course open to him was to retrace his journey and see if he could find her.

All this time he had been staring at the clock, but now he noticed the position of the hands; exactly an hour had passed. He got to his feet and picked up the clock.

Looking about him he still felt disturbed by the continuing unreality of his surroundings; but he felt less confused by them, less at their mercy.

He began to walk back towards the car.

It was only when he had reached it and climbed in that he realized Nancy Hunt and Gordon Begg were no longer there.

He looked in all directions, hoping that he would see them; but they were gone.

Had they been captured by Klosterheim and Orelli? Had Maggy White found them and forced them to go with her? Or had they simply fled, totally demoralized by their fear?

Now there was an additional reason for finding Maggy White as soon as possible.

CHAPTER FOURTEEN

THE CRUCIFIXION IN THE CATHEDRAL

As he drove back down the highway, seeing the spires of the cathedral over the roofs of the houses ahead, Faustaff wished that he had brought one of the guns he had seen on the dump. He would have felt better for possessing a weapon of some kind.

He slowed the car suddenly as he saw some figures approaching him down the middle of the highway. They were behaving in a peculiar way and seemed oblivious to his car.

When he got closer he recognized them as Orelli's men, but differently dressed. They wore unfamiliar, festive costumes of the kind normally seen at carnivals. Some were dressed as Roman soldiers; some, he gathered, as priests, and others as women. They came down the highway performing an exaggerated high-stepping walk and they wore rapt, uncomprehending expressions.

Faustaff felt no fear of them and sounded the car's horn. They did not appear to hear it. Very slowly, he drove the car around them, looking at them as closely as he could. There was something familiar about the costumes; what they represented struck a chord in him, but he could not analyze what it was, and he did not feel he had the time to work it out.

He passed them and then passed the house in which he'd been transported to E-Zero. The house still looked much more real in contrast to the others near it. He turned a bend in the street and saw the cathedral ahead. It was in its own grounds, surrounded by a stone wall. Let into the wall were two solid gate-posts and the big wrought-iron gates were open. He drove straight through them. He felt that caution would be useless.

He stopped the car at the west-front of the cathedral where the main entrance lay, flanked by tall towers. Like most cathedrals, this one seemed to have been built and rebuilt over several centuries though in general appearance it was Gothic, with the unmistakable arches of its stained-glass windows and heavy, iron-studded doors.

Faustaff mounted the few steps until he stood at the doors. They were slightly ajar and he pushed them partially open, just enough for him to pass through. He walked into the nave, the vast ceiling rising above him, and it was as empty of seats as when he had last been in it. But the altar was there and candles burned on it. It was covered by an exquisite altar cloth. Faustaff barely noticed these, for it was the life-size crucifix behind the altar which drew his attention. Not only was it life-size but peculiarly life-like, also. Faustaff walked rapidly towards it, refusing to believe what he already knew to be true.

The cross was of plain wood, though well-finished.

The figure nailed to it was alive.

It was Orelli, naked and bleeding from wounds in his hands and feet, his chest rising and falling rapidly, his head hanging on his chest.

Now Faustaff realized what Orelli's men had represented — the people of Calvary. They must certainly have been the ones who crucified him.

With a grunt of horror Faustaff ran forward and climbed on the altar reaching up to see how he could get Orelli down. The ex-cardinal smelled of sweat and his body was lacerated. On his head was a thorn garland.

What had caused Orelli's men to do this to him? It was surely no conscious perversion of Christianity; no deliberate blasphemy. Faustaff doubted that Orelli's brigands cared enough for religion to do what they had done.

He would need something to lever the nails out. Then Orelli raised his head and opened his eyes.

Faustaff was shocked by the tranquility he saw in those eyes. Orelli's whole face seemed transformed not into a travesty of Christ but into a living representation of Christ.

Orelli smiled sweetly at Faustaff. "Can I help you, my son?" he said calmly.

"Orelli?" Faustaff was unable to say anything else for a moment. He paused. "How did this happen?" he asked eventually.

"It was my destiny," Orelli replied. "I knew it and they understood what they must do. I must die, you see."

"This is insane!" Faustaff began trying to tug at one of the nails. "You aren't Christ! What's happening?"

"What must happen," Orelli said in the same even tone. "Go away, my son. Do not question this. Leave me."

"But you're Orelli — a traitor, murderer, renegade. You — you don't deserve this! You've no right..." Faustaff was an atheist and to him Christianity was one of many religions that had ceased to serve any purpose, but something in the spectacle before him disturbed him. "The Christ in the Bible was an idea, not a man!" he shouted. "You've turned it inside out!"

"We are all ideas," Orelli replied, "either our own or someone else's. I am an idea in their minds and I am the same idea in my own. What has happened is true — it is real — it is necessary! Do not try to help me. I don't need any help."

Though he spoke distantly, Faustaff had the impression that Orelli also spoke with preternatural lucidity. It gave him some insight into what he feared on E-Zero. The world not only threatened to destroy the personality — it turned a man inside out. Orelli's outer *persona* was buried within him somewhere (if he had not lost it altogether) and here was revealed his innermost self; not the Devil he had tried to be but the Christ he had wanted to be.

Slowly, Faustaff got down from the altar while Orelli's calm face smiled at him. It was no idiot's smile, it was not insane — it was a smile of fulfillment. Its sanity and tranquility terrified Faustaff. He turned his back on it and began to walk with effort towards the door.

As he neared it a figure stepped out from the shadows of the arches and touched his arm.

"Orelli does not only die for you, doctor," Klosterheim said smiling. "He dies because of you. You began the activation. I compliment you on your strength of will. I should have expected you to have succumbed by now. All the others have."

"Succumbed to what exactly, Klosterheim?"

"To the Ritual — the Activation Ritual. Every new planet must undergo it. Under normal circumstances the entire population of a fresh simulation must play out its myth rôles before it awakes. 'The work before the dream and the dream before the wakening', as some writer of yours once put it. You people have some reasonable insights into your situation from time to time, you know. Come." Klosterheim led Faustaff from the cathedral, "I can take you to see more. The show is about to start in earnest. I can't guarantee that you will survive it."

A sun now shone in the sky, bringing bright light and heavy shade to the world, though it still did not live. The sun was swollen and a glowing red; Faustaff blinked and reached into his pocket to get his sunglasses. He put them on.

"That's right," grinned Klosterheim. "Gird on your armour and prepare for an interesting battle."

"Where are we going?" Faustaff asked vaguely.

"Out into the world. You will see it naked. Every man has his rôle to play today. You have defeated me, Faustaff — perhaps you had not realized that. You have set E-Zero in motion by your ignorant actions. I can only hope that E-Zero will defeat you in turn, though I am not sure."

"Why aren't you sure?" Faustaff asked, still only half-interested.

"There are levels that even I had not prepared for," Klosterheim answered. "Perhaps you will not find your rôle on E-Zero. Perhaps you have resisted and retained your personality because you are already living your rôle. Could it be that we have all underestimated you?"

CHAPTER FIFTEEN

THE REVELS OF E-ZERO

Faustaff could not understand the full implication of Klosterheim's statement but he allowed the man to lead him out of the cathedral grounds and into a wooded park behind it.

"You know there is little left of E-1 now," Klosterheim said casually as they walked. "The war was very brief. I think a few survivors are lingering on, by all accounts."

Faustaff knew that Klosterheim had deliberately chosen this moment to tell him, probably hoping to demoralize him. He controlled the feelings of loss and despair that came to him and tried to answer as casually.

"It was only to be expected, I suppose."

Klosterheim smiled. "You might be pleased to know that many people from the other simulations have been transferred to E-Zero. Not an act of mercy on the part of the principals, of course. Merely a selection of the most likely specimens for populating this Earth."

Faustaff paused. Ahead he could make out a number of figures. He peered through the trees at them, frowning. Most of them were naked. Like Orelli's men, they were moving in a ritualistic, puppetlike manner, their faces blank. There was an approximately equal number of men and women.

Klosterheim waved a hand. "They will not see us — we are invisible to them while they are in this state."

Faustaff was fascinated. "What are they doing?"

"Oh, working out their positions in the world. We'll go a little closer, if you like."

Klosterheim led Faustaff towards the group.

Faustaff felt he was witnessing an ancient and primitive ceremony. People seemed to be imitating animals of various kinds. One man had branches tied to his head in a familiar representation of a stag. A combination of man, beast and plant which was significant to Faustaff without his understanding quite why. A woman stooped and picked up the skin of a lioness draping it around her naked body. There was a pile of animal skins in the centre of the posturing group. Some of the people already wore skins or masks. Here were representations of bears, owls, hares, wolves, snakes, eagles, bats, foxes, badgers and many other animals. A fire burned to one side of the glade.

Soon the whole group had clothed itself in pelts or masks.

In the centre now stood a woman. She wore a dog's skin around her shoulders and a crudely painted dog's mask on her face. She had long black hair that escaped from behind the mask and fell down her back. The dance around her became increasingly formal, but much faster than previously.

Faustaff grew tense as he watched.

The circle drew tighter and tighter around the dog-woman. She stood there impassively until the group suddenly stopped and faced her. Then she began to cringe, raising her head in a long drawn out canine howl, her arms stretched in front of her with the palms outwards.

With a roar they closed on her.

Faustaff began to run forward bent on trying to help the girl. Klosterheim pulled at his arm.

"Too late," he said. "It never takes long."

The group was already backing away. Faustaff glimpsed the mangled corpse of the girl lying on the ground, the dog-skin draped across her.

Bloody-mouthed, the horned man ran towards the fire and pulled a brand from it. Others brought wood that had already been gathered, heaping it around the girl. The wood was ignited and the pyre began to burn.

A wordless, ululating song began to come from the lips of the group and another dance began; this time it seemed to symbolize exaltation of some kind.

Faustaff turned away. "That is nothing but magic, Klosterheim — primitive superstition. What kind of perverse minds have your principals if they can produce scientific miracles and — permit *that*!"

"Permit? They encourage it. It is necessary to every simulation."

"How can ritual sacrifice be necessary to a modern society?"

"You ask that, after your own simulation has just destroyed itself? There was little difference, you know — only the scale and the complexity. The woman died quickly. She might have died more slowly of radiation sickness on E-1 if that was where she came from."

"But what purpose does a thing like that serve?"

Klosterheim shrugged. "Ah, purpose Faustaff. You think there is purpose?"

"I must think so, Klosterheim."

"It is supposed to serve a limited purpose, that sort of ritual. Even in your terms, it should be obvious that primitive peoples symbolize their fears and wishes in ritual. The cowardly dog, the malevolent woman — both were destroyed in that rite you witnessed."

"Yet in reality, they continue to exist. That kind of ritual achieves nothing."

"Only a temporary feeling of security. You are right. You are a rational man, Faustaff. I still fail to understand why you would not join forces with me — for I am also a rational man. You cling to primitive instincts, naïve ideals. You refuse to let your reason have full reign over you. Then you are shocked by what you have just seen. It is within the power of neither of us to change those people, but we could have taken advantage of their weaknesses and at least benefited ourselves."

Faustaff could think of no reply, but he remained deeply unconvinced by Klosterheim's argument. He shook his head slowly.

Klosterheim made an impatient movement. "Still? I had hoped that you would join me in defeat!" He laughed.

They left the park and walked along a street. On lawns, in the streets, on vacant lots and in gardens, the ritualistic revels of E-Zero were taking place. Klosterheim and Faustaff were unnoticed and undisturbed. It was more than a reversion to the primitive, Faustaff thought as they wandered through the scenes of dark carnival, it was a total adoption of the identities of psychological-mythical archetypes. As Klosterheim had said, every man and woman had their rôle. These rôles fell into a few definite categories. The more outstanding ones dominated the rest. He saw men and women in cowled cloaks, their faces hidden, driving dozens of naked acolytes before them with flails or tree-branches; he saw a man copulating with a woman dressed as an ape; another woman, taking no part herself, seemed to be ordering an orgy. Everywhere were scenes of bloodshed and bestiality. It reminded Faustaff of the Roman Games, of the Dark Ages, of the Nazis. But there were other rituals that did not seem to fit in; they were quieter, less frenetic rituals that reminded Faustaff strongly of the few church services he had attended as a child.

Some kind of attitude was beginning to dawn in his confused mind, some realization of why he had refused to agree with Klosterheim in spite of everything he had discovered since their first meeting.

If he were witnessing magical ceremonies, then they were of two distinct kinds. He knew little about anthropology or superstition, mistrusted Jung and found mysticism boring — yet he had heard of Black Magic and White Magic, without understanding the differences that people claimed for them. Perhaps what had horrified him was the black variety. Were the other scenes he had noticed the manifestations of white magic?

The very idea of thinking in terms of magic or superstition appalled him. He was a scientist and to him magic meant ignorance and the encouragement of ignorance. It meant senseless murder, fatalism, suicide, hysteria. Suddenly the idea came to him that it also meant the Hydrogen Bomb and World War. In short, it meant the rejection of the human factor in one's nature — the total acceptance of the beast. But what was white magic? Ignorance, also, probably. The black variety encouraged the bestial side of man's nature, so perhaps the white variety encouraged — what? — the "godly" side? The will to evil and the will to good. Nothing wrong with that as an idea. But man was not a beast and he was not a god; he was man. Intellect was what distinguished him from other species of animal. Magic, as far as Faustaff knew, rejected reason. Religion accepted it, of course, but hardly encouraged it. Only science accepted it and encouraged it. Faustaff suddenly saw mankind's social and psychological evolution in a clear, simple light. Science alone accepted man as he was and sought to exploit his full potential.

Yet this planet he stood on was the creation of a superb understanding of science — and at the same time these dreadful magical rituals were allowed to take place.

For the first time Faustaff felt that the creators of the simulations had gone wrong somewhere — gone wrong in their own terms.

With a shock he acknowledged the possibility that not even they understood what they were doing.

He turned to suggest this to Klosterheim, whom he had assumed was following just behind him.

But Klosterheim had gone.

CHAPTER SIXTEEN

THE BLACK RITUAL

Then Faustaff glimpsed Klosterheim just before the man turned a corner of the street. He began to run after him, pushing through the revelers who did not see him.

Klosterheim was climbing into a car when Faustaff next saw him. Faustaff shouted but Klosterheim did not reply. He started the car and was soon speeding away.

Another car was parked nearby. Faustaff climbed into it and gave chase.

More than once he was forced to swerve to avoid groups of people who were, like the others, completely oblivious of him, but he kept on Klosterheim's trail without too much difficulty.

Klosterheim was on the Long Beach road. Soon the sea was visible ahead. Klosterheim began to follow the coast and Faustaff noticed that even the seashore was not free of its rituals. There was a big, old hacienda-style house visible ahead and Faustaff saw Klosterheim turn his car into its drive.

Faustaff wasn't sure that Klosterheim had realized he was being followed. Out of caution he stopped his own car a short distance before he reached the house. He got out and began to walk towards it.

By the time Faustaff had walked warily up the drive, he found Klosterheim's car empty. Evidently the man had gone inside.

The front door of the house was locked. He walked around it until he came to a window. He looked in. The window opened into a large room that seemed to take up most of the ground floor.

Klosterheim was in there and so were a great many others. Faustaff saw Maggy White there. She was glowering at Klosterheim who wore his familiar mocking grin. Maggy White was dressed in a loose black robe. Its hood was thrown back over her shoulders. Apart from her, only Klosterheim wore any kind of conventional clothing.

The others all wore black hoods and nothing else. The women knelt in the centre, their bowed heads towards Maggy White. The men stood around the walls. Some of them held large, black candles. One of them gripped a huge mediaeval sword.

Maggy White seated herself in a thronelike chair at one end of the room. She was speaking to Klosterheim who gestured at her and left the room for a moment to reappear wearing a similar robe to the one she wore.

Maggy White disapproved but seemed to be able to do nothing to stop Klosterheim.

Faustaff wondered why she should be involving herself in a ritual. It was, even to him, evidently a black magic ritual, with Maggy representing the Queen of Darkness or whatever it was. Klosterheim now seated himself at the other end of the room and arranged his robe, smiling at Maggy and saying something which caused her to frown even more heavily.

From what he knew of such things, Faustaff supposed that Klosterheim was representing the Prince of Darkness. He seemed to remember that the woman usually had a male lieutenant.

Two of the men went out and came back with a very beautiful young girl. She was certainly under twenty and probably much younger. She seemed totally dazed, but not in the same trancelike state as the others. Faustaff got the impression that she had not undergone the psychological reversal that the rest had suffered. Her blonde hair was piled on her head and her body looked as if it had been oiled.

The kneeling women rose as she entered and they stepped back towards the wall to line it like the men.

Rather reluctantly, Maggy signed to Klosterheim who rose and walked jauntily towards the girl, parodying the ritualistic movements of the people. The two men forced the girl down so that she was lying on her back in front of Klosterheim who stared smilingly down at her. He half-turned to Maggy and spoke. The woman pursed her lips and her eyes were angry.

To Faustaff it seemed that Maggy White might be going through with something she did not like, but doing it conscientiously. Klosterheim, on the other hand, was enjoying himself, plainly taking a delight in his power over the others.

He knelt in front of the girl and began to caress her body. Faustaff saw the girl's head jerk suddenly and her eyes flare into awareness. He saw her begin to struggle. The two men stepped forward and held her.

Faustaff looked down and a saw a large flat stone, used as part of the garden's decoration. He picked it up and flung it through the window.

He had expected the people to be startled by his action, but as he clambered through the window he saw that only Maggy White and Klosterheim were staring at him.

"Leave her alone, Klosterheim," Faustaff said.

"Someone has to do it, doctor." Klosterheim said calmly. "Besides which, we are the best people for the job, Miss White and myself. We do not act from any kind of instinct. There is no lust in us — is there, Miss White?"

Maggy White simply shook her head, her lips tight.

"We have no instincts whatsoever, doctor," Klosterheim went on. "It is a source of regret to Miss White, I think, but not to me. After all, you are an example of how certain instincts can be harmful to a man."

"I've seen you angry and frightened," Faustaff reminded him.

"Certainly I might have expressed anger and fear but these were mental states, not emotional ones, or is there no difference in your terms, doctor?"

"Why are you taking part in these things?" Faustaff ignored Klosterheim's question and addressed them both.

"For amusement in my case," Klosterheim said. "I am equipped to experience sensual pleasure, also — though I do not spend a lifetime seeking it as you seem to."

"There could be more to it," Maggy White said quietly. "I've already said this to you — maybe they can experience more pleasure."

"I'm aware of your obsession, Miss White," Klosterheim smiled. "But I am sure you're wrong. Everything they do is on a puny scale." He looked at Faustaff. "You see, doctor, Miss White feels that by taking part in these rites it will somehow confirm on her a mysterious ecstasy. She thinks you have something we do not."

"Perhaps we have," Faustaff said.

"Perhaps it is not worth having," Klosterheim suggested.

"I'm not sure," Faustaff looked at the people around him. The two men were still holding the girl, though now she seemed to have lapsed into a similar state to their own. "It doesn't have to be this."

"No indeed." Klosterheim's tone was sardonic. "It could be something else. I think your friends Nancy Hunt and Gordon Begg are involved in something you would prefer."

"Are they all right?"

"Perfectly at this stage. They have come to no physical harm." Klosterheim grinned.

"Where are they?"

"They ought to be somewhere nearby."

"Hollywood," Maggy White said. "One of the film company lots."

"Which one?"

"Simone-Dane-Keene, I think. It's almost an hour's drive."

Faustaff pushed the two men aside and picked up the girl.

"Where do you think you're taking her?" Klosterheim mocked. "She won't know anything after the activation."

"Call me a dog in the manger," Faustaff said as he carried the girl towards the front door and unlatched it.

He walked out to the street, reached his car, dumped the girl in the back seat and began to drive towards Hollywood.

CHAPTER SEVENTEEN

THE WHITE RITUAL

The car was fast and the freeways clear. As he drove, Faustaff wondered about the pair he had left. From what Klosterheim had said, it was fairly obvious that they weren't human; were probably, as he'd suspected, near-human androids, more advanced versions of the robot D-squaders.

He hadn't asked the nature of the ritual in which, he assumed, Nancy and Gordon had become involved. He simply wanted to reach them as soon as possible so that he could be of help to them if they needed it.

He knew the S-D-K lot. S-D-K had been the biggest of the old-style motion picture makers on E-1. He had once visited the lot from curiosity on one of his occasional trips to E-1 Los Angeles.

Every so often he found it necessary to slow the car and steer through or around a throng of people performing what were to him obscure rites. They were not all obscene or violent, but the sight of the blank faces was sufficient to disturb him.

He had noticed a change, however. The buildings seemed in slightly sharper focus than when he had first arrived on E-Zero. The impression of newness, too, was beginning to wear off a little. Evidently these pre-activation rites had some link with the altering nature of the new planet. From his own experience he knew that it was this world's influence which produced the inability to associate properly, the quite rapid loss of personal identity, the slip back into the rôle of whatever psychological archetype was strongest in the particular psyche of the individual; but there also seemed to be a kind of feedback where the people somehow helped to give the planet a more positive atmosphere of reality. Faustaff found the idea hard to grasp in any terms familiar to him.

He was nearing Hollywood now. He could see the big illuminated S-D-K sign ahead. Soon, he was turning into the lot. It was silent, apparently empty.

He got out of the car, leaving the girl where she was. He locked the doors and began to walk in the direction of a notice which said NO. 1 STAGE.

A door was set in the concrete wall. It was covered with cautionary signs. Faustaff pushed it open and looked inside. The jungle of cameras and electronic equipment partially hid a set. It looked like a set for an historical film. There was nobody in sight.

Faustaff tried the next stage. He walked in. There were no cameras about and all the equipment seemed neatly stowed. A set was up, however. It was probably being used for the same film. It showed the interior of a mediaeval castle. For a moment Faustaff wondered at the craftsmen who had built the set so that it looked so convincing.

There was a ritual being enacted on the set. Nancy Hunt was wearing a white, diaphanous shift and her red hair had been combed out and arranged to flow over her back and shoulders. Beside her was a man dressed in black armour that looked real. Either the costume was from the film, or else it had come from the same source as all the other costumes that Faustaff had seen. The man in black armour was drawing down his visor. He had a huge broadsword in his right hand.

With a measured tread another figure came clumping from the wings. It was Gordon Begg, also in full armour of bright steel with a plain white surcoat over it. He held a large sword in his right hand.

Faustaff shouted: "Nancy! Gordon! What are you doing?"

They didn't hear. Evidently they were as much in a dreamlike state as the rest.

With peculiar movements which resembled, to Faustaff, the highly mannered motions of a traditional Japanese mime-play, Begg approached Nancy and the black-armoured man. His lips moved in speech, but Faustaff could tell that no words sounded.

In an equally formal way the black-armoured man gripped Nancy's arm and pulled her back, away from Begg. Begg now lowered his visor and seemed to challenge the other man with a movement of his sword.

Faustaff didn't think that Begg was in any danger. He watched as Nancy stepped to one side and Begg and his opponent touched swords. Shortly the black-armoured man dropped his sword and knelt in front of Gordon Begg. Begg then threw away his sword. The man rose and began to strip off his armour. Nancy came forward and also knelt before Begg. Then she got up and left the set, returning with a large golden cup which she offered to Begg. He took it and drank from it — or pretended to, since Faustaff could see it was actually empty. Begg picked up his sword and sheathed it.

Faustaff realized that he had only witnessed a small part of the ceremony and it now seemed over. What would Nancy and Gordon do?

There was a little more mime, with Nancy appearing to offer herself to Begg and being sympathetically rejected. Then Begg turned and began to move off the set, followed by everyone else. He held the golden cup high. It was obviously a symbol that meant something to him and the others.

Faustaff wondered if it represented the Holy Grail, and then wondered what the Holy Grail represented in Christian mythology and mysticism. Didn't it have a much older origin? Hadn't he read about a similar bowl appearing in Celtic mythology? He couldn't be sure.

Begg, Nancy and the rest were now walking past him. He decided to follow them. At least he would be able to keep a watchful eye on his friends to make sure they didn't come to harm. It was, he reflected, like trying to deal with a somnambulist. It was probably even more dangerous to attempt to wake them up. Sleep-walkers, he now remembered, were said to perform rituals of this kind sometimes — usually simpler, but occasionally quite complex. There must surely be a link.

The procession left the set and walked out into the arenalike compound. Tall concrete walls rose on every side.

They paused here and turned their faces to the sun, Gordon raising the bowl towards it, as if to catch its rays. A subdued chanting could now be heard coming from them all. It was a wordless chant — or at least in a language completely unfamiliar to Faustaff. It had vague affinities with Greek, but it was more like the Voice of Tongues which Faustaff had heard on a V-cast once in the South. How had it been described by a psychologist? The language of the unconscious. It was the kind of sound people used in their sleep sometimes, Faustaff found it slightly unnerving as he listened to the chant.

They were still chanting as Klosterheim made his appearance. He had found a sword from somewhere and was gleefully leading the black-hooded acolytes into the arena. Maggy White, looking rather uncertain, followed behind. She seemed to be almost as much in Klosterheim's power as the men who were with him.

Gordon Begg turned as Klosterheim shouted something in the same strange language they had been chanting in. From Klosterheim the words seemed halting, as if he had learned them with difficulty.

Faustaff knew that Klosterheim was shouting a challenge.

Gordon Begg handed the cup to Nancy and drew his sword.

Watching the scene, Faustaff was suddenly struck by its ludicrousness. He began to laugh aloud. It was his old laugh, rich and warm, totally without tension. The laughter was picked up by the high walls and amplified, its echoes rolling around the arena. For a moment everyone seemed to hear it and hesitated. Then, with a yell, Klosterheim leapt at Begg.

This action only caused Faustaff to laugh the more.

CHAPTER EIGHTEEN

THE ENCOUNTER

Klosterheim seemed bent on killing Begg, but he was such an inept swordsman that the Englishman, plainly trained in fencing, defended himself easily, in spite of the fact that his movements were so formal.

Faustaff snorted with laughter and stepped forward to grasp Klosterheim's arm. The android was startled. Faustaff removed the sword from his hand.

"This is all part of the ritual!" Klosterheim said seriously. "You're breaking the rules again."

"Calm down, Klosterheim," Faustaff chuckled and wiped his eyes. "No need to get emotional."

Gordon was still going through the motions of defense. He looked so much like Don Quixote in his armour and long moustache that his behaviour seemed funnier than ever to Faustaff who started to roar with laughter again.

Begg began to look bewildered. His movements became more hesitant and less formal. Faustaff placed himself in front of him. Begg blinked and lowered his sword. He frowned at Faustaff for a moment and then snapped down his visor and stood there rigidly, like a statue.

Faustaff raised his fist and tapped on the helmet. "Come out of there, Gordon — you don't need the armour any more. Wake up, Gordon!"

He saw that the others were beginning to stir. He went up to Nancy and stroked her face. "Nancy?"

She smiled vaguely, without looking at him.

"Nancy — it's Faustaff."

"Faustaff," she murmured distantly. "Fusty?"

He grinned. "The same."

She looked up at him, still smiling. He chuckled and she looked into his eyes. Her smile broadened. "Hi, Fusty. What's new?"

"You'd be surprised," he said. "Have you ever seen anything so funny?" He waved his hand to indicate the costumed figures about them. He pointed at the suit of armour. "Gordon's in there," he told her.

"I know," she said. "I really thought I was dreaming — you know, one of those dreams where you know you're dreaming but can't do anything about it. It was quite a nice dream."

"Nothing wrong with dreams, I guess," Faustaff said, putting his arm round her and hugging her. "They serve their purpose, but..."

"This dream was serving a purpose until you interrupted it," Maggy White said.

"But did you agree with the purpose?" Faustaff asked her.

"Well — yes. The whole thing is necessary. I told you."

"I still don't know the original purposes for the simulations," Faustaff admitted. "But it seems to me that nothing can be achieved by this sort of thing."

"I'm not sure," Maggy White replied thoughtfully. "I don't know... I'm still loyal to the principals, but I wonder... They don't seem very successful."

"You're not kidding," Faustaff agreed feelingly. "What have they scrapped? A thousand simulations?"

"They'll never succeed," Klosterheim sneered. "They've lost touch completely. Forget them."

Maggy White turned on him angrily. "This whole fiasco is your work, Klosterheim. If you hadn't disobeyed your orders E-Zero would now be well on the way to normal activation. I don't know what's going to happen now. This will be the first time that anything has gone wrong *before* full activation!"

"You should have listened to me. We need never have allowed full activation if we had been careful. We could have ruled this world easily. We could have defied the principals. At best all they could have done would have been to start afresh."

"There isn't time to start afresh. It would be tantamount to destroying their whole project, what you would have done!" Maggy glowered at him. "You tried to defeat the principals!"

Klosterheim turned his back on her with a sigh.

"You're too idealistic. Forget them. They are failures."

Gordon Begg's armour creaked. His arm moved towards his visor and slowly began to raise it. He looked out at them, blinking.

"By God," he said wonderingly. "Am I really dressed up in this stuff. I thought I was..."

"Dreaming? You must be hot in there, Gordon," Faustaff said. "Can you get it off?"

Begg tugged at the helmet. "I think it screws off," he said. Faustaff grasped the helmet and with some difficulty eased it round. Begg took it off. They began to unstrap the rest of the armour, Nancy helping. A murmur of voices around them showed that both the people who had been with Klosterheim and the people who had followed Gordon and Nancy were now waking up, confused.

Faustaff saw Maggy White stoop towards the sword and jumped up from where he was trying to unbuckle Gordon's left greave.

She had brought the sword down on Klosterheim's skull before he could reach her. He turned towards her with a smile, reached out for her, and then toppled. The top of his head had caved in completely, showing the brain. No blood came. Maggy began to hack at his body until Faustaff stopped her. She became impassive, looking down at Klosterheim's corpse. "A work of art," she said. "Like me."

"What are you going to do now?" Faustaff asked her.

"I don't know," she said. "Everything's gone wrong. All the rites you've seen are only the beginning. There's a series of huge assemblies later on — the final pre-activation rituals. You've broken the pattern."

"Surely what's happened can't make much difference on a world scale."

"You don't understand. Every symbol means something. Every individual has a rôle. It's all connected together. It's like a complicated electronic circuit — break it in one place and the whole thing seizes up. These rituals may seem horrifying and primitive to you — but they were inspired by a deeper knowledge of scientific principles than anything you're likely to have. The rituals establish the basic pattern of every individual's life. His inner drives are expressed and given form in the pre-activation rituals. This means that when he 'wakes up' and begins to lead his ordinary life, the code is imprinted in him and he will exist according to that code. Only a few, comparatively speaking, find new codes — new symbols — new lives. You're one of them — the most successful.

"Circumstances and your own integrity have enabled you to do what you have done. What the result will be, I can't think. There seems to be no division between your inner life and your outer personality. It's as if you are playing a rôle whose influence goes beyond the bounds of the principals' experiments and affects them directly. I don't think they intended to produce a type like you."

"Will you tell me now who these 'principals' are?" Faustaff asked her quietly.

"I can't," she said. "I obey them and I have been instructed to reveal as little about them as possible. Klosterheim said far too much and by that action, among others, helped to create this situation. Perhaps we should have killed you straight away. We had a number of opportunities. But we were both curious and delayed things for too long. We were both, in our ways, fascinated by you. As you can see, we let your personality assume too much control over us."

"We must do something," Faustaff told her gently.

"I agree. Let's go back to the house first and talk it over."

"What about all these others?"

"We can't do much for them — they're confused, but they'll be all right for a while."

Outside the movie lot stood the small truck in which Klosterheim had obviously brought his followers. Faustaff's car stood near it. In it a naked girl tugged at the doors and hammered on the window. Seeing them, she began to wind the window down.

"What the hell's going on?" she asked in a harsh, Brooklyn accent. "Is this a kidnapping or something? Where am I?"

Faustaff unlocked the door and let her out.

"Jesus!" she said. "What is it — a nudist camp? I want my clothes."

Faustaff pointed back at the main gate of the lot. "You'll find some in there," he told her.

She looked up at the S-D-K sign. "You're making a movie? Or is this one of those Hollywood parties I've heard about?"

Faustaff chuckled. "With a figure like that you *ought* to be in pictures. Go and see if anyone spots you."

She sniffed and began to walk towards the gate.

Gordon Begg and Nancy got into the back seats and Maggy White climbed in beside Faustaff as he started the car, turned it neatly in the street and drove towards downtown L.A.

People were wandering about everywhere, many of them still in their ritual costumes. They looked puzzled and a bit dazed. They were arguing and talking among themselves. There didn't seem to be much trouble; nobody looked afraid. There were a few cars on the road and sometimes a group of people would wave to him to stop as he passed, but he just waved back with a grin.

Everything seemed funny to him now. He realized that he was his old self again and wondered how and where he had started to lose his sense of humour.

Faustaff noticed, as he passed the spot, that the Time Dump had vanished and the anachronisms were gone too. Everything looked fairly normal.

He asked Maggy White about it.

"Those things are automatically eradicated," she told him. "If they don't fit the pattern then the simulation can't work smoothly until everything is rationalized. The pre-activation process gets rid of anything like that. Since it's been interrupted, perhaps a few anachronisms will continue to exit. I don't know. It hasn't happened before on any large scale. It's like anything else, you see. The apparatus can't be tested thoroughly until it is tried out on whatever it was designed for. This is another function of the pre-activation process.

The house, in which they traveled from E-3 to E-Zero, was still there and so was the cathedral, visible behind it.

Faustaff had a thought. He dropped the other three at the house and drove round to the cathedral. Even before he opened the door he heard shouting echoing around inside the building.

There was Orelli, still nailed to the cross. But he was far from tranquil. His face was twisted in pain.

"Faustaff!" he said hoarsely as the doctor approached. "What happened to me? What am I doing here?"

Faustaff found a candlestick that could probably be used to get the nails out.

"This is going to be painful, Orelli," he said.

"Get me down. It couldn't be any more painful."

Faustaff began to lever the nails from Orelli's flesh. He took the man in his arms and laid him on the altar. He moaned in agony.

"I'll get you back to the house," Faustaff said, picking up the ex-cardinal. "There'll probably be dressings of some kind there."

Orelli was weeping as Faustaff carried him out to the car. Faustaff felt that it wasn't the pain that was making Orelli weep, it was probably the memory of the dream he had only recently awakened from.

Driving away from the cathedral, Faustaff decided that it would be better to go to the nearest hospital. Presumably it would be equipped with antibiotics and medicated gauze.

It took him a quarter of an hour to find a hospital. He went into its empty hall and through to the emergency rooms. In a big medical chest he found everything he wanted and began to treat Orelli.

By the time he had finished, the ex-cardinal was asleep from the sedative he had administered.

Faustaff took him to a bed and tucked him in.

Orelli would be all right for a while, he decided.

He drove back to the house, parked the car and went inside. Maggy White, Gordon Begg and Nancy were sitting in the living room, drinking coffee and eating sandwiches.

The scene seemed so normal as to be incongruous. Faustaff told them what he had done with Orelli and sat down to have some food and coffee.

As they finished and Faustaff lit cigarettes for himself and Nancy, Maggy White seemed to come to a decision.

"We could use the machinery in this house to get to the principals," she said thoughtfully. "Would you like me to take you to them, Faustaff?"

"Wouldn't that be going against your instructions?"

"It is the best thing I can think of. I can't do anything else now."

"Naturally I'd like to contact your principals," Faustaff nodded. He now began to feel excited. "Though at this stage I can't see any way of sorting out the mess that everything's in. Do you know how many of the other simulations still exist?"

"No. Perhaps they have all been destroyed by now."

Faustaff sighed. "Their efforts and mine both appear to have been wasted."

"I'm not sure," she said. "Let's see. We'd have to leave your friends behind."

"Do you mind?" Faustaff asked them. They shook their heads. "Perhaps you could go and make sure Orelli's all right," Faustaff suggested. He told them where the hospital was. "I know how we all felt towards him, but he's paid a big enough price, I think. I don't think you'll hate him when you see him. I'm not sure his sanity will survive even now."

"Okay," Nancy said, getting up. "I hope you'll get back soon, Fusty. I want to see more of you."

"It's mutual," he smiled. "Don't worry. Goodbye, Gordon." He shook hands with Begg. "See you!"

They left the house.

Faustaff followed Maggy White into the other room where the equipment was.

"There's just one button to press," she told him. "But it only works for Klosterheim or me. I'd have used it before if I could have got the house to myself, but I got diverted — I had to stay to see what you did." She reached out and pressed the button.

The walls of the house seemed to change colour, rapidly going through the whole spectrum; they seemed to flow in on Faustaff, covering him with soft light, then they flattened out.

They stood on a vast plateau roofed by a huge, dark dome. Light came from all sides, the colours merging to become a white that was not really white, but a visible combination of all colours.

And giants looked down on them. They were human, with calm, ascetic features, completely naked and hairless. They were seated in simple chairs that did not appear to have any real substance and yet supported them perfectly.

They were about thirty feet high, Faustaff judged.

"My principals," Maggy White said.

"I'm glad to meet you at last," Faustaff told them. "You seem to be in some sort of dilemma."

"Why have you come here?" One of the giants spoke. His voice did not seem in proportion to his size. It was quiet and well-modulated, without emotion.

"To make a complaint, among other things," said Faustaff. He felt that he should be overawed by the giants, but perhaps all the experiences that had led up to this meeting had destroyed any sense of wonder he might have had otherwise. And he felt the giants had bungled too much to deserve a great deal of respect from him.

Maggy White was explaining everything that had happened. When she finished, the giants got up and walked through the walls of light. Faustaff sat down on the floor. It felt hard and cold and it made the parts of his body that touched it feel as if they had received a slight local anaesthetic. Its perpetual changing of colour didn't help him to feel any more comfortable.

"Where have they gone?" he asked Maggy.

"To debate what I have told them," she said. "They shouldn't be long."

"Are you ready to tell me who they actually are?"

"Let them tell you," she said. "I'm sure they will."

CHAPTER NINETEEN

CONVERSATION WITH THE PRINCIPALS

The principals soon returned. When they had seated themselves one of them spoke.

"There is a pattern to everything," he said. "But everything makes the pattern. The human failing is to make patterns out of parts of the whole and call it the whole. Time and Space has a pattern, but you see only a few elements on your simulations. Our science reveals the full dimensions and enables us to create the simulations."

"I understand that," said Faustaff. "But why do you create the simulations in the first place?"

"Our ancestors evolved on the original planet many millions of years ago. When their society had developed to the necessary point, they set off to explore the multiverse and understand it. Approximately ten thousand of your years ago we returned to the planet of our origin, having mapped and studied the multiverse and learned all its fundamental principles. We found that the society that had produced us had decayed. We expected that of course. But what we had scarcely realized was the extent to which we ourselves had been physically changed by our journeyings. We are immortals, in the sense that we shall exist until the end of the current phase of the multiverse. This knowledge has altered our psychology, naturally. In your terms we have become superhuman but we feel this as a loss rather than as an accomplishment. We decided to attempt to reproduce the civilization that had produced us.

"There were a few primitive inhabitants left on the Earth, which had long since begun a metamorphosis into an altered chemical state. We revitalized the planet, giving it an identical nature to the one it had had when civilization first began to exist in any real form. We expected the inhabitants to react to this. We expected — and there was no cause then to expect otherwise — to develop a race which would rapidly achieve an identical civilization to the one which had created us. But the first experiment failed — the inhabitants stayed on the same level of barbarism that they had been on when we first found them, but they began to fight one another. We decided to create an entirely new planet and try again. So as not to alter the balance of the multiverse, we extended a kind of 'well' into what you call, I believe, 'subspace', and built our new planet there. This proved a failure, but we learnt from it. Since then we have built more than a thousand simulations of the original Earth and have gradually been adding to our understanding of the complexity of the project we undertook. Everything on every planet has a part to play. A building, a tree, an animal, a man. All link in as essentials to the structure. They have a physical rôle to play in the ecological and sociological nature of the planet, and they have a psychological rôle — a symbolic nature. That is why we find it useful to have the populace of every new simulation (which is drawn from previous abandoned simulations) externalize and dramatize its symbolic and psychological rôle before full activation. To some extent it is also therapeutic and in many ways has the effect of simulating the birth and childhood of the adults we use. You doubtless noticed that there were no children on the new simulation. We find children very difficult to use on a freshly activated world."

"But why all those simulations?" Faustaff said. "Why not one planet which you could — judging by what you do anyway — brainwash *en masse* and channel it the way you want to."

"We are trying to produce an identical evolutionary pattern to the one which produced us. It would be impractical to do as you suggest. The psychological accretions would build-up too rapidly. We need a fresh environment every time. All this was considered before we began work on the first simulation."

"And why don't you interfere directly with the worlds? Surely you could destroy them as easily as you create them."

"They are not easily created and are not easily destroyed. We dare not let a hint of our presence get to the simulations. We did not exist when our ancestors evolved, therefore no-one should guess we exist now. We use our androids for destroying the failed simulations, or, for more sophisticated work, we use near-humans like the one who brought you here. They seem to be human and the natural assumption, if their activities are discovered and their missions fail, is that they are employed by other human beings. It is a very delicate kind of experiment, since it involves complicated entities like yourself, and we cannot afford, normally, to interfere directly. We do not want to become gods. Religion has a function in a society's earliest stages, but that function is soon replaced by the sciences. To provide what would be to your people 'proof' of supernatural beings would be completely against our interest."

"What of the people you kill? Have you no moral attitude to that?"

"We kill very few. Normally the population of one simulation is transferred to another. Only the children are destroyed in any quantity."

"*Only* the children!"

"I understand your horror. I understand your feelings towards children. It is necessary that you should have them — it is a virtue when you have these feelings in any strength — in your terms. In our terms, the whole race is our children. Compare our destruction of your immature offspring to your own destruction of male sperm and female ova in preventing birth. Your feelings are valid. We have no use for such feelings. Therefore, to us they are invalid."

Faustaff nodded. "I can see that. But I *have* these feelings. Besides which, I think there is a flaw in your argument. We feel that it is wrong to expect our children to develop as duplicates of ourselves. This defeats progress in any sense."

"We are not seeking progress. There is no progress to be made. We know the fundamental principles of everything. We are immortal, we are secure."

Faustaff frowned for a moment and then asked, "What are your pleasures?"

"Pleasures?"

"What makes you laugh, for instance?"

"We do not laugh. We would know joy — fulfillment — if our experiment were to be successful."

"So, currently, you have no pleasures. Nothing sensual or intellectual?"

"Nothing."

"Then you are dead, in my terms," Faustaff said. "Forget about the simulations. Can't you see that all your energies have been diverted into a ridiculous, useless experiment? Let us develop as we will — or destroy ourselves if we must. Let me take the knowledge you have given me back to E-Zero and tell everyone of your existence. You have kept them in fear, you have allowed them to despair, you have, in certain directions, kept them in ignorance. Turn your attention to yourselves — look for pleasure, create things to give you pleasure. Perhaps in time you would succeed in reproducing this Golden Age you speak of — but I doubt it. Even if you did, it would be a meaningless achievement, particularly if the eventual result was a race like yourselves. You have logic. Use it to find enjoyment in subjective pursuits. A thing does not have to have meaning to be enjoyed. Where are your arts, your amusements, your entertainments?"

"We have none. We have no use for them."

"Find a use."

The giant rose. His companions got up at the same time.

Once again they left the place and Faustaff waited, assuming they were debating what he had said.

*

They returned eventually.

"There is a possibility that you have helped us," said the giant as he and his companions seated themselves.

"Will you agree to let E-Zero develop without interference?" Faustaff asked.

"Yes. And we shall allow the remaining subspacial simulations to exist. There is one condition."

"What's that?"

"Our first illogical act — our first — joke — will be to have all the thirteen remaining simulations existing together in ordinary space-time. What influence this will in time have on the structure of the multiverse we cannot guess, but it will bring an element of uncertainty into our lives and thus will help us in our quest for pleasures. We shall have to enlarge your sun and replace the other planets in your system, for the thirteen worlds will constitute a much larger mass since we visualize them as being close together and easily accessible to one another. We feel that we shall be creating something that has no great practical use, within the limited sense of the word, but which will be pleasing and unusual to the eye. It will be the first thing of its kind in this universe."

"You certainly work fast," Faustaff smiled. "I'm looking forward to the result."

"No physical danger will result from what we do. It will be — spectacular, we feel."

"So it's over — you're abandoning the experiment altogether. I didn't think you'd be so easily convinced."

"You have released something in us. We are proud of you. By accident we helped create you. We are not abandoning the experiment, strictly speaking. We are going to let it run its own course from now on. Thank you."

"And thank you, gentlemen. How do I get back?"

"We will return you to E-Zero by the usual method."

"What about Maggy White?" Faustaff said, turning towards the girl.

"She will stay with us. She might be able to help us."

"Goodbye, then, Maggy," Faustaff kissed her on the cheek and squeezed her arm.

"Goodbye," she smiled.

The walls of light began to flow inwards, enfolding Faustaff. Soon they took on the shape of the room in the house.

He was back on E-Zero. The only difference was that the equipment had vanished. The room looked completely normal.

He went to the front door. Gordon Begg and Nancy were coming up the path.

"Good news," he grinned, walking towards them. "I'll tell you all about it. We've got a lot of work to do to help everybody organize themselves."

CHAPTER TWENTY

THE GOLDEN ROADS

By the time the principals were ready to create their "joke", the populations of the subspacial worlds had been informed of everything Faustaff could tell them. He had been interviewed for the Press, given V and radio time, and there had been no questioning voices. Somehow, all he said struck the worlds' populations as being true. It explained what they saw around them, what they felt within them.

The time came, and everyone was ready for it, when the thirteen planets began to phase in to ordinary space-time.

Faustaff and Nancy were back in Los Angeles when it happened, standing in the garden of the house which had first brought them to E-Zero and where they now lived. It was night when the twelve other simulations made their appearance. The dark sky seemed to ripple gently and they were there; a cluster of worlds moving in unison through space, with E-Zero in the centre, like so many gigantic moons.

Faustaff recognized the green jungle world of E-12; the desert-sea world of E-3. There was the vast continental atoll that was the only land area on E-7; the more normal-seeming worlds of E-2 and E-4; the mountainous world of E-11.

Now Faustaff received the impression that the sky was *flowing* and he realized that, miraculously, the atmospheres of the Earth-simulations were merging to form a complete envelope around the world-cluster. Now the jungle world could supply oxygen to the worlds with less vegetation, and moisture would come from the worlds predominantly of water.

He saw E-1, as he craned his neck to see them all. It seemed covered by black and scarlet clouds. It was right, he felt, that it should have been included; a symbol of ignorance and fear, a symbol of what the idea of hell actually meant in physical terms. The atmosphere did not seem to extend to E-1, for though its presence was necessary, it had been isolated.

Faustaff realized that though the principals had made a joke, it was a joke with many points to it.

"I hope they don't get too earnest about this now." Nancy said, hugging Faustaff's arm.

"I don't think they're going to be earnest for long," he smiled. "Just serious maybe. A good joke needs a spot of everything." He shook his head in wonderment. "Look at it all. It's impossible in our scientific terms, but they've done it. I've got to hand it to them; when they decide to be illogical, they go the whole hog!"

Nancy pointed into the sky. "Look," she said. "What's happening now?"

There was a further movement in the sky. Other objects began to appear; great golden structures whose reflected light turned the night to near-day; arcs of flame, roads of light between the worlds. Faustaff shielded his eyes to peer at them. They ran from world to world, spanning the distances like fiery rainbows. Only E-1 was not touched by them.

"That's what they are," Faustaff said in realization. "They're roads — roads that we can travel to reach the other simulations. See…" he pointed to an object that hung in the sky above their heads, rapidly passing as the world turned on its axis — "there's one end of ours. We could reach it in a plane, then we could walk across, if we had a lifetime to spare! But we can build transport that will travel the roads in a few days! These worlds are like islands in the same lake, and those roads link us all together."

"They're very beautiful," said Nancy quietly.

"Aren't they!"

Faustaff laughed in pleasure at the sight and Nancy joined in.

They were still laughing when the sun rose, a massive, splendid sun that made Faustaff realize that he had never really known daylight until that moment.

The giant sun's rays caught the gold of the roads so that they flamed even more brilliantly.

Used now to the code in which the principals had tried to write the history of his race, Faustaff looked at the roads and understood the many things they meant; to him, to the worlds and to the men, women and children who must now all be looking up at them.

And in its isolation, E-1 glared luridly in the new daylight.

Faustaff and Nancy turned to look at it. "There's no need to fear that now, Nancy," he said to her. "We can start getting somewhere at last, as long as we remember to relax a bit. Those roads mean understanding; communication…"

Nancy nodded seriously. Then she looked up at Faustaff and her expression turned into a spreading grin. She winked at him. He grinned and winked back.

They went into the house and were soon rolling about in bed together.

EMERGING FROM THE *benign myth of Doctor Faustaff,* *Count Renark took the main trunk road up through Lahore to Karaquazian's Bend and the back scales which had somehow become petrified and assumed a simple beauty. As he stepped to the branch road he looked up, savouring the miracle of a great scale-jumping ship of the Chaos Engineers, folding and unfolding her way rapidly down the scales and appearing to shrink as she did so, a vast cerise and scarlet caterpillar of undulating light and shade through whose luminous flesh near-human figures could be seen moving, the oddly translated Chaos Engineers, born, as they put it, to bite the fractal dust and to take the long hauls clear through the parameters of the multiverse and savour the bizarre semi-realities of the fabled Second Ether. These were creatures whose experience had given them an instinctive knowledge equipping them to leap at random through the scales of the multiverse, confident that they would sooner or later emerge into some compatible reality, able to explore territory none of their kind had ever visited before. They sought excessively for Ko-O-Ko, the Lost Universe, as their earthly versions, those Celtic Christian knights, had sought the Grail — and with the same hope of finding it or keeping it once found.*

Von Bek had no taste for the Vs which developed the mythology some believed had actually created the Chaos Engineers, but he had considerable admiration for those half-fictitious beings whose minds and bodies had been warped into alien, exquisitely beautiful forms by their adventures in the Second Ether.

He recollected his earliest years, when he had scarcely believed in all this and had encountered only one human being who claimed to have walked the roads between the worlds. His name was Emmanuel Bloom, popularly known as the Fireclown, who had set his controls for the heart of the sun and had found instead of death a new and terrible life. He knew, more than anyone, what it was like to be blown by —

THE WINDS OF LIMBO

For Judy Merril

It was a vast cavern. Part of it was natural, part of it had been hollowed out by the machines of men. Some parts were deep in dancing shadow and others were brilliantly illuminated by a great blazing mass — a roaring, crackling miniature replica of the sun itself, that hung, constantly quivering and erupting, near the high roof.

Beneath this blazing orb a tall column rose up as if to meet it, and arms akimbo upon a platform at the top stood a gross figure, clad in ragged harlequin costume. A soft, floppy, conical hat was jammed over his lank, yellow hair; his fat-rounded face was painted white, his eyes and mouth adorned with smears of red, yellow and black, and on the ragged red jerkin stretched taut upon his great belly was a vivid yellow sunburst.

Below this gross harlequin the dense crowd surrounding the column ceased its movement as he raised an orange hand that seemed to shoot from his torn sleeve like fingers of flame.

He laughed. It was as if the sun had voiced unearthly humour.

"Speak to us!" the crowd pleaded. "Fireclown! Speak to us!"

He ceased his laughing and looked down at them with a peculiar expression moving behind the paint. At length he bellowed:

"I am the Fireclown!"

"Speak to us!"

"I am the Fireclown, equipped for your salvation. I am the gift bearer, alive with the Fire of Life, from which the Earth itself was formed! I am the Earth's brother..."

A woman in a padded dress representing the body of a lion cried shrilly: "And what are we?"

"You are maggots feeding off your mother. When you mate it is like corpses coupling. When you laugh it is the sound of the winds of limbo!"

"Why? Why?" shouted a young man with a lean, mean face and a pointed chin that could pierce a throat. He leapt exuberantly while his eyes glinted and looked.

"You have shunned the natural life and worshipped the artificial. But you are not lost — not yet!"

"What shall we do?" sobbed a government official, sweating in the purple jacket and purple pantaloons of his rank, caught by the ritual enough to fidget and forget to stay in the shadows. His cry was echoed by the crowd.

"What shall we do?"

"Follow me! I will reinstate you as Children of the Sun and Brothers of the Earth. Spurn me — and you perish in your artificiality, renounced by Nature on whom you have turned your proud backs."

And again the clown broke into a laugh. He breathed heavily and roared his insane and enigmatic humour at the cavern roof. Flames from the suspended miniature sun leapt, stretched and shot out, as if to kiss the Fireclown's acolytes who laughed and shouted, surging about him, applauding him.

The Fireclown looked down as he laughed, drinking in their adoration.

In a shadow cast by the dais, detached from the milling crowd, a gaunt Negro stood as if petrified, his eyelids painted in checks of red and white, his mouth coloured green. He wore an extravagant yellow cut-away coat and scarlet tights. He looked up at the Fireclown and there were tears of hunger in his eyes. The Negro's name was Junnar.

The faces of the crowd were lashed and slashed by the leaping fire, some eyes dull, some bright, some eyes blind and some hot, overloaded with heat.

Many of the figures wore masks moulded in plastic to caricature their own faces — long noses, no noses, slit eyes, cow eyes, lipless mouths, gaping mouths. Some were painted in gaudy colours, others were naked and some wore padded clothes representing animals or plants.

Here they gathered around the dais. Many hundreds of them, loving the man who capered like a jester above them, lashing them with his wriggling rhetoric, laughing, laughing. Scientists, pick-pockets, spacemen, explorers, musicians, confidence tricksters, blackmailers, poets, doctors, whores, murderers, clerks, perverts, government officials, spies, policemen, social workers, beggars, actors, politicians, riff-raff.

Here they all were. And they shouted. And as they shouted the gross Fool capered yet more wildly and the flame responded frenetically to his dancing and his own wordless cries.

"The Fireclown!" they sobbed.

"The Fireclown!" they bellowed.

"The Fireclown! The Fireclown!" they howled and laughed.

"The Fireclown!" He giggled and he danced like a madman's puppet upon his dais and sang his mirth.

All this, in the lowest level of the multistoreyed labyrinth that was the City of Switzerland.

With a great effort the Negro Junnar turned his eyes away from the Fireclown, stumbled backwards, wrenched his body round and ran for one of the black exits, bent on leaving before he was completely trapped by the Fireclown's spell.

Behind him, the sound of the maddened crowd diminished as he ran along fusty, ill-smelling corridors until he could no longer hear it. Then he began to walk up ramps and stairs until he came to an escalator. He stepped on to the escalator and let himself be taken up to the top, a hundred feet from the bottom. This corridor was also deserted, but better lighted and cleaner than those he had left. He looked up and found a sign at an intersection:

NINTH LEVEL (Mechanics) Hogarth Lane — Leading to Divebomber Street and Orangeblossom Road (Elevators to Forty Levels)

He made for Orangeblossom Road, an old residential corridor but very sparsely inhabited these days, found the elevators at the end, pressed a button and waited impatiently for five minutes before one arrived. He entered it and rose non-stop to the forty-ninth level. Outside he crossed the bright, bustling corridor and got into a crowded lift bound for the sixty-fifth — the topmost — level.

The liveried operator recognized him and said deferentially: "Any tips for when the next election's going to be held, Herr Junnar?"

Junnar, abstracted, tried to smile politely. He shook his head. "Tomorrow, if the RLMs had their way," he said. "But we're not worried. People have faith in the Solrefs." He frowned. He had caught himself using a party slogan again. Apparently the operator hadn't noticed, but Junnar thought he saw a hint of irony in the man's eyes. He ignored it, frowned again, this time for a different reason. Obviously people were *losing* faith in the Solar Referendum Party. A sign of the times, he thought.

At length the elevator reached the sixty-fifth level and the operator called out conscientiously: "Sixty-five. Please show appointment cards as you go through the barrier."

The people began to shuffle out, some towards transport that would take them right across the vast plateau of the Top Level, some towards the distant buildings comprising the Seat of Government, various Ministries and the private accommodations of important statesmen, politicians and civil servants.

Built with the money of frightened businessmen during the war scares of the 1970s, the city had grown upwards and outwards so that it now covered almost two-thirds of what was once the country of Switzerland — one vast building. A warren with mountains embedded in it, it had begun as a warren of super-shelters *below* the mountains. The war scares had died down, but the city had remained along with the businessmen and, when the World Government was formed in 2005, it seemed the natural place for the capital. In 2031, in a bid to get full rights of citizenship for outworld settlers, the Solar Referendum Party had been formed. Four years later it had risen to power. Its first act had been to declare that henceforth they were a Solar Government running the affairs of the Federation of Solar Planets.

But since then more than sixty years had passed. The Solrefs had lost much of their original dynamism, having become the most powerfully conservative party in the Solar House.

The official at the barrier knew Junnar and waved him through. Sun poured in through the glass-alloy dome far above his head and the artificially scented air was refreshing after the untainted stuff of the middle levels and the impure air of the lowest.

He walked across the turf-covered plaza, listening to the splashing fountains that at intervals glinted among beds of exotic flowers. He was struck by the contrast between the hot excitement, the smell of sweat and the surge of bodies he had just left, and this cool, well-controlled expanse, artificially maintained yet as beautiful as anything nature could produce.

But he did not pause to savour the view. His pace was hurried compared with the movement of the few other people who sauntered with dignity along the paths. At a distance, the tall white, blue and silver buildings of the ambiguously named Private Level reflected the sun and enhanced the atmosphere of calm and assurance of the Top.

Junnar crossed the plaza and walked up a clean, graveled path towards the wide stone arch that opened on to a shady court. Around this court many windows looked down upon the cool pool in its centre. Goldfish glinted in the pool. At the archway, a porter left his lodge and planted himself on the path until Junnar reached him. He was a sour-faced man, dressed in a dark grey blouse and pantaloons; he looked at Junnar with vague disapproval as the flamboyant Negro stopped and produced his pass, sighing: "Here you are, Drew. You're very conscientious today."

"My job is to check all passes, sir."

Junnar smiled at him. "You don't recognize me, is that it."

"I recognize you very well, sir, but it would be more than my job's worth to…"

"Let me in without checking my pass," Junnar finished for him. "You're an annoying man, Drew."

The porter didn't reply. He was not afraid of incurring Junnar's disapproval since he had a strong union that would be only too ready to take up cudgels on his behalf if he was fired without adequate grounds.

So temporarily disorientated was Junnar that he allowed this tiny conflict to carry him further, and as he went into the court he shrugged and said: "It's better to have friends than enemies, though, Drew…" Immediately he felt foolish.

He took out a pack of proprietary brand marijuanas and lit one as he went through a glass-paneled door into the quiet, deserted hall of the building. The hall was lined with mirrors. He stood staring at himself in one of them, drawing deeply on the sweet smoke, collecting his thoughts and pulling himself together. This was the third time he had attended one of the Fireclown's "audiences" and each time the clown's magnetism had drawn him closer and the atmosphere of the great cavern had affected him more profoundly. He didn't want his employer to notice that.

After a moment's contemplation Junnar went to the central glass panel which was on the right and withdrew a small oblong box from his pocket. He put it close to his mouth.

"Junnar," he said.

The panel slid back to reveal a black, empty shaft. There was a peculiar dancing quality about the blackness. Junnar stepped into it and, instantaneously, was opening the inner door of a cabinet. He walked out and the door closed behind him. He was in a corridor lighted by windows that stretched from floor to ceiling and showed in the distance the thick band of summer cloud far below.

Immediately opposite him was a great door of red-tinted chrome. It now opened silently.

In the big, beautiful room, two men awaited him. One was young, one was old; both showed physical similarities, both appeared impatient.

Junnar entered the room and dropped his cigarette into a disposal column.

"Good afternoon, sir," he said to the old man, and nodded to the young man. "Good afternoon, Herr von Bek."

The old man spoke, his voice rich and resonant. "Well Junnar, what's happening down there now?"

Alain von Bek fingered the case of papers under his arm, studying his grandfather and the painted Negro as they confronted one another. They made a strange pair.

Minister Simon von Bek was tall and heavy without much obvious fat, but his face was as grim and disturbing as an Easter Island god's. The leonine set of his head was further enhanced by the flowing mane of white hair which reached almost to his shoulders, hanging straight as if carved. He wore the standard purple suit of a high-ranking cabinet minister — he was Minister for Space Transport, an important office — pleated jacket, padded pantaloons, red stockings and white pumps. His white shirt was open at the neck to reveal old but firm flesh, and on his breast was a golden star, symbol of his rank.

Junnar was sighing and spreading his hands. "If you, Minister von Bek, want to stop him you should act now. His power increases daily. People are flocking to him. He *seems* harmless, insofar as he doesn't appear to have any great political ambitions, but his power could be used to threaten society's stability."

"Could be? I'm sure it *will* be." Minister von Bek spoke heavily. "But can we convince parliament of the danger? There's the irony."

"Probably not." Alain von Bek spoke distantly, conscious of an outsider's presence. He thought he glimpsed, momentarily, a strange expression on the Negro's face.

"Helen and that mob of rabble-rousers she calls a political party are only too pleased to encourage him," Minister von Bek grumbled. "Not to mention certain members of the government who seem as fascinated by him as schoolgirls on their first dates." He straightened his shoulders which were beginning to stoop with old age. "There must be some way of showing them their mistake."

Alain von Bek chose not to argue with his grandfather in Junnar's presence. Personally, however, he thought the old man over-emphasized the Fireclown's importance. Perhaps Junnar sensed this, for he said softly:

"The Fireclown has a certain ability to attract and hold interest. The most unlikely people seem to have come under his spell. His magnetism is intense and almost irresistible. Have you been to one of his 'audiences' Herr von Bek?"

Alain shook his head.

"Then go to one — before you judge. Believe me, he has *something*. He's more than a crank."

Alain wondered why the normally self-possessed and taciturn Negro should choose to speak in this way. Perhaps one day he *would* attend a meeting. He certainly was curious.

"Who is he, anyway?" Alain asked as his grandfather paced towards the window comprising the outer wall of the room.

"No-one knows," Junnar said. "His origins, like his theories, are obscure. He will not tell anyone his real name. There are no records of his fingerprints at Identity Centre; he seems demented, but no mental hospital has heard of him. Perhaps, as he says, he came down from the sun to save the world?"

"Don't be facetious, Junnar." Minister von Bek pursed his lips, paused, then took a long breath and said: "Who was down there today?"

"Vernitz, Chief of the China Police — he is in the city on a vacation and to attend the Police Conference next Sixday. Martha Gheld, Professor of Electrobiology at Tel Aviv. All the Persian representatives currently elected to parliament…"

"Including Isfahan?" Minister von Bek was too well bred to shout, but there was astonishment in his voice. Isfahan was the leader of the Solref faction in the Solar House.

"Including all the Persian Solrefs, I'm afraid." Junnar nodded. "Not to mention a number of Dutch, Swedish and Mexican party members."

"We had advised our members not to take part in the Fireclown's farcical 'audiences'!"

"Doubtless they were all there on fact-finding missions," Alain interrupted, a faint gleam in his eyes.

"Doubtless," von Bek said grimly, choosing to ignore his grandson's irony.

"Your niece was there, too," Junnar said quietly.

"That *doesn't* surprise me. The woman's a fool. To think that she could be the next President!"

Alain knew that his cousin, Helen Curtis, leader of the Radical Liberal Movement, and his grandfather were both planning to run for President in the forthcoming Presidential elections. One of them was sure to win.

"All right, Junnar." Simon von Bek dismissed his secretary. The Negro went out through a side door opening on an inner passage leading to his own office.

When the door had closed, Alain said: "I think you place too much importance on this character, grandfather. He's harmless enough. Perhaps he could threaten society — but it's doubtful if he would. You seem to have an obsession about him. No-one else, in politics at least, seems so concerned. If the situation became serious people would soon leave him or act against him. Why not wait and see?"

"No. I seem to have an obsession, do I? Well, it may be that I'm the only man not blinded to what this Fireclown represents. I have already drafted a Bill which, if it gets passed, could easily put a stop to the fool's posturing."

Alain laid his briefcase on the desk and sat down in one of the deep armchairs. "But will it? Surely it isn't wise at this stage to back what could easily be an unpopular motion. The Fireclown is an attractive figure to most people — and as yet harmless. If you were to oppose him openly it might cost you votes in the Presidential election. You could lose it!"

Alain felt he had scored a point. He knew how important winning was to the old man. Since the formation of the Solar Referendum Party, a von Bek of every generation had held the Presidential chair for at least one term of his life — a von Bek had in fact formed the first Solref cabinet. Yet it was likely that von Bek would not be voted in, for public opinion was gradually going against the Solrefs and tending to favour the more vociferous and dynamic RLM, which had grown rapidly in strength under Helen Curtis's fiery leadership. Throughout his life Simon von Bek had aimed at the Presidency, and this would be his last chance to gain it.

"I have never sacrificed principles for mere vote-catching!" Simon von Bek said scornfully. "It is unworthy of a von Bek to suggest it, Alain. Your mother would have been horrified if she had heard such a remark coming from her own son. Though you have the look of a von Bek, the blood, whoever gave it you, is not von Bek blood!"

For a second before he controlled himself, Alain felt pain at this remark. This was the first time his grandfather had referred to his obscure origins — he had been illegitimate, his mother dying soon after he was born. Though, in his grim way, Simon von Bek had assured his grandson's education and position, he had always been withdrawn from Alain, caring for him but not encouraging friendship or love. His wife had died five years earlier and she and Alain had been close. When Eleanor von Bek died Simon had begun to see a little more of Alain, but had always remained slightly distant. However, this remark about his bastardy was the first spoken in anger. Obviously the matter of the Presidency was weighing on his mind.

Alain ignored the elder von Bek's reference and smiled.

"City Administration — if I may return to the original topic — isn't worried by the Fireclown. He inhabits the disused lower levels and gives us no trouble, doesn't threaten to come upstairs at all. Leave him alone, grandfather — at least until after the election."

Minister Simon went to the picture window and stared out into the twilight, his erect body silhouetted against the distant mountains.

"The Fireclown is a tangible threat, Alain. He has admitted that he is bent on the destruction of our whole society, on the rejection of all its principles of progress and democracy. With his babbling of fire-worship and nature-worship, the Fireclown threatens to throw us all back to disorganized and retrogressive savagery!"

"Grandfather — the man isn't that powerful! You place too much importance on him!"

Simon von Bek shook his head, his heavy hands clasping behind him.

"I say I do not!"

"Then you are wrong!" Alain said angrily, half-aware that his anger was not so much inspired by the old man's righteousness as by his earlier, wounding remark.

Simon von Bek remained with his back to Alain, silent.

At least his grandfather's solid reputation for integrity and sticking to what he thought was well earned, Alain reflected. But that reputation might not save him if the Fireclown became a political issue in the elections.

His own view, shared with a great many people, was that the Fireclown's mysterious appearance a year ago was welcome as an agent to relieve the comparative monotony of running the smoothly ordered City of Switzerland.

"Goodbye, grandfather," he said, picking up his briefcase. "I'm going home. I've got a lot of work to get through this evening."

Simon von Bek turned — a considered and majestic movement.

"You may like to know that I have approached the City Council on this matter, suggesting that they completely seal off the lower levels. I hope they will adopt my suggestion. City Administration, of course, would be responsible for carrying it out. As Assistant Director, you would probably be in charge of the project."

"If the City Council have any sense they'll ignore your suggestion. They have no evidence of law-breaking on the Fireclown's part. They can take no legal steps against him. All he has done, so far as I can see, is to address a public meeting — and that isn't a crime in this democracy you've been boasting of. To make it one would invalidate your whole argument. Don't you agree?"

"One short step back could save us from a long slide down," Minister von Bek said curtly as Alain left the room.

Entering the elevator that would take him home to the sixty-fourth level, Alain decided that he could have misjudged his grandfather over the matter of the Fireclown. He had heard a great deal about him and his "audiences" and, emotionally, was attracted by the romantic character of the man. But he had argued the Fireclown's case too strongly without really knowing it at first hand.

He left the elevator and crossed to the middle of the corridor, taking the fastway belt towards his flat. As he neared it, he crossed to the slowway with instinctive practice, produced a small box from his pocket and spoke his name into it. The door of the flat opened in the wall.

In the passage his manservant took his briefcase and carried it into the study. "We were expecting you home earlier, sir. Madeleine apologizes, but she feels the polter may be overdone."

"My fault, Stefanos." He was not particularly fond of synthetic poultry, anyway.

"And Fräulein Curtis is waiting for you in the living room. I told her you hadn't dined…"

"That's all right." Outwardly decisive, he was inwardly confused. He even felt a slight trembling in his legs and cursed himself for an uncontrolled buffoon. He had only once seen Helen, briefly, since their affair had ended, at a party.

He entered the austere living room.

"Good evening, Helen. How are you?"

They did not shake hands.

"Hello, Alain."

He could not guess why she was here but he did not particularly want to know. He was afraid he might get involved emotionally with her again.

He sat down. She seated herself opposite him in the other padded, armless chair. She was made up — which was unusual. Her lips were a light green and she had on some sort of ultra-white powder. Her eyebrows and eyelids were red. Her taste, he thought, had never been all it might. She had an almost triangular face; short, black hair and a small nose so that she looked rather like a cat — save for the make-up which made her look like a corpse.

"I hear you attended the Fireclown's 'audience' today?" he said casually.

"Where did you hear that? Bush telegraph? Have you been at a cocktail party?"

"No." He smiled half-heartedly. "But spies are everywhere these days."

"You've been to see uncle Simon, then? Is he planning to use the information against me in the election?"

"I don't think so — no."

She was evidently nervous. Her voice was shaking slightly. Probably his own was, too. They had been very close — in love, even — and the break, when it had finally come, had been made in anger. He had not been alone with her since.

"What do you think your chances are of winning it?"

She smiled. "Good."

"Yes, they seem to be."

"Will you be pleased?"

She knew very well that he wouldn't be. Her political ambitions had been the main reasons for their parting. Unlike all the rest of his family, including remote cousins, he had no interest in politics. Maybe, he thought with a return of his earlier bitterness, Simon von Bek had been right about his blood being inherited from his unknown father. He shook his head, shrugging slightly, smiling vaguely.

"I — I don't know," he lied. Of course he would be disappointed if she won. He hated the political side of her character. Whereas he had nothing against women in politics — it would have been atavistic and unrealistic if he had an objection — he felt that her talents lay elsewhere. Perhaps in the painting she no longer had time for? She had been, potentially, a very fine painter.

"It's time the Solar System had a shake-up," she said. "The Solrefs have been in for too long."

"Probably," he said non-committally. Then, desperate to get it over: "Why are you here, Helen?"

"I wanted some help."

"What kind of help? Personal…?"

"No, of course not. Don't worry. When you said it was over I believed you. I've still got the mark on my shoulder."

This had been on his conscience and her reference to it hurt him. He had struck her on her shoulder, not really intending the blow to be hard, but it had been.

"I'm sorry about that…" he said stumblingly. "I didn't mean…"

"I know. I shouldn't have brought it up." She smiled and said quickly: "Actually, I want some information, Alain. I know that you're politically uncommitted, so I'm sure you won't mind giving it to me."

"But I don't have any *secrets*, Helen. I'm not in that position — I'm only a civil servant, you know that."

"It's not really a secret. All I want is some — what d'you call it? — advance information."

"About what?"

"I heard a rumour that the City Council plan to close off the lower levels. Is that true?"

"I really couldn't say, Helen." News was traveling fast. Obviously an indiscreet councilor had mentioned Simon von Bek's letter to someone and this had been the start of the rumour. On the other hand, his grandfather, when he told him of it, had understood that he would keep the old man's confidence. He could say nothing — though the truth would put paid to the rumour.

"But you're in City Administration. You must know. You'd be responsible for the project, wouldn't you?"

"If such a project were to be carried out, yes. But I have been told nothing either by the City Council or my director. I should ignore the rumour. Anyway, why should it bother you?"

"Because if it's true it would be interesting to know which councilors backed the motion, and who egged them on. The only man with sufficient power and a great enough obsession is your grandfather — my uncle, Simon von Bek!"

"How many Solar Referendum councilors are in the Council?" he asked vaguely. He was smelling her perfume now. He remembered it with a sad nostalgia. This was becoming too much to bear.

"There are five Solrefs, three RLMs, one independent Socialist and one Crespignite who slipped in somewhere on the pensioners' vote. Giving, if you *are* so ignorant of simple politics, a majority to the Solrefs and virtual control of the Council, since the Crespignite is bound to vote with them on nearly every issue."

"So you want to tell the people that this hypothetical closing down of the lower levels is a Solref plot — a blow to their liberty."

"My very words," she said with a kind of triumphant complacency.

He got up. "And you expect me to help you — to betray confidence, not to mention giving my own grandfather's opponents extra ammunition — and let you know what the City Council decides before it is made public? You're becoming foolish, Helen. Politics must be addling your brains!"

"But it means nothing to you, anyway. You're not interested in politics!"

"That's so. One of the reasons I'm not interested is because of the crookedness that seems to get into the best of people — people who think any means to win elections are fair! I'm not naïve, Helen. I'm from the same family as you. I grew up knowing politics. That's why I stay out of it!"

"Surely you don't support this victimization of the Fireclown, Alain? He is a simple, spontaneous…"

"I'm not interested in hearing a list of the Fireclown's virtues. And whether I support any 'victimization', as you call it, is of no importance. As a matter of fact, I'm attracted to the Fireclown and consider him no danger at all. But it seems to me that both you and grandfather are using this man for your own political ends, and I'll have no part of it!" He paused, considering what he had said, then added: "Finally, there has been no 'victimization', and there isn't likely to be!"

"That's what you think. I support the Fireclown for good reasons. His ambitions and the ambitions of the RLM are linked. He wants to bring sanity and real life back to this machine-ridden world. We want real values back again!"

"Oh, God!" He shook his head impatiently. "Helen, I've got a great deal of work to do before I go to bed tonight."

"Very well. I have, too. If you reconsider…"

"Even if there was a plot to *arrest* the Fireclown I wouldn't tell you so that you could use it for political fuel, Helen." He suddenly found himself moving towards her, gripping her arm. "Listen. Why get involved with this? You've got a good chance of winning the election without indulging in dealings of this sort. Wait until you're President, then you can make the Fireclown into a Solar Trust if you like!"

"You can't understand," she said grimly, shaking herself free of his hand. "You don't realize that you have to be comparatively ruthless when you know what you're aiming for is *right*."

"Then I'm glad you know what's right," he said pityingly. "I'm bloody glad you know. It's more than I do."

She left in silence and he went back to his chair, slumping down heavily and feeling, with morose pleasure, that he had scored.

The mood didn't last long. By the time Stefanos came in to tell him his meal was waiting for him he had sunk into a brooding, unconstructive melancholy. Brusquely he told his manservant to eat the meal himself and then go out for the rest of the evening.

"Thank you, sir," Stefanos said wonderingly, chewing his ridged underlip as he left the room.

In this mood in which his confrontation of his ex-mistress had left him, Alain felt incapable of work. The work was of little real importance anyway, routine stuff which he had hoped to clear up before he took his vacation in a fortnight's time. He decided to go to bed, hoping that a good ten hours' sleep would help him forget Helen.

He had reached the point where he felt he must see the mysterious figure for himself, since so many matters seemed to be revolving around him all of a sudden.

He walked into the darkened hall and ordered the light on. The light responded to his voice and flooded the flat. The tiny escalator leading upstairs began to move, too, and he stepped on it, letting it carry him to the landing.

He went into his bedroom. It was as sparsely furnished as the rest of the flat — a bed, mellowlamp for reading, a small shelf of books, a wing on the headboard of the bed for anything he cared to put there, and a concealed wardrobe. The air was fresh from the ventilators, also hidden.

He took off his scarlet jacket and pants, told the wardrobe to open, told the cleaning chute to open and dropped them in. He selected a single-piece sleeping suit and moved moodily to sit on the edge of the bed.

Then he got up and went back to the wardrobe, removed an ordinary suit of street garments and put them on.

Rapidly, feeling that he should have taken something with him — a weapon or a notebook or an alarm signaler which would contact the police wherever he was — he left the flat and took the fastway towards the elevators.

He was going to the lower levels. He was going to find the Fireclown.

CHAPTER THREE

He was unreasoningly annoyed that the liveried operator should recognize him and stare at him curiously as he was taken down to the forty-ninth level. In the back of his mind he was thrilling to the experience, unremembered since boyhood, of exploration. He had chosen nondescript clothes so that he might move about incognito.

He was alone in the unmanned elevator as it dropped swiftly to the ninth level, causing him the added excitement of being alone and virtually helpless against danger.

He stepped boldly into the ill-lit corridor named — incongruously — Orangeblossom Road, and then advanced cautiously until he saw a sign which read: *Escalators (down) five levels.*

He rode the escalators into the chilly depths of the City of Switzerland, feeling as if he were descending into some frozen hell and at the same time making a mental note that if people were, indeed, inhabiting the lower levels, then City Administration should, out of humanity, do something about the heating arrangements.

He wished he had some warmer clothing, but that would have meant applying to Garment Centre, since he rarely went outside save on vacation, and then all necessary apparel was supplied.

But as he advanced deeper he became aware of a growing warmth and a thick, unpleasant smell that he gradually recognized as being, predominantly, the smell of human perspiration. In spite of his revulsion he sniffed it curiously.

As he walked slowly down the ramp leading to the notorious first level, reputed to be the haunt of undesirables well before the Fireclown first made his appearance, he saw with a slight shock that the light was dancing and had an unusual quality about it. As he drew closer his excitement increased. Naked flame! The light came from a great, burning torch which also gave off uncontrolled heat!

He approached it as close as he dared and stared at it, marveling. He had seen recordings of the phenomenon, but this was the first time... He withdrew hastily as the heat produced sweat from his forehead, walking along a corridor that reminded him, with its dancing, naked light, of the fairyland of his childhood fantasies. On reflection, he decided it was more like the ogre's castle, but so delighted was he by this wholly new experience that he forgot caution for a while. It only returned as he rounded another corner and saw that the roof was actually composed of living rock, so moist that it dripped condensed water!

Alain von Bek was not an unsophisticated young man, yet this was so remote from his everyday experience that he could not immediately absorb it on any intellectual level.

From ahead came sounds — the sounds of excited human voices. He had expected a vast conclave of some description, but he heard only a few people, and they were conversing. Occasionally, as he drew nearer, he heard a reverberating laugh which seemed to him so full of delighted and profound humour that he wished he knew the joke so that he could join in. If this was the Fireclown's famous laughter, then it did not strike him as at all insane.

Still, he told himself, keeping in the shadows, there were many forms of madness.

A cave came into view on his right. He hugged the left-hand wall and inched forward, his heart pounding.

The cave appeared to turn at a right-angle so that he could only see the light coming from it, but now he could make out fragments of words and phrases. At intervals there came a spluttering eruption of green light and each time he was caught in the flare.

"... shape it into something we can control..."

"... no good, it's only a hint of what we might..."

"... your eyeshield back. I'm going to..."

A hissing eruption and a tongue of green flame seemed to turn the bend in the cave and come flickering like an angry cobra towards Alain. He gasped and stepped back as the roaring laughter followed the eruption. Had he been seen?

No. The conversation was continuing, the pitch of the voices now high with excitement.

He crossed the corridor swiftly and stood in the mouth of the cave, straining his ears to make out what they were talking about.

Then he felt a delicate touch on his arm and heard a whispering voice say: "I'm afraid you can't go in there. Private, you know."

He turned slowly and was horrified at the apparition that still touched his arm. He withdrew, nauseated.

The horrible figure laughed softly. "Serves you right. They could keep me just to stop people nosing around!"

"I didn't know you had any kind of secrecy," Alain babbled. "I really do apologize if..."

"We welcome visitors, but we prefer to invite them. You don't mind?" The skinless man nodded towards the corridor. Alain backed into it, forcing himself to ignore the bile in his throat, forcing himself to look at the creature without obvious revulsion — but it was difficult.

Flesh, veins and sinews shone on his body as if the whole outer covering had been peeled off. How could he move? How could he appear so calm?

"My skin's synthetic — but transparent. Something in it takes the place of pigment. They haven't worked out a way of giving the stuff pigmentation yet — I was lucky enough to be the guinea-pig. I could use cosmetics, but I don't. My name's Corso. I'm the Fireclown's trusty henchman and deal with anyone interested in coming to his audiences. You arrived at the wrong time. We had one this afternoon."

Obviously Corso was used to random explorers, particularly those curious about the Fireclown. Deciding to play his part in the rôle Corso had mistakenly given him, Alain looked down at the floor.

"Oh, I'm sorry. When's the next one?"

"Day after tomorrow."

"I can come then?"

"Very welcome."

Alain turned to retrace his way.

"See you then," said the skinless man.

When Alain turned the corner of the corridor he had to lean against the wall for some moments before he could continue. Too many unexpected shocks this evening, he told himself.

As he began to recover his composure his curiosity started to operate again. What was going on? From what he had seen and heard, the Fireclown and a group of his friends were conducting some sort of laboratory experiment — and Corso, the skinless man, had been left on guard to turn pryers away.

Well, everyone had a right to their privacy. But his curiosity came close to overwhelming him. He began to return towards the cave when a soft voice that he recognized said:

"It wouldn't be wise. If you went back a second time Corso would know you were no innocent would-be initiate."

"Junnar!" he hissed. "What are you doing here?"

But he heard only a faint scuffling and received no reply.

Perhaps, however, the Negro's advice was good. There was no point in making anyone suspicious since he would, if discovered, be excluded from any future chance of seeing the Fireclown.

He began to return towards the ramp. What on earth had Junnar been doing in the lower levels? Was he there on his own business or on Simon von Bek's? Perhaps the Negro would tell him tomorrow, if he could find an excuse for leaving the C.A. building and visiting his grandfather's apartment.

Vaguely irritated that he had seen so little of the Fireclown's domain and nothing at all of the Fireclown himself, he finally arrived on the sixty-fourth level, took the fastway to his flat and went to bed with something of his earlier sullen mood eliminated.

The day after tomorrow he would definitely attend the Fireclown's "audience".

Very deliberately, the next morning, Alain concentrated his thoughts entirely on his job. By the time he arrived at his office in City Administration on North Top, he had turned his thoughts to the matter of elevator installation which the City Council had decided was necessary to speed up pedestrian flow between levels.

His Assistant Directorship was well earned, but he had to admit that having it was partly due to his family connections and the education which his grandfather had insisted on him having. But he was a hard and conscientious worker who got on well with his staff, and the director seemed pleased with him. He had been doing the job for two years since he had left university.

He spent the morning catching up on lost time until just before lunch when Carson, the director, called him into his office.

Carson was a thin man with an unsavoury appearance. He was much respected by those working under him. His chin, however, always looked as if he needed a shave and his swarthy face always appeared to need a wash. But this wasn't his fault. After a little time in his company the first impression of his unsavouriness vanished swiftly.

Carson said mildly: "Sit down, Alain. I wonder if you could leave the elevator matter for a while and turn it over to Sevlin to get on with. Something else has cropped up."

Von Bek sat down and watched Carson leaf through the papers on his desk. The director finally selected one and handed it to him.

It was headed *Low Level Project*, and a glance told Alain it was the proposed plan to seal off the lower levels from the upper ones.

So Helen had been right in her thinking. Simon von Bek did hold sufficient sway with the City Council to have his "suggestions" put into action.

Carson was staring at his own right thumb. He did not look up. "It will involve temporarily re-routing pedestrian traffic, of course, though to save trouble we could work at night. It would be worth paying the men double overtime to get it done as quickly as possible."

"With a minimum of fuss?" Alain said with an edge to his voice.

"Exactly."

"The Council hasn't announced this publicly, I presume?"

"There's no need to — no-one lives in the lower levels any more. There will be emergency doors constructed, naturally, but these will be kept locked. It shouldn't bother anyone..."

"Except the Fireclown!" Alain was so furious that he found difficulty in controlling himself.

"Ah, yes. The Fireclown. I expect he'll find somewhere else to go. Probably he'll leave the city altogether. I suspect he's no real right to live there in the first place."

"But the vids, the RLM — and therefore the main weight of public opinion — all regard the Fireclown in a favourable way. He has a good part of the world on his side. This isn't political dynamite — it's a political megabang!"

"Quite." Carson nodded, still regarding his thumb. "But we aren't concerned with politics, are we, Alain? This is just another job for us — a simple one. Let's get it over with."

Alain took the papers Carson handed him and got up. The director was right, but he could not help feeling personally involved.

"I'll get started after lunch," he promised. He went back to his office, put the papers in his confidential drawer, went to the roof of the C.A. building and took a cab across the spacious artificial countryside of the Top towards his grandfather's apartment, which lay close to the Solar House at South Top.

But when he got there he found only Junnar and another of his cousins — Helen's brother, Denholm Curtis.

Curtis dressed with challenging bad taste. His clothes were a deliberate attack, a weapon which he flaunted. They proclaimed him an iconoclast impatient of any accepted dogma whether reasonable or not. Above the striped and polka-dotted trappings draping his lean body was a firm, sensitive head — the heavy von Bek head with calm eyes, hopeful, seeming to be aware of detail and yet disdainful of it. Curtis's eyes were fixed on the future.

"Hello, Denholm, how are you?" He and his cousin shook hands.

"Fine — and you?"

"Not bad. And how's the Thirty Five Group? Still bent on gingering up the mother party?"

Curtis led the radical wing of the Solref party. His group was small but vociferous and carried a certain amount of weight in the Solar House. Yet, though he stuck to the traditional party of the von Bek family, he would have been much more at home in his sister's movement. But his interest was in changing the party to change the policy rather than splitting away from it and forming a fresh one.

Curtis hadn't replied to Alain's question. He glanced at the big wall-clock just as his grandfather came hurrying in through the side door.

"Grandfather." Alain stepped quickly forward but old Simon von Bek shook his head.

"Sorry, Alain. I have to get to the Solar House immediately. Coming, Denholm?"

Curtis nodded and the two of them left the room almost at a run.

Something was in the air, Alain guessed, and it wasn't the closing down of the lower levels. This seemed much more important.

"What's going on, Junnar?"

The Negro looked slightly embarrassed as their eyes met, but he spoke coolly.

"They're calling on old Benjosef to resign."

Benjosef, a dedicated member of the Solrefs, was Solar President. His two terms of office had been popular but not particularly enlightened. He had not had much public support over the last year, partly because he was slow to agree on a policy of expansion and colonization involving Mars and Ganymede.

"On what issue?"

"The planets. Ganymede and Mars are ready for settlers. There are businessmen willing to invest in them, ships ready to take them — but Benjosef is reluctant to pursue a policy of expansion because *he* says we haven't a sufficiently good organization for controlling it yet. He wants to wait another ten years to build up such an organization, but everyone else is impatient to get started. You know the story..."

"I know it," Alain agreed.

The projects to make the two planets inhabitable and fertile had been started over a hundred years previously and it had been hard enough holding private enterprise and would-be settlers back before they were ready. Benjosef had been foolish to take a stand on the issue, but he had done what he thought was right and his conviction now seemed likely to topple him.

"What are his chances of staying in power for the rest of his term?" Alain asked curiously.

"Bad. Minister von Bek and the majority of Solrefs have to stand by him, of course, but Herr Curtis and his group have sided with the RLMs. The other parties are fairly equally divided between both sides, but Herr Curtis's support should give the vote against the President."

Once again Alain was glad he had decided to have no part of politics. Even his just and stern old grandfather was going to behave like a hypocrite, giving a vote of confidence for Benjosef while encouraging Curtis to vote against him.

He decided that there wasn't much he could do, since everyone would be at the Solar House, including, of course, Helen. The current session ended in a fortnight and the next President would have to be elected during the recession. Probably, he thought ironically, both the main runners had their machines all geared for action.

"You'll be kept pretty busy from now on, I should think," he said to Junnar. The Negro nodded, and Alain continued: "What were you doing in the lower levels last night?"

"Keeping an eye on the Fireclown," Junnar said shortly.

"For grandfather?"

"Yes, of course."

"Why is he so malevolent toward the Fireclown? He seems harmless to me. Has grandfather any special knowledge that the public doesn't have?" Alain was only partly interested in what he himself was saying. The other half of his mind was wondering about the elections — and Helen.

Junnar shook his head. "I don't think so. It's a question of your point of view. Minister von Bek sees the Fireclown as a threat to society and its progress. Others simply see him as a romantic figure who wants a return to a simpler life. That's why he's such a popular cause with so many people. We all wish life were simpler — we're suckers for the kind of simple answer to our problems that a man like the Fireclown supplies."

"Simple answers, sure enough," Alain nodded, "but hardly realistic."

"Who knows?" Junnar said tersely.

"Is grandfather going to use the Fireclown as a platform?"

"I expect so. It will be taken for granted that whoever wins will encourage the expansion bill. So the other main dispute will be the Fireclown."

"But it's out of all proportion. Why should the Fireclown become a major issue?"

Junnar smiled cynically. "Probably because the politicians want him to be."

That answer satisfied Alain and he added:

"Hitler, as I remember, used the Jews. Before him, Nero used the Christians. Minority groups are always useful — they turn people's attention away from real issues which the politicians have no control over. So Fräulein Curtis and Minister von Bek are using the Fireclown, is that it? One in support, one against. People will take an interest in a battle over such a colourful figure and forget to question other policies. It sounds almost unbelievable, yet it happens. History proves that. What does grandfather plan to do about the Fireclown if he gets to power?"

"Maybe nothing," Junnar said. "Maybe nothing at all — once he's in power."

Then he smiled brightly. "No, it's not fair. After all, I am Simon von Bek's private secretary. He really is deeply concerned about what the Fireclown represents rather than the man himself."

The apparent return of loyalty in Junnar brought an awakening echo in Alain. He nodded.

"Perhaps we don't do either of them justice. I was forgetting they are both von Beks with a strong sense of family honour."

Junnar coughed. "I think I'd better go over to the Solar House myself. Can I arrange an appointment for you to see your grandfather?"

"No, don't bother."

"Are you going to the Fireclown's audience tomorrow?"

"Probably."

"I may see you there."

"Yes," said Alain. He glanced at his watch and noted that he would arrive back to his office late. He and Junnar walked into the corridor and went their separate ways.

Alain sighed as he studied the Low Level project. Basically it was a simple job to organize the sealing off of all entrances, stopping elevators and escalators and cutting off light and heating where they existed. Ten levels were to be shut down, involving the moving of less than a thousand people to accommodation higher up. The residents of levels nine and ten would welcome the change, he knew. They, at least, could be relied upon to support the operation.

No, it wasn't the project itself but the way the media would treat it, what Helen Curtis would say about it. It was going to cause City Administration and the City Council as much trouble as if they told the populace they had decided to torture and kill all pet dogs in the city. And this move would have world-wide repercussions — the Fireclown had been the subject of innumerable popular features treating him in a sympathetic manner.

Already he was convinced that his grandfather had committed political suicide by this move. But, for the moment, he wasn't worried so much about that as about the trouble he and the director would come in for.

He, in particular, would be slandered — the grandson of the man who wanted to victimize the innocent Fireclown. He would be talked of as a puppet in the hands of the old man. Doubtless he would even be shouted at in the public corridors.

He contacted City Works, waited for the manager to be located.

Tristran B'Ula was, like Junnar, a Zimbabwean from what had once been Rhodesia. The State of Zimbabwe had grown to great power in the African Federation and many of the Solar System's best administrators came from there.

"Good afternoon, Tristran." Alain was on friendly terms with the manager.

"New project I'd like to have a word with you about."

B'Ula pretended to groan. "Is it important? All my available manpower is taken up at the moment."

"The City Council wants us to give this priority. It's also highly confidential. Is there anyone else in the room with you?"

B'Ula turned, looked behind him and said: "Would you mind leaving the room for a minute or two, Fräulein Nagib?"

His pretty Egyptian secretary crossed the screen.

"Okay, Alain. What is it?"

"City Council wants us to seal off ten levels — numbers one to ten, to be precise. Concrete in the entrances, lighting, heat and water supply cut off, elevators and escalators to stop operation."

It took B'Ula a moment to absorb all this. His face showed incredulity. "But that's where the Fireclown is! What are we expected to do? Wall him up — entomb him?"

"Of course not. All residents will be moved before the project goes ahead. I'd thought of housing them in those spare corridors in Section Six of the Fifteenth Level and Sections Twelve and Thirteen of the Seventeenth Level. They'll need to be checked to make sure they're perfectly habitable. The Chemical Research Institute were going to take them over since they're getting a bit cramped, but they'll have to…"

"Just a minute. Alain. What's going to happen to the Fireclown?"

"Presumably, he'll take the alternative accommodation we're offering to everyone else," Alain said grimly.

"You know he wouldn't do that!"

"I don't know the Fireclown."

"Well, I'm having no part of it," B'Ula said rebelliously, then he switched out.

Completely taken aback, Alain sat at his desk breathing heavily. This, he decided, was only a hint of how the news would be received by the public. His colleague had always struck him as a solid, practical man who did his job well — a good civil servant, like himself. If Tristran B'Ula could be so affected by the news as to risk his position by refusing to obey the City Council, then how would others take it?

The word *Riot* popped into Alain's head. There had been no public disorder in a hundred years!

This was even bigger than he'd expected.

Another thing — B'Ula felt so strongly about it that he wasn't likely to keep the project secret. Someone had to convince the Zimbabwean that the closing off of the levels was not a threat against the Fireclown. Reluctantly, he would have to tell Carson of his little scene with the manager.

Slowly he got up from his desk. Slowly he walked into Carson's office.

CHAPTER FOUR

Benjosef had resigned.

After a meeting in the Solar House lasting well into the night as Benjosef tried to put his arguments to the Solar representatives, the old President had been shouted down.

Denholm Curtis had asked for a vote of no confidence in Benjosef. The ballot had been secret, and though Simon von Bek had seemed to support Benjosef it had been a masterly deception. He had managed to convey the image of a strong man standing beside his leader out of nothing but loyalty. In spite of favouring — or appearing to favour — Benjosef's cautious policies, Simon von Bek had risen in public esteem. Doubtless the heavy Solref vote would be his in the election. Alain was sure that his grandfather had actually voted against Benjosef. Principles the old man might have — and plenty of them — but they seemed at that moment to carry little weight against Simon von Bek's actions. This strange duality which seemed to come upon even the best politicians was not new to Alain, yet it constantly shocked him.

At 0200 Benjosef, baffled by what he considered mad recklessness on the part of the Solar House, reluctantly resigned as President, his term of office, which should have continued for another eighteen months, to finish with the current session.

Alain read and saw all this as he breakfasted, glancing from screen to screen and constructing all the details of the dramatic, and in some ways tragic, session. He rather sympathized with Benjosef. Perhaps he was old and wise, perhaps he was just old. Simon von Bek was only five years younger, but he possessed a forceful vitality that belied his age. Alain observed, judiciously, that Helen Curtis had not actually demanded the President's resignation, though other members of her party had been vociferous in attacking him. It would not have been diplomatic or polite for a would-be President to ask the current head to step down.

He sighed and finished his coffee — a new brand from which the caffeine had been removed and replaced by a stimulant described as "less harmful". The strange thing was it tasted better, though he would have liked to have denied this.

So now the fight was between his grandfather and his cousin. Would Simon von Bek see the light of day at last and ignore the Fireclown issue? As yet, of course, it had not really become an issue. It would take a political battle to make it one. Or would he plug on? Alain had a sad feeling that he would — particularly if Helen drew the Fireclown into her platform.

When he got to the office Carson was looking pale and even less savoury than usual. People were not chosen as directors of City Administration for their looks; but at this moment Alain rather wished they had a smiling, pleasant-faced he-man who could cozen the public into realizing the truth of the situation.

"What did B'Ula have to say, sir?" Alain asked.

"I was unable to contact him, Alain. I tried the Works but he must have left immediately he switched out on you. I tried his private number but his wife said he had not come back. When I tried again later he still wasn't there."

"What was he doing, I wonder?"

"I can tell you. He was broadcasting the news everywhere. Not only broadcasting but elaborating it. You can imagine what he said."

"I can imagine what would be said by some. But B'Ula…"

"I've just had Chairman Fou on the line. He says the Council is most disturbed, thinks we should have been able to judge B'Ula better. I pointed out, somewhat obscurely, that they appointed B'Ula. But it seems we're the scapegoats — from the public's point of view and evidently from the Council's."

"The news this morning was so full of 'stormy scenes in the Solar House' that they probably haven't got round to us yet," Alain said with mock cheerfulness. "But doubtless we'll be getting it in an hour or two."

"I expect so. Well, we've still got work to do. I'm going over to Works myself, to see what the men think of the project. If they oppose it as strongly as B'Ula we're going to have trouble with the unions before long."

"What will we do if that happens?"

"Brick up the bloody levels ourselves, I suppose." Carson swore.

"Black labour!" Alain said, shocked. "We'd have a system-wide strike on our hands then!" It was true.

"I'm hoping the City Council will realize the implications and back down gracefully." Carson walked towards the door. "But they didn't seem as if they were going to, judging by Chairman Fou's tone. Goodbye, Alain. Better stick to something routine until I find out what's happening."

When Alain buzzed for his filing clerk his secretary came in.

He raised an eyebrow. "Where's Levy?"

"He didn't come in this morning, Herr von Bek."

"Is he sick?"

"I don't think so. I heard a rumour he'd asked for his back-pay from the cashiers and said something about resigning."

"I see. Then will you bring me the Pedestrian Transport file? Number PV12, I think it is."

As he ploughed through the monotonous work, Alain learned from his secretary that about a quarter of the staff in the C.A. building had not turned up for work that morning. That represented over three hundred people. Where were they all? It was evident why they had left.

The whole business was growing into a monster. If three hundred people from one building alone could feel so strongly about the Fireclown, how many millions were there supporting him?

To Alain it was incredible. He knew, intuitively, that so many people could not be roused merely because of the proposed closing down of ten virtually unused levels — or, for that matter, give up their jobs in support of the Fireclown. It must be that the Fireclown represented something, some need in modern mankind which, perhaps, the sociologists would know about. He decided not to ask a sociologist and risk being plied with so many explanatory theories that his mind would be still further confused.

But what was this tenuous *zeitgeist*?

Perhaps the world would be in flames before he ever found out. Perhaps, whatever happened, no-one would ever really know. He decided he was being too melodramatic. On the other hand, he was extremely disturbed. He had a liking for peace and quiet — one of the reasons why he had rejected the idea of entering politics — and the world's mood was distinctly unpeaceful.

Facing facts, he realized that this was not a localized outbreak, that it would have to grow in magnitude before it died down or was controlled. What had his grandfather started? Nothing, really of course. His move had merely served to bring it out into the open, whatever it was.

But the people's hysteria was increasing, becoming evident everywhere. An hysteria that had not entered the human race since the war scares two centuries earlier. It seemed to have blown up overnight, though perhaps he had seen its beginnings in the worship of the Fireclown, the demand for Benjosef's resignation and other, smaller, incidents that he had not recognized for what they were.

The morning dragged. In the back of his mind something else nagged him until he realized that this was the night when the Fireclown was to hold his "audience". He felt slightly perturbed at attending it now that public anger seemed to be building to such a pitch, but he had said he would go, promised himself that he would go — and he would.

Carson came back just as Alain's secretary brought him some lunch.

"Any luck?" Alain said, offering his boss a slice of bread impregnated with beef extract. Carson refused it with an irritable wave of his hand, apologizing for his brusque gesture with a slight smile.

"None. Most of the workmen didn't turn up this morning, anyway. The union leaders deny influencing them, but someone has…"

"B'Ula?"

"Yes. He spoke to a public meeting last night, attended by most of the men who work for him. Told them that this victimization of the simple Fireclown was a threat also to *their* liberty. The usual stuff. And once the news got round, he wasn't the only one talking and rabble-rousing. At least a dozen others have used the same theme in speeches to incredibly big crowds. They didn't have to do much convincing, either. The crowds were already on their side."

"It's all happened so suddenly." Alain repeated his earlier thoughts aloud. "You wouldn't think a thing like this could grow so fast. People aren't even bothering to speak to their political representatives or beam the City Council."

"That's what's so peculiar. We might have expected angry letters demanding that we call a halt to the project — and if we'd had enough of them we should have had to. That's democracy, after all. I'd really thought the idea of law and order had finally sunk into the human race. Looks as if I was wrong."

"Disproves the Fireclown's cant about 'artificial living' producing 'artificial' men and ideas. The public's chock-a-block with human nature this morning. They seem as hysterical and as bloodthirsty as they ever were."

"Mass neurosis and all that." Carson stared at his thumb, inspecting the nail. It was dirty. However much he cleaned them his nails always seemed to get dirty a few moments afterwards.

By mid-afternoon, Carson and Alain were staring in blank incredulity at one another. At least two hundred more people had not come back after lunch. It was useless to attempt continuing work.

Another disturbing point was that they had been unable to contact the City Council. The beam had been jammed continuously. Obviously *some* people had decided to ask the City Council about the matter.

"I think we'd better go quietly to our homes," Carson said with a worried attempt at jocularity. "I'll keep a skeleton staff on and give the rest the afternoon off. I might as well, they'll probably be walking out soon, anyway."

Glad of this for his own reasons, Alain agreed.

He returned to his flat and changed into the nondescript suit he had worn earlier. He had had some trouble getting there, for the corridors were packed.

Angry and excited conversations were going on all over the place. Ordered discipline had given way to disorganized hysteria and it rather frightened him to see ordinary human beings behaving in a manner which, to him, was a rejection of their better selves.

Outside in the jostling corridor he was carried by the crowd to the elevators and had to wait for nearly a quarter of an hour as the mob's impatience grew. There just weren't enough elevators to take them all at once.

Down, down, down the levels. Into level nine and they milled down the escalators and ramps, Alain unable to go back now even if he had wanted to.

The smoke from the torches of the first level, the smell of sweat, the atmosphere of tension, the ululating roar of the crowd all attacked his senses and threatened to drug his brain as the crowd entered a huge cavern which, he knew, had once been part of an underground airstrip during the years when the city had first been planned.

And at last he saw the Fireclown, standing upon the tall column that served him as a dais, seeming to balance his huge bulk precariously on the platform.

There above him, Alain saw the spluttering mass of the artificial sun. He remembered having heard of it. The Fireclown had made it — or had it made — and somehow controlled it.

"What's this? What's this?" The Fireclown was shouting. "Why so many? Has the whole world suddenly seen the error of its ways?"

There were affirmative shouts from all around him as the crowd answered, somewhat presumptuously, for the rest of the planet's millions.

The Fireclown laughed, his gross bulk wobbling on the dais.

Thousands upon thousands of people were packing into the cavern, threatening to crush those already at the centre. Alain found himself borne towards the dais as the Fireclown's reverberating laugh swept over them.

"No more!" the Fireclown cried suddenly. "Corso — tell them they can't come in... Tell them to come back later. We'll be suffocated!"

The Fireclown seemed baffled by the crowd's size — bewildered, perhaps, by his own power.

Yet was it his own power? Alain wondered. Was not the mob identifying the Fireclown with something else, some deep-rooted need in them which was finding expression through the clown?

But it was immaterial to speculate. The fact remained that the Fireclown had become the mob's symbol and its leader. Whatever he told them they would do — unless, perhaps, he told them to do nothing at all.

The mob was beginning to chant:

"Fireclown! Fireclown! Fireclown! Speak to us!"

"How shall the world end?" he cried.

"In fire! In fire!"

"How shall it be born again?"

"In fire!"

"And the fire shall be the fire of man's spirit!" the Fireclown roared. "The fire in his brain and his belly. Too long has the world lived on artificial nourishment. The nourishment of processed food, the nourishment of words that have no relation to reality, the nourishment of ideas that exist in a vacuum. We are losing our birthright! Our heritage faces extinction!"

He paused as the mob moved like a mighty, restless tide. Then he continued:

"I am your phoenix, awash with the flames of life! I am your salvation! You see flames above." He raised an orange painted hand to the spluttering orb near the ceiling of the cavern. "You see flames around you." He indicated the torches. "But these fires only represent the real flames, the unseen flames which exist within you, and the Mother of Life which sweeps the heavens above you — the sun!"

"The sun!" the mob shrieked.

"Yes, the sun! Billions of years ago our planet was formed from the stuff of the sun. The sun nurtured life, and it finally nurtured the life of our earliest ancestors. It has nurtured us since. But does modern man honour his mother?"

"No! No!"

"No! Our ancestors worshipped the sun for millennia! Why? Because they recognized it as the Mother of Life. Without the sun man could never have been born on Earth! The Earth itself could not have been formed!"

Some of the mob, obviously old hands at this, shouted: "Fire is Life!"

"Yes," the Fireclown roared. "Fire is Life. And how many of you here have ever seen the sun? How many of you have ever been warmed directly by its rays? How many of you have ever seen a naked flame?"

A wordless bellow greeted each question.

Alain had to fight the infectious hysteria of the crowd. As if he anticipated these unspoken thoughts, the Fireclown carried on:

"We are misusing the sun. We are perverting the stuff of life and changing it to the stuff of death! We use the sun to power our machines and keep us alive in plastic, metal and concrete coffins. We use the sun to push our spaceships to the planets — planets where we are forced to live in wholly artificial conditions, or planets which we warp and change from what they naturally are into planets that copy Earth. That is wrong! Who are we to change the natural order? We are playing literally with fire — and that fire will soon turn and shrivel us!"

"Yes! Yes!"

In an effort to remain out of the Fireclown's spell, Alain encouraged himself to feel dubiously towards the logic of what he was saying. He continued in that vein for some time, drumming the words into the ready ears of the mob, again and again.

The Fireclown's argument wasn't new. It had been said, in milder ways, by philosophers and politicians of a certain bent for centuries — possibly since the birth of the industrial revolution. But, for all this, the argument wasn't necessarily right. It came back to the question of whether it was better for man to be an unenlightened savage in the caves, or whether he should use the reasoning powers and the powers of invention which were his in order to gain knowledge.

Feeling as if he had hit upon an inkling of the trouble, Alain realized that the Fireclown and those, like his grandfather, who opposed him were both only supporting *opinions*. Any forthcoming dispute was likely to be a battle between ignorance of one sort and ignorance of another.

Yet the fact remained — trouble was brewing. Big trouble unless something could be done about it.

"All religions have seen the sun as a representation of God..." the Fireclown was saying now.

Perhaps he was sincere, Alain thought; perhaps he was innocent of personal ambition, unaware of the furore he was likely to create, thoughtless of the conflict that was likely to ensue.

And yet Alain was attracted to the Fireclown. He *liked* him and took a delight in the man's vitality and spontaneity. It was merely unfortunate that he should have come at a time when public neurosis had reached such a peak.

Now a voice was shouting something about the City Council. Fragmented phrases reached Alain about the closing of the levels, an attack against the Fireclown, a threat to free speech. It was marvelous how they accepted the principles of democracy and rejected them at the same time by talk of mob action!

Marvelous — and deeply frightening. He turned to see if he could get back and out. He could not. The mob pressed closer, packed itself tighter. A horrifying vision of thousands of mouthing faces surrounded him. He panicked momentarily and then suppressed his panic. It could not help him. Little could.

The Fireclown's voice bellowed for silence, swore at the mob, reviled it. Abashed, the crowd quieted.

"You see! You see! This is what you do. So the City Council is to close off the levels. Perhaps it is because of me, perhaps it isn't! But does it matter?"

Certain elements shouted that it did matter.

"What kind of threat am I to the City Council? What threat am I to anyone? I tell you — *none!*"

Alain was mystified by these words, just as the mob was.

"None! I want no part of your demonstrations, your petty fears and puny conflicts! I do not expect action from you. I do not want action. I want you only to become aware! You can change your physical environment, certainly. But first you must change your mental attitude. Study the words you are using today. Study them and you will find them meaningless. You have emotions — you have words. But the words you have do not describe your emotions. Try to think of words that will! Then you will be strong. Then you will have no need for your stupid, overvaunted so-called 'intelligence'. Then you will have no need to march against the Council Building!"

Alain himself sought for words to describe the Fireclown's state at that moment. What had been said had impressed him in spite of his decision to observe as objectively as possible. They meant nothing much, really. They had been said before. But they *hinted* at something — gave him a clue...

Noble bewilderment. The elephant attacked by small boys. And yet concerned for them. Alain was impressed by what he felt to be the Fireclown's intrinsic innocence. But such an innocence, it could topple the world!

Placards now began to appear in the crowd:

NO TO BURYING THE FIRECLOWN!
HANDS OFF THE LOWER LEVELS!
COUNCIL CAN'T QUENCH THE FIRE OF MAN!

Amused by the ludicrous messages, Alain made out others. SONS OF THE SUN REJECT COUNCIL PLAN! was, perhaps, the best.

His mind began to skip, taking in first a fragmented scene — faces, placards, turbulent movement, a woman's ecstatic face; then a clipping of sound, a sudden idea that he could easily follow the Fireclown if he could hear the man convince him in cooler, more intellectual phrases; the flaring gash of light that quickly bubbled from the tiny sun and then seemed to be drawn back into it.

"Fools!" The Fireclown was shouting, incredulity and anger mixed on his painted face.

It seemed to Alain that the paint had been stripped away and, for the first time, he became aware of the *man* who stood there. An individual, complex and enigmatic.

But the glimpse did not last, for he felt the pressure from behind decreasing.

At least half the mob had turned away and were surging towards the cavern's exit.

And the Fireclown? Alain looked up. The Fireclown was appealing to them to stay, but his words were drowned by the babble of hysteria.

Now Alain was borne back with the crowd, was forced to turn and move with it or risk being trampled. He looked up at the dais and saw that the fat body of the Fireclown had developed a slump that hardly seemed in keeping with his earlier vitality.

As the mob boiled up to the third level, Alain saw Helen Curtis only a few yards ahead of him and to his left. He kept her in sight and managed, gradually, to inch through the stabbing elbows and hard shoulders.

On the ninth level he was just able to get into the same elevator with her. He shouted over the heads of the others:

"Helen! What the hell are you doing here?"

He saw a placard, FIRECLOWN FIRST VICTIM OF DICTATORSHIP, bob up and down and realized she was holding it.

"Do you think this will win you votes?" he demanded.

She made no reply but smiled at him. "I'm glad to see you came. Are you with us?"

"No, I'm not. And I don't think the Fireclown is either! He doesn't want you to fight for his 'rights' — I'm sure he's perfectly able to look after himself!"

"It's the principle!"

"Rubbish!"

The doors of the giant elevator slid up and they crossed the corridor to the row of elevators opposite. The liveried attendants attempted to hold the crowd away but were pushed back into their own elevators by the force of the rush. He managed to catch up with her and stood with his body tight against her side, unable to shift his position.

"This sort of thing may win you immediate popularity with the rabble, but what are the responsible voters going to think?"

"I'm fighting for what I think right," she said defiantly, grimly.

"You're fighting…" He shook his head. "Look, when we reach Sixty-five make your way home. Speak for the Fireclown in the Solar House if you must, but don't make a fool of yourself. When this hysteria dies down you'll look ridiculous."

"So you think this is going to die down?" she said sweetly.

The doors opened, the elevators disgorged their contents and they were on the move again, streaming across the quiet gardens towards the distant Civic Buildings.

It was night. The sky beyond the dome was dark. The crowd exhibited a moment's nervous calm, its pace slowed and then, as Helen shouted: "There! That's where they are!" and flung her hand theatrically towards the Council Building, they moved on again, spreading out and running.

Vid-people were waiting for them, taking shots as they surged past.

Helen began to run awkwardly, her placard waving in her hands.

Let her go, Alain thought, old emotions returning to heighten his confusion. He turned back.

No! She mustn't do it! He hated her political ambitions, but they meant much to her. She could throw everything away with this ill-considered action of hers.

Or would she? Perhaps the day of ordered government was already over.

"Helen!" He ran after her, tripped and fell heavily on a bed of trampled blue roses, got up. "Helen!"

He couldn't see her. Ahead of the crowd lights were going on in the Civic Buildings. Fortuitously, and perhaps happily for the City Council — all of whom had private apartments in the Council Building — the headquarters of the City Police were only a block away. And that building was lit up also.

He hoped the police would use restraint in dealing with the crowd.

When he finally saw Helen again she was leading the van of the mob who now chanted the unoriginal phrase: "We want the Council!"

Unarmed policemen in their blue smocks and broad belts began to muscle their way through the crowd. Vid cameras tracked them.

Alain grasped Helen's arm, trying to make himself heard above the chant. "Helen! For God's sake get out — you're liable to be arrested. The police are here!"

"So what?" Her face was flushed, her eyes over-bright, her voice high.

He reached up and tore the placard from her hands, flinging it to the ground. "I don't want to see you ruined!"

She stood there, her body taut with anger, staring into his face. "You always were jealous of my political success!"

"Can't you see what's happening to you? If you must play follow-my-leader, do it in a more orderly way. You could be President soon."

"And I still will be. Go away!"

He shook her shoulders. "Open your eyes! Open your eyes!"

"Oh, don't be so melodramatic. Leave me alone. My eyes are wide open!"

But he could see she had softened slightly, perhaps simply because of the interest he was taking in her.

Then a voice blared: "Go back to your homes! If you have any complaints, lodge them in the proper manner. The Council provide facilities for hearing complaints. This demonstration will get you nowhere! The police are authorized to stop anyone attempting to enter the Council Building!"

Helen listened until the broadcast finished. Then she shouted: "Don't let them put you off! They'll do nothing until they see we mean business."

Two hundred years of peace had taught Helen Curtis nothing about peaceful demonstration.

It was such a small issue, Alain told himself bewilderedly, such a small issue that could have been settled by a hundred angry letters instead of a mob of thousands.

The crowd was attempting to press past the police barrier.

Finally the barrier broke and fights between the police and the demonstrators broke out. Several times Alain saw a policeman lose his temper and strike a demonstrator.

He was disgusted and perturbed, but there was nothing he could do.

Wearily, he walked away from the scene. For the time being all emotion had been driven from him.

CHAPTER FIVE

Miserably, unsure of his direction, Alain let his feet carry him aimlessly.

He was sure that the riot marked some important change in the course of Earth's history, but knew with equal certainty that it would be twenty years before he could look back and judge why it had happened.

Helen, I love you, he thought, *Helen I love you.* But it was no good. They were completely separated now. He had picked an old scab. He should have left it well alone.

He looked up and found that he was approaching the building which housed his grandfather's apartment. He realized at the same time that he needed someone to talk to. There had been no-one since he and Helen had parted. The stern old man would probably refuse to listen and would almost certainly refuse to give him any advice or help, but there was nothing else for it.

He did not have a sonarkey for the matterlift, so he climbed the stairs very slowly and went to the main door of the big apartment.

A servant answered and showed him in.

Simon von Bek was sitting in his lounge intently watching the vid relaying scenes of the riots outside. He turned his great head and Alain saw that his brooding eyes held a hint of triumph.

"So the Fireclown was uninterested in power, was he?" Simon von Bek smiled slightly and pointed at the set. "Then what's that, Alain!"

"A riot," Alain said hollowly. "But though it's in the name of the Fireclown he didn't encourage it."

"That seems unlikely. You were mixed up in it for a while, weren't you? I saw you on that —" he pointed again at the screen. "And Helen, too, is taking an active part."

"Very active." Alain kept his tone dry.

"You disapprove?"

"I tried to stop her."

"So you've changed your opinion of the Fireclown. You realize I was right. If I had my way, every one of those rioters would be flung into prison — and the Fireclown exiled from the planet!"

Slightly shocked by the savagery of his grandfather's last remark, Alain remained silent. Together they watched the vid. The police seemed to be coping, though their numbers had had to be increased.

"I haven't changed my opinion, grandfather," he said quietly. "Not really, anyway."

His grandfather also paused before replying: "I wish you knew what I knew — then you'd fight the Fireclown as strongly as I'm attempting to. The man's a criminal. Perhaps he's more than that. Perhaps this is the last night we'll be able to sit comfortably and watch the V."

"We both seemed to underestimate the Fireclown's popularity," Alain mused. "Are you going to continue your campaign against him?"

"Of course."

"I should have thought you would spend your time better trying to find out *why* the public is attracted to him?"

"The Fireclown's a menace…"

"*Why?*" Alain said grimly.

"Because he threatens the stability of society. We've had equilibrium for two hundred years…"

"*Why* does he threaten the stability of society?"

Simon von Bek turned round in his chair. "Are you trying to be impertinent, Alain?"

"I'm trying to tell you that the Fireclown himself means nothing. The public is in this mood for another, a deeper, reason. I was down there in the cavern on the first level. I saw the Fireclown try to stop them from doing this but they wouldn't listen to him. *Why?*"

But the old man stubbornly refused to get drawn into an argument. And Alain felt a hollow sense of frustration. His urge to try to clarify his thoughts by means of conversation was unbearably strong. He tried again:

"Grandfather!"

"Yes?"

"The Fireclown pleaded with the crowd not to make this demonstration. I saw him. But the crowd wasn't interested in what he said. They're using him, just as you and Helen are using him for your own reasons. There is something deeper going on. Can't you see that?"

Again the old man looked up at him. "Very well. The Fireclown symbolizes something — something wrong in our society, is that it? If that's the case we cannot strike at the general, we must strike at the particular, because that is what is tangible. I am striking at the Fireclown."

Alain wasn't satisfied. His grandfather's words were reasonable, yet he suspected that no thought or sensibility lay behind them. His answer had been too pat.

"I intend to do everything possible to bring the Fireclown's activities to a halt," Simon von Bek continued. "The public may be too blind to see what is happening to them, what dangerous power the clown wields over them, but I will make them see. I will make them see!"

Alain shrugged. It seemed to him that the blind were accusing the blind.

"Politicians!" he said, suddenly angry. "What hollow individuals they are!"

Suddenly, his grandfather rose in his chair and got up, his back to the vid, his face taut with suppressed emotion.

"By God, I brought you up as a von Bek in spite of your mother's shaming me. I recognized you. I refused to take the easy way out and pay some woman to call you her own. You received the name of von Bek and the benefits of that name. And this is how you reward me, by coming to my own house and insulting me! I fostered a bastard — and now that bastard reverts to type! You have never understood the responsibilities and the need to serve which marks our family. We are not power-seekers, we aren't meddlers in the affairs of others! We are dedicated to furthering civilization and humanity throughout the Solar System! What do you understand of that, Alain whatever-your-name-is?"

"I think it most noble," Alain sneered, trying to hold back the tears of pain and anger in his eyes. His body trembled as it had done when, as an adolescent, he had been told the story of his birth. "Most noble, grandfather, all you and the von Bek clan have done for me! But you could not keep my mother alive with your high sentiments! You would not let her marry the man who fathered me! I know that much from grandmother. Some rough spaceman, wasn't it? Could you kill him by shame, the way you killed my mother?"

"Your mother killed herself. I did everything for her…"

"And judged her for everything!"

"No…" The old man's face softened.

"I've always given you the benefit of every doubt, grandfather. I've always respected you. But in this business of the Fireclown I've seen that you can be unreasoningly dogmatic, that perhaps what I've heard about you was true! Your attack on me was unfair — just as your attack on the Fireclown is unfair!"

"If you knew, Alain. If you knew just what…" The old man straightened his back. "I apologize for what I said to you. I'm tired — busy day — not thinking properly. I'll see you tomorrow, perhaps."

Alain nodded wordlessly and left, moved to an emotion towards his grandfather which, he decided, could only be love. Love? After what they had both said? It seemed to him that everything was turning upside down. The chaos of the mob, the chaos of his own moods, the chaos of his private life — all seemed to point towards something. Some cure, perhaps, for his own and the world's pain?

On the roof of the building he looked around for a car which would carry him above the riot below to North Top, where he could probably use one of the small private elevators. Above the dome the sky was clear and the moon rode the sky in a casual arc. Near the edge of the roof he saw Junnar.

The Zimbabwean was also watching the distant rioters.

"You're too late," he said cheerfully. "You missed the best of it. They're dispersing now."

"I was *in* the best of it." Alain joined him and saw that a much smaller crowd continued to demonstrate, but that most of the people were moving slowly back towards the elevator-cone.

"Did you see any arrests?" Junnar asked.

"No. Did you?"

"The police didn't seem too keen. I think they took a couple in — probably examples."

"What does all this mean, Junnar? What's happening to the world?"

"I'm not with you?" Junnar stared at Alain in curiosity.

"Nobody is, I guess. I'm sure that these riots are not just the result of the Fireclown's speeches in his cavern. I'm sure they've been brewing for ages. Why are the people so frustrated they have to break out like this suddenly? What do they want? What do they lack? You know as well as I do that mass demonstrations in the past were often nothing to do with the placards they waved and the cant they chanted — it was some universal need crying out for satisfaction, something that has always been in man, however happy and comfortable his world is. What is it this time?"

"I think I know what you mean." Junnar offered Alain a marijuana but he refused. "That down there — the Fireclown — the impatience to expand to the new Earth-type planets — the bitter arguments in the Solar House — individual frustration — the 'time for a change' leaders in the V-casts. All threatening to topple society from its carefully maintained equilibrium. You mean it's some kind of —" Junnar groped for a word — "*force* that's entered the race, that we should be doing something, changing our direction in some way?"

"I think that's roughly what I mean. I'm finding it hard to put it into words myself."

"Well, this is perhaps what the Fireclown means when he says we're turning our backs on the natural life. With all our material comfort, perhaps we should look inward at ourselves instead of looking outward at the new colony planets. Well, what do we do about it, Herr von Bek?"

"I wish I knew."

"So do I." Junnar exhaled the sweet smoke and leaned back against the rail.

"You seem to understand what the Fireclown's getting at. *You* must believe that he's innocent of causing these riots. Can't you tell my grandfather that?"

Junnar's manner changed. "I didn't say the Fireclown was innocent, Herr von Bek. I agree with your grandfather. He's a menace!" He spoke fiercely, almost as fiercely as Simon von Bek had done earlier.

Alain sighed. "Oh, all right. Goodnight, Junnar."

"'Night, Herr von Bek."

As he climbed into an automatic car and set the control, he caught a final glimpse of the Negro's sad face staring up at the moon like a dog about to bay.

To Alain, the world seemed suddenly sick. All the people in it seemed equally sick. And it was bad enough today. What would it be like tomorrow? he wondered.

Next morning he breakfasted late, waiting for Carson to call him if he was wanted at the office. All the vids were full of last night's rioting. Not only had the City Council building been attacked but others, taking advantage of the demonstration, had indulged in sheer hooliganism, smashing shop-fronts in the consumer corridors, breaking light globes, and so on. Damage was considerable; arrests had been made, but the Press didn't seem to complain. Instead, they had a better angle to spread:

C.A. MAN GRAPPLES PRESIDENTIAL CANDIDATE!
Alain von Bek attacks Fireclown supporters!

A picture showed him wrenching Helen's banner from her grasp. In the story he was described as an angry spokesman for the establishment and Helen as the heroine of the hour, going amongst the people to stand or fall with them. Maybe she had been playing her game better than he had at first thought, he decided.

On the V, a commentator's voice was heard over the noise of the riot:

"Last night, beautiful would-be President, Fräulein Helen Curtis, led a peaceful party of demonstrators to the City Council building on Top. They were there to protest against the abuse of Council power which, as everyone knows now, was to take the form of a secret closing of ten of the lowest levels of the City of Switzerland. Fräulein Curtis and her supporters saw this as a deliberate move to stop free speech, an attempt to silence the very popular figure known as the Fireclown, whose harmless talks have given many people so much comfort and pleasure.

"The peaceful demonstration was savagely broken up by large bodies of policemen who forced themselves through the crowd and began making random arrests almost before the people could lodge their protest.

"It is not surprising that some of the less controlled elements among the demonstrators resisted arrest."

Shot of demonstrator kicking a policeman in the behind.

"Reliable witnesses attest to police brutality towards both men and women.

"In the van of the police bully-boys came Alain von Bek, grandson of Fräulein Curtis's rival in the forthcoming Presidential elections — and Assistant Director of City Administration, who had already begun work on closing off the lower levels."

Shot of Alain grappling with Helen.

"But even Herr von Bek couldn't silence the demands of the crowd!"

Shot of him walking away. He hadn't realized vids were tracking him the whole time.

"And he went back to report his failure to his grandfather, Simon von Bek."

Shot of him entering the apartment building.

The cameras panned back to the riot, and the commentary continued in the same vein. He was horrified by the lies — and helpless against them. What could he do? Deny them? Against an already prejudiced public opinion?

"Obviously someone Up There," the commentator was saying, "doesn't like the Fireclown. Perhaps because he's brought a bit of life back into our drab existence.

"This programme decries the totalitarian methods of the City Council and tells these hidden men that it will oppose all their moves to encroach further upon our liberties!"

Fade-out and then fresh shots of a surly-looking individual talking to a V-man.

Reporter: "This is Herr Lajos, who narrowly escaped wrongful arrest in yesterday's demonstration. Herr Lajos, tell the viewers what happened to you."

Lajos: "I was brutally attacked by two policemen."

Lajos stood staring blankly into the camera and had to be prodded by the reporter.

Reporter: "Did you sustain injuries, Herr Lajos?"

Lajos: "I sustained minor injuries, and if I had not been saved in time I would have sustained major injuries about my head and body."

Lajos's head seemed singularly free from any obvious injuries.

Reporter: "Did the police give you any reason for their attack?"

Lajos: "No. I was peacefully demonstrating when I was suddenly set upon. I was forced to defend myself…"

Reporter: "Of course, of course. Thank you, Herr Lajos."

Back in the studio, a smiling reporter bent towards the camera.

"It's victory for Fräulein Curtis and her supporters, folks. The Fireclown won't be bothered by the Council — not so long as we keep vigilant, anyway — for the Council told the people a few minutes ago that…"

The picture faded and Carson's face appeared in its place. That was the one irritation of combining communication and entertainment in the single vidserve.

"Sorry if I butted in, Alain. Have you heard the news?"

"Something about me — or about the Council?"

"The Council — they've backed down. They've decided not to close off the levels, after all. Maybe now we can get on with some work. Will you come to the office as soon as you can?"

Alain nodded. "Right away," he said, and switched out.

As he took the fastway to the elevators, he mused over the manner in which the riot had been reported. He was certain that the police had tried not to use violence. Yet, towards the end, they might have lost their patience. These days the police force required superior intelligence and education to get into it, and modern police weren't the good-for-nothing-else characters of earlier times. Still, it could have been that because one side ignored established law and order, so did the other. Violence tended to breed violence.

Violence, he thought, is a self-generating monster. The more you let it take control, the more it grows.

He didn't know it, but he was in for a taste of it.

Two muscular arms suddenly shot out from each side of him. His face slammed against them and he lost his balance on the fastway, falling backwards and sliding along. Two figures rushed along beside him and yanked him onto the slowway.

"Get up," one of them said.

Alain got up slowly, dazed and wary.

He stared at the tall, thin-faced man and his fatter, glowering partner. They were dressed in engineers' smocks.

"What did you do that for?" Alain said.

"You're Alain von Bek, aren't you?"

"I am. What do you want?"

"You're the man who attacked Helen Curtis yesterday."

"I did not!"

"You're lying." The man flicked his hand across Alain's face. It stung. "We don't like Council hirelings who attack women!"

"I attacked no-one!" Alain prepared, desperately, to defend himself.

The fat man hit him, fairly lightly, in the chest.

On the fastway people were passing, pretending not to notice.

Alain punched the fat man in the face and kicked the thin man's shins.

Neither had expected it. Alain himself was surprised at his own bravery. He had acted instinctively. He was also shocked by his own violence.

Now the pair were pummeling him and he struck back at random. A blow in his stomach winded him, a blow in his face made him dizzy. His own efforts became weaker and he was forced to confine himself to protecting his body as best he could.

Then it was over.

A new voice shouted: "Stop that!"

Breathing heavily, Alain looked up and saw the slightly ashamed face of Tristran B'Ula.

He noticed, too, that all three were wearing a sun emblem on their clothing — a little metal badge.

The thin-faced man said: "It's von Bek — the man who wanted to close the levels. The one who attacked Fräulein Curtis last night."

"Don't be a fool," B'Ula said angrily. "He didn't want to close the levels; he was taking orders from the Council. I know him — he isn't likely to have attacked Helen Curtis, either."

B'Ula came closer.

"Hello, Tristran," Alain said painfully. "You've started something, haven't you?"

"Never mind about that. What were you doing last night?" As B'Ula approached, the two men stepped back.

"I was arguing with Helen, telling her she was stupid. Just as you're stupid. None of you know what you're doing!"

"You got a lot of Press cuttings this morning. If I were you I'd stay off the public ways." He turned to the two engineers. "Get going. You're nothing better than hoodlums. You pay too much attention to what the Press says."

Alain tried to smile. "The pot calling the kettle black. You started all this, Tris. You should have thought for a while before you began shouting the news about."

"You're damned ungrateful," B'Ula said. "I just saved you from a nasty beating. I did what I had to — I wasn't going to let the Fireclown be shoved around."

"This way, he may get worse," Alain said.

B'Ula grimaced and walked away with the two engineers. Alain looked around for his briefcase but couldn't find it. He got onto the fastway again and took the elevator to the Top, but when he arrived he didn't go to City Administration. He'd heard two people talking in the elevator. There was going to be a debate in the Solar House on last night's riots.

Careless of what Carson would think when he didn't turn up, Alain took a car towards the majestic Solar House where representatives from all over the Solar System had gathered.

He wanted very badly to see his grandfather and his ex-mistress in action.

Solar House was a vast, circular building with tall, slender towers at intervals around its circumference. Each tower was topped by a gleaming glass-alloy dome. The centre of the circle housed the main hall containing many thousands of places for members. Each nation had, like the City of Switzerland, its own councils and sub-councils, sending a certain number of candidates, depending on its size, to the Solar House.

When Alain squeezed his way into the public gallery the House was almost full. Many representatives must have just arrived back in their constituencies after the debate on the out-going President's policies only to hear the news of the riot, and returned.

Politics hadn't been nearly so interesting for years, Alain thought.

The debate had already opened.

In the centre of the spiral was a small platform upon which sat the President, Benjosef, looking old and sullen; the Chief Mediator, Morgan Tregarith, in ruby-red robes and metallic Mask of Justice; the Cabinet Ministers, including Simon von Bek in full purple. In the narrowest ring of benches surrounding the platform were the leaders of the opposition parties — Helen Curtis in a dark yellow robe, belted at the waist, with fluffs of lace at bodice and sleeves; ancient Baron Rolf de Crespigny leader of the right-wing reactionary Democratic Socialists; John Holt, thin-lipped in black, leader of the Solar Nationalists; Bela Hakasaki, melancholy-faced Hungarian-Japanese leader of the Divisionists; Luis Jaffe of the New Royalists, and about a dozen more, all representing varying creeds and opinions, all comparatively weak compared with the Solrefs, RLMs, or even the Demosocs.

Behind the circle comprising the opposition leaders all the other Solar representatives sat, first the minor lights in the Solref Cabinet — Denholm Curtis, Under-Secretary for Hydro-Agriculture, was there — then the members of the RLM shadow cabinet; de Crespigny's shadow cabinet shared a tier with John Holt's; behind them were four smaller groups; behind them again six or seven, until, finally, the rank-and-file, split into planets and continents and finally individual nations.

There were probably five thousand men and women in the Solar House, and they all listened carefully as Alfred Gupta, Minister for Police Affairs, answered a charge made by Helen Curtis that the police had used violence towards last night's crowd.

"Fräulein Curtis has accused Chief of Police Sandai of exercising insufficient control over his officers; that the men were allowed to indulge in offensive language towards members of the public, attacked these members in a brutal manner and did not allow them to lodge a protest which they had prepared for the City Council. These are all grave charges — charges which have also appeared in the Press and on our V-screens — and Fräulein Curtis mentions 'proof' of police violence having appeared on those media. If the charges are true, then this is a matter of considerable magnitude. But I suggest that the charges are fabrication, a falsification of what actually happened. I have here a statement from Chief Sandai." He held up a piece of paper and then proceeded to read from it — a straightforward account of what had actually happened, agreeing that some police officers had been forced to defend themselves against the mob, having been pressed beyond reasonable endurance.

Alain had seen one or two of the policemen attack with very little provocation but he felt, from his own observation of the previous night's trouble, that the chief's statement was fairly accurate, although painting his officers a trifle too white to ring true.

The House itself seemed fairly divided on the question, but when Helen got up to suggest that the paper contained nothing but lies she was loudly cheered. She went on, in an ironical manner, to accuse the Solar Referendum Government of deliberately provoking the riot by allowing the City Council to close off the levels. Minister for Civil Affairs, Ule Bengtsson, pointed out that it was not the government's policy to meddle in local politics and that if this matter had been discussed in the Solar House in the first place, then it might have been possible to veto the Council. But no such motion, he observed cynically, had been placed before the House.

This was indisputable.

Alain saw that Helen had decided to change her tactics, asking the President point-blank if it was not the Solar Referendum Party's fixed intention to silence and get rid of the Fireclown who, though he represented no political threat, was in his own way revealing the sterility of the government's policies in all aspects of life on Earth and beyond it?

Benjosef remained seated. His expression, as it had always been, was strangely affectionate, like an old patriarch who must sometimes chide his children. He spoke from his chair.

"You have heard Fräulein Curtis accuse my Government of underhand methods in an attempt to rid ourselves of this man who calls himself the Fireclown. I speak in honesty for myself, and for the majority of my cabinet, when I say we have no interest whatsoever in the Fireclown or his activities so long as they remain within the law. Already —" he glanced at Helen with a half-smile on his face — "it is doubtful whether his supporters have kept within the law, though I have heard that the Fireclown did not encourage last night's riot."

Alain, looking down on the old man, felt glad that someone, at least, seemed to be keeping things in fair perspective.

Then, surprisingly, the House was shaken by a tremendous verbal roar and he saw that several thousand representatives had risen to their feet and were, for the second time in forty-eight hours, shouting the President down.

He saw his grandfather glance towards the Chief Mediator. His features hidden behind his mask, the Mediator nodded. Simon von Bek got up and raised his hands, shouting to be heard. Very gradually, the noise died down.

"You do not disbelieve President Benjosef, surely?"

"We do!" Helen Curtis's voice was shrill, and it was echoed by hundreds of others.

"You think the government is deliberately seeking to outlaw the Fireclown?"

"We do!" Again Helen Curtis's statement was taken up by many of the others.

"And you also think the Fireclown wanted last night's riot?"

There was a slight pause before Helen Curtis replied:

"It was the only way his friends could help him. Personally, he is an ingenuous man, unaware of the forces working against him in the Solar House and elsewhere!"

"So you think the rioters were justified?"

"We do!"

"Is this democracy?" Simon von Bek said quietly. "Is this what my family and others fought to establish? Is this Law? No — it is anarchy. It is anarchy which the Fireclown has inspired, and you have been caught up in the mood. Why? Because, perhaps, you are too unintelligent, too impatient, to see how mankind may profit from this Law we have created! The Fireclown's babblings are meaningless. He talks of our speech having no meaning and turns sensible individuals into a maddened mob with the choice of a few emotional phrases that say nothing to the mind and everything to the belly! The Fireclown has caught popular fancy. That much is obvious." He sighed and stared around the House.

"I am speaking personally now. For some time I have been aware of the

Fireclown's potential ability to whip up the worst elements in human nature. I have seen him as a very great threat to the Solar nation's stability, to our progress, to our development and to individual liberty. And I note from last night's events that I was right..."

Alain saw in astonishment that his grandfather's level words had calmed the assembly, that they seemed to be having some effect. He had to admit that the old man seemed to be right, as he'd said. Yet, in a way, his words were *too* convincing. It was still a feeling he had — a feeling that no-one in the assembly had as yet discussed anything.

Alain thought that, for them, the Fireclown had ceased to exist. He was witnessing a clash between different ways of thoughts, not a debate about the clown at all. He remembered the old Russian technique of choosing a vague name for their enemies and then using it, specifically, to denounce them — attacking the Albanians instead of the Chinese had been one example. Everyone had known who the real enemies were, but there was never a direct reference to them. Still, that had been a calculated technique, rather a good one for its purpose.

But Alain's angry relatives were now using it unconsciously. They were attacking and defending something they were unable to verbalize but which, perhaps wrongly, they were identifying with the Fireclown.

He looked down at the great assembly and for a moment felt pity, then immediately felt abashed by his own arrogance. Perhaps he misjudged them — perhaps they were not less aware but more hypocritical than he thought.

Helen Curtis was speaking again, staring directly into her uncle's eyes as he remained standing up on the platform.

"I have never doubted Minister von Bek's sincerity in his denunciation of the Fireclown. But I do say he is a perfect example of the reactionary and conservative elements in the House who are unable to see a *change* as progress. They see their kind of progress, a progress which is inherent in their policies. I see a different kind. Theirs leads to sterility and decay. Ours, on the other hand, leads to an expansion of man's horizons. We wish to progress in many directions, not just one! That is why I see the Fireclown as a victim of the Solref Government. He offers scope and life and passion to human existence. The Solrefs merely offer safety and material comfort!"

"If Fräulein Curtis had studied the Solar Referendum manifesto in any detail," Simon von Bek exclaimed, addressing the assembly, "she would have noted that we are pledged first to forming a strong *basis* upon which future society might work and expand. Evidently, from the mob-worship of this disgusting monster, the Fireclown, we have yet to succeed!"

"You see the Fireclown as a threat! You see him as a monster! You hound this man because, in his naïve and simple manner, he has reawakened mankind's spirit!" Helen spoke directly to von Bek, her finger pointing up at him. "Then you are a hollow man with no conception of the realities!"

"So the Fireclown, Fräulein Curtis tells me, is a happy innocent, bereft of schemes or ambition, a prophet content only to be heard." Von Bek smiled at the assembly. "I say the Fireclown is a tangible threat and that this madman intends to destroy the world!"

Alain craned forward. His grandfather would not possibly have made so categorical a statement without evidence to back it up.

"Prove it!" Helen Curtis sneered. "You have gone too far in your hatred — senseless and unfounded hatred — of the Fireclown! Prove it!"

Simon von Bek's face took on a sterner expression as he turned to speak to the President.

"I have already alerted the City Police," he said calmly, "so there is no immediate danger if they work quickly. There is no question of it — I have been supplied with full proof that the Fireclown is planning to destroy the world by flame. In short, he intends to blow up the planet!"

C H A P T E R   S I X

Alain was astounded. For a moment his mood of cynicism held and he was aware of a cool feeling of disbelief as the House, hushed for a second, began to murmur.

Helen suddenly looked frightened. She stared rapidly around the House then up at von Bek, whose stern manner could not disguise his triumph.

"Acting on my information, the police have discovered a cache of plutonium war-heads..." he continued.

"War-heads!" someone shouted. "We haven't got any! They were outlawed in forty-two!"

"Presumably the Fireclown or some of his friends manufactured them. It is well know that several scientists have been aiding him with his peculiar experiments with fire."

"But he would need fantastic resources!"

Simon von Bek spread his hands, aware that his moment of power had come.

"Presumably," he said, "the Fireclown has them. I told you all that he was more than a mere irritation. His power is even more extensive than I at first guessed."

Helen sat down, her face pale. She made no attempt to question von Bek's statement. She was baffled, yet as convinced of the truth as everyone else in the House.

The crowd in the public gallery was muttering and shoving to get a closer look at Simon von Bek.

The old man's leonine head was raised. Evidently he no longer felt the need for oratory. The House was his.

"If the police discover the war-head cache we shall hear the news in a few moments." He glanced towards the towering central doorway and sat down.

As the tension built up, Alain felt he could take no more of it. He was preparing to turn back into the crowd behind him when a uniformed figure appeared at a side door and made his way down the tiers towards the platform.

It was Chief Sandai, his brown-yellow face shiny with sweat. Watched by everyone, he climbed up the few steps of the platform and approached President Benjosef respectfully.

The microphone picked up his voice and relayed it throughout the House:

"Herr President, it is my duty to inform you that, acting upon my own initiative. I have declared a state of emergency in the City of Switzerland. A cache of plutonium war-heads equipped with remote control detonators of a type used for setting off bombs from space has been found hidden on the first level. My men have impounded them and await orders."

Benjosef glanced at von Bek. "Are you sure you have found all the bombs?" he said.

"No, sir. All we know of are those we found. There could be others. These were stored in a disused war-house cavern."

"You are certain that there was no oversight when the war-house was cleared of its armaments in the past?"

"Perfectly certain, sir. These are new additions. They were being kept in containers previously used for the same purpose, that is all."

Benjosef sighed.

"Well, Minister von Bek, this is really your department now, isn't it? How did you find out about the bombs?"

"My secretary, Eugene Junnar, first reported his suspicions to me two days ago. Later investigations proved them to be true. As soon as I knew I informed the police." Von Bek spoke slowly, savouring his triumph.

Benjosef addressed Chief Sandai. "And have you any evidence to show who was responsible for this illegal stock-pile?"

"Yes, sir. It is almost certain that the man concerned is the individual known as the Fireclown. The chamber was guarded by men known to be in his employ. They at first tried to stop us entering, but offered no physical resistance. One of them has since admitted himself to be a follower of the Fireclown."

"And the Fireclown?" von Bek asked urgently.

Chief Sandai swallowed and wiped his forehead. "Not in our custody yet, sir."

Angry impatience passed rapidly across Simon von Bek's face before being replaced by a further jutting of the jaw and an expression of resolve. "You had better find him and his accomplices as soon as you can, Sandai. He may well have other bombs already planted. Have you sealed spaceports and checked all means of exit from the city itself?"

"Naturally, sir." Sandai seemed aggrieved.

"Then hurry and find him, man. The existence of the world may depend on locating him and arresting him immediately!"

Sandai galloped down the steps and strode hastily from the House.

Alain didn't wait for any further development in the debate. Simon von Bek had made his point, illustrated it perfectly and punched it home relentlessly to the assembly. It was practically certain the Presidency was his.

Pushing through the crowded gallery, he left to take an elevator down and an escalator out of the House. The news must already have leaked to the Press for V-people were swarming around Chief Sandai, who was obviously flustered and trying to shove his way past them.

Careless of who saw him and the inference that might be put on his act, Alain began to run across the turf towards the nearest elevator cone.

He was sure that his earlier judgment of the Fireclown could not have been so hopelessly wrong. It was only instinct that drove him, but he was so sure that his instinct was right that he was going back, for the second time, to the labyrinthine first level to look at the evidence for himself.

By the time he got to the lower levels another group of vociferous reporters was already on the scene. Police guards surrounded a stack of square, heavy metal boxes, unmarked, at the bottom of the ramp which led down to the first level.

Taking advantage of the police guards' occupation with the reporters, Alain worked his way round them and entered the tunnel which he had gone down earlier — the one which led to the Fireclown's laboratory.

Two guards stood on each side of the entrance. Alain produced his City Administration card and showed it to the men, who inspected it closely.

"Just want to look round, sergeant," he said coolly to one of them. "C.A. would like to know what's going on here so we can take whatever precautions are necessary."

They let him through and he found himself in a big chamber equipped with all kinds of instruments and devices. He couldn't recognize the purpose of many of them. The place was dark, lit only by an emergency bulb burning near the door. It seemed to have been vacated very rapidly, for there was evidence that an experiment had been taking place and had been hastily abandoned. The door of a cooling chamber was open; broken test tubes crunched beneath his feet; chemicals glinted in the half-light, splashed across floor, benches and equipment. He didn't touch anything but made his way to another door. It was an old fashioned steel door, nearly a foot thick, but it opened when he pushed. In the room the darkness was complete. He went back to find some means of lighting and finally settled for a portable emergency bulb, picking it up by its handle and gingerly advancing into the next room.

The acrid smell of the spilt chemicals was almost unbearable. His eyes watered. This must have been a store-room. Most of the chemical jars were still intact, so were the boxes of spare parts, neatly labeled. Yet there was nothing to suggest any warlike purpose for the laboratory. There was little manufacturing equipment. It was certain the place had only been used for research. Yet, of course, it was possible that a small manufacturing plant might have been housed in another section of the first level.

He came out of the store-room and pushed another door on his left. At first he thought it was locked, but when he pushed again it gave. Whereas the store-room had smelt of chemicals this one smelt merely damp. It was an office. Files and notebooks were stacked around, although a microfile cabinet had been damaged and its contents removed. He noticed also a small, old fashioned, closed circuit V-screen and wondered what the cameras were aimed at. He switched it on. The screen flickered and showed part of the corridor outside. He turned the control but each picture showed an uninteresting corridor, a cavern or a room, until he turned once more and the screen brightened to show a well-lighted room.

In it were two men and a woman.

The woman was unknown to Alain. But the men were unmistakable — the skinless Corso, his red, peeled body even more repulsive in good light, and the Fireclown, his great bulk seeming to undulate as he breathed, his face still painted.

Excitedly, Alain tried to get sound, but there appeared to be no sound control on the set. He had no idea where the trio were, but it was fairly certain that cameras were only trained on parts of the first level. Therefore they must be close by.

The woman came up to the Fireclown and pressed her body against him, her right arm spread up across his back, the fingers of the hand caressing him.

He smiled — somehow an extremely generous gesture considering he was now a hunted man — and gently pushed her away, saying something to her. She did not appear annoyed. Corso was more animated. He obviously felt a need for urgency which the Fireclown did not.

Alain suddenly heard a movement in the first chamber and hastily killed the set.

"Herr von Bek, sir?" the sergeant's voice shouted.

"What is it?" he replied, inwardly wishing the man dead.

"Wondered if you were all right, that's the only thing, sir — the smell in here is almost overpowering."

"I'm fine, sergeant, thanks." He heard the sergeant return to his post.

Now he noticed a smaller door leading off the room. It had no lock of any sort, just a projection at the top. He reached up to inspect it when the door wouldn't open. It was a small bar of metal apparently operated from both sides, sliding into a socket, he fiddled with it for a while, pulled at it and, at last, the right combination of chances released the mechanism and he pulled the door. Alain had never seen a bolt before.

The emergency bulb lit the place and showed him a narrow, low-roofed passage. A rusted sign hung suspended lopsidedly by one chain; the other had broken. Alain caught hold of it, disliking the touch of grimy rust on his fingers, and made out what it said: *Restricted to all personnel!* He let the sign go and it swung noisily against the wall as he continued along the tunnel. Finally he came to another door, but this one would not open at all. He went past it until he reached the end of the tunnel. This was half-blocked by the fallen bulk of another massive steel door. He pulled himself over it, wondering if anyone had ever come this way since the lower levels, which had primarily been used for storing armaments, battle-machines and military personnel, had been abandoned with the Great Disarmament of 2042.

A noise ahead of him suddenly startled Alain and he automatically switched off the emergency bulb.

Voices sounded, at first indistinct and then clearer as Alain moved cautiously closer.

"We shouldn't have left those machines intact. If some fool fiddles about with them, heaven knows what'll happen."

"Let them find out." It was the Fireclown's voice, sounding like a pulse-beat.

"And who'll be blamed?" he heard Corso say tiredly. "You will. I wish you'd never talked me into this."

"You agreed with my discoveries, Corso. Have you changed your mind now?"

"I suppose not... *Damn!*" Alain heard someone stumble. A woman giggled and said: "You're too hasty, Corso. What's the hurry? At present they're combing the corridors they know about. We have plenty of time."

"Unless they find the boat before we get there," Corso said querulously. Alain was creeping behind them now, following them as they moved along in the dark.

"I'm only worried about the fuel. Are you sure we've enough fuel, Corso?" The Fireclown spoke. Although this man had been accused of planning to blow up the world, Alain felt a glow as he listened to the rich, warm voice.

"We wouldn't make Luna, certainly, on what we've got. But we've got enough to take us as far as we want to go."

"Good."

Alain heard a low whine, a hissing noise, a thump, and then the voices were cut off suddenly. A few yards further on his hand touched metal.

He switched on the emergency bulb and discovered that he had come to a solid wall of steel. This was completely smooth and he could not guess how it opened. He tried for almost an hour to get it to work, but finally, his body feeling hollow with frustration, he gave up and began to make his way back in the direction he had come.

A short time later the ground quivered for a few seconds and he had to stop, thinking insanely that the stock-pile of bombs had exploded. When it was over, he thought he could guess what had caused it. The Fireclown had made some reference to a boat — a space-boat. Perhaps that had taken off, though how it was possible so deep underground he couldn't guess.

He was feeling intensely tired. His limbs and his head ached badly and he was incapable either of sustained thought or action. He had to keep stopping every few yards in order to rest, his body trembling with reaction. But reaction to what? To some new nervous or mental shock, or was it the cumulative effect of the past few days? He had been unable to sort out and analyze his emotions earlier, and was even less capable of doing so now.

An acute sense of melancholy possessed him as he stumbled miserably on, at last arriving back at the office. Wearily, he dumped the emergency bulb down in the main chamber, suddenly becoming conscious of a tremendous heat emanating from some source outside. When he reached the entrance the guards had gone. Somewhere in the distance he heard shouts and other noises. As he reached the opening on to the main corridor he saw that it was ablaze with light.

And the light — a weird, green-blue blaze — was coming from the Fireclown's great cavern.

A policeman ran past him and Alain shouted: "What's happening?"

"Fire!" the policeman continued to run.

Now, pouring like a torrent, the flames were eddying down the corridor, a surging, swiftly-moving inferno. There was nothing for the fire to feed on, yet it moved just the same, as if of its own volition.

Fascinated, Alain watched it approach. The heat was soon unbearable and he backed into the chamber.

Only at that moment did it dawn on him that he should have run towards the ramps. He was completely trapped. Also, the laboratory contained inflammable chemicals which would ignite immediately the blaze reached them.

He ran towards the entrance again, stupefied by the heat, and saw that it was too late. The wall of heaving flame had almost reached him.

He still felt no panic. Part of him almost welcomed the flames. But the air was becoming less and less breathable.

He wrenched open doors, looking for another exit. The only possible one seemed to be that which he'd just come back from.

It occurred to him that the Fireclown had been misjudged all round — by everyone except his grandfather who had realized the danger.

The Fireclown had released an inferno on the City of Switzerland. But how? He had never seen or heard of any flames like those which now began to dart around the corridor. He coughed and rubbed the sweat out of his eyes.

At last his brain began to function again. But too late, now, for him to do anything constructive.

Suddenly the entrance was filled with a roaring mass of fire. He retreated from it, hit his back against the corner of a bench, stumbled towards the office. As he slammed the steel door behind him he heard an explosion as the flame touched some of the spilt chemicals.

Air was still flowing in from another source in the small tunnel. He kept the door open.

The other door, sealing off the flames, began to heat and he realized, with fatalistic horror, that when it melted, as it inevitably must, he would die.

He would, he decided, leave the office and head into the tunnel at the last minute. Sitting in the darkness, his confused mind began to clear as the heat rose, and he faced death. A peculiar feeling of calm came upon him and belatedly, he began to think.

The thoughts were not particularly helpful in his present predicament. They told him of no way of escape, but they helped him face the inevitable. He thought he understood, now, the philosophic calm which came to men facing death.

For some days, he realized, he had been moving in a kind of half-dream, grasping out for something that might have been — he hesitated and then let the thought come — love. His emotions had ruled him; he had been their toy, unaware of his motives.

He had always been, to a degree, unstable in this way, perhaps because of his tendency to suppress the unpleasant ideas which sometimes came to him. Having no parents, unloved by his grandfather, his childhood had been spent in a perpetual quest for attention; at school he had been broken of his exhibitionism, and the nature of his job gave him no means of expressing these feelings. Now he sought, perhaps, that needed love in the Fireclown with his constant evoking of parent images. Certainly he had sought it in Helen, so much so that a similar need in her had clashed with his own. And now, spurred on by his grandfather's bitter references to his illegitimacy, he had embarked on a search which had led him to this — death!

He got up, abstractly watching the door slowly turning red hot.

Had many others, like him, identified the Fireclown with some need to feel *wanted*?

He smiled. It was too pat, really — too cheap. But he had hit upon a clue to the Fireclown's popularity even if he was not yet near to the exact truth.

Looking at it from another angle, he assembled the facts. They were few and obvious. The Fireclown's own psychological need had created the creed that he had preached, and it had found an echo in the hearts of a large percentage of the world's population. But the creed had not really supplied an answer to their ills, had only enabled them to find expression.

The door turned to smoky white and he smelt the steel smouldering. A slight glow filled the room and his mouth was dry of saliva, his body drained of sweat.

The world had reached some kind of crisis point. Perhaps it was, as the Fireclown had said, because man had removed himself from his roots and lived an increasingly artificial life.

Yet Alain couldn't completely accept this. An observer from another star, for instance, might see the rise and fall of man-made constructions as nothing more than a natural change-process. Did human beings consider an ant-hill "unnatural"? Wasn't the City of Switzerland itself merely a huge ant-hill?

He saw with surprise that the door had faded from white to red hot and the heat in the room was decreasing. Immediately there was some hope. He forgot his reverie and watched the change intently. Soon the door was only warm to his touch. He pushed at it but it wouldn't budge. Then he realized that the heat had expanded the metal. He waited impatiently, giving an experimental push every now and then until, at last, the door gave and he stepped into the ruined laboratory.

The fire had destroyed much, but now the room swam with liquid. An occasional spurt from the walls close to the ceiling told him the source of his salvation. Evidently this old section of the city had had to protect itself against fire more than any other part — the old automatic extinguishers had finally functioned and engulfed the fire.

In the passage outside it was the same. The extinguishers had not been tested — not even known about — for years but, activated by the extreme heat, they had finally done the job they had been designed for.

With relief, he began to run up the pitch-dark corridor, at last finding his way to the ramp. A small heap of containers was still there, but there were not so many as he had seen earlier. Had the police managed to take them, or had they been salvaged by the Fireclown? It was, of course, virtually impossible for fire to destroy the P-bombs' shielding, but how many knew that these days? How much panic, Alain wondered, had been the result of the Fireclown's holocaust?

Levels all the way up had been swept by fire. He was forced to push his body on and on, climbing the emergency stairways, avoiding charred corpses and wreckage.

Naked flame had not been used in the city for many years and fire precautions had been lax — there had been no need for them until now.

Alain wondered wryly if the Fireclown's popularity was as great as it had been yesterday.

The first group of men he met were on the fifteenth level. They were forcing open a door in a residential corridor, obviously equipped as a rescue team.

They stared at him, astonished.

"Where did you come from?" one of them asked, rubbing a dirty sleeve over his soot-blackened face.

"I was trapped down below — old fire extinguishers put out the fire."

"They may have put out the fire that the *initial* fire started," another said, "but they wouldn't have worked on the first lot. We tried. Nothing puts it out once it's under way."

"Then why is it out now?"

"Just thank the stars it *is* out. We don't know why. It suddenly subsided and disappeared between the fifteenth and sixteenth levels. We can only guess that the stuff it's made of doesn't last forever. We don't know why it burns and we don't know what it burns. To think we trusted the Fireclown and he did this to our homes..."

"You're sure it was the Fireclown?"

"Who else? He had the P-bomb cache, didn't he? It stands to reason he had other weapons, too — flame-weapons he'd made himself."

Alain passed on.

The semi-melted corridors gave way to untouched corridors full of disturbed people, milling around men organizing them into rescue teams. Emergency hospital stations had been set up and doctors were treating shock and burn victims, the lucky survivors. The lowest level had been built to withstand destruction of this kind, but the newer levels had not been. If he had been on the tenth level, or even the ninth where a few families had still lived before the blaze, he wouldn't be alive now.

Though climbing the emergency stairs and ramps was hard going, Alain chose these instead of the overcrowded, fear-filled elevators. On he climbed, grateful for the peace and quiet of the stairs in contrast to the turbulence in the corridors.

He was crossing the corridor of the thirtieth level when he saw that one of the shop-fronts — it was a consumer corridor — bore a gaudy slogan. A FREER LIFE WITH THE RLM it said. The place was the election headquarters of the Radical

Liberal Movement. Another poster — a tri-di build-up — showed the smiling face of Helen Curtis. At the top, above the picture, it said *Curtis*, and at the bottom, below the picture, it said *President*. The troublesome *for* had been left out.

He stopped and spoke to the door of the place.

"May I come in?"

The door opened. He walked into a poster-lined passage and into a large room stacked with election literature. Bundles of leaflets and posters, all brightly coloured, were stacked everywhere. There didn't seem to be anyone around.

He picked up a plastipaper poster of Helen. An audiostrip in its lining began to whisper softly: *Curtis for President, Curtis for President, Curtis for President.* He flung it down and as it crumpled the whispering stopped.

"I see that's another vote I've lost," said Helen's voice behind him.

"I had a feeling I was going to meet you," he said quietly, still staring at the fallen poster.

"It would be likely, in my own election headquarters. This is only the store-room. Do you want to see the offices? They're smart." Her voice, unlike her words, was not a bit cheerful.

"What are you going to do with all this now?" he said, waving a tired arm around the room.

"Use it, of course. What did you expect?"

"I should have thought a campaign wouldn't have been worth your time now."

"You think because I supported the Fireclown when he was popular I won't have a chance now he's unpopular — is that it?"

"Yes." He was surprised. Her spirit, it seemed, was still there. She didn't have a chance of winning the elections now. Was she hiding the fact from herself? he wondered.

"Look, Alain," she said forcefully, "I could have walked into the Presidency without a fight if this hadn't happened. Now it's going to be a tough fight — and I'm rather glad."

"You always liked a fight."

"Certainly — if the opposition's strong enough."

He smiled. "Was that leveled at me by any chance? I've heard it said that if a man doesn't love a woman enough she thinks he's strong; if he loves her too much she thinks he's weak. Was the opposition weak, Helen?"

"You're very sensitive today." Her voice was deliberately cool. "No, I wasn't leveling anything at you. I was talking about your grandfather's happy turn of luck. Our positions are completely reversed now, aren't they?"

"I don't know how I feel about it," he said, stopping the tendency to sulk. Helen's retort had stung him. "I'm not really in support of either of you. I think, on the whole, I favour the RLMs. They could still win the constituency elections, couldn't they, even if you didn't get the Presidency? That would give you a strong voice in the House.

"If they kept me as leader, Alain." Her face softened as she admitted a truth which previously she had been hiding from. "Not everyone who approved of my stand yesterday approves of it today."

"I hate to say I warned you of it. You should have known better, Helen, than to go around whipping up mobs. People have to trust politicians as well as like them. They want a modern, up-to-date President, certainly — but they also want a respectable one. When the voters sit down and think about it, even if this Fireclown business hadn't taken the turn it has, they'll choose the candidate they can feel confidence in. Fiery politics of your sort only work for short spells, Helen. Even I know that much. Admittedly, after showing yourself as a 'Woman of the People' you could have stuck to parliamentary debate to make your points and probably danced home. But now you've identified yourself so strongly with the Fireclown that you haven't a hope of winning. I should give it up." He looked at her wistfully.

She laughed shortly, striding up and down between the bales of posters. "I haven't a dog's chance — you're right. But I'll keep on fighting. Lucky old Simon, eh? He's now the man who warned the people of their danger. Who else could they vote for?"

"Don't get bitter, Helen. Why don't you start painting again? You know what you're doing in that field. Really, even I know more about politics than you do. You should never have entered them. There are people who are natural born politicians, but you're just not one of them. I've asked you this a dozen times previously, but I'd still like to know what makes you go on with it."

"One of the strongest reasons is because the more people disapprove of my actions, the harder I pursue them. Fair enough?" She turned, staring at him quizzically with her head cocked on one side.

He smiled. "In a word, you're just plain obstinate. Maybe if I'd encouraged you in your political work you might have been a well-known painter by now — and well rid of all this trouble."

"Maybe. But it's more than that, Alain." She spoke softly, levering herself up on to one of the bales. She sat there swinging her legs, looking very beautiful. She no longer wore the make-up she'd had on earlier. "But I've got myself into this now, and I'm going to stick at it until the end. Sink or swim."

He told her about his visit to the first level — omitting that he'd heard the Fireclown and his friends leaving — and of his narrow escape.

"I thought I was going to be killed," he said, "and I thought of you. I wondered, in fact, if we weren't both searching for the same thing."

"Searching? I didn't know you were the searching kind, Alain."

"Until this Fireclown business blew up, I was the hiding kind. I hid a lot from myself. But something grandfather said must have triggered something else in me." He paused. "Was it only three days ago?" he mused wonderingly.

"What did he say?"

"Oh," Alain answered lightly, "he made a rather pointed reference to the fact that my ancestry isn't all it might be."

"That was cruel of him."

"Maybe it did me good. Maybe it brought something into the open. Anyway, I started getting curious about the Fireclown. Then you visited me and I was even more curious. Perhaps because you associated yourself with the Fireclown's creed, I associated him with you and it led on from there. I went to see the Fireclown the same night, you know."

"Did you speak to him personally?" She sounded envious.

"No. I never got to see him, actually. But I attended yesterday's 'audience'. I thought I understood why you supported him. In his own heavy way he made sense of a kind." He frowned. "But the same could be said for grandfather, I suppose. That was a good speech this morning."

"Yes, it was." she was staring at him, her mouth slightly open, her breasts moving beneath her lacy bodice more rapidly than usual.

"I'm glad all this has happened," he continued. "It's done a lot of good for me, I think."

"You're glad about the P-bombs being found — about the fire, too?"

"No. I couldn't really believe the Fireclown was guilty until I saw the evidence for myself. And I still don't hate him for what he tried to do — for what he still might try to do, for that matter. I feel sorry for him. In his own way he is the naïve and generous giant you tried to tell me about."

"That's what I think. You were down there — were you satisfied that the Fireclown was responsible for stock-piling those bombs and starting the fire?"

"The evidence was plain, I'm afraid."

"It's idiotic," she said angrily. "Why should he do a thing like that? A man so full of *love*!"

"Love — or hate, Helen?"

"What do you mean?"

"He professed to love mankind — but he hated mankind's works. He hated what he thought were our faults. Not exactly true love, eh?"

"We'll never know. I wonder if he escaped. I hope he has — so long as he doesn't try any more sabotage."

For the second time in the last few days Alain found himself concealing something from his ex-mistress. He didn't tell her that he knew the Fireclown had managed a getaway, at least from Earth. Instead, he said: "Should he escape?

After all, he was responsible for the deaths of least a hundred people. The residential corridors on nine and ten all the way up to fifteen were full of corpses. Probably a great many more were roasted in their homes. A nasty death, Helen. I know. I came close to it myself. Should he escape without punishment?"

"A man like the Fireclown is probably not conscious of his crime, Alain. So who's to say?"

"He's intelligent. I don't think he's insane, in any way we can understand. *Warped*, perhaps…?"

"Oh, well, let's stop talking about the Fireclown. There's a world-wide search out for him now. The fact that he vanished seems to prove his guilt, at least for Simon von Bek and the public. I've noticed a few remained loyal to the Fireclown for some time after they found out about the bombs. If the fire hadn't started he'd probably still have strong support from people who thought the bombs were planted."

"You can't plant a stack of P-bombs, Helen. The Fireclown must have made them. He's the only one with the resources."

"That's what everyone thinks. But a few of us politicians know better, Alain."

"Nuclear weapons have been banned for years. What are you talking about?"

"Not everyone gave up all their stock-pile in the early days of the Great Disarmament, Alain. There were quite a few who hung on to some secret arms piles until they saw how things were going. Of course, when the Solar Government was found to work and the threat of war dwindled away to nothing, they forgot about them or got rid of them."

"Good God! Nuclear bombs. I'm not superstitious. War's a thing of the past. But it seems dreadful that the weapons should still be around."

"There are plenty," she said ironically. "At least enough to fight a major solar war!"

CHAPTER SEVEN

Alain, like the rest of his contemporaries, had lived so long in a peaceful world that the concept of war, particularly war fought on a nuclear scale, was horrifying. For nearly a century the world had hovered on the brink of atomic conflict, but time after time governments had just managed to avoid it. With the final outlawing of nuclear weapons in 2042, a great sigh of relief had gone up. The human race had come dangerously close to destroying itself, but at last it could progress without that fear forever pressing on it.

And now Helen's casual reference to a solar war!

"You don't mean that as a serious suggestion, did you?" he asked her.

"Alain, the Solar Cabinet, myself and one or two other party leaders have been aware of the existence of nuclear arms for some time. Simon von Bek, in his speech before the House this morning, could not reveal that, because if the news leaked we might well have a fresh panic on our hands. Anyway, it suited his purpose to suggest that the Fireclown manufactured them. The Fireclown might have been able to make his, but he could just as easily have *bought* them."

"*Bought* —?" Alain gasped. "Bought them from whom?"

"From one of the men who specialize in such things. Over the years there has been a constant 'black market' in nuclear arms. The police have been aware of it and they have been vigilant. Many of those who discovered forgotten caches have been arrested and the weapons destroyed. But some haven't. And these men would welcome physical conflict — preferably on Earth or between Earth and *one* of the other worlds, so that they could get to safety on the unthreatened world. If one side began an attack with nuclear arms, the other would have to defend itself — and the dealers could then get any price that they wanted."

"But, surely, arms dealing on such a scale is impossible!"

"Not if the cards are played right. And it has been evident to me for some

time that someone *is* playing their cards right. If he gets the hand he wants —
bang! Suddenly, overnight, without any kind of warning and none of the
psychological protection people perhaps had a hundred years ago, we'd be
plunged into a war of colossal destruction."

"I can't believe it!"

"Perhaps it's better. Remember, this is only what the dealers wish for — it
might not happen. That's why it's so secret. It might be possible to remove the
danger once and for all with none of the public knowing it was there. The RLM
shadow cabinet have a plan to prevent the eventuality; Simon von Bek has
another. I think ours is better. Now you know one of the reasons I'm in politics
and why I stay in."

"I'll accept that," he said a trifle dubiously. "Do you think the Fireclown's
tied up with any of these dealers?"

"If he's tied up with one, he's probably tied up with them all. Those we
haven't caught are the most powerful and have very likely formed themselves
into a syndicate. That's what the rumours say, at any rate."

"I saw no evidence of a plant when I explored the Fireclown's level. So it's
probable that he could have bought the P-bombs."

"There's another angle to it," Helen said thoughtfully. "Admittedly I may
not have been wholly objective about the Fireclown, but what if the dealers
had *planted* the P-bombs on him, knowing that someone would eventually find
out?"

"Why should they do that?" Alain bent down and picked up a handbill, his
eyes fixed on it. It was another picture of Helen, this time in an heroic pose.
Fifty words of text underneath briefly outlined her ideals in purple adjectives.

"The arms dealers want a war — preferably one that wouldn't have too
destructive results and wouldn't involve all three habitable planets. First, hint
that the Fireclown has a stock-pile, supply the evidence to be found, take
advantage of the scare — and the possibility of the Fireclown possessing more
weapons — then unload a ready-made batch of weapons for 'defense' of the
Solar Government. That way, you see, there might not be a war at all — but
the dealers would profit just the same."

"That sounds close to the truth — if the dealers did frame the Fireclown,
of course. But we have proof that he caused the destruction of fifteen levels.
How do you explain that? That fire was impossible to extinguish. He had
obviously made it, in the same way he manufactured that weird artificial sun in
the cavern."

"He may have been pushed into it — self-defense."

"No, I don't think so."

"There's one way we can get more information," she said briskly, jumping down off the bale. "We can go and see Simon von Bek. He'd know more about it than anyone."

"Do you want to do that?"

"I'm curious. More than that, Alain." She smiled nervously. "I may be able to wheedle something out of the old patriarch that would be advantageous to me in the election. If I could prove that Fireclown was framed it would help a lot."

He shook his head, wondering at her incredible optimism. "All right," he said. "Let's go."

Simon von Bek received them with the air of the conquering Roman general receiving the defeated barbarian leaders. All he needed, Alain thought, was a toga and a laurel crown.

He smiled urbanely, greeted them conventionally, offered them drinks, which they accepted.

"Come into the study," he said to his grandson and niece. He led the way. He had furnished the place with deliberate archaism. There were even a few family portraits — of the best-remembered members of the von Bek clan. The first Denholm, Alain and Simon von Bek hung there, as well as the two women Presidents of the Solar Government. A proud and slightly sombre-looking group. The bookcases were of mahogany, filled primarily with books on politics, history and philosophy. The novels were of the same type — political novels by Disraeli, Trollope, Koestler, Endelmans and De la Vega. Alain rather envied his grandfather's one-track mind. It made him good at his career.

"To tell you the truth," Simon von Bek said heavily. "I feel sorry for you both. You were misled, as most people were, and this business must have left you slightly in the air. It hasn't done you much good politically, has it, Helen? A pity — you've got good von Bek stuff in you — strong will, impersonal ambition…"

"And an eye to the main chance." She smiled. "Though you'll probably say, uncle Simon, that I lack self-discipline and could do with a spot more common sense. You'd probably be right about the self-discipline. I lost out on that one — I think I'm finished now, don't you?"

Alain admired her guile.

Simon von Bek nodded regretfully. He probably did regret his niece's political demise, just as he obviously regretted Alain's never having shown an interest in politics. "Still, you were rather foolish, y'know."

"I know," she said contritely.

He turned to Alain. "And you, my boy? I suppose you understand why I was so adamant earlier?"

"Yes, grandfather."

The old man seemed to warm to both of them. "I shall be President, no doubt, when the next session begins. It was really my last opportunity to take such high responsibility — family tradition demands a von Bek of every generation to serve at least one term. I was hoping that you, Alain, would follow on, but I suppose the task will fall to Helen's son and Denholm's. I wish my daughter…" He cleared his throat, seemingly moved to strong emotion, although Alain thought the last line had been a bit stagey. It was probably for his benefit. He wondered why he should have felt such momentary love for his grandfather at their earlier interview.

"What made you suspicious of the Fireclown in the first place?" Helen said, in the manner of a whodunit character preparing the detective for his denouement.

"Instinct, I suppose. Could have told you there was something fishy about him the first time I heard of him. Made Junnar go down and have a look the first opportunity he could. There was also another business which I can't really talk about…"

"He knows about the illegal stock-piles, uncle," Helen said forthrightly.

"Really? A bit unwise to spread it around, isn't it?"

"I'm not in the habit of betraying confidences, grandfather," Alain said tritely, with a hard look at Helen.

"No. I suppose it's all right. But presumably Helen has impressed you with the need for secrecy?"

"Of course," Helen said.

"Well, I had a feeling he'd been connected with the dealers. They're the only group of criminals powerful enough to hide a man and help him change his identity. I guessed that he had probably come from their hideout, though this was all conjecture, you understand. The police investigated him and could find nothing to indicate it, though they agreed with me."

"So, in fact, unless it can be established that the P-bombs are part of the old stock, there is nothing to connect him with the dealers?" Helen said, trying hard not to show her disappointment.

"I have already been in touch with the laboratory analyzing the bombs. They tell me they *are* old stock — you would have discovered that soon, anyway, at the next Committee meeting. Obviously we can't tell the public that."

"Obviously," said Helen, "though it might have strengthened my own case in the House slightly."

"Not to any important degree."

"What's this committee?" Alain asked curiously.

"We call it the One Hundred Committee, after a slightly less effective British anti-nuclear group which existed in the middle of the twentieth century.

Actually there are only ten of us. The Committee is pledged to locating every single nuclear weapon left over from the old days and seeing the offenders punished where possible. We work, of course, in close collaboration with the highly secret ARP — the Arms Removal Police. Our work has been going on for years. Helen is the secretary and I am the chairman. Other important politicians comprise the remaining eight."

"Very worthy," said Alain. "Are you effective?"

"We have been in the past, though our job is becoming more difficult since the dealers work together, pooling their resources. They would welcome an opportunity to sell what they have — perhaps Helen has already told you."

"Yes, she has. But it occurred to me that you could offer to buy the dealers out now. Surely it would be better to pay their price and have the arms without waiting for a crisis to decide you?"

"That's our main bone of contention," Helen put in. "Uncle doesn't agree with buying them now. I want to do that."

"The fantastic price these brigands would demand would beggar the Solar nation," Simon von Bek said gruffly to his grandson. "We must do it in secret and justify the expenditure at the same time. It would be impossible. I feel they'll overstep the mark at some stage, then we'll catch them."

"The expenditure's worth it!" Helen said. "We could recuperate from poverty, but survival in a nuclear war…!"

"If we caught the Fireclown, then," Alain said slowly, "it might give us a lead to the arms dealers."

"Possibly," von Bek agreed, "though he might not admit to it. Secondly, he might not even know who the dealers are. They are naturally extremely cautious. However, they are certainly going to take advantage of the trouble the Fireclown has caused. The man must be caught — and destroyed before he makes any more trouble!"

"Grandfather!" Alain was shocked. The death penalty had been abolished for more than a hundred years.

"I'm sorry — I'm extremely sorry, Helen. You must forgive an old man's tongue. These concepts were not quite so disgusting when I was a young man. Certainly we must imprison or exile the Fireclown."

Alain nodded.

"It's funny," he said, "that the Fireclown should preach a return to nature; that, in fact, science leads to mankind's destruction, and yet he should be planning that same destruction — or at very least is a tool of those who would welcome it."

"Life," said the old man with the air of a philosopher, "is full of that sort of paradox."

C H A P T E R   E I G H T

"I'll see you home," Alain said lightly as they left the apartment.

"That would be nice," she said.

They walked slowly through the gardens, repaired and beautiful again. The starlight was augmented by soft beams from the roof structure which had the appearance of many tiny moons shining down, each one casting a single, exquisite beam. The Top had been well designed. To live here was the ambition of every young man and woman. It gave people, thought those at the Top, something to aim for.

"If only I could speak to the Fireclown personally," Helen said wistfully. "Then at least I'd be able to form a better idea of what he's really like."

Alain preferred to say nothing.

They reached the door of her apartment on the sixty-third level and went in. Familiar smells greeted him, smells which he always associated with Helen — fresh, slightly scented, of soap and oils. It was strange, he reflected, that women's apartments always seemed to smell better than men's. Maybe it was an obvious thought. He noticed he was breathing a little more quickly, slightly more shallowly.

Neither recognized by outward expression the thought that was in their minds, yet each was aware of the other's emotions. Alain was slightly fearful, for he remembered the conflict between them as well as their old happiness and realized that Helen probably did, too.

"Would you like a nightcap?" she invited.

"I'd prefer coffee, if you've got it." Unconsciously, he had given her her opportunity. He was torn now, half-afraid of what seemed likely to happen.

She came over to him as he sat down in a comfortable chair beside a small shelf of book-tapes.

She leaned down and stroked his face lightly.

"You look dreadfully tired, Alain."

"I've had a hard day." He smiled. He took her hand and kissed it.

"I'll go and get the coffee," she said.

When she came back she had changed into a pair of chaste pyjamas and a robe of thick, dark blue material. She had a tray of coffee — real coffee from the smell. She put it down on a table and drew up a chair so that the table was between them.

Helen, he thought, *Oh, Helen, I love you.* They were staring at each other, both wondering, perhaps, if this reunion would take on the same pattern as their previous affair.

"We're wiser now," she said softly, handing him his coffee. "It's a von Bek trait — we learn by our mistakes."

"There are always different mistakes to be made," he warned her. It was the last attempt to retreat from the situation and allow her to do the same, as gracefully as possible.

"That's experience," she said, and the fears were forgotten. Now they looked at one another as if they were new friends.

When they made love that night it was entirely different from anything either had ever before experienced. They treated one another delicately, yet passionately, as if a return to their earlier, less self-conscious love would plunge them back into the turmoil of four months before.

In the morning Alain's arm was aching painfully from having cradled her head all night. He raised her head gently and propped himself on his elbow, tracing the softness of her shoulder with his fingers. She opened her eyes and seemed to be looking at him like a respectful stranger. Presumably there was a similar expression in his own face, for he felt he shared her emotion. He kissed her lightly on the lips and pushed back the bed clothes, swinging himself out of the narrow bed.

He sat slightly hunched on the edge, studying his head and torso reflected in the mirror opposite.

"I've got an idea where the Fireclown is," he said suddenly.

She was half-asleep and didn't seem to hear him.

He didn't repeat himself then but went into the kitchen to make coffee. He was feeling rather tired now and his legs shook a little as the machine came alive and produced two beakers of hot coffee. He transferred the coffee into cups and took them back.

She was sitting up.

"What did you say about the Fireclown? You know where he is?"

"No, but we might be able to guess." He told her about overhearing the trio in the passage.

"Why didn't you tell me about this yesterday?"

"That was yesterday," he said simply. She understood and nodded.

"They took off in a small space-boat. I've thought about it since and I think there must be a launching ramp leading through the rock to somewhere outside the city. Those old bombs had to be launched from somewhere."

"That sounds logical. You say he remarked that they didn't have enough fuel to make Luna. They may have made a transcontinental flight."

"Unlikely. You can't land even a small rocket without at least a few people observing it. I've got a feeling they're orbiting — maybe waiting for someone to pick them up."

"Or they may have gone to St Rene's?"

"Why should they do that?" The Monastery of St Rene Lafayette was the home of a group of monks who practised a form of scientific mysticism. Little was known about the Order and it was thought that the monks were harmless. The monastery was, in fact, an abandoned space-station which the monks had taken over. The world had decided they were quaintly mad and had all but forgotten them.

"Well," Helen said, sipping her coffee, "it's just a connection that my mind made. I associated one 'crank' with a group of others, I suppose."

"Unless they *were* orbiting, it's the only place they could have gone," Alain agreed. "I wonder how we could find out."

"By going there, perhaps."

"We'd need a boat. We haven't got one."

"My brother has. A nice job — one of the latest Paolos."

"Would he let us take it?"

"We don't need to ask. I often use it. I have a pilot's licence, the audiolocks respond to my voice, the ground staff at the port know me — we'd have a good chance of getting away with it."

"And going to our deaths, maybe. The Fireclown appears to be more ruthless than we thought, remember?"

"But are the monks? They are bound to give sanctuary to those they term 'unclears', I believe."

"It's worth a try." He got up. "I'm going to have a bath. Is my green suit still here?"

"Yes."

"Good." He glanced at the chronom on the wall. "It's still early. If we leave now we could..." He turned to her. "Where is your brother's ship?"

"Hamburg — she's a sea-lander."

"A fast cab could get us there in an hour. You'd better get up and get ready." He grinned at her as she sprang out of bed.

Hamburg Spaceport was surrounded by a pleasant garden-city with a population of less than two millions. In contrast to the capital city of Switzerland, its buildings were single- or double-storeyed. Beyond the spaceport buildings water glinted in the summer sun, beneath a pale and cloudless blue sky. As the cab spiraled down towards the landing roof a huge bulbous ship suddenly erupted from the waves, water boiling to steam as it lumbered upwards.

Helen pointed: "The *Titan*, bound for Mars and Ganymede, probably carrying one of the last seed consignments they need."

By the time the cab brought them down on the roof the ship had disappeared. From his lodge, the only building on the roof, an official in a brown velvet cutaway and baggy, cerise pantaloons came sauntering towards them. He was a firm-faced man with a smile.

"Good morning, Fräulein Curtis. Sorry to hear about yesterday," he said. "Many people's faith in the Fireclown seems to have been misplaced."

"Yes, indeed," said Helen, forcing a smile in response to his. "I'm planning to make a pleasure trip until the fuss dies down. Is the *Solar Bird* ready?"

"I expect so. She was being checked in the locks, I believe. She should be okay now. Do you want to go straight down?"

"Yes, please."

He took them into his lodge, a neat office with a big window overlooking the sea which was still heaving and steaming after the *Titan*'s take-off. A small elevator cage was set in one wall. The man opened the gate for them, glancing at Alain in a speculative way. Alain returned his stare blandly and followed Helen into the elevator. It began to hiss downward.

A man in coveralls let them out, a plum, red-faced man with a mechanics' badge on his sleeve.

"Good morning, Fräulein Helen. Nice to see you."

"Good morning, Freddie. This is Herr von Bek — Freddie Weinschenk."

They shook hands and Weinschenk led them along an artificially lit corridor. Alain had never been in Hamburg before, but he knew the general design of a modern spaceport. They were now below ground level, he guessed, heading along a tunnel which led under the sea-bed.

Finally, Freddie ordered a door to open and they were in a dark, cool chamber with metal walls. From one wall, the back half of a small space-yacht projected, seeming, at first, to be stuck on the wall until Alain realized that the other half lay outside and that they were actually in a pressure chamber.

"Thanks, Freddie." Helen went up to the airlock and spoke to it. It began to slide open; then slowly the four doors all opened and they went into the cramped cabin of the ship. Freddie shouted from outside:

"If you're leaving immediately, fräulein, I'll start the chamber up."

"Thanks, Freddie. See you when we get back."

Helen went to the control panel and touched a stud. The airlocks closed behind them. She switched on the exterior viewer so they could see the chamber. Freddie had left and Alain saw that the room was swiftly being flooded. Soon it was full and the wall surrounding the ship began to expand away from the ship itself and he saw the ramp extending outwards into open sea.

"We'll make a soft take-off," Helen said, strapping herself in the pilot's couch. Alain got into the other couch. "We don't want anyone to think we're in a hurry," she added.

"The softer the better," he smiled. "I've only been into space once and I didn't much care for the trip. She was an old chemical ship and I was certain she was going to break down every inch of the journey."

"You'll see a lot of difference in the *Solar Bird.*" She activated the drive. "It's unlikely they could improve a nuclear ship any further. They'll have to start thinking of some new type of engine now, I suppose, just as the old type starts getting familiar and comfortable."

The control panel was alive now, its instruments measuring and informing.

Alain felt a double pounding beat for a second or so, and then the ship was speeding up the ramp, leaving it, plunging up through water and then was in daylight, racing into the sky.

She switched on the chart-viewer, selected the area of space she wanted. It showed her the position of the space-station monastery and gave her all the information she needed.

"I hope our hunch is right," she said and turned round to see that Alain had blacked out.

There had been no reason for this at all, since the mounting pressure outside was completely countered by the ship's internal mechanisms. It was probably some kind of reflex, she decided.

"I'm a fool," he said when he was awake again. "*Did* anything happen, or was it just my imagination."

"Just imagination, I'm afraid. But you needed the sleep, anyway."

"Where are we?"

"In orbit. We should be getting pretty close to the station in a little while. For the time being I'm going to pretend we're in trouble — that way we'll lull any suspicions the monks might have if they *are* harbouring the Fireclown."

Soon the wheel of the big station came in sight, the sun bright on its metal. There were two ships they could see hugged in its receiving bays, a big one and a little one. The big one was of unfamiliar design. They could see its title etched on its hull from where they were. *Pi-meson.*

"Funny name for a ship," Alain commented.

"The monks — if it *is* their ship — have got funny ideas." She reached out to press a red stud. "That's the May-day signal. With any luck they should get it."

In a moment their screen flickered and a face appeared on it — a thin man, lean-nosed and thin-lipped.

"Would it be impertinent to deduce that you are in trouble?" he said.

"It wouldn't be, no," Helen replied. "Can you help us?"

"Who knows? Can you maneuver your ship so that we can grapple, or shall we send out help?"

"The steering seems to be all right," she said. "I'll come in."

She coasted the ship until they were near one of the empty bays and the station's magnegraps pulled them into the bay.

When, finally, they climbed from their ship into the unpleasant air of the monastery they were greeted by the thin-faced monk. He was dressed in a blue habit that did nothing for his already pale face. His hair was short but he had no tonsure. His eyes and cheeks were sunken but, in his own way, he looked healthy enough. He held out a skeletal hand with incredibly long fingers.

"I am Auditor Kurt," he said as Alain shook hands. "It is good that we can be of service to you. Please come this way."

He took them into a small, barely furnished room and offered them tea, which they accepted.

"What exactly is wrong with your ship?" he asked politely.

"I'm not sure. I'm not familiar with the type — it's new. I could not get the landing jets to work when I tested them preparatory to re-entering the atmosphere. It's just as well I did test them." She had personally jammed the jet control. It could be fixed easily.

"You were lucky to be so close." The monk nodded.

Alain was wondering how he could find out if Fireclown was here.

"I'm extremely interested in your Order," he said conversationally. "I'm something of a student of religions — perhaps you can tell me about yours?"

"Only that we were founded as long ago as 1950, although this Order did not come into existence until 1976 and did not come here until about twenty years ago. We are a branch of the original faith, which did not pay a great deal of attention to its mystical aspects until we founded the Order of St Rene. St Rene is not the true name of our inspired founder — that is secret to almost all — but that is the name we use for him."

"I should like to see the monastery. Is that possible?" Alain looked around the small room, avoiding the monk's intent gaze.

"Normally it would be possible — but, ah, we have repairs going on in many parts... We are not really prepared for visitors."

"Oh? Then whose is the ship, other than ours, in the receiving bay?"

"Which one?"

"There are two. The *Pi-meson* and the *Od-Methuselah*."

"Both ours," the monk said hastily. "Both ours."

"Then why did you ask which one I spoke of?"

The monk smiled. "We monks have devious minds, I'm afraid. It is the nature of our calling. Excuse me, I'll go and check that the mechanics are repairing your ship." He rose and left. They heard the door seal itself behind him. They were locked in.

Alain sipped his tea.

"If the Fireclown's here, they're not likely to let on to outsiders who'd take the news back to Earth," he said.

"We'll have to think of a means of getting a look around this place. Have you noticed the atmosphere? It's weird."

The atmosphere of the place fitted well with the space-station monastery circling in space, away from the things of Earth. It had a detached air of calm about it, and yet there was a feeling of excitement here, too. It was possible, of course, that he was imagining it, for he was very excited himself.

"Do you think they know what he's up to? Or is he just making use of their habit of affording people sanctuary?" Alain asked her.

"They seem unworldly, to say the least," she replied, shivering a little, for the room was not well heated.

The door opened and Auditor Kurt came back.

Your boat has been fixed, my friends. I see from the registration plates that it is owned by Denholm Curtis — an important man on Earth, is he not?"

"He's my brother," Helen said, wondering if the monk was getting at anything in particular.

Alain became aware at last that they might be in danger. If the Fireclown was here and knew they were here, too, he might decide it was risky to let them go.

"So you are Helen Curtis. Who, then, is this gentleman?"

"I'm Alain von Bek."

"Ah, yes, Simon von Bek's grandson. From what I have seen of recent V-casts, Fräulein Curtis and Minister von Bek are at odds over certain issues. Which side do you support, Herr von Bek?"

"Neither," Alain said coldly. "Just call me a disinterested spectator."

A peculiar expression came on the monk's face for a second. Alain could not work out what it indicated.

"I should say you were the least disinterested..." the monk mused. Then he said briskly: "You asked earlier if you could look over the monastery. To tell you the truth we are not always willing to let strangers inspect our home, but I think it would be all right if you wanted to take a quick tour before you leave."

Why the monk's sudden change? Was he planning to lead them into some sort of trap? Alain had to take the chance.

"Thanks a lot," he said.

They began to walk along the curving corridor. This part, the monk told them, was reserved for the monks' cells. They turned into a narrower corridor which led them to another similar to the one they'd just left, though the curve was tighter.

"Here is what we term our clearing house." The monk smiled, opening a door and letting them precede him through. It was a fairly large room. Several monks sat on simple chairs. They were dressed in brown dungarees. The monk in the centre was dressed, like Auditor Kurt, in a blue habit, and was chanting some sort of litany.

"How would you worry somebody?" he chanted.

"By destroying their confidence," the other monks mumbled in reply.

"How would you make somebody happy?"

"By casting forth their engrams," said the monks in unison.

"How would you help somebody?"

"Teach them to be clear."

"By the Spirit of the Eight Dynamics," intoned the blue-clad monk, "I command thee to cast forth thy engrams forthwith!"

The monks seemed to freeze, concentrating intently. Above them, behind the monk in the blue habit, a weird machine whirred and buzzed, dials swinging around strangely marked faces, lights flashing.

Alain said respectfully: "What are they doing?"

"They are attempting to learn the ultimate secret of the Great Triangle," Auditor Kurt whispered.

"Ah," Alain nodded intelligently.

They left this room and entered another. Here a great screen was blank and there were comfortable chairs scattered around before it.

"Sit down," said Kurt. "We are expecting a special event, today."

Alain and Helen sat down and watched the screen.

They fidgeted for over half-an-hour as nothing happened, and Kurt continued to watch the screen impassively, not looking at them.

Alain's sense of danger was heightened and he had a feeling the monk was deliberately keeping them in suspense.

Then, all at once, big letters began to form on the screen until a whole sentence was emblazoned there.

ANOTHER BROTHER CLEAR! said the message. It meant nothing to either of them.

Alain turned to the monk, half-suspicious that a trick had been played on them, but the monk was looking ecstatic and incredibly pleased.

"What does it *mean?*" Alain asked desperately.

"What it says — the hampering engrams have been exorcized from one of our brothers. He is now a clear and ready to become a Brother Auditor, as I am. It is a time for rejoicing in the monastery when this comes about."

Alain scratched his head and looked at Helen, who was equally perplexed.

"Well," beamed thin-faced Auditor Kurt, "now you have seen a little of our monastery."

Half-convinced that he was the victim of a practical joke, Alain nodded mutely. He was no nearer to finding out if the Fireclown was here, although perhaps a check on the *Pi-meson* when they got back to Earth would help them.

"Thank you for showing us," Helen said brightly. She, too, was obviously uncertain of what to do next.

"Oh —" the monk seemed to remember something — "there is one other thing I should like to show you before you leave. Will you follow me?"

They walked until they were close to the centre of the space-wheel and came to a small door in the curved wall of Central Control. Auditor Kurt ordered it open. It hissed back and they stepped through.

"Good afternoon, Herr von Bek," said the Fireclown amiably.

CHAPTER NINE

"So you *did* come here," Helen blurted out.

"I have no idea how you deduced it." He grinned. "But I must praise your intelligence. I hope no-one else on Earth thinks as you do."

Alain kept silent. They would be safer if they didn't tell the Fireclown how they had worked out his hiding place. He looked around. Corso and the woman were also there, lounging in their seats and staring amusedly at the rest.

He felt dwarfed by the Fireclown's bulk, not only physically — the man stood at least six foot six — but also psychologically. He could only stare stupidly, unable to say anything. Yet it was peculiar. Now that they were face to face he did not feel afraid any longer. The man's strange magnetism was tangible, and once again he found himself liking the Fireclown, unable to believe that he had committed an act of mass murder and plotted to blow up the Earth.

"So you are Alain von Bek," mused the Fireclown, as if the name had some special meaning. His face was still heavily painted, with wide lips and exaggerated eyes, but Alain could make out the features under the paint a little clearer. They seemed thoughtful.

"And why are you here, anyway?" Corso said, moving his repulsive red and glinting body in the chair.

"To ask questions," Helen said. She was pale and Alain could understand why — the skinless man took a lot of getting used to.

"Questions!" The clown's body moved in a great shrug. He turned his back on them and paced towards his seated friends. "Questions! By the solar firmament! What questions can I answer?"

"They are simple — and demand only simple replies, if you are truthful with us."

The Fireclown whirled round and laughed richly. "I never lie. Didn't you know that? I never lie!"

"But perhaps you mislead," Alain said quietly. "May I sit down?"

"Of course."

They both sat down.

"We want to know if you planned to blow up the world," Helen said with a trace of nervousness in her voice.

"Why should I? I wanted to save it, not hurt it."

"You did a good job with the fire which swept Switzerland," Alain retorted.

"Am I to blame for that? I warned them not to tamper."

"Are you trying to tell us you weren't responsible for that fire?" Alain said grimly.

"I've been watching the V-casts. I'm aware of what's being said of me now. They are fickle, those people. If they had really listened to me this would not have happened. But nobody listened properly."

"I agree with that." Alain nodded. "I saw them — they were using you as a means of rousing their own latent emotions. But you should have known what you were doing and stopped!"

"I never know what I am doing. I am..." The Fireclown paused and glared at him. "I was *not* responsible for the fire. Not directly, at any rate. Some of those policemen must have tampered with my fire machines. They are very delicate. I have been experimenting with means of controlling chemical and atomic fire. I produced that little artificial sun and could have produced more if I had not been interrupted by those meddlers."

"Why are you experimenting with fire? What's your purpose?" Helen leaned forward in her chair.

"Why? I have no reasons. I am the Fireclown. I have no purpose save to exist as the Fireclown. You do me too much honour, Fräulein Curtis, to expect action and plans from me. For a time I spoke to the people in Switzerland. Now that's over I shall do something else." He roared with laughter again, his grotesque body shaking.

"If you have no plans, no thought for the future, then why did you buy P-bombs from the arms dealers?"

"I know nothing of bombs or dealers! I had no inkling that those bombs were in my cavern!"

Either he was blinded by the Fireclown's overpowering presence or the man was telling the truth, Alain felt. He seemed to have a lusty disregard for all the things that concerned Helen and himself. He did not seem to exist in the time and space that Alain shared with the rest of the human race, seemed to tower over it, observing it with complete and amused detachment. But how far could he trust this impression? Alain wondered. Perhaps the Fireclown was the best actor in the world.

"You must know something of what's happening!" Helen exclaimed. "Your appearance at a time of acute crisis in society's development could not be mere coincidence."

"Society has had crises before, young lady." Again he shrugged. "It will have others. Crises are good for it!"

"I thought you ingenuous, then I changed my mind. I can't make you out at all." She sank back into the chair.

"Why should you make me out? Why should you waste time trying to analyze others when you have never bothered to look within yourself? My own argument against machines and machine-living is that it hampers man from really looking into his own being. You have to take him away from it, put him in the wilderness for a short time, before you can see that I speak truth. In my way I worship the sun, as you know. Because the sun is the most tangible of nature's workings!"

"I thought you represented a new breakthrough in ideas," Helen said quietly. "I thought you knew where you were going. That is why I supported you, identified myself and my party with you."

"There is no need to seek salvation in others, young lady!" Again he became disconcertingly convulsed with that weird and enigmatic laughter.

She got up, bridling.

"Very well, I've learnt my lesson. I believe you when you say you weren't planning destruction. I'm going back to Earth to tell them that!"

"I'm afraid Herr Corso here, who advises me on such matters, has suggested that you stay for a while, until I am ready to leave."

Alain saw his logic. "When are you leaving?" he said.

"A few days, I expect. Perhaps less."

"You won't, of course, tell us where." Alain smiled at the Fireclown for the first time and when the man returned his smile, grotesquely exaggerated by the paint around his lips, he felt dazzled, almost petrified with warmth and happiness. It was the Fireclown's only answer.

Why did the Fireclown have this ability to attract and hold people just as if they were moths drawn to a flame?

Auditor Kurt had left the room while they were conversing. Now he returned with another man behind him.

"A visitor for you, Fireclown."

Both Alain and Helen turned their heads to look at the newcomer. He was a small, dark man with a moody face. A marijuana was between his lips.

"I commend you on your choice of rendezvous," he said somewhat mockingly. His hooded eyes glanced at the others in the room, stopped for a moment on Alain and Helen. He looked questioningly at the Fireclown. "I hope you haven't been indiscreet, my friend."

"No," said the Fireclown shortly. He chuckled. "Well, Herr Blas, have you brought what I wanted?"

"Certainly. It is outside in the ship I came with. We must talk. Where?"

"Is this not private enough for you?" the Fireclown asked petulantly.

"No, it is not. I have to be over-cautious, you understand."

The Fireclown lumbered towards the door, ducking beneath it as he made his way out. "Corso," he shouted from the corridor, "you'd better come, too."

The skinless man got up and followed Blas from the room. The door closed.

"Blas," Helen said forlornly. "So the Fireclown has been lying to us."

"Who is he?"

"Suspected head of the arms syndicate." She sighed. "*Damn!* Oh, damn the Fireclown!"

The woman, a full-bodied brunette with a sensuously generous mouth, got up from her seat.

She stared down at Alain, regarding him closely. Helen glared at her.

"And what part do *you* play in this?" she asked.

"A very ordinary one," she said. "The Fireclown's my lover."

"Then your lover's a cunning liar," Helen snorted.

"I shouldn't condemn him until you know what he's doing," the woman said sharply.

The three of them were alone together now that Kurt had left too.

"You're disappointed, aren't you?" the woman said, looking candidly at Helen. "You wanted the Fireclown to be some sort of saviour, pointing the direction for the world to go. Well, you're wrong. And those who think he's a destroyer are wrong also. He is simply what he is — the Fireclown. He acts according to some inner drive which I have never been able to fathom and which I don't think he understands or bothers about himself."

"How long have you known him?" Helen asked.

"Some years. We met on Mars. My name's Cornelia Fisher."

"I've heard of you." Helen stared at the woman in curiosity. "You were a famous beauty when I was quite young. You disappeared suddenly. So you went to Mars. Hardly the place for a woman like you, was it? You must be over forty but you don't look thirty."

Cornelia Fisher smiled. "Thanks to the Fireclown, I suppose. Yes, I went to Mars. The life of a well-known 'beauty', as you call me, is rather boring. I wasn't satisfied with it. I wasn't satisfied with anything. I decided that I was leading a shallow existence and thought I'd find a deeper one on Mars. Of course I was wrong. It was merely less comfortable —" she paused, seeming to think back — "though the peace and quiet helped, and the scenery. I don't know if you've seen it since the revitalization plan was completed but it is very beautiful now.

But I never really lost my ennui until I met the Fireclown."

"He was a Martian, then?" Alain knew there were a few families of second and third generation colonists responsible for working on the revitalization project.

"No. He came to Mars after a spaceship accident. He's from Earth originally. But I don't know much more about him than you do. Once you've been with the Fireclown for a short time, you learn that it doesn't matter who he is or what he does — he's just the Fireclown, and that's enough. It's enough for him, I think, too, though there are strange currents running beneath that greasepaint. Whether he's in control of them or not, I couldn't say."

"His connection with Blas seems to disprove part of what you've said." Alain spoke levelly, unable to decide what to think now.

"I honestly don't know what he and Blas are doing." Cornelia Fisher folded her arms and walked towards her handbag which lay on the chair she'd vacated. She opened it and took out a packet of cigarettes. Alain tried to look unconcerned but he had never seen a nicotine addict before. She offered them defiantly. They both refused, with rapid shakes of their heads. She lit one and inhaled the smoke greedily. "I'd swear he's not buying arms. Why should he? He has no plans of the kind Earth condemns him for having."

"Maybe he doesn't tell you everything," Helen suggested.

"Maybe he doesn't tell me anything because he hasn't got anything to tell me. I don't know."

Alain went to the door and tested it. It was shut firmly.

"Judging by the evidence," he said, "I can only suppose that the accusations made by my grandfather against the Fireclown are basically correct. Those P-bombs were part of the arms syndicate's stock — and we have seen that the Fireclown already knows Blas, who you say, Helen, is the head of the syndicate."

"It's never been proved, of course," she said. "But I'm pretty sure I'm right."

"Then the world *is* in danger. I wonder if the Fireclown would listen to reason."

"His kind of reason is different from ours," said Cornelia Fisher.

"If I see him again, I'll try. He's too good to get mixed up in this sordid business. He has a tremendous personality — he could use his talents to…" Alain's voice trailed off. What could the Fireclown use his talents for?

Cornelia Fisher raised her eyebrows. "His talents to do what? What does safe little Terra want with men of talent and vision? Society doesn't need them any more."

"That's a foolish thing to say." Helen was angry. "A complex society like ours needs expert government and leaders more than ever before. We emerged from muddle and disorder over a hundred years ago. We're progressing in a definite direction now. We know what we want to do, and if Blas and his friends don't spoil it with their plots and schemings we'll do it eventually. The only argument today is *how*. Planned progress. It was a dream for ages and now it's a reality. Until this arms trouble blew up there were no random factors. We had turned politics into an exact science, at long last."

"Random factors have a habit of emerging sooner or later," Alain pointed out. "If it wasn't the nuclear stock-piles it would have been something else. And those random factors, if they don't throw us too far out of gear, are what we need to stop us getting complacent and sterile."

"I'd rather not be blown to smithereens," Helen said.

"The Fireclown isn't a danger to you, I know." Cornelia Fisher sounded as if she was less convinced than earlier.

"We'll soon know if the ARP fail to get hold of those stock-piles." Helen's voice sounded a bit shaky. Alain went over to her and put his arm round her comfortingly.

A short time later the Fireclown returned, seemingly excited. Blas was not with him. Alain couldn't guess at Corso's expression. He could only see the red flesh of his face, looking like so much animated butcher's meat.

"Did you get some more P-bombs?" Helen asked mockingly.

The Fireclown ignored her.

Corso said: "What are you hinting at, Fräulein Curtis?"

"I know Blas is head of the arms syndicate."

"Well, that's more than we do. Blas is supplying us with materials for our ship, the *Pi-meson*, which we badly need. There has been no talk of armaments."

"Not a very convincing lie," Helen sneered.

Now Corso also ignored Helen. He watched the Fireclown in a way that a mother cat might watch her young — warily yet tenderly. Corso seemed to play nursemaid to the clown in some ways.

"It will take time to fit," said the Fireclown suddenly. "But thank God we could get them. We couldn't possibly have made them ourselves."

His gaudy red and yellow costume swirled around him as he turned to grin at Alain.

"I wonder if you'd want to," he mused mysteriously.

"Want to what?" Alain asked.

"Come for a trip in the *Pi-meson*. I think it would do you good."

"Why me? And what kind of good?"

"You could only judge that for yourself."

"Then you could dispose of us in deep space, is that it?" Helen said. "We've seen too much, eh?"

The Fireclown heaved a gusty sigh. "Do as you like, young woman. I've no axe to grind. Whatever takes place on Earth has no importance for me now. I tried to tell the people something, but it's obvious I didn't get through to them. Let the darkness sweep down and engulf your hollow kind. I care not."

"It's no good." Helen shook her head. "I can't believe anything you say. Not now."

"If you had it wouldn't have made any difference." Corso's ghastly face grinned. "The rest of the world lost faith in their idol, and the world hates nothing so much as an idol who turns out to have feet of clay! Not, of course, that the clown wished to be one in the first place."

"Then why did you start that set-up on the first level? Why did he make speeches to thousands. Why did he let them adore him at his 'audiences'?" Helen's voice was high, near-hysterical.

As Alain watched and listened, a mood of absolute detachment filled him. He didn't really care about the pros and cons any more. He only wondered what the Fireclown's reasons were for suggesting the trip.

"The Fireclown was originally living down there in secret. We were working on our machines. We needed help — scientists and technicians — so we asked for it, got it. But the scientists told their friends about the Fireclown. They began to ask him about things. He told them. All he did, in the final analysis, was supply an outlet for their emotional demands."

Helen fell silent.

Alain came to a decision.

"I'd like to take that trip," he said — "if Helen can come, too."

"Good!" The Fireclown's resonant voice seemed suddenly gay. "I should like to take you. I'm glad. Yes. Glad."

Both Alain and Helen waited for the Fireclown to add to this statement, but they were disappointed. He went and leaned against a bulkhead, his great face bent towards his chest, his whole manner abstracted.

Was he thinking of the trip? Alain wondered. Or had he simply forgotten about them now they had agreed to go?

Somehow, he felt the latter was the more likely answer.

The Fireclown seemed a peculiar mixture of idiot and intellectual. Alain decided that he was probably insane, but what this insanity might lead to — the destruction of Earth? — could not easily be assessed. He must wait. And perhaps he would learn from the trip, wherever it took them. Mars, possibly, or Ganymede.

Helen was getting understandably restless. Five hours had passed and the Fireclown still stood in the position he had taken up against the bulkhead. Corso and Cornelia Fisher had talked sporadically with Alain, but Helen had refused to join in. Alain felt for her. She had placed all her hopes on gaining information from the Fireclown and, he guessed, she had desperately wanted him to disprove the allegations now being made against him on Earth. But, frustratingly, they were no nearer to getting an explanation; were worse confused, if anything.

If he had been studying any other individual, Alain would have suspected the Fireclown of sleeping with his eyes open. But there was no suggestion of slumber about the clown's attitude. He was, it seemed, meditating on some problem that concerned him. Possibly the nature of the problem was such that an ordinary man would see no logic or point in solving it.

The Fireclown seemed to exist in his own time-sphere, and his mind was unfathomable.

At last the grotesque giant moved.

"Now," he rumbled, "the *Pi-meson* will be ready. We have been lucky to find shelter with the monks, for they are probably the only men who can come close to understanding the nature of the ship, and doubtless they will have done their work by now. Come." He moved towards the door.

Alain glanced at Helen and then at the other two. Corso and Cornelia Fisher remained where they were. Helen got up slowly. The Fireclown was already thumping up the corridor before they reached the door.

"I hope you know what you're doing," she whispered. "I'm afraid, Alain. What if his plan *is* to kill us?"

"Maybe it is." He tried to sound self-possessed. "But he could do that just as easily here as in deep space, couldn't he?"

"There are several ways of dying." She held his hand and he noticed she was shivering. He had never realized before that anyone could be so afraid of death. Momentarily he felt a sympathy with her fears.

They followed the gaudy figure of the Fireclown until they reached the bay section.

Auditor Kurt was there.

"They have just finished," he told the Fireclown, spinning the wheel of the manually operated airlock. "Your equations were perfectly correct — it was we who were at fault. The field is functioning with one hundred per cent accuracy. Five of us were completely exhausted feeding it. Blas being able to supply those parts was a great stroke of luck."

The Fireclown nodded his thanks and all three stepped through the short tunnel of the airlocks and entered a surprisingly large landing deck. Alain, who had seen the *Pi-meson* from space, wondered how it could be so big, for a considerable portion of spaceships was taken up with engines and fuel.

Touching a stud, the Fireclown closed the ship's lock. A section of the interior wall slid upwards, revealing a short flight of steps. They climbed the steps and were on a big control deck. The covered ports were extremely large, comprising more than half the area of the walls. Controls varied — some familiar, some not. And there were many scarcely functional features — rich, red plush couches and chairs, fittings of gold or brass, heavy velvet curtains of yellow and dark blue hung against the ports. It all looked bizarre and faintly archaic, reminding Alain, in a way, of his grandfather's study.

"I shall darken the room," the Fireclown announced. "I can operate the ship better that way. Sit where you will."

The Fireclown did not sit down as Alain and Helen sat together in one of the comfortable couches. He stood at the controls, his huge bulk blotting out half the instruments from Alain's sight. He stretched a hand towards a switch and flicked it up. The lights dimmed slowly and then they were in cold blackness.

Helen gripped Alain's arm and he patted her knee, his mind on other things as a low whining arose from the floor.

Alain sensed tension in the Fireclown's movements heard from the darkness. He tried to analyze them but failed. He saw a screen suddenly light with bright whiteness, colour flashed and swirled and they saw a vision of space.

But against the darkness of the cosmos, the spheres which rolled on the screen, flashing by like shoals of multicoloured billiard balls, were unrecognizable as any heavenly bodies Alain had ever seen. Not asteroids by any means, not planets — they were too solid in colour and general appearance; they shone, but not with the glitter of reflected sunlight. And they passed swiftly by in hordes.

Moved by the beauty, astonished by the unexpected sight, Alain couldn't voice the questions which flooded into his mind.

In the faint light from the screen the Fireclown's silhouette could be seen in constant motion. The whining had ceased. The spheres on the screen began to jump and progress more slowly. The picture jerked and one sphere, smoky blue in colour, began to grow until the whole screen itself glowed blue. Then it seemed to burst and they flashed towards the fragments, then through them, and saw — a star.

"Sol," commented the Fireclown.

They were getting closer and closer to the sun.

"We'll burn up!" Alain cried fearfully.

"No — the *Pi-meson* is a special ship. I've avoided any chance of us burning. See the flames!"

The flames… Alain thought that the word scarcely described the curling, writhing wonder of those shooting sheets of fire. The control deck was not noticeably warmer, yet Alain felt hot just looking.

The Fireclown was roaring his enigmatic laughter, his arm pointing at the screen.

"There," he shouted, his voice too loud in the confines of the cabin. "There, get used to that for a moment. Look!"

They could not help but look. Both were fascinated, held by the sight. And yet Alain felt his eyes ache and was certain he would be blinded by the brightness.

The Fireclown strode to another panel and turned a knob.

The port coverings began to rise slowly and light flowed in a searing stream into the cabin, brightening everything to an extraordinary degree.

When the ports were fully open, Alain shouted his wonder. It seemed they were in the very heart of the sun. Why weren't they made sightless by the glare? Why didn't they burn?

"This is impossible!" Alain whispered. "We should have been destroyed in a second. What is this — an illusion of some sort? Have you hypno —?"

"Be quiet," said the Fireclown, his shape a blob of blackness in the incredible light. "I'll explain later — if it is possible to make you understand."

Hushed, they let themselves be drawn out into the dancing glare.

Alain's soul seemed full for the first time, it even seemed natural that he should be here. He felt affinity with the flames. He began to identify with them, until he *was* them.

Time stopped.

Thought stopped.

Life alone remained.

Then blackness swam back. From far away he observed that his rigid body was being shaken, that a voice was bellowing in his ear.

"… you have seen! You have *seen*! Now you know. *Now* you know! Come back — there is more to see!"

Shocked, it seemed, back into his body, he opened his eyes. He could see nothing still, but felt the grip on his shoulders and knew that the Fireclown, his voice excited — perhaps insane — shouted in front of his face. "That is why I call myself the Fireclown. I am full of the joy of the flames of life!"

"How…?" The word stumbled hoarsely from his lips.

But the Fireclown's hands left his shoulders and he heard the man screaming at Helen, shaking her also.

There could be no fear now, Alain decided. Though, earlier, he might have been perturbed by the Fireclown's ravings, he now half-ignored them, aware that there was no need to listen.

What he demanded now was an explanation.

"How could we have seen that and lived?" he shouted roughly, groping out to seize the Fireclown's tattered clothing and tug at it. "*How?*"

He heard Helen mumble. Satisfied, the Fireclown moved away from her, jerking himself free from Alain's grip.

He got up and followed the Fireclown through the blackness, touched his body again, sensing the tremendous strength in the man.

The Fireclown shook with humour again.

"Give me a moment," he laughed. "I have to feed the ship further directions."

Alain heard him reach the control panel, heard him make adjustments to studs and levers, heard the now familiar whine. He groped his way back to Helen. She put her arms round him. She was crying.

"What's the matter?"

"Nothing. Really — nothing. It's just the — the emotion, I suppose."

The lights came on.

Arms akimbo, the Fireclown stood grinning down at them.

"I see you are somewhat stunned. I had hoped to turn you mad — but you are obviously too entrenched in your own narrow 'sanity' to be helped. That grieves me."

"You promised me you would explain," Alain reminded him shakily.

"If you could understand, I said, if you remember. I'll explain a little. I am not yet ready to tell you my full reason for bringing you with me. Now, see…" He turned and depressed a stud and a section of one port slid up to reveal normal space, with the sun flaring — still near, but not so near as to be dangerous. "We have returned to our ordinary state for a while. Now you see the sun as any traveler would see it from this region of space. What do you think of it?"

"*Think* of it? I don't understand you."

"Good."

"What are you getting at?"

"How important do the conflicts taking place on Earth seem to you now?"

"I haven't..." He couldn't find the words. They were important, still. Did the Fireclown think that this experience, transcendental as it might have been, could alter his view of Earth's peril?

Impatiently, the Fireclown turned to Helen.

"Is your ambition to become President of Earth still as strong as it was, Fräulein Curtis?"

She nodded. "This — vision or whatever it was — has no bearing on what are, as far as you're concerned, mundane problems relating to our society. I still want to do my best in politics. It has changed nothing. I have probably benefited from the experience. If that's the case, I shall be better equipped to deal with Earth affairs."

The Fireclown snorted, but Alain felt Helen had never sounded so self-confident as she did now.

"I still want to know how you achieved the effect," Alain insisted.

"Very well. Put simply, we shunted part of ourselves and part of the ship out of normal time and hovered, as it were, on its edges, unaffected by many of its rules."

"But that's impossible. Scientists have never..."

"If it was impossible, Alain von Bek, it couldn't have happened and you couldn't have experienced it. As for your scientists, they have never bothered to enquire. I discovered the means of doing this after an experience which almost killed me and certainly affected my thought processes.

"The sun almost killed me, realize that. But I bear it no malice. You and I and the ship existed in a kind of time freeze. The ship's computer has a 'mind' constructed according to my own definitions — they are meaningless to the rigidly thinking scientists of Earth but they work for me because I am *the Fireclown!*

"I am unique, for I survived death by fire. And fire gave my brain life — brought alive inspiration, knowledge!" He pointed back at the sun, now dwindling behind them.

"There is the fire that gave birth to Earth and fed its denizens with vitality. Worship it — *worship it* in gratitude, for without it you would not and could not exist. *There* is truth — perhaps the sum of truth. It flames, living, and *is*; self-sufficient, careless of *why*, for *why* is a question that need not — cannot — be answered. We are fools to ask it."

"Would you, then, deny man his intellect?" Alain asked firmly. "For that is what your logic suggests. Should we have stayed in the caves, not using the brains which —" he shrugged — "the sun, if you like, gave us? Not using an entire part of ourselves — the part which sets us over the animals, which enabled us to live as weaklings in a world of the strong and the savage, to speculate, to build and to *plan*? You say we should be content merely to exist — I say we should *think*. And if our existence is meaningless then our thoughts might, in time, give it meaning."

The Fireclown shook his painted head.

"I knew you would not understand," he said sadly.

"There is no communication between us," Alain said. "I am sane, you are mad."

The Fireclown, for the first time, seemed hurt by Alain's pronouncement. Quietly, without his usual zest, he said: "I know the truth. I know it."

"Men down the ages have known a truth such as the one you know. You are not unique, Fireclown. Not in history."

"I am unique, Alain von Bek, for one reason if none other. I have seen the truth for myself. And you shall see it, perhaps. Did you not become absorbed into the fire of the sun. Did you not lose all niggling need for meaning therein?"

"Yes. The forces are overwhelming, I admit. But they are not everything."

The Fireclown opened his mouth and once more bellowed with laughter. "Then you shall see more."

He closed the port and the room darkened.

"Where are we going?" Helen demanded grimly, antagonistically.

But the Fireclown only laughed, and laughed, and laughed, until the strange spheres began to roll across the screen again. Then he was silent.

CHAPTER ELEVEN

Hours seemed to pass and Helen dozed in Alain's arms. Alain too, was half-asleep, mesmerized by the coloured spheres on the screen.

He came fully awake as the spheres began to jerk and slow. A bright red filled the screen, divided itself into fragments.

More spheres appeared, but these were suns.

Suns. A profusion of suns as closely packed as the planets to Sol. Huge, blue suns, green, yellow and silver suns.

A thousand suns moving in stately procession around the ship.

The screens slid up from the ports and light, ever changing, flickered through the cabin.

"Where are we?" Helen gasped.

"The centre of the galaxy," the Fireclown announced grandly.

All around them the huge discs of flame, of all colours and all possible blends of colour, spun at extraordinary speeds, passing by in an orbit about an invisible point.

Alain, once again, could not retain his self-possession. Something within him forced him to look and wonder at the incredible beauty. These were the oldest suns in the galaxy. They had lived and died and lived again for billions of years. Here was the source of life, the beginnings of everything.

Though the Fireclown would probably have denied it, the vision was — profound. It had significance of such magnitude that Alain was unable to grasp it. Philosophically, he resigned himself to never knowing what the experience implied. He felt that the Fireclown's belief of existence without significance beyond itself was preposterous, yet he could see how one could arrive at such a conclusion. He himself was forced to cling to his shredding personality. The whirling stars dwarfed him, dwarfed his ideas, dwarfed the aspirations of humanity.

"Now," chuckled the Fireclown in his joyous insanity, "what is Earth and all its works compared with the blazing simplicity of — *this!*"

Helen spoke with difficulty. "They are — different," she said. "They are linked, because they all exist together, but they are different. This is the order of created matter. We seek an order of cognizant matter and the stars, however mighty, however beautiful, have no cognizance. They might perish at some stage. Man, because he thinks, may one day make himself immortal — not personally, perhaps, but through the continuance of his race. I think that is the difference."

The Fireclown shrugged.

"You have wondered what is real, have you not? You have wondered that we have lost touch with the realities, we human beings; that our language is decadent and that it has produced a double-thinking mentality which no longer allows us contact with the natural facts?"

He waved his hands to take in the circling suns.

"Intelligence! It is nothing, it is unimportant, a freak thrown up by a chance combination of components. Why is intelligence so esteemed? There is no need for it. It cannot change the structure of the multiverse — it can only meddle and spoil it. *Awareness* — now, that's different. Nature is aware of itself, but that is all — it is content. Are we content? No! When I go to Earth and try to convey what I know to the people, I am conscious of entering a dream world. They cannot understand me because they are unaware! All I do, sadly, is awaken archetypal responses in them which throws them further out, so they run around like randy pigs, destroying. Destroying, building, both acts are equally unimportant. We are at the centre of the galaxy. Here things exist. They are beautiful but their beauty has no purpose. It is *beauty* — it is enough. They are full of natural force but the force has no expression; it is force alone, and that is all it needs to be.

"Why ascribe meaning to all this? The further away from the fundamentals of life we go, the more we quest for their meaning. There *is* no meaning. It is here. It has always been here in some state. It will always be here. That is all we can ever truly know. It is all we should want to know."

Alain shook his head, speaking vaguely at first. "A short time ago," he said, "I was struck by the pettiness of political disputes, horrified by the ends to which people would go to get power — or 'responsibility' as they call it — feeling that the politicians in the Solar House were expending breath on meaningless words..."

"So they were!" the Fireclown bellowed back at him approvingly.

"No." Alain plugged on, certain he was near the truth. "If you wished to convince me of this when you took us on this voyage, you have achieved the opposite. Admittedly, as one observes them at the time, the politicians seem to be getting nowhere, society detaches itself further and further from the kind of life its ancestors lived. Yet, seeing these suns, entering the heart of our own sun, has shown me that this stumbling progress — *unaware* gropings in the dark immensity of the universe, if you like — is as much a natural function as any other."

Gustily, the Fireclown sighed.

"I felt I could help you, Alain von Bek. I see you have fled further back into your fortress of prejudice." He closed the port covers. "Sit down — sleep if you wish. I am returning to the monastery."

They berthed and entered the monastery in silence. The Fireclown seemed depressed, even worried. Had he seen that, for all his discoveries, for all his vision and vitality, he was not necessarily right? Alain wondered. There was no knowing. The Fireclown remained still the enigmatic, intellectual madman — the naïve, ingenuous, endearing figure he had been when Alain first saw him.

Auditor Kurt greeted them. "We are looking at our weekly V-cast. Would you like to come and watch? It might interest you."

He took them to a small room where several monks were already seated. Corso was there, too, and Cornelia Fisher. At the door the Fireclown seemed to rouse himself from his mood.

"I have things to consider," he told them, walking away down the corridor.

They went in and sat down. The V-screen was blank. Evidently the amount of viewing allowed the monks was limited.

Corso came and sat next to them. Alain was getting used to his apparently skinless face.

"Well," he said good-naturedly, "did your voyage enlighten you?"

"In a way," Alain admitted.

"But not in the way he intended, I think." Helen smiled a trifle wistfully, as if she wished the Fireclown had convinced them.

"How did he hit on the discovery that enables him to travel so easily and to such dangerous parts?" Alain said.

"Call it inspiration," Corso answered. "I'm not up to understanding him, either, you know. We were co-pilots on an experimental ship years ago. Something went wrong with the ship — the steering devices locked and pushed us towards the sun. We managed, narrowly, to avoid plunging into the sun's heart and went into orbit. But we were fried. Refrigeration collapsed slowly. I suffered worse in some ways. It took my skin off, as you can see. My fellow pilot — the Fireclown to you, these days — didn't suffer so badly physically, but something happened to his mind. You'd say he was mad. I'd say he was sane in a different way from you and me. Whatever happened, he worked out the principle for the *Pi-meson* in the Martian hospital — we were rescued, quite by chance, by a very brave crew of a freighter which had gone slightly off course itself. If that hadn't happened, we'd both be dead now. We were in hospital for years. The clown pretended amnesia and I did the same. For some reason we were never contacted by Spaceflight Research."

"How did you get the money to build the *Pi-meson?*"

"We got it from Blas, the man you accused of being an arms dealer. He thinks the ship is a super-fast vessel but otherwise ordinary enough. He supplied us with computer parts this time."

"Where is Blas now?"

"The last I heard he had a suite at the London Dorchester."

"The Dorchester? That's reasonable — a man could hide in the Mayfair slums and nobody would know."

"I think you don't do Blas justice. He's an idealist. He wants progress more than anyone. He wouldn't have any part in blowing the world up. At least..." Corso paused. "He's a funny character, but I don't think so."

Alain was quiet for a while. Then he said:

"After that trip, I think I do believe you when you say you're not implicated in the arms dealers' plans — not knowingly, anyway. At least the Fireclown has satisfied me on that score, even if he didn't achieve his main object." He turned to Helen. "What about you?"

"I agree." She nodded. "But I'd give a lot to know Blas's motives in helping you." She looked at Corso. "Are you telling us everything?"

"Everything I can," he said ambiguously.

The V-screen came to life. A news broadcast.

The newscaster bent eagerly towards the camera.

"It's fairly sure who the next President will be, folks. Simon von Bek, the one man to recognize the peril we are in from the infamous Fireclown's insane plot to destroy the world, is top of this station's public opinion poll. His niece, the only strong opponent in the elections which begin next week, has dropped right down. Her violent support of the Fireclown hasn't helped a bit. Rumour circulates that Fräulein Curtis and Minister von Bek's grandson, Alain von Bek, have disappeared together. Strange that two people who were seen publicly fighting in the recent riots should have teamed up."

Shot of Simon von Bek in his home, a smug expression on his powerful old face.

Reporter: "Minister von Bek, you were the first to discover the bomb plot. How did it happen?"

Von Bek: "I suspected the Fireclown from the start. I don't blame people for being duped by his talk — we're all human, after all — but a responsible politician has to look below the surface..."

Reporter (murmuring): "And we're all very grateful."

"I made sure that a constant check was kept on his activities," Simon von

Bek continued, "and thus was able to avert what might have been a terrible crime — the ultimate crime, one might say. Even now the threat of this man still trying to bombard the Earth from some secret hiding place is enormous. We must be wary. We must take steps to ensure his capture or, failing that, ensure our own defense."

"Quite so. Thank you, Minister von Bek."

"Everything's calm again in Swiss City," announced the newscaster as he faded in, "and we're back to normal after the riots and subsequent fire which swept sixteen levels yesterday. The Fireclown's victims number over three hundred men, women — and little children. We were all duped, folks, as Minister von Bek has pointed out. But we'll know better next time, won't we? The freak hysteria has died as swiftly as it blew up. But now we're watching the skies — for the search for the Fireclown seems to prove that he has left Earth and may now be hiding out on Mars or Ganymede. If he's got bombs up there, too, we must be ready for him!"

Although angered, Alain was also amused by the V-man's double-thinking ability. He, like the rest, had done a quick about-face and now Simon von Bek, ex-villain and victimizer, was the hero of the hour.

But the hysteria, he realized, had not, in fact, died down. It had taken a different turn. Now there was a bomb scare. Though he hadn't planned it that way, Alain thought, Simon von Bek could easily be falling into the arms syndicate's plot, for this scare was just what they needed to start trouble. As soon as he got the chance he was going to tell the police about Blas and the Dorchester — or else go there himself and confront the arms dealer.

He didn't bother to watch the V-cast but turned to Helen.

"We'd better try to get the Fireclown to let us go as soon as possible," he said worriedly. "There's things to be done on Earth."

"Apart from anything else," she pointed out, "I've got an election to fight!"

A chuckle behind her, full-throated and full of humour, made her turn and look up at the Fireclown's gaudy bulk filling the doorway.

"You are persistent, Fräulein Curtis. Even a journey into the heart of the sun does nothing to change your mind. You'll be pleased to hear that we are leaving very soon and you'll be able to return to Earth. But first..." He looked directly at Alain, stared into his eyes so that Alain felt a strange thrill run through him, partly fear, partly joy. There was no doubt that the Fireclown's magnetism was something apart from his strange ideas. "I must talk with you, Alain von Bek — alone. Will you follow me?"

Alain followed. They entered a room decorated with marvelous oil paintings, all of them depicting the sun seen in different ways.

"Did you do these?" Alain was impressed as the Fireclown nodded. "You could have put more across to the public by displaying them than with all that talking you did," he said.

"I didn't think of it. These are private." The Fireclown indicated a metal bench for Alain to sit on. "No-one comes here but me. You are the first."

"I feel honoured," Alain said ironically. "But why me?"

The Fireclown's huge chest heaved as he took an enormous breath. "Because you and I have something in common," he said.

Alain smiled, but kindly. "I should say that's extremely unlikely judging by our earlier conversations."

"I don't mean ideas." The Fireclown moved about — like a caged lion. There was no other analogy to describe his restless pacing, Alain thought. "I regret that I've been unable to convince you. I regret it deeply, for I am not normally given to regretting *anything*, you know. What happens, happens — that is all. I should have said we have *someone* in common."

"Who?" Alain was half-dazed already, for he thought he knew what the Fireclown was going to say.

"Your mother," grunted the Fireclown. The words took time coming out of this man, normally so verbose.

"*You are my son, Alain.*"

CHAPTER TWELVE

"My father..." Alain groped for words, failed, became silent. The Fireclown spread his large hands, his painted fool's face incongruous now.

"I was, in spite of anything you may have heard, much in love with your mother. We planned to marry, though Simon von Bek wouldn't hear of it. I was a common space-pilot and she was Miriam von Bek. That was before we could find the courage to tell him you were going to be born. We never did tell him — not together, anyway."

"What happened?" Alain spoke harshly, his heart thumping with almost overwhelming emotion.

"I got sent on a secret project. I couldn't avoid it. I thought it would only last a couple of months but it kept me away for nearly two years. When I got back Simon von Bek wouldn't let me near you — and your mother was dead. Von Bek said she'd died of shame. I sometimes think he shamed her into dying." The Fireclown broke into a laugh but, unlike his earlier laughter, this was bitter and full of melancholy.

Alain stood up, his body taut.

"What's your real name? What did you do? What did my grandfather say?"

The Fireclown ceased his laughter and shrugged his great shoulders.

"My real name — Emmanuel Blumenthal — Manny Bloom to my friends..."

"And fans," Alain said softly, remembering a book he'd had confiscated as a child. His grandfather had, meaninglessly he'd thought, taken it from him with no explanation. The book had been called *Heroes of Space*. "Manny Bloom, test pilot of the *Tearaway*, captain of the Saturn Expedition. That was the secret project, wasn't it? Saviour of Venus Satellite Seven."

"Co-pilot of the *Solstar*..." the Fireclown added.

"That's right — the *Solstar*, an experimental ship. It was supposed to have gone off course and crashed into the sun. You were reported dead."

"But a Martian freighter, carrying contraband so that it dare not notify the authorities or land in an official port, rescued us."

"Corso told me. That was ten years ago, as I remember. Why have you never contacted me? Why didn't you get custody of me when you came back from Saturn and found my mother was dead?"

"Simon von Bek threatened to ruin me if I went near you. I was — heartbroken. Heartbroken — yes — but I reckoned you'd have a better chance than any I could give you."

"I wonder," Alain said gloomily. "A kid would have been happy just knowing his father was Manny Bloom — Commander Manny Bloom, frontiersman of space!" The last phrase held a hint of irony.

"I wasn't like the stories, though I thought I was when younger. I loved my own legend then, had it in mind nearly all the time. I wasn't naturally brave. But people behave as other people expect them to — I acted brave."

"And now you're the Fireclown, shouting and raving against intelligence — championing mindless consciousness with your fingerprints burned off, I suppose, and no records of who you really are. That's part of the general mystery solved, anyway. And part of my own — the main part."

"And now you know I'm your father, what will you do?"

"What can the knowledge possibly affect?" Alain said sadly.

"Your subconscious." The Fireclown grinned, half-enjoying a private joke against his son.

"Yes, that, I suppose." He sighed. "What are you going to do?"

"I have work that holds me. Soon Corso, Cornelia and I will journey out beyond the Solar System in the *Pi-meson*. There I shall conduct certain experiments on my own mind and on theirs. We shall see what good intelligence serves — and what great good, I suspect, pure consciousness achieves. Then we shall walk the roads between the worlds. Do you want to come, Alain?"

Alain deliberated. He had no place with the Fireclown. There were things to sort out on Earth. He shook his head.

"It grieves me to see you reject a gift — maybe the greatest gift in the multiverse!"

"It is not a gift that suits my taste — father."

"So be it," the Fireclown sighed.

The *Solar Bird* soared down into Earth's atmosphere and streaked across oceans and continents before Helen switched on its braking jets and plunged into Hamburg spaceport.

The berth was ready for her and she steered into it. The water drained from the interior chamber.

Alain preceded her out of the airlock.

As he stepped into the chamber, a man entered through the other door.

"My God, von Bek, where've you been?" It was Denholm Curtis, a mixture of worry and anger on his face.

Alain didn't answer immediately but turned to help Helen out of the ship. He didn't need the pause since he had already worked out his answer.

"We've been to see my father."

"Your father! I didn't know you..."

"I only found out who he was recently."

"I see. Well..." Curtis was nonplused. "I wish you and Helen had told me."

"Sorry. We had to leave in a hurry. Your ship's perfectly all right."

"The ship's not important — it was you and Helen..." Curtis pursed his lips. "Anyway, I'm glad that's all it was. What with the threat of the Fireclown making an attack and everything, I thought you might have been kidnapped or killed." He smiled at his sister, who didn't respond. Helen had been silent for most of the trip. "But rumours about the pair of you are rife. Scandal won't do either of you any good — least of all Helen. Uncle Simon's popularity is rising incredibly. Overnight he's become the dominant man in Solar politics. You've got a tough fight on — if you still *intend* to fight."

"More than ever," Helen said quietly.

"I've got a car upstairs. Want to come back with me?"

"Thanks," they said.

As her brother lifted his car into the pale Hamburg sky Helen said to him: "What do you think of this Fireclown scare, Denholm?"

"It's more than a scare," he said. "It's a reality. How can we be sure he hasn't planted bombs all over the world — bombs he can detonate from space?"

Alain felt depressed. If Denholm Curtis, who rebelled habitually against any accepted theory or dogma, was convinced of the Fireclown's guilt then there was little chance of convincing anyone else to the contrary.

"But do you realize, Denholm," he said, "that we have only the word of one man — Simon von Bek — and circumstantial evidence to go on? What if the Fireclown isn't guilty?"

"The concept's too remote for me, I'm afraid," Denholm said with a curious glance at Alain. "I didn't think anyone doubted the Fireclown had planned to detonate his cache. There were enough bombs there to blow the world apart."

"I doubt if he planned anything," Helen said.

"So do I." Alain nodded.

Denholm looked surprised. "I can understand you being uncertain, Helen, after your support of the Fireclown. It must be hard to find out you've been wrong all the way down the line. But you, Alain — what makes you think there could be a mistake?"

"There's the one big reason — that all the evidence against the Fireclown is circumstantial. He might not have known about the bombs, he might not have been responsible for the holocaust that swept the levels. He might not, in fact, have had any plan to destroy anything at all. We haven't captured him yet, we haven't brought him to trial — but we've all automatically judged him guilty. I want to see my grandfather — he's the man who has convinced the world that the Fireclown is a criminal!"

Curtis was thoughtful. "I never thought I'd get caught up in hysteria," he said. "But, although I'm fairly sure the Fireclown is guilty, I admit there's a possibility of his being innocent. If we could prove him *innocent*, Alain, the war scare would be over. I'm already perturbed about that. You know the government has been approached by the arms syndicate?" This last remark to Helen.

"It's logical." Helen nodded. "And we've also considered the chance that this whole thing has been engineered by the dealers — not the clown."

"That crossed my mind, too, at first," Denholm agreed. "But it seems too fantastic."

"Let's go and have this out with the Man of the Moment," Alain suggested. "Can you take us to grandfather's apartment, Denholm?"

"Take you? I'll come with you."

As the trio entered Simon von Bek's apartment, they were greeted by Junnar.

"Glad to see you're both all right," he said to Alain and Helen. "Minister von Bek is in conference with the President, Chief Sandai, Minister Petrovich and others."

"What's it about?" asked Alain, unwilling to be put off.

"The Fireclown situation."

"So that's what they're calling it now!" Alain said with a faint smile. "You'd better disturb them, Junnar. Tell them we've got some fresh information for them."

"Is it important, sir?"

"Yes!" Helen and Alain said in unison.

Junnar took them into the sitting room, where they waited impatiently for a few moments before he came back, nodding affirmatively.

They entered Simon von Bek's study. The most powerful politicians in the Solar System sat there — von Bek, Benjosef, gloomy-faced Petrovich, Minister in the Event of Defense, hard-featured Gregorius, Minister of Justice, smooth-skinned, red-cheeked Falkoner, Minister of Martian Affairs, and tiny, delicate

Madame Ch'u, Minister of Ganymedian Affairs. Beside the mantelpiece, standing relaxed and looking bored, was a man Alain didn't recognize. His eyes were at once amiable and deadly.

Simon von Bek said harshly: "Well, Alain, I hope you've got an explanation for your disappearance. Where have you been?"

"To see the Fireclown." Alain's voice was calm.

"But you said…" Denholm Curtis broke in.

"I had to tell you something, Denholm. That was before I decided to come here."

"The Fireclown! You know his whereabouts?" von Bek glanced at the tall man by the mantelpiece. "Why didn't you tell us immediately you knew?"

"I didn't know for certain until I found him."

"Where is he?" Von Bek turned to address the tall man. "Iopedes, be ready to get after him!"

"I met him in space," Alain said carefully. "We went aboard his spaceship. He won't be in the same region of space now. He wouldn't let us go until he'd moved on."

"Damn!" Simon von Bek got up. "We've got every ship of the three planets combing space for him and you discovered him by chance. Did you learn anything?"

"Yes." Somewhere, in the last few actionful days, Alain had found strength. He was in perfect control of himself. He addressed the entire group, ignoring his fuming grandfather.

"I believe the Fireclown to be innocent of any deliberate act of violence," he announced calmly.

"You'll have to substantiate that, Herr von Bek," purred Madame Ch'u, looking at him quizzically.

"How do you know?" Simon von Bek strode over to his grandson and gripped his arm painfully.

"I know because I spent some hours in the Fireclown's company and he told me he had nothing to do with the bomb plot or the burning of the levels."

"That's all?" Von Bek's fingers tightened on Alain's arm.

"That's all I needed," Alain said, and then in a voice which only his grandfather could hear: "Let go of my arm, grandfather. It hurts."

Simon von Bek glared at him and released his grip. "Don't tell me you're still being gulled by this monster! Helen — you saw him, too — what did you think?"

"I agree with Alain. He says the policemen tampered with his delicate flame-machines and that's what caused the holocaust. He says he knew nothing of the bombs. I suspect they were planted on him by the arms syndicate — in order to start the scare which you're now helping to foster."

"In short," Alain said, "I think this whole business has been engineered by the syndicate."

The room was silent.

Alain pressed his point. "I think you've all been blinded by the apparent discovery that the Fireclown wasn't what he at first seemed. Now you've turned completely against him — you believe him capable of any crime!"

"Herr von Bek —" Petrovich spoke with an air of assumed patience — "we are the government of the Solar System. We are not in the habit of jumping to ill-considered and emotional conclusions."

"Then you're not human," Alain said sharply. "Everyone can make mistakes, Minister Petrovich — especially in a heated atmosphere like this."

Petrovich smiled patronizingly. "We have considered the place of the arms syndicate in this business. We are sure they are taking advantage of the situation — but we are convinced that they did not 'engineer it', as you say."

Simon von Bek roared: "My grandson's an immature fool! He has no understanding of politics or anything else. When the Fireclown lisps his innocence he believes him without question. Helen Curtis is just as bad. Both of them, to my own knowledge, were on the Fireclown's side from the start. Now they refuse to see the facts!"

The tall man, Iopedes, began to walk towards the door. Simon von Bek called after him. "Iopedes — where are you going?"

"The young people said the Fireclown had left the area of space he was originally occupying. That could indicate he's gone to Mars or Ganymede. It's a better lead than we had, at any rate." Iopedes left.

"Who's he?" Alain said.

"Nick Iopedes, the ARP's top agent. He's been commissioned to bring the Fireclown to justice — by any means he has to employ."

"You're turning the system into a police state!" Helen said angrily.

"There's a state of emergency existing!" Simon von Bek said coldly. "The world — perhaps the Solar System — is threatened with destruction."

"In your mind and in the minds of those you've managed to convince!" Alain retaliated. "Have any bombs exploded? Has any threat been made?"

"No." This was Benjosef, who had hitherto seemed detached from the argument taking place around him.

"And the arms syndicate has approached you with a bargain, I hear." Alain laughed sharply.

"That is true," Benjosef agreed. Quite obviously, he was no longer in control of his cabinet. Simon von Bek dominated it now, as if he had already superseded Benjosef. The old man seemed to accept the situation fatalistically.

"So there's your answer — the syndicate plant the bombs and start the scare.

Then they sell you more bombs to 'defend' yourselves against a non-existent menace! Then what? Another scare — another move by the syndicate — until the seeds of war have been thoroughly planted. Everybody's armed to the teeth and the possibility of conflict between the planets is increased!"

"Oh, that's very pat," Simon von Bek sneered. "But it doesn't fit the evidence. You know what you've done? You've been to see the Fireclown and instead of gaining information which could help us capture him, you've listened to his sweet protestations of innocence and thrown away a chance to help save the world!"

"Really?" Alain said in mock surprise. "Well, I disagree. It seems to me that *you* are taking the world to the brink of destruction, grandfather, by your blind hatred of the Fireclown."

"Leave, Alain!" Simon von Bek's voice shook with anger. The assembled ministers look disturbed and embarrassed by what was, in the main, a family row.

Alain turned and walked out of the door, Helen following him. Denholm Curtis remained in the room, a frown on his face.

Outside, Helen smiled faintly. "Well, we seem to have antagonized everyone, don't we?"

"I'm *sure* we're right!" Alain said. "I'm certain of it, Helen. That trip the Fireclown took us on convinced me. He's too interested in his weird philosophizing to be capable of any plots against the system."

Helen took his arm.

"It's our opinion against theirs, I'm afraid."

"We've got to do something about convincing the ordinary people," Alain said as they descended the steps to the ground floor. "This is still a democracy, and if enough people protest they can be ousted from power and a more sane and rational party can solve the situation better."

"They're sane and reasonable enough," she pointed out. "They just don't happen to believe in the Fireclown's innocence."

"Then what are we going to do about it?"

She looked up at him. "What do you expect? I'm still in the running for President, Alain. I'm still leader of my party. We're going to try and win the election."

CHAPTER THIRTEEN

Director Carson, head of City Administration, looked hard at Alain and nodded understandingly.

"It would be best if you resigned," he agreed. "Though, as far as it goes, you're the ablest assistant I've ever had, Alain. But with things as they are and with you outspoken against Simon von Bek and for the Fireclown, I doubt if City Council would want you to stay on, anyway."

"Then we're both in agreement," Alain said. "I'll leave right away, if that's all right with you, sir."

"We'll manage. Your leave is due soon, anyway. We'll settle up your back-pay and send it to you."

They shook hands. They liked one another and it was obvious that Carson regretted Alain's leaving C.A. But he'd been right.

"What are you going to do now?" Carson said as Alain picked up his briefcase.

"I've got another job. I'm Helen Curtis's personal assistant for the Presidential campaign."

"You're going to need a great deal of luck, then?"

"A great deal," Alain agreed. "Goodbye, sir."

The Radical Liberal Movement's Campaign Committee met at its headquarters. They sat round a long table in the large, well-lighted room. One of the walls comprised a huge V-screen — a usual feature of the windowless apartments in the City of Switzerland.

Helen sat at the head of the table with Alain on her right, Jordan Kalpis, her campaign organizer, on her left. The two heads of the RLM's Press and Information Department sat near her — Horace Wallace, handsome and blank-faced, Andy

Curry, small, freckled, and shifty-eyed — both Scots who had hardly seen Scotland and were yet anachronisms in their pride for their country. National feeling hardly existed these days.

Also at the table were Publicity Chief Mildred Brecht, an angular woman; Vernikoff, Head of Publications and Pamphlets; Sabah, Director of Research, both fat men with unremarkable faces.

Helen said: "Although you've all advised me against it, I intend to conduct my campaign on these lines. One —" she read off a sheet of paper before her — "an insistence that other steps be taken to apprehend whoever was responsible for storing those bombs on the first level. Although we'll agree it's possible that the Fireclown was responsible, we must also pursue different lines of investigation, in case he was not. That covers us — the present policy of concentrating on the pre-judged Fireclown does not."

"That's reasonable," Sabah murmured. "Unless someone reveals that you personally believe the Fireclown innocent."

"Two —" Helen ignored him — "that more money must be spent on interstellar space-flight research — we are becoming unadventurous in our outlook."

"That's a good one." Mildred Brecht nodded.

"It fits our 'forward-looking' image." Curry nodded, too.

"Three, tax concessions to Mars and Ganymede settlers. This will act as an incentive to colonizers. Fourth, price control on sea-farm produce. Fifth, steps must be taken to re-locate certain spaceports now occupying parts of the sea-bed suitable for cultivation..." The list was long and contained many other reforms of a minor nature. There were several short discussions on the exact terms to use for publicizing her proposed policy. Then the means of presenting them.

Mildred Brecht had some suggestions: "I suggest we can stick to old fashioned handbills for the main policy outline. World-wide distribution to every home on Earth. Large size power-posters for display on Earth and the colonies..." She outlined several more means of publicizing the campaign.

Jordan Kalpis, a swarthy, black-haired man with prominent facial bones and pale blue eyes, interrupted Mildred Brecht.

"I think, on the whole, we're agreed already on the main points of Fräulein Curtis's policy as well as the means of publicizing them. We have a sound image, on the whole, and some nice, clear publicity material. The only troublesome issue is that of the Fireclown. I would like to suggest, again, that we drop it — ignore it. Already we have lost a lot of headway by the swing in public opinion from support to condemnation of the Fireclown. We can't afford to lose more."

"No," Helen said firmly. "I intend to make the Fireclown situation one of my main platform points. I am certain we shall soon find evidence of the

Fireclown's innocence. If that happens, I shall be proved right. Von Bek proved the hysteric he seems to be, and public faith in me should be restored."

"It's too much of a gamble!" Kalpis insisted.

"We've got to gamble now," Helen said. "We haven't a chance of winning otherwise."

Kalpis sighed. "Very well," and lapsed into silence.

Alain said: "When's the first public speech due to be made?"

"Tomorrow." Helen fidgeted with the papers before her. "It's at the City Hall and should be well-attended."

The huge area of City Hall was packed. Every seat was occupied, every inch of standing space crammed to capacity. On the wide platform sat Alain, Helen, Wallace and Curry, staring out at the rows of heads that gaped at them from three sides. Behind them on a great screen pictures were flashed — pictures of Helen talking to members of the public, pictures of Helen with her parents, pictures of Helen visiting hospitals, old people's homes, orphanages. A commentary accompanied the pictures, glowingly praising her virtues. As it finished, Alain got up and addressed the crowd.

"Fellow citizens of the Solar System, in just a few weeks from now you will have voted for the person you want to be President. What will you look for in your President? Intelligence, warmth of heart, capability. These are the basic essentials. But you will want more — you will want someone who is going to lead the Solar nation towards greater freedom, greater prosperity — and a more adventurous life. Such a woman is Helen Curtis…" Unused to this sort of speech-making, Alain found he was quite enjoying himself. Enough of the von Bek blood flowed in him, he decided, after all. He continued in this vein for a quarter of an hour and then presented Helen to the crowd. The applause was not as great as it might have been, but it was satisfactory.

Helen's platform manner was superb. At once alert and confident, she combined femininity with firmness, speaking calmly and with utmost assurance.

She outlined her policy. At this stage she ignored the Fireclown issue entirely, concentrating her attack on the sterile Solrefs and their Presidential candidate Simon von Bek. She ignored hecklers and spoke with wit and zest.

When she finished she was applauded and Alain von Bek got up, raising his arms for silence.

"Now that you have heard Fräulein Curtis's precise and far-thinking policy," he said, "are there any questions which you would like to ask her?"

Dotted around the auditorium were special stands where the questioner could go and be heard throughout the hall. Each stand had a large red beacon on it. Beacons began to flash everywhere. Alain selected the nearest.

"Number seven," he said, giving the number of the stand.

"I should like to ask Fräulein Curtis how she intends to work out the controlled price of sea-farm produce," said a woman.

Helen went back to the centre of the platform.

"We shall decide to price by assessing cost of production, a fair profit margin, and so on."

"This will result in lower prices, will it?" the woman asked.

"Certainly."

The red light went out. Alain called another number.

"What steps does Fräulein Curtis intend to take towards the present ban on tobacco production?"

"None," Helen said firmly. "There are two reasons for keeping the ban. The first is that nicotine is harmful to health. The second is that land previously used for tobacco is now producing cereals and other food produce. Marijuana, on the other hand, is not nearly so habit-forming, has fewer smokers and can be produced with less wastage of land."

There were several more questions of the same nature, a little heckling, and then Alain called out again: "Number seven-nine."

"Fräulein Curtis was an ardent supporter of the Fireclown before it was discovered that he was a criminal. Now it's feared that the Fireclown intends to bombard Earth from space, or else detonate already planted bombs. What does she intend to do about this?"

Helen glanced at Alain. He smiled at her encouragingly.

"We are not certain that the Fireclown is guilty of the crimes he has been accused of," she said.

"He's guilty all right!" someone shouted. A hundred voices agreed.

"We cannot condemn him out of hand," she went on firmly. "We have no evidence of a plot to attack or destroy the planet."

"What would you do if he *was* guilty," shouted the original speaker — "sit back and wait?"

Helen had to shout to be heard over the rising noise of the crowd.

"I think that the Fireclown was framed by unscrupulous men who want a war scare," she insisted. "I believe we should follow other lines of investigation. Catch the Fireclown, by all means, and bring him to trial if necessary. But meanwhile we should be considering other possibilities as to how the bombs got on the first level!"

"My parents were killed on the eleventh level!" This was someone shouting from another speaking box. "I don't want the same thing to happen to my kids!"

"It's sure to unless we look at the situation logically," Helen retaliated.

"Fireclown-lover!" someone screamed. The phrase was taken up in other parts of the hall.

"This is madness, Alain." She looked at him as if asking for his advice. "I didn't expect quite so much hysteria."

"Keep plugging," he said. "It's all you can do. Answer them back!"

"Von Bek for President! Von Bek for President!" This from the very back of the hall.

"Von Bek for insanity!" she cried. "The insanity which some of you are exhibiting tonight. Blind fear of this kind will get you nowhere. I offer you *sanity!*"

"Madness, more likely!"

"If you listened to me like sensible adults instead of shouting and screaming, I'd tell you what I mean." Helen stood, her arms folded, waiting for the noise to die down.

Alain went and placed himself beside her.

"Give her a chance!" he roared. "Give Fräulein Curtis a chance!"

When finally the noise had abated somewhat, Helen continued:

"I have seen the Fireclown since the holocaust. He told me that policemen tampered with his machines and caused the fire. He had nothing to do with it!"

"Then he was lying!"

"Calm down!" she begged. "Listen to me!"

"We listened to the Fireclown's lies for too long. Why listen to yours?"

"The Fireclown told you no lies. You interpreted what he said so that it meant what you wanted it to mean. Now you're doing the same to me! The Fireclown is *innocent!*"

Alain whispered. "Don't go too far, Helen. You've said enough."

She must have realized that she had overshot her mark. She had been carried away by the heat of the argument, had admitted she thought the Fireclown innocent. Alain could imagine what the V-casts would say in the morning.

"Are there any other questions?" he called. But his voice was drowned by the angry roar of the crowd.

"Not exactly a successful evening," he said as he took her home. They had had to wait for hours before the crowd dispersed.

She was depressed. She said nothing.

"What's the next stage in the campaign?" he asked.

"Next stage? Is it worth it, Alain? I'm getting nowhere. I've never known such wild hysteria. I thought we got rid of all that a century ago."

"It takes longer than a hundred years to educate people to listen to reason when someone tells them their lives are liable to be snuffed out in an instant."

"I suppose so. But what are we going to do? I didn't expect such a strong reaction. I didn't intend to say that I thought the Fireclown was innocent. I knew that was going too far, that they couldn't take direct opposition to what they now believe. But I got so angry."

"It's just unfortunate," he said comfortingly, though inwardly he was slightly annoyed that she had lost her self-control at the last minute. "And it's early days yet. Maybe, by the time the campaign's over, we'll have more people on our side."

"Maybe they'll just ignore us," she said tiredly as they entered her apartment.

"No, I don't think that. We're nothing if not controversial!"

Next day, the RLM Political Headquarters received a deputation.

Two men and two women. The men were both thin and of medium height. One of them, the first to advance into the front office and confront Alain, who had elected to deal with them, was sandy-haired, with a prominent Adam's apple and a nervous tic. The other was less remarkable, with brown hair and a mild face in which two fanatical eyes gleamed. The women might have been pretty if they had dressed less dowdily and paid more attention to their hair and make-up. In a word, they were frumps.

The taller woman carried a neat banner which read: THE END OF THE WORLD DRAWS SLOWLY NIGH. LATTER-DAY ADVENTISTS SAY "NO" TO FALSE GODS. STOP THE FIRECLOWN.

Alain knew what they represented. And he knew of the leader, had seen his face in innumerable broadcasts.

"Good morning, Elder Smod," he said brightly. "What can we do for you?"

"We have come as the voice of the Latter-Day Adventists to denounce you," Elder Smod said sonorously. The Latter-Day Adventists were now the strongest and only influential religious body in existence today, and their ranks were comprised so obviously of bewildered half-wits and pious paranoiacs that public and politicians alike did not pay them the attention that such a large movement would otherwise merit in a democracy. However, they could be a nuisance. And the main nuisance was Elder Smod, second-in-command to senile Chief Elder Bevis, who was often observed to have fallen asleep during one of his own speeches.

"And why should you wish to denounce me?" Alain raised his eyebrows.

"We've come to denounce the Radical Liberal Movement for its outrageous support of this spawn of Satan, the Fireclown!" said one of the frumps in a surprisingly clear and musical voice.

"But what have the Latter-Day Adventists to do with the Fireclown?" Alain asked in surprise.

"Young man, we oppose the supporters of Satan."

"I'm sure you do. But I still don't see what connection…"

"Satan seeks to destroy the world by fire before the good Lord has his chance. We cannot tolerate that!"

Alain remembered now that the original twentieth century sect had announced that they were the only ones who would be saved when the world was destroyed by fire. They had been a little chary of announcing the date but, egged on by slightly disenchanted supporters, they had finally given an exact date for the end of the world — 2,000 AD, claiming the Third Millennium would contain only the faithful. Sadly, when the Third Millennium dawned, it contained fewer of the faithful than before, since many had not wholly accepted the fact pointed out to them by the movement's elders, that the Bible had earlier been misread as to the date of Christ's birth. (A speedy and splendid juggling with the Christian, Jewish and Moslem calendars had taken place on January 1st, 2,000 AD). But, in spite of the discredit, the movement had grown again with the invention of a slightly altered interpretation — i.e., that the world would not perish in a sudden holocaust but that it would begin — and *had* begun — to perish from the year 2,000 — giving an almost infinite amount of time for the process to take place. However, the coming of the Fireclown scare, with its talk of destruction, had evidently thrown them out again!

"But why, exactly, have you come to us?" Alain demanded.

"To ask you to side with the righteous against the Fireclown. We were astonished to see that there were still foolish sinners on Earth who could believe him innocent! So we came — to show you the True Way."

"Thank you," said Alain, "but all I say — and I cannot speak for the RLM as a whole — is that the Fireclown is *not* likely to destroy the world by fire. We have no argument."

Elder Smod seemed a trifle nonplused. Evidently he considered the Fireclown a sort of johnny-come-lately world-destroyer, whereas his movement had had, for some time, a monopolistic concession on the idea.

Alain decided to humour him and said gently: "The Fireclown could be an agent for your side, couldn't he?"

"No! He is Satan's spawn. Satan," said Smod with a morose satisfaction, "has come amongst us in the shape of the Fireclown."

"Satan? Yet the clown predicted a return of fire to the world unless, in your terms, the world turned its back on Mammon. And one cannot worship both…"

"A devil's trick. The Fireclown is Satan's answer to the True Word — *our* word!"

It was no good. Alain couldn't grasp his logic — if logic there was. He had to admit defeat.

"What if we don't cease our support of the Fireclown?" he asked.

"Then you will be destroyed in the flames from heaven!"

"We can't win, can we?" Alain said.

"You are like the rest of your kind," Elder Smod sneered. "They paid us no attention, either."

"Who do you mean?"

"You profess not to know! Ha! Are you not one of that band who call themselves the Secret Sons of the Fireclown?"

"I didn't know there was such a group. Where are they?"

"We have already tried to dissuade them from their false worship. A deputation of our English brothers went to them yesterday, but to no avail."

"They're in England? Where?"

"In the stinking slums of Mayfair, where they belong, of course!" Elder Smod turned to his followers. "Come — we have tried to save them, but they heed us not. Let us leave this gateway to Hell!"

They marched primly out.

Mayfair. Wasn't that where Blas had his hideout? Perhaps the two were connected. Perhaps this was the lead that would prove, once and for all, whether the Fireclown planned mammoth arson or whether the syndicate had framed him.

Alain hurriedly made his way into the back room where Helen and Jordan Kalpis were planning her tour.

"Helen, I think I've got a lead. I'm not sure what it is, but if I'm lucky I'll be able to get evidence to prove that we're right about the Fireclown. He's still got some supporters, I just learned, in London. I'm going there."

"Shall I come with you?"

"No. You've got a lot of ground to make up if you're going to get near to winning this election. Stick at it — and don't lose your self-control over the Fireclown issue. I'll get back as soon as I've got some definite information."

"Alain, it's probably dangerous. Blas and his like take pains to protect themselves."

"I'll do the same, don't worry," he said. He turned to Kalpis. "Could we have a moment, Jordan?"

Jordan walked tactfully out of the room.

Alain took Helen in his arms, staring down at her face. She had a half-startled look, half-worried. "Alain…"

"Yes?"

She shook her head, smiling. "Look after yourself."

"I've got to," he said, and kissed her.

C H A P T E R   F O U R T E E N

Mayfair mouldered.

Nowhere on the three planets was there a slum like it, and riches, not poverty, had indirectly created it.

As Alain walked up the festering streets of Park Lane, a light drizzle falling from the overcast afternoon sky, he remembered the story of how it had got like this. Mayfair was the property of one man — a man whose ambition had been to own it, who had achieved his ambition and was now near-senile — Ronald Lowry, the British financier, who refused to let the government buy him out and refused, also, to improve his property. The original residents and business houses had moved out long since, unable to stand Lowry's weird dictatorship. The homeless, and especially the criminal homeless, had moved in. Like Lowry, they weren't interested in improving the property, either. For them, it was fine as it was — a warren of huge, disused hotels, office blocks and apartment buildings. Lowry was rich — perhaps the richest man in the world — and Lowry, in spite of his senility, had power. He would not let a single government official set foot on his property and backed up his wishes by threatening to withdraw his capital from industries which, without it, would flounder and give the government unemployment problems, re-location problems and the like. Until a less cautious party came to power, Mayfair would continue to moulder, at least for as long as Lowry lived.

The scruffy, old-world architecture of the Hilton, the Dorchester and the Millennium Grande towered above Alain as he passed between them and the jungle that grew alongside Hyde Park. Hyde Park itself was public property, neat and orderly, well maintained by London's City Council, but roots had spread and shrubs had flowered, making an almost impenetrable hedge along the borders of the park.

Wisely, he did not head immediately for the Dorchester, where Blas was supposed to be, but went instead to a café that still bore the name of the Darlington Grill. The *specialité de la maison* these days, however, was fish and chips — from the smell.

The majority of the men were gaudily dressed in the latest styles, but some were down at heel — not necessarily criminals, but pridies, people who refused to accept the citizens' grant which the government allowed to all who were unable to work, whether because of physical or emotional reasons. These were extreme emotional cases who, if they had not come to the official-free area of Mayfair, would have been cured by this time and rehabilitated. Mayfair, Alain thought, was indeed a strange anachronism — and a blot on the three planets. Ronald Lowry's vast financial resources had produced the only skid-row now in existence!

Alain had taken the precaution of getting himself a green luminous suit and a flowing scarlet cravat which made him feel sick whenever he saw himself in a mirror. On his head was perched, at a jaunty angle, a conical cap of bright and hideous blue, edged with gold sateen.

He saw by the list chalked on a board at the end of the café that his nose hadn't lied. The only food was turbot and chips. The liquor, it seemed, was a product of a local firm — a choice between wheat, parsnip or nettle wine. He ordered a wheat wine and found it clear and good, like a full-bodied Sauterne. It was only spoiled by the disgusting aroma of illicit cigarettes, smoked by several of the nicotine addicts who lounged in what was evidently a drug-induced euphoria at the greasy tables.

Before he had left the City of Switzerland, Alain had procured one of the badges previously worn by the Fireclown's supporters — a small metal sun emblem which the disillusioned Sons of the Sun had rid themselves of when public sympathy for the Fireclown had changed to anger. He wore it inside his cap.

He looked around over the rim of his glass, hoping to see a similar emblem, but he was disappointed.

A sharp-faced little man came in and sat at Alain's table. He ordered a parsnip wine. A few drops spilled on the table as the proprietor brought it.

Alain decided that he would have to chance the possibility that the café fraternity were sufficiently angered against the Fireclown to cause trouble. He took off his hat, lining upward so that the sun emblem was visible.

The sharp-faced man was also sharp-eyed. Alain saw him stare at the badge for a moment. Then he looked at Alain, frowning. In the spilled liquor on the table he drew, with a surprisingly clean finger, a similar design.

"You're one of us, eh?" he grunted.

"Yes."

"Fresh to Mayfair?"

"Yes."

"You'd better come to the meeting. It's a masked meeting, naturally. We've got to protect ourselves."

"Where do I go?"

"South Audley Street — a cellar." The man told him the number and the time to be there. Then he ignored Alain, who finished his drink and ordered another. A little later he got up and left.

Alain could understand the need for secrecy. The police would be searching for any clue to the Fireclown's whereabouts. He wondered if this group knew. Or did they have any real contact with the Fireclown at all? Perhaps in an hour's time, at six o'clock, he would know.

At six he entered the broken-down doorway in South Audley Street and found himself in a long room that had evidently been a restaurant. Through the gloom he could make out chairs still stacked on tables. He walked over rotting carpets, through the piled furniture to the back of the place. A door led him through a filthy, dilapidated kitchen. At the end of a row of rusted stoves he saw another door. Opening it, he saw that it closed off a flight of concrete steps leading downwards. He advanced into a cellar.

About five or six masked figures were already there. One of them, stocky and languid in his movements, Alain thought he recognized.

One of the others, a woman in a red and yellow hood that covered her whole face, came up to him. "Welcome, newcomer. Sit there." She pointed to a padded chair in a shadowed corner.

From a brazier at the end of the cellar flames danced. Huge, grotesque shadows were spread along the floor and up the walls as the men and women began to come down the cellar steps and sit on the damp-smelling chairs.

"Thirty-nine, plus the newcomer — forty in all," the stocky man said. "Close the door and bar it."

The stocky man went and stood by the brazier. Alain wished he could place him, but couldn't for the moment.

"We are come here," he intoned, "as the last loyal Sons of the Fireclown, to honour our leader and prepare for his return. We are pledged to carry out his work, even if we risk death in so doing!"

Alain realized suddenly that these people were using the Fireclown's name, just as the majority had done earlier, to support some creed or obsession of their own. The whole tone of the meeting did not fit with what he knew of the Fireclown, his father. Probably, he thought, he understood the Fireclown better than anyone — particularly since he could recognize certain traits in the Fireclown that had a milder expression in himself.

Certainly, he decided, this group was worth observing, for it might help clarify the rest of the questions that needed clarifying before he could act in an objective way.

What if the arms syndicate were operating this group for their own purposes? It was possible that they had got hold of these people who seriously wished to put the Fireclown's *outré* philosophy into practice and were making them act against the Fireclown's interests.

Then he had it. The identity of the intoning man — *Blas*!

Now, he felt, there was substance for his theory that the arms syndicate was using the Fireclown as a patsy — a fall-guy to carry the can for their devious plans for world conflict. He bent forward as Blas came to the important point.

"You have each been given incendiary bombs to plant in some of the major buildings around the globe. The burning buildings will act as beacons, heralding the return of the Fireclown with his bolts of fire for the unclean and his gift of a new world for you, the true believers. Are you all sure of what you must do?"

"Yes!" each man and woman responded.

"Now." Blas's masked face was cocked to one side as he suddenly regarded Alain. "The newcomer is not yet a full Son of the Fireclown. He must prove himself to us."

Alain suddenly realized the menace in the words. He sensed, from the atmosphere in the room, that this was not normal procedure.

"Come here, my friend," Blas said quietly. "You must be initiated."

There was a strong chance that Blas recognized him. But what could he do? For the moment he would have to go through with it.

He got up slowly and walked towards the fiery heat of the brazier.

"Do you worship the Flame of the Sun?" Blas asked theatrically.

"Yes," he said, trying to keep his voice level.

"Do you see the fire as the Fire of Life?"

He nodded.

"Would you bring forth the fires of life in yourself?"

"Yes."

"Then —" Blas pointed at the brazier — "plunge your hand into the flames as proof that you are a brother to the Flame of the Sun!"

Ritual! If Alain needed confirmation that these people had nothing to do with the Fireclown in any real sense, he had it now. The Fireclown scorned ritual.

"No, Blas," he said scornfully, and turned to the masked gathering. "Don't listen to this man. I know the Fireclown — he is my father — he would not want this! He would hate you to debase yourselves as you are doing now. The Fireclown only uses fire as a symbol. He speaks of the human spirit, not —" he gestured at the brazier — "natural fire!"

"Silence!" Blas commanded. "You seek to disrupt our gathering! Do not listen to him, brothers!"

The Sons of the Fireclown were glancing at one another uncertainly.

Blas's voice spoke almost good-humouredly in Alain's ear. "Really, von Bek, this is nothing to you. Why do you interfere? Admit to these fools that you lied and I'll let you go. Otherwise I can probably convince them, anyway, and you'll be roasted on that thing there."

Alain glanced at the blazing brazier, gouting flames. He shuddered. Then he leapt at it and kicked it over in Blas's direction. Blas jumped away from the burning coals, shouting something incoherent.

Alain pushed through the confused crowd and reached the door, wrenched the bar away and fled up the steps. He ran through the darkened restaurant and out into the crumbling street a few seconds ahead of his closest pursuer. He dashed down towards Grosvenor Square, an overgrown tangle of trees and shrubs. In the last of the evening light he saw the monolithic tower of the old American Embassy, fallen into decay long since.

A flight of steps led up to the broken glass doors. He climbed them hurriedly, squeezed through an aperture and saw another flight of steps leading upwards.

By the time he had reached the second floor, let his feet lead him into a maze of corridors, he no longer heard the sounds of pursuit and realized, thankfully, that he had lost them. He cursed himself for not wearing a mask. He should have guessed that Blas and the spurious Sons of the Fireclown had some connection.

And now it was almost certain that Blas, unknown to the Fireclown, was playing both ends against the middle. But he'd still have to find out more before he could prove the Fireclown's innocence.

He had only one course of action. To go to the Dorchester, where Blas had his hideout. He knew he wasn't far from Park Lane, since he had studied a map thoroughly before he left. He waited for two hours before groping his way down to a different exit from the one he'd left and stumbled through the jungle of Grosvenor Square, climbing over fallen masonry and keeping in the shadows as he walked down Grosvenor Street and into Park Lane.

He threw away his hat and reversed his jacket as an afterthought so that the reversible side showed mauve shot with yellow, hunched his shoulders to disguise his outline and hid his face as much as possible, then continued down towards the Dorchester.

Luckily, the street was almost deserted and he passed only a couple of drunks sitting against the wall of a bank, and a pretty young girl who hailed him with pretty old words. She reviled him softly in language even older when he ignored her.

Reaching the side entrance of the Dorchester, he found the door firmly locked. He continued round to the front. Lights were on in the lobby and two tough-looking men lounged outside. He couldn't get past them without them seeing him, so he walked boldly and said:

"I've come to see Herr Blas — he's expecting me. Which suite?"

"First floor," said the guard unsuspiciously.

Alain found the lobby in surprisingly good repair. Even the elevators looked in working order, although there was a good deal of litter about. He took the stairs, reached the first floor which was in semi-darkness, and saw a light coming from under a pair of big double doors. He paused outside and strained his ear to catch the mumble of voices from within. He was sure he recognized both of them — one was probably Blas's, anyway.

The other, he realized after a moment, was the voice of Junnar, his grandfather's secretary!

He took from his pocket the squat laser pistol he had brought with him at Helen's request and walked into the room.

"The plot," he said with forced lightness, "thickens. Good evening, gentlemen."

Blas took the cigarette out of his mouth with an expression of surprise. "Good evening, von Bek," he said amiably. "I didn't think we'd seen the last of you. If you're not going to be impetuous we can explain everything, I think."

"Herr von Bek," Junnar said sadly, "you should have stayed out of this from the start. What's the gun for?"

"Self-protection," Alain said curtly. "And I don't need much explanation. I've had an inkling of this for some time. Grandfather put you up to planting the bombs on the Fireclown — am I right?"

Junnar's silence was answer enough. Alain nodded. "He'd use any means to prove the Fireclown a criminal, even if it meant supplying the proof himself, in a very simple way. You got the bombs from Blas and planted them. But you bit off more than you could chew when you started this war scare. What are you up to now? Doing another deal with Blas over the arms he wants to supply the government with as a 'defense' against a non-existent plot?"

"That's about it," Blas admitted.

Alain felt physically sick. His own grandfather, head of the house of von Bek, descendant of a line of strong, honest and fervently dedicated politicians, had descended to faking evidence to prove his own theory about the Fireclown. And, in consequence, he had started a wave of hysteria which he was virtually unable to control. He wondered if Simon von Bek now regretted his infamy. He probably did, but it was too late.

And this was the man the public were almost bound to elect President.

"You bloody, treacherous pigs!" he said.

"You'd have to prove all this," Blas said softly, his self-assurance still apparently maintained.

Alain was still in a quandary. All his life the concept of clan loyalty to the von Beks had been drummed into him. It was hard to shake it off. Could he betray his own grandfather, who in a peculiar way he still loved, at the expense of the father responsible for his bastardy?

Slowly, standing there with the laser gun in his hand, its unfamiliar grip sticky with sweat, he came unwillingly to a decision.

He waved the gun towards the door. "After you," he said.

"Where are we going?" Junnar asked nervously.

"The City of Switzerland," Alain told them. "And just remember what a laser can do. I could slice you both in two in a moment. It's going in my pocket, and my hand's going to be on it all the way."

"You're rather a melodramatic young man," Blas said resignedly as he walked towards the door.

C H A P T E R F I F T E E N

Under Alain's direction, Junnar brought the car down on the roof of the von Bek's apartment block.

"Climb out, both of you," Alain ordered. They obeyed him.

They descended to Simon von Bek's apartment and Junnar made the door open. They went through.

"Is that you, Junnar?" von Bek called from his study.

Alain herded them in.

He saw a terrible expression of sheer fear cloud his grandfather's face as they entered.

Hollowly, Alain said: "I know everything, grandfather."

Simon von Bek remained seated at his desk. Slowly he put down his stylus and pushed the papers from him.

"What are you going to do then, Alain?"

"Denounce us, I expect," Blas said cheerfully. "May I sit down, von Bek?" He turned to Alain.

"Both of you sit," Alain ordered, his hand still on his pocketed gun.

"You'd have to prove it," Simon von Bek said slowly, in an old man's voice. "It's the word of an emotional young man against that of a respected minister. I could say you were raving. Neither Junnar nor Blas would testify against me."

"Why?" Alain demanded. "Why, grandfather?"

"There are a number of reasons, Alain. It was my last chance to become President. A von Bek of every generation has been President at least once. I couldn't let family tradition die — it would have been a disgrace."

"Isn't what you did a disgrace? Isn't it a crime?"

"You don't understand. Politicians can't always use clean methods. I was right. The Fireclown's no good, Alain. It was the only way to show the public..."

"That was only a matter of opinion. The fact is you framed the Fireclown in order to prove your own theory about him — and because Helen was bound to win the election if you didn't do something desperate. It was the only way to change public opinion radically. Because of that, Sandai's police tampered with the Fireclown's flame-machines — and three hundred people were killed."

"I didn't want that to happen."

"But it happened — *you* were responsible for their deaths!"

"I feel guilty…"

"You *are* guilty! And you fell neatly into Blas's plan, didn't you? He supplied you with the bombs with which you framed the Fireclown. And now, because you daren't admit the whole thing was manufactured by you, he's holding the government up to blackmail. There is a possibility of mass destruction if this hysteria builds up — but even if that doesn't happen the money that Blas will demand will impoverish the Solar nation for years. And he's got you neatly in his trap — he can dictate any terms he wants. If you were elected President you would be his puppet. Blas would run the Solar nation. And he nearly succeeded, didn't he?"

"As your grandfather pointed out," Blas said equably, "you still have to prove all this, young man."

"I intend to, Blas. Grandfather — you're going to confess, before it's too late. You're a von Bek! You must!"

Simon von Bek wet his lips and stared down at the desk.

"Are you going to confess, grandfather?"

"No," said Simon von Bek. "No, I am not."

It had been Alain's only chance, and it had failed. As his grandfather and Blas had said, it was his word against theirs. Already he had the reputation as a die-hard supporter of the Fireclown. Who would believe him now that Simon von Bek had turned the Solar System against the Fireclown? What could he do now?

His idealism, his belief that his grandfather would act in accordance with the principles he had so plainly shed was shattered. He was drained of emotion and could only stand staring down at the old man.

"Stalemate, von Bek." Blas crossed his legs.

There must be proof, Alain thought. There must be proof somewhere.

He knew that if he could prove his grandfather's guilt he could stop Blas's plan for controlling the Solar System, avert the threat of a war almost bound to come about with so much hysteria in the air, prove the Fireclown innocent and allow Helen to become President.

Everything hinged on what was, in fact, a means of betraying his grandfather.

He gave Blas a disgusted glare.

"Yes, stalemate. But if I walk out of here now, you daren't do anything for fear that I'll say too much. You can't rig evidence against me the same way as you did to the Fireclown." As an afterthought, he added: "You could kill me, of course."

"No!" Simon von Bek rose from his chair. "Alain, come in with us. In a few weeks the world will be ours!"

Alain went towards the door. "You accused me once of having none of the noble von Bek blood, remember? If that's what flows in your veins, thank God I haven't got any!"

He flung down the gun and left.

Outside, he walked slowly towards the elevator cone, brooding and unable to think coherently. All he had was definite knowledge of his grandfather's perfidy, knowledge that he was unable yet to prove. Still, the knowledge itself was something.

He went down to the thirtieth level and made his way to the RLM Headquarters.

He entered the front office, still stacked with posters. Jordan Kalpis was there, his bony face full of worry.

"Von Bek! What did you find out?"

"Where's Helen? I'll tell you later."

"At a meeting in the Divisional Hall on forty. There's some pretty bad heckling going on. The crowd has turned nasty."

"Right. I'm going over there."

Alain went out into the corridor and took the fastway to the elevator, rose ten levels and took the fastway again to the Divisional Hall. Every ten levels had a Divisional Hall, comprising a meeting hall and the offices of the local sub-council officials. Outside, the posters of Helen had been torn down.

There was a fantastic noise coming from inside. Alain entered the crowded hall and glimpsed Helen at the far end on the platform. A man beside him threw back an arm. Alain saw it held a piece of raw meat. As the man's hand came up to hurl the meat, Alain grabbed it and wrenched it savagely back. He didn't give the man time to see who had stopped him but pushed his way down the aisle. All kinds of refuse flew on to the platform as he hauled himself up.

Helen's face was bleeding and her clothes were torn. She stood rigidly, defiantly shouting at the mob.

"Helen!"

She saw him. "Alain! What —?"

"Get out of here — they're not listening to you!"

She seemed to pull herself together.

Now the mob surged forward, faces twisted, hands grasping. He heard someone shout: "She wants us burned to death."

She — wants — us — burned — to — death!

A gem of a phrase, Alain thought as he kicked the first man who tried to climb the stage. It fed the hysteria which spawned it. He found himself hating humanity and his kicks were savage.

Andy Curry's freckled face appeared from the side exit. "Quick! Here!"

They ran in and Curry ordered the door locked.

"I can only say I told you so," Curry said dourly. "You shouldn't have made the speech in the first place, Fräulein Curtis."

"I avoided all mention of the Fireclown," she said furiously, "and they didn't give me a chance!"

Curry picked up the VC in the passage. He pressed two studs.

The word *Police* flashed on the screen and an operator's face followed it.

"I'm speaking from Divisional Hall, level forty," Curry said swiftly. "There's a riot going on down here. We're besieged. We need help."

The operator looked at him. "Helen Curtis meeting — is that right?"

"That's right."

"We'll have a squad there right away," the operator told him in a voice that indicated he should have known better than to start trouble.

The police dispersed the crowd and the captain told Alain, Helen and Curry that an escort was ready to see them home. He sounded unsympathetic, as if he was helping them unwillingly.

When they reached Helen's door the leader of the escort said: "If I were you, Fräulein Curtis, I should stay inside. You're liable to be attacked otherwise."

"I've got an election to fight," she pointed out.

"You'll have people to fight if tonight's trouble's repeated — and I don't doubt it will be if you insist on setting yourself up to resist the whole climate of public opinion! We've got enough on our hands with the Fireclown investigation — crowds demanding to know when we're going to catch him, rabble-rousers shouting that we must prepare for war, and all the rest of it."

The escort leader shrugged. "We can't be held responsible if you deliberately risk being mobbed."

"Thank you, officer." Alain followed Helen into the apartment. The door closed.

"So I'm supposed to stay boxed in here, am I?" she said bitterly. "Meanwhile I've got to try and convince people that they're wrong."

"It's useless," he said hollowly, going into the sitting-room and slumping down in a chair.

"What did you find out in London?"

"Everything."

"Even what Blas is up to?"

He told her, slowly and wearily, all that had happened.

"So we *were* right," she said thoughtfully. "But uncle Simon — that's incredible."

"Yes, isn't it?" He smiled cynically. "And our hands are virtually tied. We've got to do some cool thinking, Helen."

She was calmer now. She seemed to notice, for the first time, that he was exhausted.

"We'd better sleep on it," she said. "We may feel more optimistic in the morning."

As they breakfasted, Alain switched on the V. "Let's see what's happened in the world this morning," he said.

"… petition urging the government to speed up its defense plans," mouthed the newscaster. Then he leaned forward urgently. "For those who missed our early edition, the first attacks by the Fireclown have begun. Two nuclear bomb explosions have been observed — one in the Atlantic and one in the Gobi Desert. So far nobody has been reported hurt, but it will be impossible to know for certain for some time yet. Where will the Fireclown's next bomb strike? Swiss City? New York? Berlin? We don't know. Emergency shelters are being erected and bomb detector teams are covering the areas around the main cities to try and discover hidden bombs. Meanwhile, in Britain, mystery fires have devastated important public buildings. The National Gallery is smouldering wreckage — the marvelous architectural beauty of Gateshead Theatre is no more. Precautions are being taken to protect other such buildings throughout the planet. There is little doubt that the Fireclown — or his die-hard supporters here — was responsible!"

"That's all Blas's work," Alain said angrily. "How are we going to prove it?"

"Look," Helen pointed at the screen. Simon von Bek had appeared, looking dignified and grave.

"My fellow citizens of the Solar System, I am speaking to you in troubled times. As I predicted a short while ago, the Fireclown has attacked the globe. He has been offered no hostility, we have intended him no harm. But nevertheless he has attacked. We must defend ourselves. If we had to manufacture bombs and other weapons for defense we should be wiped out before we had any chance. Luckily the Solar Government has been offered arms." Von Bek paused as if saddened by the task he had to perform. "A group of men — criminals we should have called them but a few hours ago, but now we are more than thankful to them — have offered us a supply of arms. We are going to purchase them, on your behalf, and set them up around the planet This will have to be done swiftly, and already bodies of volunteers are working on emergency installations. Let us hope we shall be in time to avert our peril. When I next speak to you, perhaps we shall know."

"The devil!" Helen swore. "He's obviously completely in Blas's power. He knows that Blas will use him to control Earth — that we're threatened with a military dictatorship, and yet, in his pride, he still refuses to stop. Doesn't he know what he's doing?"

"He's gone so far now that he can't go back. His hate for the Fireclown and love for his own political ambitions have combined and, in a sense I'm sure, turned him insane! Maybe he can't even see the extent of his treachery."

"We've got to do something to stop him, Alain." Helen spoke quietly.

"Like what?"

"First we'll try to convince Sandai. Then, if that fails, we'll have to kill him."

"Helen! Killing him won't do any good. What could we do? Set up another dictatorship to control the people? Don't you see that if we continue this violence we'll breed more violence *ad infinitum*? We've *got* to use legal means against him. Otherwise, society as we know it is finished!"

"Then what other alternative is there?"

"First well see Sandai," he said. "Then we'll decide."

CHAPTER SIXTEEN

It took time to get to see Sandai. It took over a day. By the time they walked into his office they were looking very tired indeed. So was Sandai.

"If you've come to tell me that the Fireclown's innocent of these outrages," he said, wiping his olive forehead, "I'm not interested."

Alain stood over the seated police chief, his hands resting on the man's desk.

"That's part of it, Chief Sandai. But that's not all. I have heard the man responsible confess his guilt to me!"

"You've what?" Sandai looked up, astonished.

"The man responsible for framing the Fireclown, for setting off the bombs and causing the fires in Britain, is a man named Blas."

"Blas? François Blas? He's suspected head of the arms syndicate." Sandai looked thoughtful. "It's a possibility, Herr von Bek. But what proof have you? How did you find out?"

"I heard that Blas had his headquarters in Mayfair. I went there and discovered he was running an organization calling themselves the Sons of the Fireclown."

"So Blas is working for the Fireclown?"

"No. The thing was definitely spurious. Blas was using it for his own ends. Later I broke into Blas's apartment and confronted him with what I knew and what I suspected. He denied nothing. He told me to prove it — which I couldn't do. I then brought him and another man back to the capital..."

"Who was the other man?"

"Junnar, my grandfather's secretary."

"You mean you suspect he's been working against Minister von Bek? That's fantastic — if it's true."

"He's been working *with* von Bek," Alain said firmly. "Blas and my grandfather are hand-in-glove — they plan to use the war scare they've created and the fear of the Fireclown to hold the Earth to ransom. You heard yesterday's announcement — about von Bek having to buy bombs from the syndicate. It's a set-up, Chief Sandai!"

"Young man, you're evidently deranged." Sandai stood up and patted Alain's arm sympathetically.

"Listen to him!" Helen said urgently. "Listen, Chief Sandai. It sounds impossible, but it's a fact."

"And the proof?" Sandai said gently.

"As circumstantial as that against the Fireclown," Alain pointed out.

"But the Fireclown is a renegade — your grandfather is virtually the leader of the Solar System. That's the difference, von Bek. I'm sorry, but your defense of the Fireclown doesn't hold up. Why don't you admit that and work with the rest of us to avert the menace?"

"It's the truth," Alain said. He felt the energy go out of his body, his shoulders slump.

"I'm very busy," Sandai said. "You'd better leave now."

As they crossed the sunny gardens of the Top, Helen said to him: "That didn't work. What do we do now, Alain?"

"Watch the world die," he said hopelessly.

"The whole lot of them deserve death for what they're doing," she said cautiously.

"Maybe. But the law banished the death sentence over a hundred years ago. We want to preserve the law, Helen, not demolish it further!"

"If only we could contact the Fireclown. Maybe he could help us."

"He's journeying off somewhere in that ship of his, conducting his experiment. There's no hope there, anyway. He's not interested in Earth's problems, you know that."

They reached the elevator cone and entered it with a dozen others.

As they descended a man stared hard at Helen.

"Aren't you Helen Curtis?" he said roughly.

"I am."

The man spat in her face.

Alain jumped at him, punching savagely. The attendant shouted for them to stop. Hands grabbed Alain. The man punched him in the stomach and then in the head.

"Stinking fire-bug!"

Alain felt bile in his throat. Then he passed out.

He came to in a few seconds. The lift was still going down. Helen was bending over him. The lift stopped. "You'd better get out, both of you," the attendant said.

Alain got to his feet.

"Why?" he grunted.

"You're making trouble, that's why."

"We didn't start it."

"Come on, Alain," Helen said, taking his arm. "We'll walk."

He was weak with pain as they stumbled into the corridor. Also he was insensately angry.

She helped him on to the fastway and supported his weight until his strength returned.

"That shows you how much anything we say is worth," she said quietly. "Hatred and violence are everywhere. What harm would a little more do? The good would outweigh the bad, Alain."

"No," he gasped. "No, Helen. Simon von Bek sold his principles. I'm not selling mine."

"So," she said when they were back in her apartment, "what do we do? Just wait here and watch the world collapse?"

"Switch on the set so we've got a good view," he said. She went over and turned on the V.

They watched glumly as the announcer reported another explosion in the Pacific, two more in Central Africa, killing a large number of people who lived in small communities in the blast area. Work was under way on the defense project. Simon von Bek was directing the preparations.

"They don't need to bother with the farce of electing him," Helen said. "He's as good as President now!"

"You mean Blas is," Alain told her. "He's the one pulling the strings."

Helen reached over to the V and pressed out a number.

"Who are you calling?"

"My brother," she said. "Denholm's about the only person who can help us now."

Her brother's face came on the screen. "Hello, Helen, I'm rather busy — is it important?"

"Very important, Denholm. Could you come over?"

"If it's another defense of the Fireclown..."

"It is not."

Her brother's expression changed as he stared at her image. "Very well. Give me an hour — all right?"

"Okay," she said.

"How can Denholm help us?" Alain said. "What's the point?"

"We'll tell him all we know. The more people of importance who are told about it, the better chance we have."

Denholm came in, placed his gaudy hat on a chair arm and sat down.

"Alain," Helen said, "tell Denholm everything — from the time we went to see the Fireclown until our interview with Sandai."

He told Denholm Curtis everything.

When he had finished, Curtis frowned at him. "Alain," he said, "I think I believe you. Uncle Simon's been behaving a trifle mysteriously in some ways. The alacrity with which he managed to contact the dealers when the government finally decided to buy the arms was astonishing. It could mean that he's abused his position as chairman of the One Hundred Committee!"

"What do you mean?"

"Supposing in some way he had got hold of a list of the dealers and the location of their caches? Supposing he held on to it without letting the other committee members know, contacted Blas and concocted this scheme? Suppose then they worked out a plan to take advantage of the Fireclown, get Simon von Bek elected as President, and then run the world as they wanted to run it? Von Bek might have got in touch with Blas originally with a view to smashing the syndicate. But Blas might have proposed the whole idea. We all know how much uncle Simon hates the Fireclown. It would have been the perfect means of getting rid of him. Maybe he intended to capture the Fireclown. Maybe the original deal was simply over a few bombs. But Blas has provided the Fireclown with the means of producing a super-ship, and he was fairly certain that the Fireclown would escape when the chips were down. He did. The war scare started, aided by the police tampering with the flame-machines. Simon von Bek couldn't back out — and Blas had him where he wanted him."

"That sounds logical," Alain agreed.

"But all this needs proof to back it up." Denholm Curtis pursed his lips thoughtfully.

"It comes back to that every time." Helen sighed.

"There'd be only one way. To find the man who was von Bek's original contact with Blas, and get him to confess."

"But how?" Alain asked. "Where do we look?"

"We check the files of the One Hundred Committee — that was probably how von Bek found his contact. You're still secretary, Helen. Where are the files?"

"Right here. In the safe."

"Get them."

She got them — dozens of spools of microfilm. They fitted them into the projector.

It was more than six hours before they found what they were looking for. A reference to one Nils Benedict, suspected of trying to sell arms to a super-reactionary Crespignite splinter group. They had turned him over to the police. The police had been unable to find any evidence against him. Simon von Bek had interviewed him while in custody and reported that, in his opinion, the man was innocent. Simon von Bek had been, apart from the police, the only man to question Benedict. Benedict had a Brussels address.

"Do you think that's him?" Alain said, rubbing his eyes.

"It's the only one it could possibly be. What do we do now?"

"Pay Nils Benedict a visit, I suppose," Helen suggested.

A smaller, less complex version of the City of Switzerland, Brussels had an altogether different character. Every inch of stonework was embellished with red lacquer, and over this bright designs had been laid. Gilt predominated.

The structure rose fourteen levels above the ground, five below, covering an area of five square miles. The roof landing space was limited so that they were forced to land outside the city and take a monorocket which let them off on the tenth level. Benedict lived on level eight.

They reached his apartment. They had already decided that Denholm would do the talking, since he was less likely to be suspect than the other two.

"Nils Benedict," he said to the blank door, "this is Denholm Curtis. I've got some good news for you."

The door opened. A tall, rangy man in a dressing gown of green silk stared curiously at Curtis.

"Are you from von Bek?" he asked as the door closed behind them.

Alain took the lead. "We want to contact Blas in a hurry. Can you arrange it?"

"Sure. But why? I thought he was in direct contact nowadays."

That was enough. Now they knew for certain.

"Oh, he is," Alain said. "But we thought it would be nice for you and Simon von Bek to meet again after all this time."

Benedict had been uncommonly slow, he thought, for a man who was supposed to live by his wits. The man seemed gradually to realize that something was wrong. He backed into his living room. They followed.

The answer was there. Benedict was an addict. The stink of mescaline was in the room; nightmarish murals covered the walls. He was a mescamas who got his kicks from descending into his own psychological hell.

Helen said in a strained voice: "I'll wait outside."

"Come on, Benedict," Denholm said roughly.

"I have rights, you know," Benedict said thickly. "Why does von Bek want to see me?"

"Are you scared of von Bek?"

"He told me I'd be killed if I ever got in touch with him again."

"There's not a chance of that, I promise," Alain said.

Benedict was still wary. Alain suddenly hit him under the jaw. He collapsed.

"Let's get him dressed," Denholm said. "It wouldn't be proper for him to go out without his correct clothes on."

They had surprisingly little difficulty getting Benedict to Helen's apartment. Organization of the usual kind seemed to have gone to pieces during the fake emergency.

While Helen tried to revive Benedict and Denholm tied his hands, the V began to flash. Alain answered it. Chief Sandai looked out at him.

"You're not the only madman in the system, it seems," he said. "I thought about what you told me and thought I couldn't do any harm to assign a few men to go undercover to Mayfair and check your story. It held up. We found Blas and Junnar there. We're holding them, under the emergency laws which Simon von Bek insisted we make, as suspects in an arson plot. We got one of the Sons of the Fireclown, too. But we're going to need more proof — and I'm still not convinced that your tale about Simon von Bek is true!"

Alain stepped aside so Sandai could see Benedict.

"Recognize this man, Chief?"

"I've got a feeling I do, but I can't place him. Who is he?"

"He's Simon von Bek's original contact with Blas. He's a mescamas. If we withhold his supply for a short time he should tell us everything he knows."

"If it's true, you've had a big stroke of luck, young man."

"It'll be the first we've had," Alain said dryly. "Can you come over and pick us up? It might be wise to have an escort."

Sandai nodded. The screen blanked.

Blas alone remained seemingly at ease. Benedict was slumped hopelessly in his chair, perhaps even enjoying the experience of defeat. Junnar had his back to them, staring out of the window over the mountains. The police prison had a wonderful view.

Blas said: "Chief Sandai, what evidence do you have for these fantastic charges? Confront Simon von Bek with them. He will laugh at you!"

Sandai turned to Denholm Curtis. "Where's von Bek now? You've convinced me."

"He's at a special meeting in the Solar House. Members are asking him questions on his war policy. He's bound to answer since we still retain a vestige of democracy."

"What are you going to do, Chief?" Alain asked.

"Something spectacular," Sandai said. "It's probably the only thing we can do now to break von Bek's power in front of the assembly. Otherwise it may be too late."

"After what I've been through in the last day or so," Helen said grimly, "I'm beginning to doubt that anyone can topple uncle Simon!"

Standing nobly before the mighty assembly of Solar Representatives, Simon von Bek answered their questions in a grave and sonorous voice. He was the image of the visionary and man of action. The weight of responsibility seemed to rest heavily upon his broad shoulders, but he bore it manfully, not to say hypocritically.

Alain watched him on the screen outside the main entrance to the Assembly Chamber itself. He, Denholm and Helen stood in a group to one side. Chief Sandai, four policemen and the fettered trio of Junnar, Blas and the slobbering Benedict stood to the other.

They chose their moment well, when a member for Afghanistan asked Simon von Bek what the police were doing in the Fireclown investigation.

Sandai pushed the button operating the double doors. The doors swept open and the party pushed forward.

"The police," Sandai called, "have caught most of the men responsible for the present situation." He gestured dramatically towards the shackled men. "Here they are — there is only one man missing!"

Alain saw that Simon von Bek's face bore an expression similar to the look he'd had on the night he'd accused him.

But he held up well, Alain decided, considering everything.

"What does this interruption mean, Chief Sandai?"

Sandai spoke laconically. "Using the emergency powers vested in me by the Government of the Solar System I am holding under arrest the three men you see there — François Blas, suspected arms dealer, Nils Benedict, a contact for the arms syndicate — and Eugene Junnar, personal assistant to Minister Simon von Bek. All the men admit to being implicated in a plot, instigated by Minister von Bek, to frame the Fireclown, start a war scare by means of nuclear bomb explosions and incendiaries, and thus assure Minister von Bek of full political power as President of the Solar System!"

Blas said: "He's lying, Minister von Bek."

But Nils Benedict, not of Blas's calibre, continued the theme. "We didn't admit anything, sir! I haven't said a word about the deal!"

Simon von Bek thundered: "Be quiet! You have abused your powers, Sandai. I demand that you leave the hall immediately!"

But the hubbub from the rest of the representatives drowned out anything else he might have wished to say.

Alain walked swiftly down to the central platform and mounted it.

"We have witnesses, now, grandfather! We have the proof you told us to get!"

Benjosef rose from his seat.

"What's the meaning of this, Herr von Bek?"

"My grandfather, sir, has betrayed every trust you and the system have ever put in him." Briefly, Alain outlined the facts.

Benjosef turned to Simon von Bek who stood rigidly, as if petrified, in his place. "Is this true, von Bek?"

"No!" von Bek came alive, his face desperate — wretched. "No! Can't you see this is the work of the Fireclown's supporters, an attempt to disgrace me and confuse us in our hour of peril? My grandson is lying!"

But Simon von Bek had lost all self-control. His wild denial had convinced the assembly of his guilt. He knew it. He stared around him, his breathing irregular, his eyes wide. He advanced toward Benjosef.

"I run the Solar System now, Benjosef — not you! You can't do anything. The people are with me!"

"Possibly," Benjosef said mildly, with a slight air of triumph, "but evidently this assembly is not." Benjosef seemed pleased at his would-be successor's downfall. "I was aware, Minister, that you wished to oust me as President — but I did not expect you to take quite so much trouble." He gestured to the police chief. "Sandai — I'm afraid you had better arrest Minister von Bek."

Simon von Bek leapt from the dais, stumbled and fell. He got up, evidently in pain, and stood there panting as Sandai stepped cautiously towards him.

"You fool! I could have made the world a better place. I knew it was going soft. I could have stopped the rot! You are under my orders, Sandai — don't listen to Benjosef."

Sandai slipped a pair of electrogyves from his belt.

"No!" Simon von Bek was sobbing now. "The Fireclown will destroy us! He will destroy you all — as he destroyed my daughter!"

Alain looked up in surprise. So his grandfather had known all along that the Fireclown was his father! That explained, even further, his insensate hatred of the Fireclown.

He went up to the old man, pitying him now.

"Grandfather, I know you have suffered, but…"

Old Simon von Bek turned his great head and looked into Alain's eyes. His expression was that of a bewildered, tearful child.

"It was for her sake," he said brokenly. "For hers and yours, Alain."

The gyves hummed and curled about von Bek's wrists. His head bowed, his seamed face now tear-streaked, he allowed Sandai to lead him out of the assembly hall.

Benjosef stepped from the platform and touched Alain's arm. "I'm sorry you had to do what you did, my boy. I must admit I never liked your grandfather — always thought him, well, somewhat weak, I suppose. That was why I, and many members of the party, never promoted him to a more prominent position; why he had never, until now, been nominated as a Presidential candidate. Evidently I was right, at least." He turned to Helen Curtis. "The world is going to be grateful to you both, I suspect. The climate of opinion is going to take yet another reversal before the elections are finally held. I hope you make a good President, Fräulein Curtis."

"Thank you, sir," said Helen, looking worriedly at Alain.

Alain ran a hand across his face. He swallowed with difficulty and glowered at the ground. Then he shook Benjosef's hand off his arm.

"I'm glad you're all proved right," he said bitterly. "I'm bloody glad about the happy ending."

And he walked straight up the aisle and out of the Solar House, his pace fast as he crossed the lawns. His heart pounding, his eyes warm, his fists clenched and his mind in a mess.

Chapter Seventeen

Two days later Alain emerged from the cavern on the first level, where he had been avoiding everyone, and ascended to the Top, passing a great many power-posters proclaiming Helen Curtis for President. Listening to the conversation, his faith in the stupidity of human nature was fully restored. In the swift movement of events, the public had changed their loyalty from the Fireclown to Simon von Bek, and now to Helen Curtis. Why did they need heroes? he wondered. What was wrong in people that they could not find what they needed within themselves? How did they know Helen was any better than the rest?

Vids announced the complete rounding up of the members of the arms syndicate and the discovery of every nuclear cache left in existence. That was one good thing. The Vs also said that order had been completely restored. Alain wondered. On the surface, perhaps, it was true. But what of the disorder that must still exist in the hearts and minds of most members of the public?

He reached the Top and entered Police Headquarters. After a few moments he was shown into Chief Sandai's office.

"Herr von Bek! There has been a general search out for you! You and Fräulein Curtis are the heroes of the hour. Every V station in the Solar System has been after you."

"In that case," Alain said coolly, "I'm glad they couldn't find me. I want to see my grandfather, Chief — if that's possible."

"Of course. He made a full confession, you know. He's been very subdued since his arrest — hasn't given us any trouble."

"Good. Well, can I see him now?"

Not exactly every home comfort had been provided for Simon von Bek, but his room hardly looked like a prison cell with its pleasant view of the clear summer sky, the cloud-wreathed mountain peaks in the distance. It was well furnished. There were books, writing materials and V-prints on the small desk by the window.

His grandfather was staring out at the mountains, his chair pushed back from his desk, when Alain entered.

"Grandfather."

The old man turned. And it *was* an old man who stared gauntly up at his grandson. All the vitality had left him. He seemed completely enervated.

"Hello, Alain. Glad to see you. Do sit down." He gestured vaguely towards the only other chair in the room.

"How do you feel?" Alain asked inanely.

Simon von Bek smiled thinly. "As well as can be expected," he said. "How are you?"

Alain seated himself on the edge of the chair. "I'm sorry I had to do it, grandfather, but you know why it was necessary."

"Yes. I'm glad, in a way, that you did — though I can hardly bear the shame. I don't know if you'll understand, Alain, but I *was* insane, in a way. I was caught up in a nightmare — my ambition, my hatred, my schemes ran away with me. Do you know that when my fortunes turned after the Fireclown business I seemed to be living in a dream thereafter? I feel as if I've just woken up. I remember I accused you of having none of the good von Bek blood. I shouldn't have done that, and I'm sorry. I tried, in my way, to apologize almost as soon as I'd said it. But it seems you had better stuff in you than I. I've always been conscious of my inherent weakness, that I wasn't of the same breed as our ancestors, but I always fought it, Alain. I tried not to let it get the better of me. It did, of course, but in a different way."

"You didn't really hate the Fireclown for anything he was doing, did you?" Alain spoke softly. "You hated him for loving my mother, and giving her a son — me. You knew he was Manny Bloom all the time."

"Yes." Simon von Bek sighed and stared out of the window again. "I knew he was Manny Bloom. I was responsible for sending him on the Saturn mission. That was my first major mistake, I suppose. But I couldn't see my daughter marrying an ordinary spaceman, however much of a hero he was in the public eye. I didn't realize you were going to be born. He was away for two years. When he came back you were here — and your mother had killed herself."

"Killed herself! I didn't know…"

"I'd told her Manny Bloom was dead — killed in a space accident. I didn't expect those consequences, of course. That was the first death I was responsible for, indirectly. As Minister for Space Transport I was in the perfect position to send Manny Bloom wherever I chose. I bided my time — then I really *did* try to kill him."

"What? You mean the rocket that went too near the sun?"

"Yes. I bribed the technician responsible for the final check — had him fix the steering rockets so that the ship would plunge into the sun. I heard the ship had gone off course and I thought I was rid of him. But somehow he survived — and he came back, to haunt me as it were, as the Fireclown."

"So you really created your own nemesis. You caused my father to drift towards the sun and that experience resulted in his strange mental state. Ultimately he appeared as the Fireclown and, because of your hatred against him, brought about your ruin without ever consciously wishing for vengeance against you."

Simon von Bek nodded. "I appreciate the irony of it all," he said. "It's one of the things I've been thinking about, sitting here and waiting for my trial."

"When is it to be?"

"They haven't fixed it yet. It's going to be a big one — will probably take place after the Presidential elections."

"Helen will be able to influence the judges then," Alain said. "She'll probably try to get you the lightest possible sentence."

"The lightest sentence would be death, Alain. And that, I'm afraid, is outside even the President's powers to exact."

Alain remembered Helen's proposal to assassinate Simon von Bek. In many ways, he thought, everyone would have welcomed it. It was painful to see this once respected and powerful man in such a wretched state, no matter how much he deserved it.

Simon von Bek got up, extending his hand. "It was good of you to come, Alain. I wonder if you would mind leaving now. This — this is somewhat hard to…" He broke off, unable to express his shame.

"Yes, of course." Alain went forward and shook Simon von Bek's hand. The old man tried to make the grip firm, but failed.

Feeling considerably more affection for his grandfather than he had ever had in the past, Alain left the cell, left Police Headquarters and stood for a long time by a splashing fountain, staring into the clear water and watching the darting goldfish swimming in the narrow confines of the pool. Did they understand just how narrow their little universe was? he wondered. They seemed happy enough, if fish could be happy. But if they weren't happy, he reflected, neither were they sad. They had no tradition but instinct, no ritual but the quest for food and a mate. He didn't envy them much.

C H A P T E R E I G H T E E N

In the following weeks Alain led a fairly solitary life, taking little interest in the elections, scarcely aware of the fact that Helen was almost certain to win since there were no candidates in the field with her popularity. Denholm Curtis, who had played some part in the denunciation of von Bek, was now the Solref's candidate for the office, but he didn't stand much of a chance. Helen was busy, but she had tried to contact him from time to time. He would see her when he was ready.

The election date came. The votes were counted. Helen was President.

The day after her election she came to see him and he let her in.

"I thought you were angry with me," she said as she accepted a drink. "I thought, perhaps, you'd decided not to see me again. I know you've had a bad series of emotional shocks, Alain — but I could have helped you. I could have been some comfort, surely."

"I didn't need comfort, Helen. I needed to be alone with myself. And anyway, you couldn't have afforded to waste time on me — you had problems of your own."

"What do you propose to do now?" She couldn't disguise the fact that she was anxious.

"Ask you to marry me, Helen."

"I accept," she said thankfully. "I thought…"

"We all tend to see other people's emotions as reflecting on ourselves. It's a mistake. People's emotions are rarely created by anyone else. I think we might be happy, don't you?"

"In spite of my work?"

"In spite of that, yes. I don't expect to see much of you for some time. But maybe that's for the best."

A buzz began to sound on her wrist.

"I'm sorry." She smiled. "I get issued with this thing — I'm on call, as it were, all the time. I didn't expect it to start so soon."

She went to his V and pressed a number.

"President Curtis," she said to the slightly perturbed-looking man on the screen. She put the drink down on the set.

"Madame — there is probably no danger but I have just received news that a strange spaceship has landed somewhere near Algiers. It's believed to be the Fireclown's."

"No need for declaring a state of emergency now." She smiled. "It will be good to see him again." She switched out and turned to Alain. "He's your father — want to be part of a deputation?"

"If it's just the two of us, yes."

"Come on then. Let's see what his experiments have proved."

Before Helen could go she was forced to leave notification of her whereabouts. Her Presidential duties had not really begun as yet, but from now on her time would never be her own. In his new state of mind, Alain decided he could bear it so long as she only served one term.

The *Pi-meson* rested on its belly, its pitted hull gleaming in the African sun. As yet, nothing had been heard from the ship. It was as if it was empty, bereft of life.

As their car settled beside it, the huge airlock began to open. But nothing else happened.

"What now?" Helen looked to Alain for guidance.

"Let's go in," he said, leading the way over to the ship and clambering into the airlock.

On the big landing deck Alain touched the stud operating the sliding wall. It opened and they climbed into the control deck. It was darkened. No light passed the closed ports.

"Father?" Alain spoke into the silence, certain someone was here. "Fireclown?"

"Alain…" The voice was rumbling, enigmatic, thoughtful.

"Yes — and Helen Curtis. We've got something to tell you." He was slightly amused at his decision to announce his engagement formally to his strange father.

A single light shone now from the corner. Alain could just make out the slumped bulk of the Fireclown. A short distance away Cornelia Fisher stirred. Corso seemed prone, but Alain thought he heard him mumble under his breath.

"Is anything wrong, father?"

"No." The Fireclown raised his huge body up from the couch. His gaudy tatters curled about him, his conical hat still bobbed on his head and his face was still painted. He chuckled. "I thought you'd come here first. I wouldn't have admitted anyone else."

"Helen and I are getting married, father."

"Ah… really?" The Fireclown didn't sound very interested. His manner had become, if anything, more detached and alien.

"A lot's been happening on Earth, sir," Helen put in, "since we last met. You're no longer an outcast."

The Fireclown's body shook with laughter which he at first suppressed and then let roll from his mouth in roaring gusts. "No — longer — an — outcast. Ha! Ha! Ha! Good!"

Nonplused, Alain glanced at Helen, who frowned back at him.

"It is not I who am the outcast, young lady — not in the cosmic sense. It is the human race, with their futile, worthless *intelligence!*"

"I still don't understand…" Helen said bewilderedly.

"I took you to the heart of the sun — I took you even to the heart of the galaxy and you still failed to understand! Consciousness is not the same as intelligence. Consciousness is content to exist as it exists, to be what it is and nothing more. But intelligence — that is a blot on the cosmos! In short, I intend to wipe out that blot. I intend to destroy intelligence!"

"Destroy intelligence? You mean, destroy life in the Solar System!" Alain was horrified.

"No, my son, nothing so unsubtle. For one thing, human life is the only culprit — the only thing that offends against the law of the multiverse. I have journeyed the roads between the worlds and have found nothing like it anywhere else. Intelligence, therefore, is a weed in the garden of infinity, a destroying weed that must be dealt with at once."

"You are mad!" Alain said desperately. "It's impossible to destroy intelligence without destroying those who have it!"

"According to human logic, that is true. But according to my logic — the Fireclown's logic — that is false. I have perfected a kind of fire — call it 'Time Fire' — which will burn away the minds of those it strikes without consuming them in body. My Time Fire will destroy the ability to think because thought takes time."

The Fireclown reached out his hand towards a stud and depressed it. The wall hummed down. He went over to the controls and began to operate them. "I waited for you to arrive because I still retain some human sentiment. I did not want to make my son go with the rest. I will convince you, anon, that I speak truth and you will agree with me. You will want only consciousness!"

Alain strode towards his father and grasped his huge arm. "It can't work — and even if it could, who are you to take such a task upon yourself?"

"I am the Fireclown!"

The screen in front of them showed that the ship had once again set up its own peculiar field. The spheres began to flash past.

"See those!" The Fireclown pointed. "They are chronons — Atoms of Time! Just as there are atoms of matter, the same is true of time. And I control those atoms as ably as the physicists control their electrons and protons. They are the stuff of my Time Fire!"

Astounded, Alain could only believe his father. He turned to Corso, who was opening his eyes, a dazed look on his red face. "Corso! Do you want any part of this? Stop him! Cornelia —" the woman stared at him blankly — "tell him to cease!"

The Fireclown put his painted, bellowing face close to Alain's. "They cannot understand you. They hear you — but they hear sound alone! They are the first to gain from the Time Fire. They are fully aware but they have no intelligence to mar their awareness."

"Oh, God!" Helen looked aghast at the blank-faced pair.

"Where are we going?" Alain yelled at his insane father.

"I intend to put the ship into a time-freeze. Then, as the globe passes beneath me, I will unleash the Time Fire, covering the world with its healing flames!"

"No, father!"

"Don't try to tamper with the controls, Alain. If you do you will disrupt the time field and we might well perish."

The spheres — the chronons — flashed past. Alain stared at them, fascinated in spite of the danger. Atoms of Time. He had heard the chronon theory before, but had never believed it had any reality in fact. But there was no other explanation he could think of for the Fireclown's ability to ignore the laws of matter and venture into the sun's heart, travel swiftly through the galaxy to its centre and remain unharmed. Unharmed bodily, at least. His mind had obviously been unable to stand up against the impressions it had seen.

Faster and faster the chronons rolled past on the screen.

Concentrating on his controls, the Fireclown ignored them.

"What are we going to do, Alain?" Helen said. "Do you think he's right about this Time Fire?"

"Yes. Look at Corso and Cornelia for proof. He is a genius — but he's an idiot as well. We've got to stop him, Helen. Heaven knows what destruction he *can* work — even if it isn't as bad as he boasts!"

"How!"

"There's only one way. Destroy the controls!"

"We could be killed — or frozen forever in this 'time freeze' of his!"

"We've got to take the risk."

"But what can you do? We've no weapon, nothing to destroy them with!"

"There's one thing we can do. I'm going to grapple with him. He's incredibly strong so I won't be able to hold him for long. While I keep him occupied, go to the control panel and press all the studs, change the position of all the levers, twist all the dials. That should do something. Ready?"

Conscious that this might be the last time he saw her before they perished, he gave her a long, eloquent look. She smiled.

He leapt at the Fireclown's back and got his arm around his father's thick neck.

The great arms went up and the hands closed over his wrists. The Fireclown shook him off.

"I've spawned a fool! You could cause us to slip into a time vortex we could never get out of!"

Alain grabbed the Fireclown's legs and, surprisingly, though the clown was still a trifle off-balance, pulled him down.

Helen dashed towards the controls and began depressing studs and pulling levers.

"No!"

The Fireclown raised himself on one elbow, his other hand outstretched in a warning gesture.

The light began to fizz, to change colour rapidly. The ship shuddered. He was blinded by the glare, his head ached. He felt the Fireclown move and flung himself at his father. With a movement of his arm and body the Fireclown shook him off again.

Then the deck seemed to vanish and they seemed to hang in space. All around him now Alain saw the spheres whirling. The great chronons, each the size of the moon, spun in a dazzling and random course.

The Fireclown bellowed like a baleful bull from somewhere. He heard Helen's voice shouting. He could make no sense of their words. He tried to move but his body was rigid, would answer none of his commands.

Then the chronons changed colour and began to expand.

They burst! A chaotic display of coloured streamers smeared themselves all around him and dissipated swiftly.

Alain tried to breathe but couldn't.

Instead, he sucked in water!

It took seconds for him to realize that he was under the sea. He struggled upwards and at last reached the surface, drew air into his lungs. He was in the middle of an ocean, no land in sight.

There was no evidence that a ship had crashed. Had it entered the water so smoothly that it hadn't made a ripple?

But — another thought came — he should have been *in* the ship! How had he got out?

Another head broke the surface. He swam towards it. The Fireclown! The paint streaked his face. He was panting and cursing. Then Helen's head came up!

"What happened!" Alain gasped. "Father — what happened?"

"Damn you! You broke the time field — I've lost my ship!"

Overhead Alain heard the drone of an air-car. He looked up, waving frantically. It was an amphibian and it seemed to be looking for them. It came down low and landed.

Puzzled faces stared out of the cabin. Someone emerged on to the small, flat deck and a line flashed out over the water. Alain caught it, swam towards Helen and handed it to her. She was pulled swiftly in and, once aboard, the line was sent back. Alain handed it to the Fireclown.

The man refused to take it. Automatically, he kept himself afloat, but his face had an expression of melancholic suffering.

"Take it, father!"

"Why should I? What purpose do I fulfill by continuing to live? I have failed."

Impatiently, Alain tied the rope around the passive Fireclown and watched the great bulk being towed in. The Fireclown made no move to release himself or help himself on to the deck.

Alain took the line as it came out once again.

"How did you know we were here?" he asked the vessel's captain.

"We saw a peculiar kind of explosion in this area. We thought we'd better investigate. Sorry it took us so long. We've been circling over this area for three hours. Can't think how we missed you the first time."

"Three hours! But..." Alain stopped. "What time is it now?"

The captain glanced at his chronometer. "Fourteen hundred, almost."

Alain was about to ask the date but he decided against it. It seemed that they had been deposited in the ocean exactly half-an-hour before they entered the Fireclown's ship. But what had happened to the ship? he asked the morose Fireclown who had slumped himself moodily in a corner of the cabin.

"I told you — you broke the time field. What happened was simple — we existed in a different time location, the ship in another. The ship should make its appearance between now and the next million years!"

Thereafter, his father refused to answer further questions.

CHAPTER NINETEEN

The trial of Simon von Bek and the trial of the Fireclown were held at the same time, but in different courts. The V stations were torn between which should have most prominence.

The *Pi-meson* had been found, intact, in Wyoming. Scientists had already stripped it of its time mechanisms and were investigating them. The Fireclown offered them no help when asked.

The relationship between the late protagonists came out, and scandal blended with sensation to feed the V networks.

Simon von Bek was not very entertaining, however. He admitted all charges and was found guilty on all charges. Even the judge did not exercise that strange prerogative which judges seem to think themselves entitled to — his summing up contained no list of his personal biases. It was quick and clean. Simon von Bek was banished to a confined bunk in one of the pressure domes in the asteroid belt.

The Fireclown was more verbose, his case harder to try since it had no precedent. He could not be tried for his philosophical beliefs, or even for his unique intentions to destroy intelligence. The charge, when it was finally decided, read: "Plotting to disrupt human society to a point where it could no longer function".

His long speeches in his defense — or rather in defense of his creed — agreed with the charge.

"I am the victim of crude intelligence," he told the bewildered jury. "Intelligence which has no business to exist in the multiverse. I have been pulled down by it as it will pull down the human race in time. I tried to help you but, for all your vaunted minds, you could not understand. Perish, then, in spirit. Set yourselves against the law of the multiverse! Your punishment will come soon enough and be well merited!"

Though still puzzled, the jury decided the Fireclown's own punishment soon enough. They found him guilty but insane. He would be sent to a mental hospital on Ganymede.

Meanwhile, the scientists continued to puzzle over his bizarre equations and could arrive at no conclusion. In time, perhaps, they would, for once on the track they would never leave it.

For the time being, public hysteria died down, and society once again settled into an ordered existence. Helen Curtis began to put her reforms to the assembly and they were accepted or rejected after discussion. Progress would be slow and would always follow behind the demands of the reformers, but at least in this manner it might retain its dynamism. Helen was comparatively satisfied.

Their wedding date was fixed.

And then came the final drama.

Alain, once more looking for a job, scanned the list of specialist agencies, and sipped coffee. The V buzzed and he switched it to receive. Helen's face appeared on the screen.

"Alain — the Fireclown's escaped!"

He put down his cup with a clatter. "What! How?"

"You know how strong he was. He overpowered a guard, got hold of his gun and held up the entire Police Headquarters. He made them release uncle Simon and they left in a stolen police car together."

"Where have they gone?"

"We don't know."

"I'm coming over. Are you at the House?"

"Yes."

When he reached the Presidential apartments Helen and some of her advisers were staring at the huge wall-screen. A commentary boomed:

"Our cameras have succeeded in tracking the escaping spaceship *Pi-meson*, containing convicts Manny Bloom, better known as the Fireclown, and Simon von Bek!"

Deep space. The ship in clear focus.

"The ship, degutted of its weird time devices but retaining its ordinary drive, has so far outdistanced all pursuers."

"That answers my question," Alain said from behind Helen. "Where are they going?"

"They seem to be heading for Venus. They could just about survive there and certainly escape the police. The revitalization project is two-thirds complete," said Helen, adding in puzzlement: "A strange pair to be traveling together!"

"They've got things in common," Alain pointed out. "In their different ways they were both reactionary idealists. They wanted things simpler than they in fact are."

The ship passed Venus.

"Where in the universe are they heading for?" Helen said, baffled.

Alain thought he knew.

He watched helplessly as the ship carrying his father and grandfather plunged on.

"Perhaps it's for the best — for them and for us," he whispered.

The Pi-meson *passed the orbit of Mercury.*

They watched as it wheeled and sailed in towards the sun.

It vanished, consumed almost immediately, as it followed its unveering course into the heart of Sol.

The watchers were silent. Helen turned her face up towards Alain and studied his expression. She glanced back at the screen.

In a few short weeks a new Age had come to Earth and gone as swiftly. It had left a strange mood behind it — and perhaps a new science. Sociologists and psychologists attempted to explain the sudden ebb of hysteria that had seized the people. There were a dozen theories, all complex, all with their merits. One attempted to explain it as the result of the transition period between "natural" (or biological) living and "artificial" (or machine) living. It concluded that until the artificial became the natural and human psychology altered accordingly we should experience many such disturbances.

It was a likely explanation. But there might have been another, far simpler explanation.

Perhaps the world had just been — *bored.*

THE SHIP COUNT RENARK had seen was one of the most famous. She was the Now The Clouds Have Meaning, perhaps the best known of all the famous Chaos Engineers' ships. Her voyages were legends. Her escapes were fabulous. Her created realities were amongst the most complex. Yet, as with all these great entities, she carried a certain sadness about her, for, like her crews, she had given up immortality for this long and enormously exciting life-span.

Still, thought Captain Billy-Bob, captain of the Now The Clouds Have Meaning, death was a very distant reality and there were so many fresh scales to explore. She made a polite enquiry of her new lover and ally, Ra, First Beast of the Skimlings.

"We are used to such scales," said the Skimling impatiently. "We run the roads between the worlds. We know the subtle shades which guide us through the fastest drops. We see no danger or novelty in what you present to us."

Billy-Bob apologized. "Then you will go with us to the Greenheart Diamond?"

"Of course."

Weeping, they embraced before the pale blues and creams of the Outer Halo which rimmed the shapes of those vast cathedrals of light and colour known as Karaquazian's Bend. Massive black globes rolled overhead, purposefully towards some unseen horizon.

The Spammer Gain had called them and when Spammer called all was beauty; terror was inevitable. Life became infinitely sweet.

"Aaahhh," breathed the handsome First Beast, fingering his unstable scars, "our time is here again. What adventures we shall find together, eh, captain!"

And he clapped a paw of liquid silver upon the fluttering carapace of his fellow Chaos Engineer.

There was a sigh from the crew as the Now The Clouds Have Meaning began her first long graceful slide down the scales, her hull ticking and twitching with every shift, her tongues licking hungrily at the strands of colour which curled about her, providing her with the energy to make another jump.

Why had Spammer called? What was the exact nature of the catastrophe? And where was von Bek?

THE SHORES OF DEATH

For Harry Harrison

"Let me assert my firm belief that the only thing we have to fear is fear itself."

— Franklin D. Roosevelt

When she told her father she was pregnant he said, "We'll have to get rid of it," but almost immediately his morbid, introverted mind was fascinated by the idea of permitting the birth; so he put his arm around his daughter's soft shoulders and murmured, "It is wrong, however, to take life, particularly when life is so scarce in this region of the world. Let us see if the child lives after birth. Let nature decide…"

They lived in a grotesque tower in the twilight region. Moulded several centuries before from steel and fibreglass by a neo-naturalist architect, its asymmetrical lines gave it the appearance of something that had grown, living, from the ground and then atrophied. Red dust blew around it and sparse brown lichen covered its lower parts.

The tower threw a black shadow across the rock and the shadow never shifted, for the Earth had not turned on its axis since the raid from space ages before, when the space-dwelling creatures had paused with casual ease to stop the world spinning, looted what they required, and passed on in their insane, ceaseless passage through the universe.

One of the birdlike mammalian bipeds had been left behind and from him it was learned that his race was seeking the edge of the universe. When they discovered it, they would fling their ships and themselves into the oblivion of absolute lifelessness. From what could be understood of the alien's explanation, his people were driven by a racial guilt which had existed for aeons. This was all mankind could learn before the alien had killed himself.

After hearing the alien creature's story, the few survivors of the raid had accepted their fate realizing the comparative insignificance of their own disaster when compared with the grandiose madness of the space-dwellers.

Now the Earth, with perpetual day on one side, perpetual night on the other, and a twilight and dawn region between the two, circled on around the sun.

Psychological alterations had been bound to result from the drastic environmental changes that had occurred in the different regions of the planet. The alterations had been beneficial to some and not to others. In the sparsely populated twilight region, where Valta Becker and his daughter lived in love, the inhabitants had turned in on themselves, rarely leaving their heavily-guarded towers, devoting their time to eccentric pursuits, pleasures and experiments of a dark, narcissistic nature.

Children were scarcely ever born in the twilight region, so inbred were the inhabitants. It was customary, in the event of conception, to destroy the foetus. Valta Becker's decision to let his incestuous offspring live was the decision of a man whose mental and emotional appetites had become dulled. Having convinced his daughter that she must endure her pregnancy, he waited in morbid anticipation for the birth.

In the season of the winds, in the postraid year 345, a son was born to Valta Becker and his pale daughter Betild.

It was a lonely, unlucky birth, and Betild died of it after a few months.

Strangely for a child of incest, Clovis Becker clung to his life and grew strong and healthy in time. He flourished in spite of his father's careless and disappointed attitude towards him. His father, expecting a freak of some kind, half hoping that his offspring should be a girl so that he could continue to experiment, lost interest in Clovis as the boy grew healthier and healthier. Clovis was as delicate-boned and slender as Betild and Valta, but there was a toughness about him and a will to survive that was intensified, perhaps, by the unconscious understanding of the circumstances by which he had entered the world. It was this will to live, apparent since birth, that was his most remarkable characteristic.

His brain was good, his intelligence broad, and, because of his father's lack of interest in him, Clovis Becker grew into an independent, self-reliant boy. When he was twelve, his father died. Clovis burned the body, locked up the baroque tower and set off for the daylight region which, for several years, it had been his ambition to visit.

Here, Clovis Becker discovered a world absolutely different from the one he knew. The society was the nearest thing to perfection that had ever existed; vital without being violent, stable without being stagnant. This society had resulted from a number of factors, the most important being a small population served by a sophisticated technology and an equally sophisticated administrative system. The arts were alive, there was universal literacy, the philosophies flourished. To Clovis the world was paradise and he was taken into it kindly and made welcome. He quickly responded to the frank and healthy outlook of the daylight people and had soon adapted to their way of life as if he had always known it.

Only in the deep places of his mind were the dark influences of his first twelve years dormant rather than exorcized. Perhaps it was these that led to his interest in the administrative life of the daylight region so that he sought power whilst thinking he sought to serve. He began by getting elected to local committees, rose to become a member of the upper council and at last supreme administrator, Council Chairman. He was much admired by everyone. He was respected for his understanding, his ability to take the right decisions at all times, his awareness of the processes governing both individual human life and society in general. It was agreed that he was the best Council Chairman there had ever been.

A much respected man, Clovis Becker; famous for his philosophical writings, his easy stoicism, his unselfish energy, his kindness and his wisdom. There were many to match him in most of the qualities, but none who combined them as he did. Clovis Becker was the golden man, almost the god, the darling of his world.

Clovis Becker was in his fifth year of office when the scientists announced the catastrophe.

For several generations no children had been born to the daylight people. With life-spans of up to three hundred years, people did not feel the need to reproduce very often. Those who tried and failed thought little of it. Everyone assumed that the reason for the lack of children was because everyone else had decided not to have any.

Then a couple complained. Other couples complained. It was discovered that a large section of the population had indeed tried to have children and had failed.

Urgent experiments and tests were made.

Physics and biology were fields in which little new research had been done for at least two hundred years; it was felt that there was no need for any more information than was available to assure comfortable living.

The climate of the times had not produced anyone sufficiently interested in the two disciplines to do new research. The increase in harmless omega radiation had been measured and noted in the previous century. It was believed that the radiation was a by-product of the mysterious energies which the space-dwellers had used to stop the world spinning. The radiation had seemed, in fact, beneficial to many plants. It had produced the flower forests, it destroyed weeds, it appeared to contribute to people's youthfulness.

The tests showed that it also affected semen and ova. In short, it had made every man and woman on daylight Earth barren.

This was not at first thought particularly disastrous. Expeditions were sent to the twilight regions to seek people who could still reproduce.

But, whether or not they had resisted the effect of the omega radiation, the denizens of the twilight regions had inbred to the state of impotence. Valta Becker had been the last father, Clovis Becker the last child of the twilight.

A few expeditions were made by robot machines into the cold nightlands, but there, as was already known, nothing lived.

In space, then?

A thousand years before, at great expense and at the cost of many lives, Mars and Ganymede had been transformed into facsimiles of Earth. They were lush worlds and they had supplied food and minerals to Earth when they had been needed. After the raid from space, they had lost their usefulness, for the population had greatly decreased. Now only a few existed on either planet, simply to ensure that they continued to produce food and minerals in case they were ever needed. The wardens of Mars and Ganymede and their small staffs were replaced every three months because three months was almost the maximum time that men could live away from Earth and remain sane.

It was because of this that space-travel to distant solar systems had been discontinued not long after man had first gone into space; it had been discovered that in spite of their ability to reproduce exactly Earth atmosphere and other conditions on ship or, as in the case of Mars and Ganymede, even on planets, somehow men could not bear being away from Earth for long.

There were psychological explanations, physiological explanations, semi-mystical explanations for this being so, but the fact remained: Men who were on average away from Earth for little over three months went mad with pain and a terror that welled up from the recesses of their minds and could not be controlled. Even in space, on the journey to Mars, men had to undergo the *space ache*. The word had been coined to describe the indescribable experience of leaving the mother planet. Space ache — a combination of mental and physical agony — came soon after your ship had passed the half-way point on the journey to Mars. It was possible, by complicated methods, to relieve the space ache, but not to avert it.

Thus the faint hope that those men who guarded Earth's colonies for a few months every year would not have received as much omega radiation as those who had never left Earth.

It was proved that they had, while on Earth, received more than enough radiation.

There was a legend — a mere fiction, everyone knew — that a colony had been founded on Titan soon after the raid and that the colonists had managed to adapt, losing something of their humanity in the process. Half-human or not, their seed could be used.

It was an illustration of the point of desperation reached that a volunteer expedition was sent to Titan and did not return.

There was no escape from the truth after that. The space-dwellers had, probably without realizing it, effectively destroyed the human race. In two hundred years everyone would be dead. Two hundred years was the life expectancy of the youngest person on Earth. Her name was Fastina Cahmin.

When the realization dawned that the mortality of the race could not be averted a new mood swept through the society of daylight Earth. The people gave themselves up to pleasure-seeking, and a party began. It was a kind of Wake; a premature Wake held by the soon to be deceased. Too sophisticated to let it control them as yet, the people of the daylight suppressed their hysteria or gave vent to it harmlessly, in their arts and pleasures.

Clovis Becker resigned his chairmanship of the council and mysteriously disappeared.

The shock of realizing he was never to propagate himself had re-awakened the dormant elements in Becker's psyche.

He became wholly driven by what had caused him to survive his birth and early childhood so successfully. He became wholly driven by his intense will to live.

The long party continued and the signs of the suppressed hysteria began to show — in the fashions, art and in the topics of conversation. From time to time people wondered where Clovis Becker had gone and why he had gone, though it had not taken them long to get used to instances of irrational actions by men once thought completely adjusted. It had been surprising, though, that Clovis Becker, their demigod, should break so soon — unless he was seeking still for a remedy for their plight. They told themselves that this must be so. It was comforting to know that Becker was making this sacrifice, even though it was absolutely certain that no hope was left.

Clovis Becker was gone a year and then he returned to his friends and his people.

They celebrated his home-coming with a party. It was really just part of the ever-present party. It was more elaborate than usual that was all.

B O O K   O N E

THE ROADS BETWEEN THE WORLDS

C H A P T E R O N E

S O M E T H I N G T O F E A R

It was a noisy party, a colourful party, a splendid, exciting party, and it swirled all around him in the huge hall. It was packed full of life; full of heads and genitals and bellies and breasts, legs and chests and arms and hands; people with pumping hearts under their ribs, rushing blood in their veins, nerves at work, muscles moving. Most of their costumes were colourful and picturesque, though here and there stood a dark-clad sexless individual in heavy clothes, wearing a mask and with its head shaven. But most of them drank down the liquor and ate up the food and they danced and flirted and they talked all the time. It is necessary, he thought.

The walls of the hall were of pseudo-quartz, translucent and coloured like writhing rainbows. Pillars, arches and galleries, rising from the floor, were of the same subtle manufacture. Music filled all parts of the hall and there was laughter, excited voices. The throng seemed in good humour.

He tried to relax and join in the pleasure. A roboid waiter, humanlike but running on hidden casters, paused with a tray of drinks. Clovis Becker reached out from his seat in the corner and took a wine-glass; but as he did so he saw his pursuer again. The enigmatic face was merged with the blackness, but Becker recognized the awkward way in which the man held his head, as if he had weak neck muscles and was keeping the head erect by an effort. Becker stared at him, but there was no response from the dark figure, no sign that he knew Becker was looking at him.

Becker sipped his drink, wondering whether to ignore the man or cross the hall and confront him. But he felt afraid.

To succumb to the fear would be irrational, he realized. Fear could be understood and controlled. There seemed no reason to be afraid of the mysterious figure. Becker frowned and stood up, stepping down from the little dais and joining the heaving, almost solid mass of people on the floor. Being very tall, he could look over their heads and keep his attention on the still figure of the man who stood in the shadow on the far side of the hall.

Almost involuntarily, Becker began to move forward. Everything but himself and the other figure seemed unreal. He was hardly aware of the warm bodies pressing against his and now even the noise of the party seemed distant.

He had held off confronting this man for too long. He had had opportunities on Mars and Ganymede to speak to him face to face. He had seen him more than once on Earth, too; but he had given in, every time, to his irrational reluctance to admit that the man existed, or that his constant presence near him was anything more than coincidence.

He knew the man only as Mr Take. He had discovered that much from the passenger list of the ship they had both taken to Mars. The outdated form of address the man chose to use before his name was another unusual thing about him, smacking of the pointless eccentricities of the twilight people. It was even likely that Mr Take was not his real name.

Repressing his fear, Becker moved more rapidly towards him.

Overhead a fat man levitated, laughing in a way that had not been heard a year ago. The laughter was brittle, hysterical. The fat man ascended erratically towards the nearest gallery where similarly laughing men and women reached out, trying to grab him. He was giggling so much himself that he could hardly control his flight, threatening to crash on the heads of the crowd below. He had a bottle in his hand and, as he veered about in the air like a gigantic, drunken bumble bee, the bottle spilled its contents, raining golden wine down into the hall. Some of it caught Becker in the eyes. He paused to wipe his face, and when he looked at the corner again, Mr Take had gone.

Carefully scanning the hall, Becker saw Take moving slowly towards one of the big oval entrances. The crowd, like the foaming wake of a ship, seemed to divide about him as he walked.

Becker shrugged. He felt relieved that the man was leaving.

Then Take turned. He still held his head in that strange way, but now he looked directly at Clovis Becker. Take's frame was thin; his head was long and pale, his sombre eyes hooded, colourless.

Becker shrugged again, emphatically, and felt someone touch his hand. It was his old friend, Narvo Velusi, the man who had chosen to protect him when, over twenty years before, he had first come to daylight Earth. Narvo Velusi was two hundred and ninety years old; a man nearing death. There were few signs of this on Velusi's face. The flesh was old, but firm, the blue eyes alert and the hair dark. He had a square face and a bulky, wide-shouldered body. When he spoke his tone was mild but vibrant.

"Are you enjoying the party, Clovis?"

Clovis felt slightly offended by the presence of the hand on his arm. He took a step back. He had never considered Velusi's age before, but now he did and the thought was unpleasant. He controlled himself and smiled.

"Wonderful, Narvo. It was good of you…"

"You don't look happy, though. Perhaps I was thoughtless? I should have given you time to rest before I suggested the party. After all, you only got back this afternoon…"

"No, I meant it. It's a relief to be back here and a pleasure to be with so many people." He looked for Take, but the dark man had gone. "Did you invite a person who calls himself Mr Take?"

Velusi shook his head. "Did you hope to meet him? He could be here. It's open house — to welcome you back."

"No — he was here. He's gone."

"I still think you seem ill at ease, Clovis."

Becker tried to smile again. "I suppose I am a little tired. I'll stay though. It would be ungracious to leave so soon."

"Not at all. Let's go. Your house has been prepared for you. If you —"

"No. I'll stay. Have you heard of this Mr Take? A strange man." Becker described him.

"He sounds it. I should know a man like that — but I don't. Why are you so interested in him?"

"I've seen him before. Not just on Earth — on Mars and Ganymede, too. He seems to have been following me."

Velusi pursed his lips. Becker knew that he was too polite to ask him directly where he had been and why he had been gone so long. Velusi was evidently hoping to hear more. Becker was half-ashamed of himself for being so secretive with his old friend, but he had long ago made up his mind to share his ideas with no-one else.

"We can find out who and where this Take is tomorrow," Velusi said with a smile. Once again he took Becker's arm. Once again Becker felt a trace of revulsion at the touch but let Velusi steer him towards the nearest gravishute. "Come on, Clovis, cheer up. Let's go and meet some friends. I think you know most of them."

Becker made himself relax as Velusi stood aside to let him enter the gravishute entrance. The gravishute was a circular shaft going from top to bottom of the house. At its base was a force-beam generator. A single button by the entrance could control the strength of the beam so that one could drift gently down or be pushed gently up. Inside the opening was a simple hand-grip which could be grasped to halt one's progress.

The harnessing of this power had contributed a great deal to Earth's present civilization, and all techniques were now based on it, as earlier they had been based on nuclear energy.

They drifted up to the highest gallery, several hundred feet above the floor of the hall. There were only a few people here lying on couches, talking quietly. Most of them were old acquaintances. Becker greeted them politely. He sat down on a couch beside Velusi.

Several of the men and women there were ex-officials of the council. Since the disaster, most people had followed Becker's example and resigned their jobs so that now only a skeleton staff looked after the administration. It was all that was needed.

Becker was surprised to see Brand Calax, Warden of Ganymede, in conversation with Andros Almer, ex-Controller of Public Communications. Calax should have been in the middle of his three-month duty on Ganymede. Why was he here?

Miona Pelva, a red-headed woman running to fat, smiled at Becker. She had been Deputy Chairman under his chairmanship. She had not been fat then. She was not the only person who had let herself go since last year's news.

"How was space?" She was evidently as eager as Velusi to hear him answer the questions they had all been asking about him.

"Awful," he smiled.

"Isn't it always? Any after-effects of the space ache?" She shook her head in sympathy, her floppy purple headdress waving. "A *year* away! Was it all spent in space?"

"Not all."

"Somebody said they thought you'd gone back to the twilight region for a while." The speaker was a sharp-featured man wearing a golden gauze mask over his upper face. The fashion of wearing masks had grown up since Becker had left. Symptomatic of the suppressed hysteria now dominating daylight Earth, Becker thought.

"Really?" said Becker, thinking that people's manners also seemed to have declined in the year.

Velusi changed the subject. "Have you been to see Carleon's new novel, Quiro?" he asked the man in the golden mask. "You must see it, Clovis. The mood mobiles are very impressive."

Becker felt more comfortable as the conversation went on to more general topics. A little later he rose and went over to speak to Brand Calax and Andros Almer. The men seemed to be arguing quite fiercely but broke off as he greeted them.

"Sit down, Clovis," Almer said cheerfully. "The council's gone to pieces since you left — but I suppose there's no need for it any more. Brand and I were discussing this idea of his about sending another expedition to Titan. Do you think it's a good idea?"

Becker shrugged. "I doubt if it would achieve anything but a few more deaths. Besides, who'd volunteer now?"

Brand Calax was a squat man with a pointed, black beard. He wore an orange turban, a red, knee-length coat, open at the neck and flared at the waist, and low-heeled boots. Some said he had been born in space. Certainly he had a stronger resistance to the space ache than anyone else.

"I would," Calax said. "I could take it — I doubt if anyone else could."

"It's a long journey," Becker said.

Andros Almer scowled. He had a dark, tanned face, slightly slanting eyes and cheekbones, full lips and a supercilious expression that always seemed a little studied. "A pointless journey," he said.

"You agree we should not give up," Calax growled. "What else is there to do?"

"Anything would be better than risking your life or your sanity in a voyage through space to a planet that is barely habitable in search of a group of people *thought* to have gone there just after the raid and who would probably be dead if they had!" Almer drew a deep breath and was going to continue when Brand Calax broke in.

"I told you I had found evidence that a large expedition did land on Titan. I circled the world myself. I saw the remains of ships. I saw suggestions that attempts had been made to begin a settlement of some kind."

"You saw these things from a great distance!" Almer said. "You brought back no proof that you actually saw ships and buildings. Your eyes might have deceived you. Maybe you saw what you hoped to see! Why didn't you land?"

Becker listened intently to the two men.

"Because I had little fuel left and because the space ache was getting me," Calax said sharply. "I was in a converted ferry. They haven't a big range!"

"And that's the only survey you made." Almer spread his hands. "Flimsy evidence, surely? Yet you came back to Earth to ask for a special ship to be built so that you can bring some of these 'survivors' back to Earth. Even if there were ships and buildings — do you think anyone could have lasted on a world like Titan?"

"It's possible," Calax said. "I spent nine months at a stretch away from Earth once."

"Nine months — and you're scarcely typical of the rest of us. These people are supposed to have been on Titan for four hundred years!"

Calax turned to Clovis Becker. "It's just possible, isn't it, Clovis?"

Becker shook his head. "Not likely, though. You want to build a ship, eh, to take you to Titan and bring back the people you think are there?"

"The descendants of the original expedition," Calax said brusquely. "It's a chance worth taking, I think. If I hadn't been away when the first expedition was made, I'd have volunteered. I could have made it."

"Possibly," said Almer. "I still think we should be concentrating on something more positive — creating semen and ova artificially, for instance."

"It's been tried. Not one of our scientists has got anywhere." Calax helped himself to wine.

Becker sensed that a genuine dislike existed between the two. There seemed no reason for it. There seemed to be no argument, either. If Calax wanted to go to Titan, surely that was his risk?

He started to say as much when suddenly they all looked up. The hubbub of the party, which had been in the background all the time, had cut off sharply.

Becker moved to the edge of the gallery and leant over the invisible force-rail.

People were streaming rapidly from the hall. All the other galleries had been cleared. Through every exit, people hurried silently. They seemed tense.

Then they had gone and the hall was still and silent.

There was party litter everywhere and the light breeze from the entrances stirred it. That was the only movement.

Almost in the centre of the hall, near a couch, Becker saw a dark shape on the floor. It was the figure of a man.

As Almer, Calax, Velusi and the others reached the rail, Becker turned and made for the gravishute. He descended rapidly, crossed the hall to where the figure lay.

The man was dressed in the high fashion of the moment, his head shaved, his rust-coloured mask obscuring his entire face, belted coat of deep blue spread out around him on the floor.

Becker knelt beside him and felt his pulse.

He was dead.

Velusi and Almer crossed the hall towards him.

"What's the matter with him?" Almer asked.

"Dead," said Becker. He peeled off the mask. The man was old. Evidently he had died of a heart attack probably brought on by the excitement of the party.

Velusi turned away, clearing his throat. Almer looked embarrassed.

"Why did they all just leave like that?" Becker asked. "So suddenly — not trying to help him or anything..."

"They probably decided to carry on with the party somewhere else," Velusi said. "That's what usually happens — they go on somewhere else..."

"I don't understand," Becker said. "You mean they just leave a corpse where it lies?"

"Usually," said Almer. "You can't blame them, can you?"

"I can't understand them, either!" Becker said disapprovingly. "What's happening here nowadays, Andros?"

"Can't you guess?" said Velusi quietly. "Are you sure you can't understand them, Clovis?"

CHAPTER TWO

SOMEONE TO LOVE

Fastina Cahmin had waited a year for Clovis Becker to return, but on the day of his arrival she had been asleep. She could go without sleep for extraordinarily long periods and could spend an equally long time catching up on it. She woke, after three days asleep, to learn that Becker had come home. Andros Almer had told her in a letter he had left while she slept.

Fastina Cahmin was a widow whose husband had been one of the Titan expedition volunteers. She was twenty-eight and the youngest woman in the world. She was the last child of the day side of the Earth as Clovis Becker was the last child of the twilight region.

She was tall, with a slender, full-breasted figure and golden skin. Her hair was black and her eyes were a deep, luminous blue. She had a small, oval face and a wide mouth. Perhaps because her life-span would be so long, she took a sensual pleasure in living that was nowadays rare.

Before her husband's death she had known Clovis Becker only socially, but she had been completely in love with him for several years. Her husband had loved her with similar single-mindedness and she believed, without remorse, that it was because he had realized her own obsession that he had volunteered for the Titan expedition.

She read Almer's letter.

> *Fastina,*
>
> *My selflessness knows no bounds. We heard today that Becker is on the Mars ship and should arrive this afternoon. Remember what you told me. I hope you are unlucky.*
>
> *With love,*
> *Andros*

She smiled affectionately. She liked Andros. He had been the one who had brought the news of her husband's presumed death. At the same time, knowing what her feelings had been towards her husband, he suggested that she should come and live with him. She had refused, telling him that she would first propose to Clovis. If he rejected her, which was likely, she would then accept Andros. That was what the letter was about.

She put the letter on the table beside her bed and touched a stud on the control panel. The wall shimmered and became transparent. It was a fine day. The sun, at permanent zenith, shone down on the sea. The tideless expanse of water was completely still and blue. The white beach that led up to her house was deserted, as it almost always was. In daylight Earth, people lived far apart. Their houses were self-sufficient and transport swift. There was no need for cities. The nearest thing to a city had been the few buildings which had housed the administrative offices.

Fastina lived in an area that had once been Greece, although there were no artificial boundaries of that sort any more. The planet's real boundaries were now formed by the twilight region.

She contacted Central Information on her V-screen, and asked: "Where is Clovis Becker at this moment?"

The screen replied.

"He was last observed half-an-hour ago entering the south-western flower forest."

Fastina put on her best dress. Its crimson fabric was virtually weightless and drifted around her like a cloud of blood. She took the gravishute to the roof of her house. There her air carriage waited. Its golden body had been moulded to the shape of a fantastic bird with spreading wings. There was a cavity in the back, lined with deep red cushions. Up to four people could rest in it in comfort.

She climbed into the carriage and put a small, ultrasonic whistle to her lips. She blew a particular signal and the air carriage drifted upwards over the beach and the sea. Like a fabulous creature it swept gracefully towards the south-west and the flower forest.

A little while later she walked through the flower forest, hoping that she might bump into Clovis Becker. She walked with a long, easy stride, smiling as she breathed in the scents of the huge blooms hanging above her and around her.

Everywhere rose the shining green and brown trunks of the flowers and the scents were so heavy that they drugged her into a state of pleasant light-headedness. She looked up at the leaves, the petals, the heat-hazy sky and the sun. Beneath her feet were petals of all colours; large petals of pale purple, small ones of dark purple, pink, pale yellow and mauve. There were petals of yellow, scarlet, cerise and crimson, petals of soft blue and orange, sometimes ankle deep. And there was every shade of sunlit green, from near-black to near-white, where flower trees stood tall and cool or clustered to the ground.

She turned down a path that was thick with the cerise flowers fallen from the trees above her. It was cooler in this avenue and, although like all her people she had become used to the great heat of the world, she appreciated the shade.

She did not, as she had hoped, bump into Clovis Becker. She bumped into Andros Almer instead and knew at once that it was not accidental. Obviously he had guessed she would come here.

Almer had succumbed to fashion, it seemed. He was wearing a gauze mask that gave his face a blue tinge. He wore a deep blue pleated shirt, black, tight trousers and a loose, black cloak that was gathered in at the waist and belted. He paused, bent and picked up one of the fallen cerise flowers, offering it to her with a smile.

She smiled back and accepted it. "Hello, Andros. Have you seen Clovis?"

"Ah," he said lightly. "If I were vain, I'd be so offended..."

She laughed. "I hope you are vain, Andros. Didn't Alodios write 'Vanity makes for variety in a man, whereas humility offers only the humdrum'? I'd hate you to be humdrum."

"You hate me anyway," he said with a mock frown. "Besides, if what you say is the truth then Clovis should not attract you, for his lack of vanity is well known. He's a perfect man, all virtue and no vice — a whole man. A whole man offers no surprises, Fastina. Change your mind or risk his acceptance. He would *bore* you to death!"

"I see you're not completely given to the fashion," she said lightly. "You can still force yourself to say the word..."

"Death is all I want if you won't have me, Fastina."

"Don't die, Andros. It would embarrass all those poor people. After all, it's our duty to stay alive, isn't it? Just in case."

"Just in case there's a miracle and the world starts spinning and jostles our genes so that overnight we all find ourselves parents of triplets?" Andros laughed, but now his laughter was sharper. "That's the soundest hope, you know. There are wilder ones about. Brand Calax believes there are people on Titan just throbbing with healthy seeds. The only trouble is the gravity's a bit heavy and they look like walking pancakes. The big bangers might have a better idea — they want to go out in one mighty explosion. They seriously suggested we make a bomb big enough to blow up every human artifact in the world."

"Why blow them up?"

"They think they've no right to exist. They've gone off sex as well — no love-making without progeny, they say. What a syndrome!"

"Poor things. I'd never have thought people could change so much."

"It's fear," he said. "And they've got every right to be afraid. You're lucky — you don't seem to worry at all."

"I'm worried, of course, but I can't believe it altogether."

"You should have been on the council when we gradually realized the whole truth. You'd believe it." He pulled at his dark clothes, fingered his mask. "Look at all this — I *like* the fashion, but you can see what's creating it. I must be as scared as anyone else. I haven't started shaving my head, yet, or wearing those sweltering black masks and robes — but don't be surprised if I get to like the idea in a few months."

"Oh, Andros, you're too intelligent to go that far!" She smiled.

"Intelligence has very little to do with it. Can I take you to the meeting?"

"Is there a meeting?"

"Is there a meeting! Your senses must be more distracted than I guessed. That's why Clovis is here. Everyone interested is in the Great Glade discussing Brand Calax's idea. It'll be decided today whether to let him have the materials to build his ship or not. I hope they laugh him out of the glade!" The last sentence was spoken with such vehemence that she glanced at him in surprise. *Was* Andros becoming unbalanced? She could hardly believe it.

"When does the debate start?" she asked, taking his arm gingerly.

"It's already started. Come on, we'll go there now." He put the ultrasonic whistle to his lips and shortly afterwards his carriage moved down through the flower trees, hardly disturbing a leaf. It hovered a foot above the ground, its ornate metal scroll-work glistening red and yellow. Andros helped her on to the plush cushions and lay down on the couch opposite her. He blew on the instrument and the carriage rose into the hot sky. Through its transparent floor, she saw the mass of brightly coloured flowers, some measuring twenty feet across, moving swiftly past.

She said nothing as they flew along and Andros seemed to respect her silence and stared with apparent interest at the flowers until the carriage had found a space for itself among the hundreds of other carriages hovering above the Great Glade where that part of Earth's society sufficiently concerned with the problem of a second Titan flight had met to debate. For a moment she thought she saw Andros glance at her in a peculiar way, but she dismissed the idea, guessing that it came from her own abnormal mental state.

"I see you're not wearing a gravstrap," Andros said, reaching under the couch. He handed her the thin, tubular belt and fitted a similar one under his arms. She did the same, clipping the thing together over her breastbone. They left the carriage and drifted down among the packed tiers until they found two vacant chairs and seated themselves.

Below them, on the central dais, Brand Calax was speaking. He still wore his turban and red coat.

She did not listen closely to Brand Calax until she was sure Becker was there, sitting with his arms folded, dressed in a simple high-collared white shirt, black trousers and with small dark lenses over his eyes to protect them. From his seat in the first tier, he seemed to be listening intently to Calax. Beside Clovis sat old Narvo Velusi, dressed soberly in a russet toga, his high-heeled black boots stretched out before him, his body bent forward slightly. His square, heavy face was turned towards Calax.

Calax's voice seemed harsh to Fastina. He was speaking urgently and bluntly.

"In about two hundred years there won't be any of us left in the world. The human race will be nothing but a few bones and a few buildings. Surely it's better to keep trying to stop that happening? Everyone on Earth seems to have drawn in on themselves — there's an apathy I never expected to see. Do you want to die? From what I've seen in the past few days, that's the last thing you wish. Besides — I'm only saying I want to risk my own life on Titan. I know what the gravity's like and I know that that combined with space ache is too much for the average man to take for more than a day or so. But I'm used to space — I can even live with the space ache for longer than I'd need to stay on Titan, just to make sure there isn't any hope there. I'm asking for materials we'll never need to use for anything else. What's the matter with everyone? Why don't you just let me go ahead? I'm the only one who might be hurt!" Calax wiped his forehead and waited for the response. None came. "We've got to go on trying," he said. "It's a valuable human trait to go on trying. We survived the raid. We can survive this."

"This is the aftermath of the raid," said Almer from the audience. The silvery phonoplates hanging in the air around the auditorium picked up his words and amplified them for the others. "We only *thought* we'd survived it."

Narvo Velusi got up and looked at the mediator who sat on the dais behind Calax. The mediator was a fair-haired man with a blond moustache which he kept stroking. He nodded and Velusi walked on to the dais as Calax left it.

"I think I can tell Brand Calax why we are reluctant to grant him the resources to build his ship," said Velusi quietly. "It is because we have now become so fearful that we are even afraid to hope. We are rational people normally — our society is still probably the most perfect in history. Yet we can all sense it going sour on us — our reason doesn't seem to be helping any more. I think this is because, though we know why we are behaving unreasonably, what has happened to us is bigger than reason. It strikes at our deep psychic drives — our animal drives, for that matter. We are no longer immortal as a race. We had always assumed we would be. We are beginning to behave irrationally and I think this will get worse, no matter what we do to try to stop it. I feel that Brand Calax should be allowed to do as he thinks fit — but I share the general opinion that he will be doing it for nothing."

Velusi's calm, slow words seemed to impress his listeners. Fastina saw people nodding agreement with him. She too sensed his sanity, his understanding of the situation they were all in.

Someone else spoke from the audience.

"May we hear what Clovis Becker thinks?"

Velusi glanced at Becker.

Becker remained seated. He said. "I can add nothing more to what Narvo Velusi has said. I am sorry."

People looked disappointed. Evidently the rumour that Becker had been seeking some solution had been wrong.

Velusi continued:

"There is little hope. It would be stupid to hope. If our destiny is to die, let us try to do it well."

A woman laughed shrilly. They saw her rising towards her air carriage on her gravstrap. A few others followed her. A group of faceless, sexless people in their masks and dark clothes also returned to their air carriages. The vehicles wheeled away through the bright, hot sky.

Brand Calax jumped back on to the dais. "And let's do it fighting! Will you give me my spaceship?"

The mediator stopped stroking his moustache and got up. "Who agrees?" he asked the crowd.

Hands rose. The mediator counted them.

"Who disagrees?"

Fastina watched Andros raise his hand.

The mediator counted again.

"Brand Calax, the resources you need are at your disposal," said the mediator formally.

Calax nodded his thanks, touched his gravstrap and rose into the air.

Fastina saw Clovis Becker stand up, obviously preparing to leave. He was pointing into the air, towards a white air carriage hovering above him. Narvo Velusi was nodding. They were obviously deciding to travel in that carriage.

Impulsively she touched the control of her gravstrap and was lifted upwards, guiding herself gently towards the white carriage.

Andros shouted after her, but he did not follow.

She reached the carriage before Becker and Velusi. She drifted over the side and sat down on one of the couches.

Clovis was not the first man she had confronted with a proposal of marriage, but her heart was beating rapidly as he and Velusi reached the craft and saw her sitting there.

Clovis recognized her and smiled. "Hello, Fastina."

"Hello, Clovis. Welcome back. How are you feeling after your mysterious travels?"

"He's better today," Velusi said, settling on to a couch and raising a whistle to his lips, "you should have seen him yesterday, Fastina!"

Becker did feel better that morning, having slept well during the period they still called "night". He felt more his old self. He sat down next to Fastina and kissed her lightly on the forehead. They had never been lovers, but she had always flirted with him and he had always responded cheerfully.

Before he blew the appropriate signal, Velusi asked: "Do you want a lift, Fastina?"

"Not really," she said. "I came to see Clovis. If you're busy, I'll wait…"

"That's all right," Becker told her. "It's nice to see you again. Come and have some lunch at my house."

She looked at him, wondering how deep his affection was. She could tell that he was attracted to her, but she knew he was not the man to begin a casual love affair on the strength of a mild attraction.

The carriage was moving away from the flower forest, passing over the occasional house. Now that there was no need for towns, public services were maintained by a big underground computerized network. The houses were mobile and a man and his friends or family could land their buildings in the scenery of their choice. Becker's house was situated at the moment close to the lake that had once been known as Lake Tanganyika. Europe, Africa, the Middle East, India and parts of Russia faced the sun, as did a tiny part of the South American continent. Most of South America, all of North America, nearly all of China, and all of Japan and the Australias lay in the night region. The habitable world was, in fact, what had been the known world before the great explorations of the Renaissance.

Soon they could see the lake ahead, like a sheet of blue steel flanked by hills and forests. Herds of animals grazed below. While the human race had decreased, the animals had proliferated; perhaps because their life cycles were shorter, they had adapted to the omega radiation in time. It was ironic, thought Becker as his carriage dropped towards the mosaic roof of his tall house, that if human longevity had not been increased they would probably be all right as far as the survival of the race was concerned. With what had once been the normal cycle of life and death, genes might have built up a gradual resistance. It was too late to do anything about it now, though.

When the car had landed, Clovis helped Fastina out of it. She smiled, breathing in the rich, heavy air. Africa directly faced the sun and its vegetation was even lusher than it had been. She glanced at Clovis and was about to comment on the view when she thought she caught a peculiar look in his eyes, as if he stared at some secret part of her that she did not know existed — some physical organ of hers which stored the secrets of her unconscious ambitions and her future.

She thought of him for an instant as an ancient, sombre shaman who might cut the organ from her living body and toss it steaming in the still air to make some unholy divination. He smiled at her quietly as he gestured for her to precede him into the gravishute which gaped in the centre of the roof. Perhaps, she thought, he had not been looking into her soul, but his own.

Dropping into the dark hole of the shute, she felt as if she were condemning herself to an irrevocable destiny. Whether her destiny would be good or bad she could not tell.

I'm in a funny state of mind, she thought, as she drifted down. A disordered state of mind, no doubt about that. It must be love…

Later they stood drinking aperitifs on the balcony outside the dining room. It looked out over the lake. A great cloud of pink flamingos flew past, high above the lake. There was a sense of peace now and the silence of the countryside was broken only by the distant call of some wild canine in the forest.

"When we're gone, at least this will remain," said Velusi leaning on the invisible force-rail. "When people bothered to debate these abstract issues, some used to think that the human race was a freak — a sport of nature — that we had no business being here at all and no place in the scheme of things. Perhaps they were right."

Fastina smiled. "It doesn't matter now."

"Not to us," Velusi replied, "but there are people about even today who think that the space-dwellers were some sort of mystic agency — you know, like in the old religions — whose purpose was to eliminate human beings, to straighten the biological record, as it were. It matters to them — it's becoming their creed."

"You mean those peculiar people who shave their heads and so on?" Becker asked.

"Yes, poor things," Velusi sighed. "We don't change much, do we? Only a short time ago we had nothing to fear. Our population was small, we had everything we wanted, the world was good — we lived in a paradise, though we didn't know it…"

"I knew it," Becker murmured.

"Yes, I suppose you did," Velusi continued. "I remember when you first came to live with us how you would go on and on telling us how perfect our society was compared with the one you'd just left. I could never properly understand why a certain kind of person actually chose to live in the twilight…"

"Can you now?" Fastina asked.

"In a way, yes. Those people with their shaven heads are living in a kind of mental twilight already. If you have that mentality, then I suppose you choose to live where it can survive best. That's what I was going to say. In a world without fear the human virtues flourish and become dominant. We've had no violence, no major neuroses for centuries. The space-dwellers somehow managed

THE ROADS BETWEEN THE WORLDS

to put us in our place, made us realize our limitations, made us cultivate the best of what we had. But now fear is back, isn't it? Fear was largely responsible for creating the primitive religions, and fear, of one sort or another, was what fostered the unpleasant elements in even the sophisticated religions. Fear produced repressive societies, totalitarian governments, wars, and the major proportion of sexual perversions, as well, of course, as the multitude of mental perversions — perverse philosophical theories, political systems, religious creeds, even artistic expression. Think of the numbers of talented creative people who spent their lives trying to bend their gifts to express some insane notion of the way things should be." Velusi gestured with his glass. "Well, it seems we're back where we started. There's nothing we can do about it — when in the past did a really irrational person ever listen to reason? I'm not a pessimistic man, but I get the feeling that we're going to enter a new dark age which will only end when the last man or woman on Earth dies — and at this rate that could be even sooner than we think..."

"You sound like an ancient prophet yourself, Narvo." Becker drained the remainder of his drink. "The apocalypse is at hand, eh?"

CHAPTER THREE

SOMETHING TO HIDE

They ate in Becker's dining room. It was not large. Its walls were decorated with abstract frescoes, vaguely reminiscent of Mayan art. The room was just a little gloomy.

After the meal, Narvo Velusi got up to go. He had guessed the purpose of Fastina's visit.

"I'll see you tomorrow, Clovis," he said. "And I'll tell you then about my own equally unreasonable project." He waved cheerfully and entered the gravishute entrance.

"I wonder what that could be," Becker murmured when he had gone. "I hope it's nothing drastic."

Fastina poured more wine for both of them. "Narvo wouldn't do anything drastic would he? Do you think he's right about what he said? It sounded ominous — and it did seem reasonable."

Becker stretched out in his big chair. "We haven't changed much in all those thousands of years, Fastina. We have the same drives, the same ambitions — presumably the same fears producing the same results. I know that I've felt afraid at times, recently…"

"But you've been in space. That's different."

"Not just in space. In fact it's nothing to do with space or any other kind of environment — it's in *me*. I think it always has been."

"Is that what made you go off so suddenly?"

He laughed. "You're still trying to find out about that, aren't you? I promised myself I'd tell no-one why I left or what I'm looking for…"

"So you're looking for something." She smiled back. "Not someone, by any chance?"

He shook his head. "Not a woman, Fastina, if that's what you're getting at.

I don't need to look, anyway, when the nicest woman I've ever known is sitting ⟩site me." He spoke half-jokingly and she looked at him carefully, trying to ⟩ if the statement had been anything more than a pleasant compliment. ʏʊɪ an instant he returned her gaze steadily, then looked at the wine. He reached out and refilled their glasses. They were both drinking more than usual.

"It is someone as well," he continued. "Someone with something I want — and even then I'm not sure they have it."

"You're not being fair, Clovis," she said lightly. "You're making it sound more and more intriguing!"

"I'm sorry, Fastina. I suppose there's no harm in mentioning the name of the person. It's Orlando Sharvis…"

He glanced at her intently, as if looking for a sign that she recognized the name. It was vaguely familiar, but nothing more.

"No," she said. "It doesn't mean anything. I won't press you any further, Clovis. I'm sorry to have sounded so curious. You're back now, that's the main thing."

He rubbed his lips, nodding abstractedly. "For the time being, anyway," he said quietly.

Now she could not disguise her anxiety. She leant towards him over the table. "You're not leaving again?"

"It might be necessary." He touched her hand. "Don't worry about it, Fastina. My own feelings are as stupid as anyone's. Maybe I'll see sense and forget all about them."

She held his hand tightly and now they looked directly into each other's faces.

"We should enjoy life," she said hesitantly. "Shouldn't we? While we can?"

Still holding her hand, he got up and came round to the couch.

He took her in his arms, pressing her to his body. "Perhaps you're right," he said. His voice was trembling, grim, distant.

He kissed her suddenly and she responded, though now she was afraid of him, afraid of something she had released in him. His love-making became urgent, desperate.

"The bedroom," he murmured and they got up together, walking towards the gravishute.

His frantic and tense manner disturbed her, but she knew it was far too late to do anything but let him lead her into the shaft. They rose up together. His grasp on her arm was painful.

They reached the bedroom entrance and he caught the hand-grip, pulling them both to the side of the shaft. They entered his room. It had been darkened and only a little light came through the outer wall.

Surprised, she saw the silhouette of a man against it. A man who held his head in a peculiar way.

In a world without crime, locks and alarms did not exist, so that the man could have entered the room when and how he chose. He was guilty of a crime; an invasion of privacy at very least.

That was not what shocked Becker so much as his recognition of the man. He paused by the gravishute entrance, still gripping Fastina's arm.

"What do you want here, Mr Take?" he said.

The man did not move, did not speak.

Almost for the first time in his adult life, Clovis Becker allowed anger to get the better of him. He let go of Fastina's arm and plunged across the room towards the dark figure.

"This time I'm getting my explanation," he said, reaching out towards Take.

The intruder moved just before Becker's hands touched him. He moved faster than it should have been possible for an ordinary man to move. He made for the gravishute, but Fastina blocked the entrance with her body. He veered aside and stood stock still again. Then he spoke. His voice was melodious and deep.

"You will never be able to touch me, Clovis Becker. Let me leave here. I mean you no harm, I hope."

"No harm?" Becker was breathing heavily. "You've been haunting me for months! Who are you? What do you want from me?"

"My name is Take."

"A good name for a thief. What's your real name?"

"I did not come here to steal anything from you. I merely wished to confirm something."

"What?"

"What I guessed you are looking for."

"Be quiet!" Becker glanced anxiously at Fastina.

"You are ashamed?" asked Take.

"No, but it doesn't suit me to reveal what I'm looking for. You can see the sense of that, can't you? Conditions here are no longer normal. I'm not sure you know what it is, anyway."

"I know."

Then Take had leapt to where Fastina stood, pushed her gently aside and jumped into the gravishute, so swiftly that it was impossible to follow his movements.

Clovis ran across the room and followed him into the shute. Above him he heard Take's voice calling a warning.

"You are a fool, Clovis Becker — what you're looking for isn't worth the finding!"

Reaching the roof, Becker saw a small carriage taking off.

His own car was back at the Great Glade. He could call it on his ultrasonic whistle, but it would take too long to get here.

He watched Take's car disappear in the direction of the mountains. He shielded his eyes, trying to see exactly where it was heading, but it was no good.

His face clouded with anger, he walked slowly back over the bright, mosaic roof to the gravishute shaft.

Fastina appeared. Her hair was disheveled, her expression concerned.

"I couldn't stop him," she said. "I'm sorry."

He took her hand gently, controlling his anger. He shrugged.

"That's all right. He moved too quickly."

"Have you ever seen a man move as fast as that? How does he do it? You know him, don't you?"

"I've seen him — but that was the first time I've spoken to him. I must find out where he comes from. How *could* he know what I'm looking for?"

"If he's staying on daylight Earth, then Central Information could find him for you," she suggested. "But he looked like a twilighter to me — there was something about him…"

"I know what you mean. Forget about him. I'll get in touch with Central Information later, as you suggest."

Then he grasped Fastina, pulling her towards him, bending her head back to kiss her, pushing his hands over her body, feeling her arms circle him and her nails dig into his back.

"Oh, Clovis!"

As they lay in bed later he decided to tell her what he was looking for. Since he had made love to her, his original obsession had become more remote and the need for secrecy, at least with her, less important Also it would be a relief to talk about it to her.

He began to speak. In the darkness, she listened.

"My father used to talk about Orlando Sharvis," he said, his voice faint and reminiscent. "He was a scientist who lived in the days before the raid. There was never a genius like him, my father said. He had mastered every discipline. Sharvis was not a seeker after knowledge in the ordinary sense, but he had a monumental curiosity. He would experiment for its own sake, just to see what could be made to happen. When the world stopped, he built a laboratory in the twilight region and gathered a group of people about him. They were not all scientists. They decided to build a spaceship to Sharvis's specifications and go to Titan, to set up a colony…"

"The Titan expedition — the original one?" She raised herself on her elbow and faced him. "So there was an expedition."

"Yes. Sharvis's experiment, so my father said, had revealed a way of staving off the effects of the space ache for long periods. Sharvis believed that they could stay on Titan long enough to adapt to the conditions there even if adaptation had to be artificially aided. Sharvis's biological experiments had already got him into trouble in his youth. There had been a war — the Last War we call it now — between the monopolistic commercial companies. Sharvis had been chief of research with one of the companies and had experimented on living prisoners. When the war was over — you remember that it was responsible for the radical change in our society that led to the establishment of our present one…"

"I know that much. The commercial organizations destroyed one another. Paseda's party stepped in, nationalized everything and abolished the money system. Go on."

"After it was all over, Sharvis was a wanted criminal, but he managed to go into hiding during the confusion. He would have been caught eventually, I suppose, if it hadn't been for the raid. His experiments, inhuman though they were, had taught him a great deal about human biology. He believed that he could operate surgically to counter the space ache and accelerate adaptation. He made the initial operations on Earth, then they left for Titan."

"So there is a chance that there are people on Titan?"

"I thought so — but there aren't."

"How do you know?"

"I went there in a ship I obtained on Ganymede."

"But surely you couldn't have survived long enough to —?"

"It wasn't pleasant, but I was there long enough to discover that Sharvis's colony had arrived, that it had survived for a while… but when I got there all I discovered were skeletons. They were scarcely human skeletons, either. Surgically, Sharvis had changed his Titanians into monsters. I looked for Sharvis himself — or at least a sign of him — but there was nothing. As far as I could tell Sharvis had left Titan."

"But he would be dead by now," she said. "He must have been born at least a hundred years before the raid."

"That's what I was coming to. You see, my father told me that Sharvis was immortal. He said that Sharvis had the power to make others immortal as well."

"And yet you've spent a year looking for him and haven't found a trace. Doesn't that prove that your father was wrong?"

"There *have* been rumours. I believe that Alodios discovered where Sharvis was."

"Alodios!"

Alodios, the great artist, had disappeared at about the same time as Becker. His disappearance had been even more inexplicable than Becker's.

"Yes. I came back to see if I could pick up the trail again — find out where Alodios went."

"What about Take?"

"I know nothing of Take — unless he is Sharvis's agent."

"But you still haven't told me what you want Sharvis for. Do you think he might have a means of reviving our fertility — or creating artificial sperm in some way?"

"He might have. But my reason for finding him is rather more selfish."

She kissed his shoulder softly, moving her left hand over his chest.

"I can't believe you're selfish, Clovis."

"Can't you?"

Once again she felt that disturbing, desperate grip on her body as he caressed her.

"I'll tell you what I want from Sharvis," he began grimly, but she put her mouth to his and kissed him.

She no longer wanted to know what he was looking for. She was afraid for herself and for him.

"Don't tell me," she murmured. "Just love me, Clovis. Love me."

CHAPTER FOUR

SOMETHING TO FORGET

As they were preparing to get up some hours later, the V-screen in the corner signaled. Becker wondered who it was and whether to ignore it. He decided to answer it since he had anyway meant to get up earlier. He went to a cupboard and took a yellow cloak from it, wrapping it round him.

He activated the screen.

Andros Almer's face appeared. He could see into the darkened room and his expression changed as he saw Fastina lying in the bed.

"So you weren't unlucky, after all," he said to her.

She smiled regretfully. "Sorry, Andros."

Becker looked perplexed. "What do you want, Andros?"

"I've just had news that a ship is heading for the Sector Eight landing field," Almer said, still looking at Fastina. "Due to get here soon."

"What of it?"

"Well, as far as we can tell, the ship's coming from Titan. We think it's the Titan expedition returning."

"Impossible."

"Maybe. I'm going to meet it, anyway. Something could have activated the automatic return system. I thought you might like to see it, too, Clovis. I screened Brand Calax, but he's busy, he says, with the plans for his own expedition. My guess is that he just doesn't want to see proof of the truth. Fastina might like to come, too. After all…"

"Thanks, Andros, we'll probably see you at the field." Becker switched off. "Your husband could be on it," he said. "Do you think you want to see him?"

"I'll come," she said, swinging her legs to the floor.

The ship came silently down. It landed on the deserted field under the blazing, motionless sun. It was a big, complex ship of a golden plastic alloy that was turned to deep red by the sunlight. It landed with a faint whisper of sound like a murmur of apology, as if aware that its presence was unwelcome.

Three figures started forward over the yielding surface of the spacefield. In the distance, to their right, were the partially abandoned hangars and control rooms: slim buildings in pale yellow and blue.

The voice in Becker's earbead said: "Shall we open up?"

"You might as well," he said.

As they reached the spherical ship, the lock began to open, twenty feet above them.

They paused, listening for a familiar sound they did not want to hear.

There was no sound.

Drifting up on their gravstraps, they paused at the open airlock. Becker looked at Fastina. "Andros and I will go in first — we've seen this sort of thing before. You haven't…"

"I'll go with you."

The smell from the airlock was nauseating. It was a combination of foul air and rotting tissue.

Andros Almer pursed his lips. "Let's go, then." He led the way through the airlock into a short metal tunnel.

The first body was there.

It was a woman's body. It was naked, contorted and it stank. The grey flesh was filthy, the hair was matted, the upturned face was twisted, with wide eyes and lips snarling back from the teeth; the cheeks were hollow. The flesh showed signs of laceration and her fingernails seemed imbedded in her right breast.

"Ierna Colo," Almer murmured. "Pyens Colo's daughter. I told the old fool to make her stay behind."

Fastina turned away. "I didn't realize…"

"You'd better wait outside," Becker said.

"No."

In the main control cabin they found two others. A man's body lay over a woman's. For some reason the man's body had corrupted much faster while the woman's was still almost whole. She seemed to be embracing him, the rictus of her mouth giving her the appearance of reveling in obscene joy — though it was really plain that she had been trying to ward the man off.

"Hamel Berina," Almer said. It was Fastina's husband.

"The woman's Jara Ferez, isn't it?" Fastina asked weakly. "Jara Ferez?"

"Yes," Becker replied. Jara had always liked Hamel. That was probably the reason why she had volunteered for the expedition.

The remains of the rest of the crew were also there. Some of the bones had been gnawed, some split. A skull had been broken open.

Face taut, Andros operated the door to the galley. He glanced inside.

"Enough supplies for at least another six months," he said. "We made the controls simple enough, in case things got really bad. All they had to do was break the seals on the packs."

"But they didn't, did they?" Fastina said, her voice breaking.

"You'd think they'd retain some survival instincts," Becker murmured.

"Isn't that a definition of madness, Clovis?" Andros cleared his throat. "Something that makes you act against your natural instincts? Look — that's how we lost contact."

He pointed at the smashed cameras above. Their protective cases had been torn open. Everything breakable had been destroyed. Machinery was twisted, papers torn, streamers of tape were scattered everywhere.

Andros shook his head. "All those tests we made on them, all that time we spent training them, conditioning them — all the precautions we took…" He sighed.

Becker picked up a torn length of tape and began twisting it round his finger.

"They were intelligent people," Andros went on. "They knew what to expect and how to fight it. They had courage, initiative, common sense and self-control — yet in six months they became insane, bestial travesties of human beings. Look at them — grotesque animals, more debased than we could guess…"

He glanced at a wall. He pointed at the pictures drawn on it in what seemed to be dried human blood. "That sort of thing was done quite early on, I should think." He kicked at a pile of filthy rags. "Titan! We can't survive in space for a matter of months, let alone centuries. These people were sacrificed for nothing."

Becker sighed. "We could revive the woman — Jara — for about ten minutes. She's not too far gone."

Andros rubbed his face. "Is it worth it, Clovis?"

"No." Becker's voice was hollow. "It's unlikely they were able to get at the recorders. They should tell us what happened."

"We don't really need to check, do we?" Almer said.

Becker shook his head slowly. He put his arm round Fastina's shoulders. "Let's get out of this ship."

As they left the airlock and drifted towards the spaceport buildings the voice in Becker's earbead said: "Any instructions?"

"Destroy it," Becker said. "And don't release the news. Morale's bad enough as it is."

They climbed into Almer's car on the edge of the field.

The ship had an automatic destruction mechanism that could only be operated from base. All ships had the same device in the event of space ache getting out of hand as it had done on the Titan vessel.

Behind them the golden ship crumpled. There was a brilliant flash and they heard the sharp, smacking sound as it was vaporized.

Fastina's face was pale.

"Do you think Calax will change his mind now?" Becker asked Almer.

Almer sneered. "Calax? Not after we've destroyed the evidence. Mark my words, he just won't believe us."

"You think we should have kept the ship to show him?"

"I doubt if he'd have let us show it to him," Almer said. "Calax doesn't obey any rational instincts as far as I know."

"You seem to have some personal grudge against Calax," Becker said. "It's almost as if you hate him."

"I hate everyone," Andros said savagely. "I hate the whole horrible mess."

Becker stretched back on his couch, trying to get the images in the ship out of his mind. He could see them all, still; twisted faces, contorted bodies, filth, wreckage, bones.

Memento mori the world could do without, he thought. That was why he had told them to destroy the ship. If they ran away from a dying man at a party, what would that sight do to them?

Fastina was sitting upright, staring over the countryside as they moved along. Becker knew it would be stupid to try to comfort her at this stage. She was in a state of shock.

"What do you want to do now?" Almer was asking him. "Can I take you both back to your house, Clovis?" His voice sounded ragged.

"No thanks, Andros. Take us to the Great Glade, my car's there."

The air carriage wheeled in the cloudless sky as Almer accelerated and headed for the south-western flower forest.

CHAPTER FIVE

SOMETHING OMINOUS

Four days later, Clovis Becker left Fastina at his house and went to see Tarn Yoluf of Central Information.

Fastina had recovered from her shock but was still occasionally pensive. She had been unable completely to rid her mind of the sight of her dead husband in the spaceship and at length Becker had decided to leave her alone for a while so that she could, as she had suggested, sleep for a couple of days and hope that that would be enough to clear her head of the images in the ship and the guilt that she felt when she remembered them.

The horror he had witnessed had, for the moment at least, convinced Clovis Becker of the futility of his own search for the legendary Orlando Sharvis. Doubtless Sharvis had died on Titan, too.

Situated on the edge of a flower forest, the Central Information building stood two storeys above ground and fifty storeys below. Tarn Yoluf's big, computer-lined office looked out over the sunlit forest and a smooth intervening lawn.

Yoluf sat at his desk surrounded by V-screens and control consoles. He was a tall, slim man in middle age. He had very fair hair and a pale, anaemic face. His eyes were pale blue and in contrast to the rest of his features his very full red lips looked as if they had been painted. He was wearing a high-collared lilac shirt and green tights.

Becker told him that he wanted to know the whereabouts of Take. Yoluf started at once. He punched buttons and operated controls but after an hour his records had come up with nothing.

"I'll try my sections, Clovis," he said. His voice was extremely high-pitched. "But not all of them are operating these days."

Later he sat back in his chair and spread his long hands in apology.

"No trace yet, Clovis."

Becker shrugged. The problem of Take had become less important since he had made his decision. "I'm sorry to have troubled you, Tarn. The man's made me uncomfortable, that's all. As I said, he seems to have been following me for some time. The other day I discovered him in my house…"

"Surely not?" Yoluf looked shocked. "Uninvited?"

"Yes. I thought if I could find him and warn him about doing anything like it again, it would be sufficient to make him leave me in peace. For all I know he's vanished for good, anyway."

"You mentioned that his reflexes were abnormally fast. Your description of him could hardly fit anyone — but we're stumped, Clovis. He sounds like a twilight man, but we've records of all surviving twilight people and he's not amongst them. Twilighters are about the only people who'd invade a man's house like that…"

Becker nodded. "Thanks, anyway, Tarn."

Yoluf chewed his lower lip. "Hang on for a moment, Clovis. There's still a chance…"

"It's not really important…"

"I'd rather make sure we've checked everywhere." He turned to one of his consoles and began pressing more buttons. "You know what we need? A passport system like the old days. To hell with the freedom of the individual. How am I supposed to run an information centre without a decent system?"

Becker smiled and sat down in the chair opposite Yoluf. "You're a frustrated bureaucrat."

"We wouldn't be where we are today without the bureaucrats, Clovis." Yoluf jokingly wagged his finger. "It was the civil servants who helped turn over the State from its old restrictive form into the present one. Don't underestimate the bureaucratic mentality. You might think that the administration's decision to wind itself up was a good idea — I don't."

"It simply happened that way," Becker said good-humouredly. "Since we only had a short time to go we suggested that anyone who wished to give up their work could do so. Many are still continuing. You are, for one."

"It's not the same, Clovis. Where's yesterday's smooth-running administrative machine? Bits! Bits without links or a properly working motor. If the machine were running right do you think it would take this long to find your mysterious friend?"

"I suppose not," Becker admitted as Yoluf fussed with his controls. "You think some sort of emergency government should be formed?"

"I don't make decisions of that order. That's up to you. But anyone can see that our civilization's crumbling to pieces day by day. We need a firmer government — not none at all!"

"Firmer government? You're really beginning to sound like someone from pre-raid days. What good do firmer governments ever do that isn't overbalanced by the harm they cause."

"You used the word 'emergency' yourself, Clovis. Isn't this one? Ah, here's Mars..."

A light was blinking above one of the V-screens and a face appeared on it. The colours were in bad register and the man's face was a dirty green.

Yoluf pointed at the screen. "There's another example of what's happening. See that colour? We can't get a mechanic to fix it. At this rate there'll be complete chaos in a matter of months. Didn't they always say that when communications began to break down that was a sign of the beginning of the end? We'll all be dead sooner than we think..." The signal buzzed and Yoluf flicked a switch. "Yes?"

The man on the screen was already talking. "... no information regarding the man you call Mr Take. No ship registered to him. No-one of his description or name has landed in a passenger ship. We haven't checked everywhere. Some of the old mine pits are deep enough to hide a small ship..."

Yoluf's tone was exasperated. "Then keep trying." He broke contact well before his message could get to Mars. He shook his head. "I used to be all but omniscient a year ago — as far as people's public lives were concerned. Now all I get are mysteries! We were asked about your whereabouts and lost you half the time. We're still being asked about Alodios and we can't find *him*. Now this man Take can't be traced. You're looking at a broken man, Clovis! Somebody who's gone from omniscience to impotence in less than twelve months. I'm going insane!"

"Aren't we all?" smiled Becker. "What did happen to Alodios?"

"I told you, we don't know. We found his air carriage without any trouble. It was in the twilight region. Sector 119."

"I know the area — near the sea, isn't it?"

"Yes. South American continent."

"Do you think he killed himself?" Becker was now almost certain that this was what had happened to the great artist. There had been one or two other suicides, especially among artists.

"That's what I do think," Yoluf said emphatically, "but not everyone will have it. I have to keep trying with the best means at my disposal, which isn't saying a great deal these days..."

"Ah, well," said Becker as he got up to leave, "struggle on as best you can, Tarn."

Yoluf shrugged. "What's the point?"

"None, I suppose. If you do hear anything of Take you'll let me know, will you?"

"If I can get in touch with you," said Yoluf bitterly, turning his attention back to his instruments.

*

On his way to visit Narvo Velusi, Becker saw smoke rising in the distance. He was crossing a great, grassy plain that covered the region once known as northern France. The breeze whispered through the grass and around the air car and a few white clouds moved slowly through the deep blue sky. As always, the sun hung motionless above him. In this area it was in a position of mid-afternoon.

It was definitely thick, black smoke he could see ahead. It was very unusual to see smoke at all. Curious, he guided the car towards it.

Later he saw that it was a building; an ordinary mobile house. Strictly speaking the house was not burning, but its contents were. Becker took the car down to see if there was anyone in trouble.

On the far side of the building, obscured at first by the billowing smoke, he saw a small group of figures standing watching the blaze. There were about eight people there, all dressed in black robes like ancient monks' habits, their heads shaven and their faces covered in masks of the same black material.

There was little doubt, Becker decided, that the fire had been started deliberately.

As he circled closer the bald skulls went back and masked faces peered at him. He felt bound to shout to them.

"Anything wrong? Can I help?"

One of them called back: "You can help cleanse the universe of evil by joining us, brother."

Becker was astonished. The word "evil" was an archaic term rarely heard these days.

"What are you doing?" he called.

"We are ridding the world of the artifacts of mankind," answered another tonelessly.

"Who are you?" Becker could hardly believe that these people were from daylight Earth. Twilight Earth had had, at one time, its share of peculiar cults, but that was normal and even the cults had died out in later years as the twilight folk became more and more introverted.

"We are the guilty!" a new voice screamed up at him.

With a shudder, Becker took the car into a rapid climb and fled away.

He looked back once at the smoke. It seemed to him that it came from the first signal fire that heralded the apocalypse he had joked about a few days earlier.

He knew that, unless it was checked, it would soon be one of many fires. His own upbringing in the twilight region had made him familiar with the darker side of human nature, but he had never expected to see anything like it in the daylight world.

How could this cult's activities be checked? There was no method known to his society; there had been no violence there for centuries. To take the reactionary step, as Yoluf had half-jokingly suggested, of forming a "firmer" government was unthinkable to people trained to respect the freedom of the individual at all costs. Yet here was a situation that could only be fought by a society of the old sort.

There was no doubt about it, he thought, as he passed over the forests of the Rhine and neared Narvo Velusi's house, Narvo had been right: Fear created fear and violence created violence.

It was with a feeling of despair that he landed on the roof of his old friend's house.

No-one more than himself had appreciated the social and natural paradise of daylight Earth, no-one had valued it more or realized how ideal it had been.

Now, it seemed, the world he had loved was not even to die gracefully.

Fear was back and with it the old terrors, the old mental aberrations, the old superstitions, the old religions. He knew the pattern. He had studied it in the text books. He knew how little power rational argument had when faced with minds turned sick by fear. He knew how quickly a cult of the kind he had seen could proliferate and dominate a society and then split internally and become several warring sects. And his society, without means of fighting the cult, was probably the most vulnerable in history.

His paradise threatened to become a hell and there was little he could think of doing that would stop the process now that it had begun.

CHAPTER SIX

SOMETHING TO HOPE FOR

"They call themselves the Brotherhood of Guilt," Narvo Velusi said, pouring Becker a drink. "Originally they simply decided to give up sexual relations because it was pointless — though it hadn't stopped anyone in the past. Well, you can guess what followed that decision, can't you? The masks and the rest were explained by them as being necessary so that a person's sex could not be distinguished. Up to now they have been harmless, in that they haven't actually done anything violent. This burning you mention must be the first — we'd have heard of others. I suspect that the house belongs to one of their number. It's an odd syndrome, Clovis, but one we could have anticipated if we had not been so obsessed with the idea of our ultimate fate."

"What do you mean?" Becker noticed his hand was trembling as he took the drink and walked towards the window to look out over the forest of dark pines that lay below the hill on which Narvo Velusi had sited his house.

"Well, while denying nature in themselves, they say that what is not 'natural' is 'evil' — you're quite right, that is the word you heard them use — and that therefore all human artifacts are evil."

Becker shook his head. "It doesn't make sense, Narvo." He took a sip of his drink. "I know these peculiar ideas never do, but it's not that I really meant. I can't understand how a well-adjusted society could go rotten in such a brief time. Even in the past things didn't happen so rapidly."

Narvo joined him at the window. "You're quite right — but in the past they had various means of resisting and controlling such outbreaks. They were a recurring cancer in the body of society, but usually they were promptly cauterized from the main body — segregated in some way. Sometimes they were not cut out in time — so you got the fanatical Christianity of what the Christian society later called their 'middle ages' — and the equally fanatical black magic cults and secret societies. A few hundred years later, when non-religious leaders were dominating the world, you got the madness of Nazism; still later there was the meritocratic system which virtually controlled the whole world at one stage. And every time, of course, human society managed, through violence and struggle, to rectify itself and destroy the cancer. But now, Clovis, there will not be time to do any such thing…"

"Are you sure?" Becker's tone was bleak.

"The only thing that would save us," Narvo smiled ironically, "is salvation itself. If our poisoned cells could be revived. It is a pattern, you see. There's always a pattern."

"Isn't there something positive we can do, Narvo? Isn't there some goal we could give people — even…?" He broke off and stared at his friend miserably.

"Even if it means lying to them?" Velusi said gently. "Perhaps there is, but you can see what's happening, can't you? A lie or two might halt the process for a little while, but it wouldn't stop it for long enough. And how would lying affect us, Clovis? There's no doubt in my mind that we should find ourselves corrupted, needing to gather more and more personal power in order to control the means of communication, keep the truth from the majority. It has started, you see. Even we are affected by what is happening. We can't fail to be."

Becker threw down his glass. It bounced across the sunlit room and struck a wall. "Can't we divert them? Can't we appeal to their better instincts? All these people were sane, rational human beings up to a few months ago. Their ethical instincts have only been buried. If we can revive them…"

"An ethic is simply a system of survival," Velusi said. "What does an ethic mean when there is no chance of survival?"

Becker put his hands to his face, shaking his head mutely.

Velusi went over and picked up his glass. It was unbroken. He filled it and took it back to Becker.

"Clovis," he said after a while, "I mentioned the other day that I had a scheme — a scheme as irrational as Brand Calax's, but one that might work to some extent."

"What is it?"

"It's a stupid plan. It seems ludicrous even to me when I think about it. It is just something I thought of. I want to build a big transmitter — a bigger radio transmitter than any that has ever existed. And then I want to send a message on it."

"A message? Why? What message?" Becker tried to clear his head and give his attention to the old man.

"Just a message that will travel through space — that will go to the other intelligent races in other star systems and galaxies. We know they exist — the space-dwellers told us that much. It will be a message that will survive long after we have perished. It'll be a kind of monument — it'll just say that we once lived. They probably won't even be able to understand the message…"

"What will it say?"

Velusi went over to a deep, high-backed chair and sat down.

"Just 'We are here'," he said.

"Just that?" Becker shrugged: "But we won't be…"

"I know, but someone might follow the message back — the transmitter will continue to work after we are dead, you see. Another race might find us, discover our records, and we'll live on in a way — in their minds and their books. Do you see, Clovis?" Velusi looked up eagerly at him.

Clovis nodded. "I do, Narvo, but is there any point? I mean, could you convince the others that the transmitter would be worth building?"

"I'm going to try at the Great Glade tomorrow. The message could be picked up by all manner of creatures, you see. Perhaps some of them will be like us. The message will convey our pride in our existence, our gratitude to the biological accident that gave us the ability to reason." Velusi sighed, looking up at Becker. "I know it's pathetic, Clovis, but it's the best thing I could think of."

"It's better than anything I can think of," Becker said, putting his hand on the old man's shoulder. He saw that Narvo Velusi was crying. "I'll come with you to the glade tomorrow. I'll back you up. Work on the transmitter will employ hundreds of people. It will be therapeutic at very least, eh?" He made an effort and smiled at his friend.

"It will be a kind of immortality," Velusi said, weeping openly now. "Won't it, Clovis?"

"Yes," Becker said in pity, "a kind of immortality."

CHAPTER SEVEN

SOMEWHERE TO GO

Fastina sat in bed eating the meal Becker had brought her. "So Narvo convinced them?" she said with her mouth full.

"Many of them. Obviously I don't know as much about human nature as I thought. They're wondering where to site the transmitter and everything." He sat down beside her on the bed. "How do you feel?"

She grinned at him. "Fine. How are you? Have you given up the search for Sharvis?"

"There doesn't seem any point in going on with it."

She put down her fork and took his hand. "I'm glad, Clovis. We've got the best part of two centuries together. We should be grateful."

He smiled. "Do you think we can stay together that long?"

"The first hundred years are the worst," she laughed. "Anyway, you're a very mysterious person and I'm sure it will take that long to get to know you. I'm not as simple as I look, either." She gave him the tray. "I'd like to get up and go out now. Where shall we go?"

"Anywhere," he said. "Anywhere you like."

Lying side by side, naked under the hot sun, they let the air car drift out above the sea. Virtually tideless now, the South Atlantic went sparkling to the edge of the world.

They talked idly, holding hands. He spoke of his childhood and his morbid, melancholy father; of his mother, who had also been his sister. He spoke without rancour or embarrassment, for the times were now distant and unreal. The twilight world had become the same strange place to him as it had always been to her. He told her how Velusi had had his house in Kashmir the year he had walked towards the sun. He had arrived there, almost dead with fatigue and starvation.

Velusi and his wife had liked him. Velusi had probably been a little amused by him, too. They had adopted him and Velusi had begun to teach him all that the old man knew himself; though Clovis had already known a great deal from his own reading in his father's tower. Velusi was then Deputy Chairman of the Council and had been able to instruct Clovis Becker in the ideas and methods of the politics of the daylight region. He had encouraged him to go into public life when the time came.

"I wanted to, anyway. I admired this world so much, you see."

The carriage drifted on. They raised the canopy and made love. They ate and drank. Later, they settled the car on the water so that it rocked on the gentle waves. They swam in the warm ocean, splashing and laughing in the salt sea, making it foam around the hull of the carriage.

Time passed and they did not care. They became filled with a euphoric happiness and a pleasure in each other's company that could only be felt away from society. They both experienced a love that they knew to be elemental and probably never to be repeated. They wanted it to last. They had brought no means of telling the time and they had all they needed to eat. They sailed on across the calm Atlantic, hardly even talking now, but smiling a great deal and laughing sometimes, too, and staying very close together as if they feared that once they parted they would not find each other again.

There were no strong winds on the ocean, no cold nights, no wild tides. The sea was at peace and so were they. They saw a whale. It was a huge adult blue whale, nearly a hundred and twenty feet long, the largest beast that had ever lived. It was moving over the surface at speed, sometimes lifting its great bulk clean out of the water. They followed it. It swam along gently for a while and then dived deep into the ocean. They saw a school of fifty or so dolphins not long after, chasing one another through the sea.

Still later, they saw seabirds wheeling in flocks in the distance.

The sun was far behind them now, not far from the horizon, and it was a little cooler but still pleasant.

The carriage was swept by a sudden current towards an island. It was thickly wooded and a yellow beach ran down to the sea. The sky behind the island was orange and darkening and they knew that this was almost the twilight region; but the island was pleasant and they ran about in the sand, picking up seashells and pieces of coral. They went to sleep on the beach, with their toes pointing towards the sea.

When they woke up, it seemed colder, and an animal was screaming from behind them in the jungle. They laughed, but ran down to the air carriage and wrapped themselves in cloaks.

Then he took the carriage into the sky and headed swiftly towards the sun.

They landed on the ocean again when they were back, and swam and made love again, but their earlier pleasure was gone and soon they went home into Africa and his house beside Lake Tanganyika.

Even here they ignored the V when it signaled and spent a great deal of their time together in bed, or walking along the shore of the lake arm in arm.

One day Fastina sighed. "If only we could have children," she said, dabbling her bare foot in the lake and looking out over the tree-covered hills that were framed against the hot sky. "Look what there is for them to enjoy."

Becker decided to go to Narvo Velusi's house and see how the work on his transmitter was going.

A month had passed.

The time, he thought, as he headed towards Europe in the air carriage shaped like a golden bird in flight, meant nothing to Fastina, with her barren womb.

It seemed, however, that they were bound together now, perhaps until death. How the link had been forged, he did not understand, but it *had* been forged and neither would ever be able to stay away from the other for long. There might never be pleasure again, only pain, but that would not matter.

He could not explain his knowledge: Love, as he understood it, was not what they had, but love was there in all its forms. Hate was there, too, now, and anger and a melancholy bitterness, and a need for her body that was not any sort of love or hate, but a blind hunger that terrified him. He could understand how such unbearable emotion could drive lovers to suicide.

It was unbearable now. That was why he needed to go away from her and yet seek other company than his own.

The automatic force-screen leapt around the carriage as he pushed it to its maximum speed.

The tension had begun to leave him as he saw the Rhineland ahead and reached Velusi's house.

C H A P T E R   E I G H T

S O M E T H I N G   T O   F I G H T

The huge apparatus took the form of a gigantic sculpture in blue steel and gold wire. It overlooked the Black Sea, rising hundreds of feet high, each piece shining and vibrating slightly in the breeze. It was still surrounded by its tall scaffolding. Its central sections at base were almost half a mile in diameter; between them ran delicate webs, threads of copper, coils of silver, triangles and squares of shimmering greens and reds.

On a high platform above the apparatus stood two figures dwarfed by the great structure.

"There's still a lot to do," Narvo Velusi said to Clovis Becker. "We haven't begun to install the power yet."

Becker folded his arms and looked down at the transmitter. He knew that it could have been built in a more compact form and cased in some kind of cabinet, but he understood why Velusi had chosen to build it this way. It was not only visible to all those involved in working on it, it was also extremely beautiful, somehow complementing the simplicity of the message they intended to send.

"It's very impressive, Narvo," he said.

"Thank you. It really does seem to have cheered a lot of people up." He smiled. "The work's going faster than I anticipated. We might have to invent a few technical hitches."

A black air carriage began to circle down towards them. It came level with the platform. In it stood a man wearing a loose, flowing black cloak that enclosed his whole body. Attached to the cloak was a hood of the same material. The hood hid the man's face in shadow.

"May I join you?"

Becker recognized the voice as Andros Almer's.

"Hello, Andros," he said, as the man stepped from the car and on to the platform.

Andros nodded to them and pushed his hood back slightly to peer down at the transmitter. Far below tiny figures could be seen at work.

Becker saw that he was wearing a dark blue mask over the top half of his pale face. The mask was edged in scarlet and like the hooded cloak was of heavy, rich material. On Almer's hands there were matching gloves in dark blue, worked with scarlet, and on his feet were soft, red, knee-length boots.

"'We are here', eh?" Almer's voice was dry. "Perhaps 'We were here' would be a better message, Narvo?"

Velusi looked uncomfortably at Becker. "Andros thinks there are better uses for the transmitter, Clovis."

Almer turned with a swirl of his heavy cloak, raising one gloved hand. "I have no intention of interfering, Narvo. It is your project. It simply seemed a good idea to broadcast rather more information, to give whoever heard it a better idea of who we were and where to find us."

"That would defeat the whole spirit of the idea, surely?" Clovis frowned. "Can't you see that, Andros?"

"It simply seems a waste, that's all, Clovis." Almer's voice was acid now. "To build this great contrivance and make so little use of it." Almer shrugged. "I wonder what other projects of this kind we'll see in the near future?"

"What do you mean?" Velusi said, pushing his old hand through his hair. Becker noticed that it was beginning to grey. "Other projects?"

"I'd admit that this one isn't as hopeless as Calax's Titan ship — at least it has a definite, understandable purpose…"

"The Titan ship has a purpose," Becker interrupted, "if only to occupy Calax's mind. How's the building going?"

"Oh, rapidly, rapidly. Yes, soon Calax will be off for Titan and that's the last we shall see of him — unless he returns in the manner of the first expedition." Almer moved arrogantly towards his air car. "Well, give my regards to Fastina, Clovis. I must get back to my own affairs. My men are waiting…"

"Your *what?*" Becker was incredulous. He had only heard a phrase like that in an historical V-drama.

Andros ignored him, stepped into his air car and swept away.

"What did he say, Narvo?" he asked.

"His men." Narvo repeated quietly, looking down at the transmitter to avoid Becker's eyes.

"*His!*" The concept of other people "belonging" to a particular person was even more archaic than the term "evil" which he had heard a month earlier. "Was he joking, Narvo? What's he doing?"

Velusi's tone was over-controlled when he replied. "The Brotherhood of

Guilt fired several more houses while you were away. They didn't actually burn the houses, of course, because they won't catch fire, but they destroyed everything that could be burned inside them. And the last two houses they set fire to didn't belong to their own members — a woman was badly burned trying to put the blaze out in her house. Some people, particularly Andros, didn't see why the Brotherhood should be allowed to go about destroying at will while everyone looked on passively…"

"So they formed themselves into a group against the Brotherhood, is that it?"

Velusi nodded. "I think *vigilante* is the term they found from somewhere. Andros became their leader — he seemed to like the idea, Clovis."

"I see you were right," Becker sighed. "It was bound to happen, as you said. But I find it hard to believe a man of Andros's training and intelligence would give himself over to such an idea…"

"He argues an old theme, Clovis. Desperate times, he says, require desperate measures."

"So now there are two sources of that cancer you mentioned," Becker murmured, "and if the pattern stays true, there will be more."

"Well, the way it was in the past was that the cancers helped destroy one another, but, as I told you, I doubt if there will be time left for that now." Velusi touched his gravstrap. "Come, let's get back to the ground. You've seen the transmitter. What about coming to my house for a meal?"

As they sank down gently, Becker said: "I think I'd like to have a look at Brand's spaceship, if you don't mind, Narvo."

"Very well. It's only a couple of hundred miles from here."

They were using Fastina's air car and when Velusi had walked around talking to some of the people working on the transmitter, they got into it and headed for the mountains of Turkey where Calax's Titan ship was under construction.

As they rode towards Turkey, Velusi said: "It's not a question of knowledge and reason, you see, Clovis — it's essentially a question of temperament and strength of mind. Andros had given up. Brand, in his way, has given up, too. In the past we were always ruled by our unconscious drives — even when we knew they were there — reason simply tempered instinct. Andros knows what's happening to him, but he doesn't seem to care any more. I think it's because of Fastina…"

"She told me that he was attracted to her, but I didn't think it was a very strong attraction."

"Deep enough, perhaps. Ah, we're nearing the mountains."

In a wide valley, the heavy outlines of Calax's ship could be seen as they descended. The sharp peaks of the mountains, formed into their present shape by the upheavals that had come with the raid, surrounded the valley. The spaceship hull was complete and men were currently fitting its machinery.

They found Brand Calax inside the ship directing the positioning of the compact drive unit. Becker was surprised to see how gaunt and grim-faced he had become. He greeted them civilly enough. "Hello Narvo — Clovis. It's coming along. When we're finished she'll be the best ship ever built. I've got complete simulated Earth environment which will help stave off the space ache. She's about the fastest thing there is, which will help get me there and back quicker and allow me to spend more time on Titan. If there's —" they all stood aside to let the mechanics through as they carried various pieces of equipment into the drive chamber — "if there's anyone on Titan, I'll find 'em."

Becker could have told Brand Calax the truth about Titan, but he had decided that it would not be fair to spoil the man's dream. Even if he died, Calax had the right to die in the manner he chose.

Calax peered into the drive chamber, checking something against the plans he held in his hand. He straightened up, leaning on his other hand against the cold, dark metal of the bulkhead. Later, the interior would be coated with several layers of other materials, and the shell itself was in fact three divided layers with force-fields between them.

"People have been really kind," Calax said. "I've had more than I need volunteering to help put the ship together. I'm going to call her *The Orlando Sharvis*, after the man who commanded the colonizing expedition…"

Though startled to hear the name, Becker said calmly: "Sharvis wasn't a particularly heroic figure, by all accounts. Didn't he do biological experiments on living human beings, things like that?"

"Maybe he had to," Calax said: "Besides, it depends how you look at it. Sharvis had vision and guts. I don't care about the rest of his character, good or bad."

Becker walked around the ship. It was relatively cold in there and he shivered slightly as he went to the entrance and peered out. The airlock had not been installed as yet. He blinked in the strong sunlight, reached into a pocket and brushed darkened lenses over his eyes.

In the foothills of the mountains he thought he saw some people standing motionless, watching the ship.

"Who are those men over there?" he called to Calax.

Brand Calax joined him. "They're from that damned Brotherhood of Guilt cult. They've been there for days. They don't do anything but stare at us, but I'm afraid they may try some sort of attack. From what I've heard they've already done damage. I'll say that for Andros Almer, he was wise to act swiftly and protect us against them."

"Have they shown any sign that they would attack?" Velusi asked from behind him.

"No, but you know what they think of machinery and the like. A ship like this would be a prime target for them I shouldn't wonder."

"You're probably right." Becker touched his gravstrap and drifted down to the ground. The other two followed him.

"Miona Pelva and Quiro Beni have joined them, I heard," said Velusi, referring to two ex-councilors they had known.

"Incredible!" said Calax. "Decent, intelligent people."

The masked, bald, heavily-robed men and women stared in their direction. Whereas earlier they had worn clothes of any dark material, now they all wore brown.

"Some of them flog one another, by all accounts," Calax said as he led them towards a temporary building where he had his living quarters. "It's part of the punishment for their guilt apparently. I may be stupid, but I can't see what they feel to be guilty about. Still, so long as they don't interfere with me, they can stand there for the next two hundred years for all I care."

"You think they might start something?" Becker asked as they reached the single-storey building and went inside. The room they entered was functional and undecorated. They sat on hard chairs while Calax operated the food dispenser in the corner.

"They might," Calax nodded, "but they've no weapons as yet, only fire. If they want weapons, of course, they'll have to manufacture them in some way and luckily Andros is keeping a firm check on the stores of supplies they'd need. I think we'll be all right."

Becker turned to Velusi. "What authority has Andros to do all this? Has anything been voted on at all?"

"More or less," Velusi said. "A lot of people agreed to give him temporary powers to deal with the emergency."

"I see." Becker accepted the plate Calax put before him.

"There's only one way of countering this that I can see," Velusi told Becker as they ate. "And that's for you to re-form the official council before it's too late."

"How many of us are there left?" Becker asked cynically. "If some of them have joined the Brotherhood and Andros is going it alone, there can't be many."

"We can hold a new election or co-opt fresh members," Velusi suggested.

Becker nodded reluctantly. He did not like to admit to his old friend that his heart was no longer in politics, that, in spite of the threat of the Brotherhood and Andros Almer's vigilantes, he was too obsessed with his personal affairs to consider seriously becoming chairman of the council again.

"You are still the most respected man in public life, Clovis," Velusi told him. "The majority of the people would follow your leadership willingly. It would give us the chance to put a stop to Almer's ambitions before he gained too much power."

"Are you sure the people would be behind me, Narvo?" he asked. "And would there be time to stop Almer?"

"You could find out!" Brand Calax had been listening. He leaned across his plate, gesticulating with his spoon. "Narvo's thinking straight at last. My feeling is that someone like Almer's needed to deal with the Brotherhood, but we could find ourselves needing someone to deal with Almer in time. Let's act now."

"It would mean restricting people's liberty..." Becker shook his head, perplexed. "I couldn't do it. My conscience..."

"We've got to make the best of a bad situation, Clovis," Velusi reminded him. "Now Almer's evidently got an appetite for power he'll want more. It's obvious."

"I'd have to think more seriously about it," Becker said. He was playing for time, he knew. He did not want the responsibility any longer.

"You'd better make up your mind soon, Clovis," Calax warned him. "When I come back from Titan with my good news I want to find a few people still alive to hear it."

They left a short time later. The little group of Brotherhood members were still standing there, watching them impassively.

Brand Calax returned to his ship, *The Orlando Sharvis*.

B O O K   T W O

THE SHORES OF DEATH

315

C H A P T E R   O N E

M E N   O F   A C T I O N

Becker soon discovered that he could not stay away from Fastina for long and he decided to return home after only three days at Narvo Velusi's house. A further incentive to leave was offered by Velusi's somewhat accusing eye; the old man was plainly waiting impatiently for Becker to make his decision.

He left for Lake Tanganyika.

"I'll decide what to do once I'm there," he told Velusi.

The golden air car took him home and he found Fastina asleep.

Resisting an urge to wake her, he wandered around the house and along the lakeside for several hours, trying to justify to himself the decision he had already made not to become chairman again. He ought to agree to Velusi's idea if he felt badly about the state of things, he knew. He was being as selfish and irrational as those he despised. It was as if there were a tangible poison in the air that destroyed one's strength of mind.

Yet he could not face Velusi if it was to tell the old man that he was not going to help form a government. Perhaps he could act as a token chairman, and let Velusi do the real work? But that was no good; the people would soon realize he was not active.

He had made the right ethical decisions all his life, up until the news of the race's sterility. First he had gone off on that wild goose chase after Orlando Sharvis, thus indirectly affecting the morale of the public, and now he was taking no pains to rectify the situation while he could.

Was there some instinct in him that was driving him to help destroy the society he valued? An instinct that had been buried since he had left the twilight regions? An instinct inherited, perhaps, from his father?

Fear was encouraging the dark side of human nature to flourish again. Was it also reviving a dark side of his own nature that he had thought to be dead?

He could now sympathize, to some extent, with the feelings that had led people to join the new cult. First came the fear, then the dark thoughts, then the guilt in having the thoughts. It had been a common enough syndrome in the past.

He sat down on a rock and stared into the calm water of the lake.

Perhaps it would be best for himself if he agreed to Narvo's suggestion? The practical problems of organizing a new administration might divert his mind into healthier channels. He had already given in to one selfish impulse and it did not seem to have benefited himself or anyone else.

He decided to do nothing for a couple of days and then contact Narvo to say that he was ready to head a new government.

He felt more at ease as he walked back towards his house.

After he had prepared himself a light meal and eaten it, he went back up to the bedroom. Fastina was still sleeping. There was a slight smile on her lips and she seemed very much at peace. He envied her.

He took off his clothes and had a shower, then he moved desultorily around the house, sorting through his Vs for something to look at or read, but nothing appealed to him.

A little later he got into bed beside Fastina. She stirred slightly and he put his arm around her shoulders, enjoying the sensation of her soft skin and hair against his body, feeling the old affection returning.

Soon he was also asleep.

Fastina was not beside him when he awoke, but she returned shortly with warm drinks for them both. She handed him his and came back to bed. They sipped their drinks in silence. Both were thoughtful and relaxed.

After a while he kissed her and they made love gently, handling each other carefully as if each was infinitely precious and fragile.

Some hours later, when they were eating breakfast on the balcony overlooking the lake, he told her what he had been doing and what he had seen. He mentioned Almer and she did not seem surprised to learn what had happened to him.

"Andros even anticipated it himself," she said. "He seemed to like the idea in a way, I think. He was always a little perverse."

Becker told her about Velusi's suggestion that he become chairman of a new government.

She frowned. "It would be a good idea, I suppose. It would be useful to have some sort of mediating influence between those vigilantes of Andros's and the Brotherhood. But it would take up a lot of your time, wouldn't it, Clovis? I think you ought to do as Narvo suggests — but I don't really want you to."

"I don't want to. Every instinct is against it. I'd prefer simply to retire here, or move the house to some other spot where it would be hard to find."

"Run away, Clovis? That's not like you."

"I ran away once, Fastina, when I was a child. I ran away a second time just over a year ago — though I told myself I was looking for something. I could run away a third time, couldn't I? It *is* like me..."

"Like all of us," she said. "Sometimes. What do you want to do, Clovis? Which impulse is strongest?"

"That's the trouble — I'm completely torn between my emotional need to keep away from it all, and my feeling that it is my duty to get involved. Oh, there are easy roads out — I could indulge in a spot of self-pity, I could argue that in the long run it all comes to the same thing — death. I could build up a bit of resentment, I suppose, at their foolishness. Perhaps, eventually, I will take one of those ways out — if the situation gets worse for me. But really, if I'm to remain true to my own ideals, I must join with Narvo and form the damned government. It's partly a question of self-interest, anyway. The more power Andros gets, the more he'll want to use it — and I have the impression he doesn't feel particularly friendly towards me."

"You know why that is..."

"I know." He stared gloomily at the great flight of flamingos wading in the shallows of the lake. In this timeless world of everlasting day it seemed impossible that violence and hatred could intrude and, what was more, begin to hold sway so rapidly.

"I can't help," she said.

"You don't have to. It's my problem. I'll do what I decided earlier. I'll leave it for a day or two until I feel calmer about it. Then I'll probably go and see Narvo."

He walked into the room, leaving the balcony. "I don't want to stay in the house, though. What shall we do?"

She joined him in the room. "We'll go to my house," she suggested, "and then we'll decide. All right?"

He sighed. "All right. A good idea. You're coddling me, Fastina. There's no need to — but it's kind of you."

"Come on," she said. "Let's go to the car."

He went up to her and hugged her. "Don't worry." he said. "I'm just off-balance at the moment, that's all."

She kissed him lightly on the chin and took his hand, leading him towards the gravishute. He followed passively, like a tired child.

He spent much longer than he had intended at her house in Greece. He took to going for protracted walks along the beach, thinking about nothing in particular. He put off contacting Narvo day after day. He dozed or slept a great deal of the time. He hardly spoke to Fastina at all, but she was there whenever he was hungry or wished to make love and if she was disturbed by the remote look in his eyes, the impassive features, she kept her feelings hidden.

One day, just after he had returned from the beach, she gave him a drink and said: "Narvo called earlier. He asked if you were here. I told him you were. He said that it was even more important than ever that you get in touch with him."

He nodded abstractedly.

"Will you contact him?" she asked.

"Yes, I'd better."

He walked slowly to the screen and spoke Velusi's name into the console. Narvo's face appeared almost immediately.

"I expected to hear from you earlier, Clovis. Is anything wrong?"

"No. I meant to talk to you, but…" He cleared his throat. "Why did you ask me to call you? Fastina said it was important."

"There's fighting going on, Clovis — between Almer's vigilantes and the Brotherhood people. Outside my house at this minute!"

"What?" Becker began to feel more alert. "How did it happen?"

"The Brotherhood tried to set fire to the house. I was asleep. They were running about everywhere with brands when I woke up. I tried to get them to leave. They wouldn't listen — they set hands on me — threatened me. I panicked, I'm afraid. I called Almer. Could you come over, Clovis?"

Becker nodded grimly. "Yes, of course. At once."

The fire had not really had time to get a grip on the relatively few things that were flammable, but the stink of burning was coming up through the gravishute as Becker landed the air car on the roof.

Down the hillside, among the trees, he could see the brown-clad Brotherhood struggling with men in black, hooded cloaks like the one he had seen Almer wearing. In the general manner of their dress, there did not seem to be much difference between them.

He dropped through the gravishute and found Narvo Velusi in his living room. The old man was trembling violently, sitting in his deep armchair and staring through the transparent wall at the fighting men in the woods below. Velusi looked older than he had ever seemed before. His clothes were smudged and torn, his hands dirty and bleeding.

Horrified, Becker knelt down beside the chair and looked into his friend's face. "Narvo?"

Velusi was in a state of shock. He turned his head slightly and his lips moved and even tried to smile.

The room was disordered. Furniture was overturned, fabric charred and water saturated the floor coverings. Becker had never seen such a sight at close hand. He patted Velusi's arm and went to the wall to look out at the battle.

Men were rolling about on the ground punching one another. Others were using sticks torn from the trees to strike one another. Becker was horrified. He touched the appropriate control and the wall became blank and solid again.

In the semi-darkness, he drew up a chair beside Velusi and sat down, trying to comfort the old man. He fetched him a drink and put it into his hand.

After a while, Velusi raised the glass to his lips and sipped the drink. A long, infinitely tired sigh escaped him.

"Oh, Clovis," he murmured, "I blamed you for your apathy, but now I feel that it's not worth continuing to try to do anything. You knew it was too late, didn't you?"

"Nothing of the sort. I was just trying to come to grips with my conscience, that was all. Later, when you feel better, we'll go to the Great Glade and tell the people we intend to re-form the council."

There was a sound from behind them and a tall, black-cloaked figure emerged from the gravishute. His chest was rising and falling rapidly. He was dressed exactly as Almer had been, save that his mask was without the scarlet edging and his boots were black, his gloves undecorated.

He walked over to the cabinet and, unasked, poured himself a drink. He drained the glass and put it down with a thump.

"We've dealt with them," he said harshly. "I'm glad you called us in time. This is the first real chance we've had to have a proper go at them."

"What happened?" Becker asked hesitantly, not really wanting to hear.

"We captured a couple of the maniacs. We'll put them in a safe place somewhere where they can't affect anybody any more."

Becker no longer questioned the archaic terms the man used so freely. It would not be long, he thought, before the words "arrest" and "prison" would become familiar again. He felt afraid of this masked, earnest man with his brisk manner. The state of mind, reflected in the fact that he and his fellows wore uniform clothing, was one of basic insecurity.

"Was anyone badly hurt?" Velusi asked.

"Only one of them. He is no longer with us."

"Where is he?"

"He — he is no longer with us." The masked man helped himself to another drink.

"You don't mean he's dead?" Becker got up. "You killed him?"

"If you insist on the term, yes, he's dead. There was no intention of taking his life. It was accidental. But it has its advantages now that it's happened. It will warn the cult off from further violence…"

"Or incite them to vengeance," Becker said scornfully. "What's happened to your education, man? Remember your history, your psychology, your sociology!"

"The present situation is unique as you well know," the vigilante replied forcefully.

"Only in one respect — certainly not in any other."

"We shall see. I must say I expected more gratitude when I came here. We probably saved your friend's life." The man's tone was deliberately rude and there had not been quite such a breach of manners before in all Becker's experience. He felt unable to deal with the man's impoliteness; he had no precedent.

"This is Narvo Velusi…" he began.

"I know very well who he is. You are Clovis Becker. I'm supposed to respect you, I gather. Well, I did once, but what have you done to help the present situation? Velusi has embarked upon a useless, time-wasting project with that transmitter of his — and you have done nothing at all. Very well, I accept that you are men of peace and enlightenment. Such men are not particularly useful these days. Men of action are needed — like our leader."

"Andros Almer?"

"We do not use personal names. We have dispensed with the old associations until the Brotherhood is under control. You seem ill-informed for men of affairs. Perhaps things have moved too rapidly for you — perhaps you are unused to people making rapid decisions?"

"Hasty decisions, perhaps?" Becker suggested coolly.

The man laughed harshly and turned to go. "Decisions, anyway." He gestured with one gloved hand. "Look down on us from your remote height if you wish, but, if it weren't for our decisions and our action, Narvo Velusi might be badly injured, at very least, by now. You should be grateful to us. We are giving you the security to continue with your pleasant philosophizing!"

"I came here today to discuss reforming the administration," Becker told him angrily. "We intend to hold a meeting in the Great Glade today and co-opt new members on to the council."

"Noble of you. But a little belated, I would say."

The man drew his hood further over his face and entered the gravishute.

"Tell Almer we shall need him there!" Becker called after the man, half-placatingly. He realized he should have responded rather more neutrally than he had done. There was no point in angering Almer or his vigilantes. The best thing to do would be to get Almer on to the council and also, perhaps, a member of the Brotherhood cult, since it would be only fair to have all sides represented.

He smiled ironically, then.

When, in the past, had such attempted conciliations worked when the parties concerned were so full of anger and distrust?

CHAPTER TWO

MEN OF JUDGMENT

As soon as the meeting began, Becker realized that it was all but useless. The proportion of black-cloaked vigilantes and brown-habited cult members in the auditorium was slightly higher than the proportion of ordinary men and women. He had not realized how quickly groups of that sort could grow.

Hovering above, in their black air cars, were several more of Almer's vigilantes. Almer himself sat on the platform with Narvo Velusi and Becker. He leaned back casually, with his arms folded and his legs crossed; the very picture of arrogance. His hood was flung back, but he wore his mask still.

Looking around the auditorium, Becker saw that the fashion for wearing masks — albeit brightly coloured ones — had also increased. There were scarcely twenty people there who did not wear a mask of some kind.

Velusi had recovered. His hands were still bruised and his shoulders were not held as straight as normal, but he gave the appearance of being relaxed. He stood up to open the meeting.

"As you have heard," he began, "Clovis Becker has agreed to head a new administration which will be specifically concerned with dealing with the various problems that have arisen since the old council disbanded."

He was speaking very carefully, Becker thought, making sure he offended no-one.

"The new administration," Velusi continued, "will attempt to ensure that people will have security and, perhaps, a sense of purpose…"

He went on in this vein for some time, but Becker could tell that Velusi's diplomatic words were making no impression at all. The Brotherhood of Guilt was fanatical and convinced of their own right to act as they saw fit. The vigilantes evidently despised the kind of argument Velusi was using. As for the ordinary people, they could look around them and see how useless it was to try to reconcile the opposed groups by means of placatory words.

"And so we require volunteers," Velusi concluded. "Preferably people who have served on a council of some kind in the past. Would those willing raise their hands?"

All the Brotherhood members raised their hands. Most of the vigilantes raised their hands. Two ordinary people raised their hands, glanced about, and lowered them again.

Becker realized that a mockery was being made of the whole anarchic-democratic system they had lived by for so long.

The idea of forming a new administration on a sane and rational basis had been doomed from the start, it was now plain. Perhaps he had instinctively realized this and for that reason had been slow to act?

Velusi was evidently at a loss.

"Perhaps if you could remove your masks..." he began.

Becker got up. He thought he heard Almer chuckle from where he sat, still in the same casual posture.

"We want a balanced representation," said Becker as levelly as he could. "Could we have a few more volunteers from the —" he pretended to smile — "non-aligned men and women here?"

No more hands were raised.

Suddenly there was a scream from above them. Everyone looked into the air. A black-cloaked man was falling towards the ground. He landed with a smack just short of the platform. Becker rushed towards him but he could tell from the way the body lay that he was dead. He began to peel off the mask, to see who it was.

The man seemed to have fallen from his air car, yet he was wearing a gravstrap. It had not been switched on.

He heard a shout. People were still looking upwards.

There, drifting away from the air car on a gravstrap, was a brown-habited member of the Brotherhood.

It was evident that he had come up behind the vigilante and pushed him out of his car before he could operate his gravstrap.

Vigilantes were now rising into the air to give chase, others were grappling with Brotherhood members in the tiers of the auditorium.

Becker still had his hand on the dead man's mask and now he felt someone touch his shoulder. He looked up into the shadowed face of Andros Almer.

"Don't remove his mask," Almer said icily. "Didn't you know that that was one of the reasons for wearing them — so we shall not know who are dead and who are living?"

Becker straightened and stood looking at Almer.

"This is superstition, Andros!"

"Is it? We think it is practical." There was a triumphant, bantering note in Almer's voice now. "We are a practical group of men. It was a worthy decision to make, Clovis, about forming a government, but as you can see it is unnecessary. I suggest you and Narvo go home and stay out of all this. We can look after things perfectly well."

Becker looked to where a great mass of men were fighting. The whole auditorium was in confusion. In the air two cars crashed head on with a great splintering sound. Men dropped out of them and began fighting in mid-air.

"As you can see, there is too much violence for a man like yourself to cope with, Clovis," Almer said patronizingly, with soft amusement. "There's a new order now — one well-equipped to deal with this sort of thing. I would rather see you safely away from the unpleasantness…"

Becker felt the anger coming back with renewed strength. He wanted to strike Almer.

"You helped produce this situation, Andros — you are doing nothing to get rid of it! Look what happened earlier. Your men killed a Brotherhood member. Now a Brotherhood member kills one of your men. You can only make things worse!"

"We shall see."

As Narvo Velusi and Clovis Becker flew back towards their air car, a voice from below cried "*Cowards!*"

Bewildered and outraged by the turn of events, the two men headed towards Fastina's house on the Greek coast, hurrying away from the noise and confusion in the Great Glade.

They flew over the flower forest. Its heavy scents and richly coloured flowers half-surprised them as they looked down.

"There is nothing we can do, after all," Velusi said after a while. "That was the defeat of reason you saw back there — symbolized and displayed."

Becker nodded.

"What do we do now, Narvo?"

"I don't know. Stay out of it for a while. What else can we do?"

"It depends what happens," Becker said. "For how long will Almer confine himself to fighting only the Brotherhood? When will he begin to arrest those he suspects of being 'secret' members? There is even the chance that the Brotherhood will get the upper hand and destroy him and his vigilantes. It would not matter."

"At least Almer speaks for order," Velusi said.

"Of a sort," Becker agreed. "But there will be no difference between them in a short while."

"I suppose not." Velusi seemed no longer interested. His voice was heavy with despair.

"Perhaps we should take Almer's advice and stay out of things," Becker said. "It's not our world now, Narvo — it's becoming unrecognizable. Let them sort out their own problems."

Velusi nodded.

A little later the old man said: "We can ignore them, Clovis, easily enough. But will they ignore us?"

A month later, lying on the white beach, half-submerged in the warm sea, Clovis Becker heard the thump of someone running towards him.

It was Fastina. He stretched out a hand to her, smiling, but she shook her head. "It's the news, Clovis. Narvo said you'd want to see it."

She began to run back and he followed her more slowly.

Velusi was hunched forward, watching the V-screen on which, lately, news bulletins had begun to be broadcast. The screens had not been used for such things since Central Information had been set up to serve anyone who wished to know something. But information was now restricted and channeled into the regular hourly bulletins operated from the old Central Information building, which was under the control of Almer's vigilantes.

The scene on the screen showed the Great Glade. The glade was now surrounded by a force-wall nearly a mile high. This was to restrict passage to and from it.

On the enlarged platform stood three members of the Brotherhood. They had been stripped naked, but their shaven heads were sufficient to tell what they were. Two were men and one was a woman. They were dirty and there were recent scars on their bodies. By the look of them, they could hardly stand with exhaustion and starvation.

Black-cloaked vigilantes ringed the platform. They all bore swords in their hands; long blades of bright steel. So far these were the only weapons that had been manufactured, but in a world otherwise without weapons, they were sufficient to suit the vigilantes' purpose.

In a high chair, raised above the floor of the platform, sat a man who could be recognized as Almer by his red boots and scarlet-trimmed mask and gloves.

He was not called Almer now, by his men, but simply "leader".

Almer's voice came from the V-screen.

"I judge you guilty of complicity in the murder of another citizen," Almer was saying. "And sentence you to die so that your fellows will learn by your example."

"No!" Becker looked incredulously at his friends. "Has it reached this stage already?"

"I said it would be rapid," Velusi said tonelessly. "In a society not equipped to withstand this sort of thing, people like Almer and his vigilantes can develop as quickly as they wish to."

Becker saw the ring of vigilantes turn inwards, their swords raised.

The Brotherhood people fell to their knees, making no attempt to rise.

The swords fell, rose, and fell again, sparkling with blood in the strong sunlight.

Then the vigilantes stepped back from the corpses.

They had been butchered beyond recognition.

Becker controlled his need to vomit. He could not move to switch off the set, but watched in fascination as Almer stepped haughtily down from his chair and stood near the bloody pile of flesh and bone.

Almer looked down at it for a moment and then disdainfully drew in his cloak and walked around it, leaving the platform and crossing to a specially cleared space in the auditorium where his black air car stood guarded by four of his men.

The auditorium, Becker could now see, was packed.

CHAPTER THREE

MEN OF CONSCIENCE

After that, they switched off the V-screen for good. They moved the house from Greece to the deep jungles of Sri Lanka, close to Anuradhapura, the ancient city of the Mahavansa, with its great domes and ziggurats dating from almost five hundred years before the Christian era. Thousands of years old, the buildings had survived tidal waves and earthquakes and the encroachment of the jungle. No-one lived there now. No-one visited the city. They could site the house in the shade of a temple, disguise it with tree branches, and be invisible from the air.

Months passed and they found comparative happiness in the jungle city. It was everlasting afternoon, mild and golden. Monkeys and brightly coloured birds moved through the foliage and over the old, vine-covered stones of the buildings. Jungle and city seemed merged into one ancient entity.

Occasionally Narvo Velusi would take the air car and go to the Black Sea to supervise work on his transmitter. Almost a colony had formed there, he told the others, of people who wanted nothing to do with Almer or the Brotherhood. He would bring back extra supplies every time he visited the transmitter and once he made a point of calling on Brand Calax, who had not been bothered by the Brotherhood since Almer had come to power and had been full of praise for the vigilantes' system.

One day, when they were picnicking on the grassy slope of a ziggurat, they saw an air car come drifting down through the trees. Instinctively they looked for cover, but then Velusi recognized the carriage.

"It's Brand. He asked where we were and I had to tell him. He promised he would keep the secret."

They knew that if anyone really wished to seek them out it could be done systematically, using instruments, but they hoped that the old maxim "out of sight, out of mind" would hold true as far as Almer or the Brotherhood were concerned. They were simply being cautious, they told themselves.

Brand guided his car down until he was hovering beside them.

"I tried to get you on the screen," he said, "but I couldn't get through. So I thought I'd come personally and say goodbye."

He was paler and gaunter still, but he seemed very cheerful.

"The ship is complete, is it?" Becker said. Like the other two, he wore a loose kilt around his middle and he was very brown.

"Yes. We blast off tomorrow. I'll be back in six months of course…"

"Of course," said Becker.

"… and I shouldn't wonder if I won't have a couple of healthy Titanians with me in *The Orlando Sharvis*."

Velusi, who still did not know that Becker had already been to Titan, said slowly: "Are you sure you'll manage the voyage both ways, Brand?"

Calax laughed. "Surer than ever. I'll make you all eat your words when I come back."

Fastina smiled. "You'll do a lot of good if you do find some Titanians, Brand." The smile trembled and her expression was pitying before she turned her head away, pretending to pack up the picnic things.

Calax had not noticed her face and he grinned. "I know it."

He brought the air car a little closer, so that they could climb aboard. "I hope you'll offer me a drink to celebrate. You guide me, and I'll take you back to your house."

In the main room, which was full of the golden-green light of the forest, Calax sat down and stretched his legs.

"You know, I'm in agreement with a lot that Almer's doing. He's got strength and conviction and he knows what he wants to do. A few people have got hurt, I realize, but it was no more than they deserved. I can't understand his constant antipathy towards my Titan project. It's such a negative attitude for such a positive man to hold."

"I would have said his whole attitude was negative," Fastina said, leaning against the transparent wall and looking at the trees which grew right up to the house. They were gnarled old trees and had probably been there since before the raid.

"I don't see that," Calax told her. He looked back at Becker and Velusi who were standing together behind his chair. "And I don't understand why you're hiding from him like this. What harm would he do you? He's only interested in controlling the madmen who've joined this cult. I know he's had to take emergency measures to check the thing growing and so on, and I don't say he has to kill these people, but someone like him was needed. He filled a demand, you know. He was what everyone but the Brotherhood wanted."

"Yes," said Velusi, "you're probably right. But better safe than sorry, eh?"

"He won't try to do anything to people like you — ex-members of the council! He wouldn't dare, for one thing, and he wouldn't need to for another. I just don't know why you're worrying."

"Neither do we," Becker put in. "Just call it the example of history. We're probably being over-pessimistic. But when a man like Almer goes insane, anything that conflicts with his view of things is likely to be regarded as a threat."

"Almer insane? He's not insane, Clovis. He follows this fashion of masking and so on, and maybe he's a bit more brutal than he should be, but that's not insanity — not strictly."

Velusi laughed. The laugh was a little strained. "Let's not argue any more. We should be drinking to the success of your trip, Brand."

After Calax had left, the three of them sat in the room looking at the monkeys playing over the half-ruined temple. They chattered and squawked, knocking one another from theirs perches, leaping wildly from level to level and from stone to stone.

As they watched the monkeys they began to relax and smile.

"I think I'll re-connect the V tomorrow," Becker said, "just to see Brand taking off. I don't think he'll be back."

"There's a chance," Velusi said.

"I don't think so." Becker got up. "When he finds that there's no human colony on Titan, I don't think he'll want to come back. I think he knows there isn't a chance. He wants to go there to die, that's my guess."

"He could die just as easily here if he wanted to kill himself," Fastina said.

"That's not the point. He wants to die trying — doing something. You can't blame him."

When he and Fastina went to bed that night, their love-making was cruel and desperate.

The next day they sat down to watch the take-off on the V-screen. It was not being covered on Almer's official broadcasts, but there were cameras trained on the ship. The cameras were of the ordinary domestic kind, but they were sufficient to show the mountain valley and the great steel ship ready on its launching pad.

There was no commentary, no count-down that they could hear, as the ship began to warm up.

The ship was built to a design that was nowadays unusual. It was a slender, tapering thing, with circular fins at its base.

Its drive began to murmur, its hull began to tremble slightly, and then it was rising slowly into the air.

They said nothing as they watched *The Orlando Sharvis* climb upwards, beginning to gather speed; but they gasped when the explosion came.

The whole hull burst apart in blue and orange flames. Pieces of the ship were flung in all directions and they saw them begin to fall while the antigravity drive unit continued alone to sail upwards, as if unaware that the ship it had powered had broken into a thousand fragments.

They heard the roar of the explosion and the screen rattled and reverberated as its speakers were unable to take the strain. They could almost feel the heat of the blast.

"Sabotaged," whispered Fastina. "It must have been."

"But by whom?" Velusi was badly shaken. "Who killed him?"

The scene faded and a masked member of the vigilantes appeared on the screen.

"We have just received news that Brand Calax's Titan ship, *The Orlando Sharvis*, has blown up," said the man. "It is suspected that members of the notorious Brotherhood of Guilt or their sympathizers were responsible for this destruction. Brand Calax, the heroic ex-Warden of Ganymede who was embarking on a lone expedition to seek survivors of the rumoured Titan colony..."

"Too quick," Becker said. "What do you say, Narvo?"

The old man nodded. "They were expecting it. They knew it was going to happen. They're the ones who did it. Almer did not want Calax to build the ship in the first place. I thought it was strange that he didn't interfere with him. They sabotaged the ship, unquestionably."

"... those responsible will be found and punished," the vigilante was saying. "This is perhaps the worst crime the so-called Brotherhood has yet committed. Be certain, however, that we shall protect you against further outrages of this kind."

"They don't need further outrages," Fastina said. "And there can't be anything like it. Why has Almer done this?"

"For several reasons," Velusi murmured, "to consolidate his own position because he probably wants a reason for extending his power, to make the people even more reliant on him than they are already, to punish Brand Calax for his 'obstinacy' and not listening to 'reason'... The man's clever and psychotic at once. The combination is pretty rare, by all accounts." Velusi shook his head sorrowfully. "Poor, Brand — he wanted to die, but not like that."

"I'm going to see Almer," Becker said suddenly.

Velusi did not take him seriously. "What good would that do?"

"He still has his conscience. He still has to justify these actions to himself."

"He's too far gone — he can justify anything now."

"I might as well try, anyway. And I might get the chance to see Yoluf at Central Information. He would possibly give me a chance to broadcast the truth. This can't go on unchecked…"

"You think you can check him now? We tried and failed. Now he has more power than ever."

Fastina broke in. "It would be dangerous, Clovis. Don't go."

"I'm afraid of him, Fastina — as we all are. I must try to face him nonetheless."

Velusi shook his head. "We must be more subtle, Clovis. The only thing we could do would be to get together a group of our own and undermine Almer's power gradually."

"While he murders at will?"

Velusi sighed. "Very well, go to see him, but be on your guard, Clovis."

CHAPTER FOUR

MEN OF REASON

Almer's headquarters were in the old Main Administration Building just south of the flower forest that enclosed the Great Glade. Though still surrounded by its smooth lawns, it seemed to have been turned into a fortress, guarded by vigilantes armed with swords and a force-field that was partially visible; the shimmering air that indicated its presence gave it extra menace.

Strangest of all, a flag flew from the roof of the building. The letter "M" had been worked on it and beneath this were the smaller words "For Order". The M could stand for militia or even, Becker guessed, for some dead-language word. Although not personally familiar with such things, he had seen enough similar examples in his history Vs.

Well before he had reached the force-barrier an amplified voice roared from a phonoplate close by.

"Stop! It's forbidden to approach Main Admin by air!"

Becker stopped the car as two vigilantes on gravstraps came speeding up from the ground. They dropped into his car and stood looking down at him. He rose, frowning.

"I have come to see An — your leader," he said. "Tell him that Clovis Becker is here." He spoke with deliberate firmness.

They both seemed to relax a trifle then and one of them spoke apparently into the air. Becker knew that his voice was picked up by the tiny earbead transceiver in his ear. The man relayed Becker's message and then waited for a reply.

Becker stood there impatiently for several minutes until at length the vigilante looked up and said: "It's all right. They'll make an opening in the screen. Go through carefully — the thing's charged with enough energy to stun you badly."

The two men left his air car and returned to the ground. Becker saw a gap appear in the screen well above the level of the lawn and he guided his air car through it to land on the roof of the building.

Two more guards were waiting for him there. They were swathed, like the others, in their heavy black hoods and cloaks, but their masks and gloves were edged in yellow braid. This was evidently some sign of rank or function. This evidence of further erosion of individuality depressed Becker. He let them lead him to the gravishute.

They fell several storeys and then entered what had once been the big council meeting room. Where there had been seats for almost a hundred people, there was now only one chair at the far end near the darkened wall. It was the same black, high-backed chair that Becker had seen on his V-screen several months before when Almer had had his men murder the Brotherhood members. The chair was equipped with an anti-gravity generator, for it hovered about a foot off the floor.

The walls were now lined with scores of V-screens and just in front of Almer's chair was a console that evidently controlled them.

Almer sat in the chair, even more arrogant in posture than ever. He signaled to the guards and they left.

Becker faced Almer alone.

He began to walk down towards the masked man.

When he had covered half the distance, Almer drawled: "No further please, Clovis."

Becker stopped, puzzled. "Why is that?"

"I have enemies. It is impossible to trust anyone. Besides, after today's wanton murder of Brand Calax and the destruction of his ship…"

"That's what I came to see you about."

"You know, perhaps, which members of the Brotherhood were responsible?" Almer's tone was sardonic.

"I know that they were not responsible."

"Oh? Then who was it?" Almer crossed his legs and settled deeper in his chair. "You? Have you come to confess, Clovis?"

"You were responsible, Andros. It was quite plain — your news bulletin came too rapidly and too fluently after the explosion…"

"Did it now? We live and learn. Thank you, Clovis."

"All these lies! This myth you are building! Your evasion of reality, both personally and publicly, is almost unbelievable, Andros. You hide in your hoods and masks, you hide in half-baked ideas, you hide, now, in outright lies. For your own sake, listen to me!"

"I'm listening," said Almer banteringly.

"There comes a point in a situation like this where you become so far removed from actuality that your own system of lies defeats you. It has happened often enough in the past. Your lie becomes your reality — but it is only yours.

You begin to operate according to a set of self-formulated laws that conflict with the actual laws of existence. If you continue, you will realize that eventually. But if you listen to me now, you will be able to rectify the position and..."

Almer began to laugh. "Thank you, Clovis, thank you. What if a sweet-hearted man you are. You have come to save me from myself, eh?"

"I suppose so."

"Oh, Clovis, don't you see that it doesn't matter about *my* reality and *the* reality any more? We have only so long to live. We can do what we like. I can play kings here — you can play hermits wherever you've hidden yourself. We are both in hiding — but you hide in your detachment while I hide in my *attachment*."

"I don't see..."

"Yes you do, yes you do. You hide by refusing to become involved in all this — I hide, if you like, by involving myself in it up to the chin. More than that, Clovis, I act as the catalyst, do you see? I cause things to happen that much faster!" Andros began to laugh again.

"You aren't as insane as I thought you were," Clovis said quietly. "Or at least..."

"I know I am? Is that what you want to say?"

"It will do."

Almer chuckled. "You don't have to tell me that this process will result in mutual destruction eventually. But I am following the rules, Clovis. I am doing all the things I should. I am repressive, I aggravate a situation by publicly murdering people, I sabotage spaceships, I lie and distort the truth and then arrest people on false charges." He leaned forward, still smiling. "And I wait to see how far I can go before some resistance is offered by thoughtful people like yourself, Clovis..."

"You expected me here?"

"Sooner or later. I've been disappointed on the whole — I expected opposition earlier. My public killings were actually popular. I had underestimated the people. I had underestimated the power of fear."

"So I am here. And obviously I cannot appeal to you to stop."

"I have anticipated all your arguments, I believe."

"All but one. Haven't we a duty to help people lead happier lives than these?"

"Duty? I am no Messiah, Clovis. But you are, perhaps?" Andros Almer's tone not only mocked him but somehow struck an unpleasant chord deep inside Becker. He began to wish very much that he had not come to see Almer.

"You are an arrogant man, Andros Almer."

"Arrogant? Arrogant? Oh, come now, Clovis!"

"You imply that I'm arrogant…"

"Aren't you? Clovis — I am merely moving with the tide of events."

"And turning them to your advantage."

"Someone would have done. You, under other circumstances, perhaps?"

"Perhaps."

"Well, then?"

Becker shrugged. "I left things too late. If I had stayed…"

"Things might be the same today — only you would be sitting in this fine chair." Almer slapped the arm.

"I don't think so."

"Maybe not. But they would be the same tomorrow or the next day. You are slower to accept the obvious, that's all."

"I like to think you're wrong, Andros." Becker sighed. "But I suppose it is possible that I would have found myself forced into the position you now occupy. I did anticipate that — and that was one of the reasons I chose to do nothing until too late."

"There you are then!"

A signal on one of the central V-screens had been blinking urgently for some moments. Almer had ignored it up to now. He drifted in his chair to the console and reached out a gloved hand to touch a stud.

A masked and hooded vigilante appeared on the screen.

"About twenty suspects have been rounded up, leader," said the man. "Half are actual Brotherhood members and the rest are thought to be secret sympathizers."

"They are the ones on the list I gave you?" Almer asked.

"Most of them. We still have to locate one or two."

"Good work. Find them soon."

Becker shook his head. "I take it these are people you regard as dangerous. You intend to accuse them of destroying the spaceship?"

"Quite so." Almer turned his attention back to the vigilante who was still on the screen. "And the other matter? How is that progressing?"

"We expect the result very soon, leader."

"Excellent!"

The man faded from the screen.

"What 'other matter'?" Becker asked.

"Oh, I expect you will hear of it shortly," Almer told him. "Now, Clovis, I must supervise the questioning of our suspects. If there is nothing else…?"

"Plainly there is nothing I can do?"

"Certainly there is nothing you can *say*, Clovis, that will affect me. Goodbye."

Becker turned and went to the gravishute entrance. The guards were still there, hovering just inside. They escorted him back to the roof.

Almer's last statement seemed to have been something of a challenge.

As Becker flew back towards Sri Lanka, he let the golden air car drift slowly while he tried to gather his thoughts. Almer seemed to want him to take some sort of positive action against the vigilantes and Almer himself. In short, Almer wanted to fight Becker, perhaps to test himself and almost certainly to "win" Fastina from his rival.

Becker had no intention of playing this game, but Almer might try to force him to in some way. Almer had impressed Becker with one thing; the man could only be brought down by violent means now.

Becker was still horrified at the idea of using violence and yet could think of no subtle method.

About half-an-hour after he had left Almer's fortress, he glanced behind him and noticed several flying objects coming closer. They were probably air cars and they were moving very rapidly. Soon they could be seen plainly. There were five black air cars, and standing in them, their cloaks billowing out behind them, were vigilantes.

Becker frowned. Was Almer already trying to force his hand?

The cars caught up with him and began to surround him and Becker saw the men draw the straight swords with which they were all armed.

"What's going on?" he called.

"We have been ordered to take you into custody, Clovis Becker!" one of them shouted back. "Turn your car about and come with us."

"What is the reason?"

"Suspicion of complicity in sabotage."

"Oh, this is stupid. I was nowhere near Calax's spaceship for months. Even Almer can't make that sound right!"

"The charge is not connected with the Titan ship. You are thought to have helped sabotage the giant radio transmitter project initiated by Narvo Velusi."

Now Becker knew what the other matter was that Almer had mentioned earlier.

"You have destroyed Velusi's transmitter, is that it?" he said levelly. "You are contemptible."

"Come with us."

Becker touched the control that operated the car's force-shield and instantly the car was enclosed in an invisible bubble of force. The vigilantes did not seem to have noticed this action. Becker felt in his pocket and took out the ultrasonic whistle there, trying to remember the code he needed. He had never had occasion to use it before.

One of the vigilantes gestured impatiently with his sword and his voice was muffled now by the screen.

"We are prepared to use violence if you do not come willingly," he said.

Becker took the whistle from his pocket and blew three long blasts on it.

The car began to hurtle upwards and he was flung to the couch as it went into an emergency climb. If he had not been protected by the screen, Becker could not have survived the rapid ascent into the ionosphere. As it was the only air he had was that trapped inside the bubble.

He looked down. The cars were climbing very slowly it seemed.

His chest felt sore and he could hardly get to his feet again. He looked out over the planet, searching for what he needed. Then he saw them. A group of cumulus clouds to his west. If he could dive into them, he might stand a chance of evading the vigilantes.

The clouds were traveling in roughly the same direction he had been going before the vigilantes turned up.

He settled himself back into the couch and felt under the ledge of the car to find the manually operated control board. He swung it out and his fingers moved over the studs, giving the car its directions.

The car dipped and began to dive, like the huge bird it resembled.

Becker was again pressed deep into the cushions as the car hurtled downwards. He could not see if the vigilantes were following him.

Then he was in the obscuring mist of the clouds. He quickly cut the car's speed and calculated the speed at which the clouds its were traveling.

Gently, he began to move along, using the clouds as a cover.

He would have to wait and see if the vigilantes had discovered his trick.

Several hours later, Becker knew that it had worked. He had been forced to switch off the screen and let the cold, clammy mist into the car, but it was the only way he could breathe.

The quality of the light told him that he was entering the twilight region and he judged that it was safe to leave the clouds and descend into the warmer air.

Dropping from the clouds, he saw that he was over the ocean and he guessed that it was probably the Bay of Bengal. He checked his instruments and set his course for Sri Lanka, traveling rapidly.

Soon the island was in sight and he swept lower and lower over the jungles until he could make out the buildings of Anuradhapura below.

With a feeling of relief, he circled into the jungle, guiding the car among the trees to land on the mosaic roof of the house.

There were two other air cars already there. They were black and they were familiar. He was sure that one of them was Andros Almer's.

Panic-stricken, Becker dashed for the gravishute. It now seemed likely that the attempt to arrest him had been designed to keep him away from the house while Almer and some of his vigilantes went there. Perhaps the vigilantes had even let him escape.

He dropped into the shaft and drifted down to the entrance of the main room. He could hear voices. He reached out and grabbed the hand-grip, hanging there and peering cautiously into the room.

Almer only had two others with him. They were holding Fastina who was struggling.

Almer himself stood over Narvo Velusi. There was a sword in Almer's hand and there was blood on the sword.

It took Becker a while to realize the truth that Velusi was in fact dead and that Almer was his murderer.

Almer was chuckling. "If that doesn't force Becker to do something desperate, nothing will." He turned to Fastina who looked away from him in disgust. "It's quite traditional, really, Fastina. Now we take you off with us — and the noble prince has to rescue the fair princess from the wicked baron." He laughed again. "What a game!"

Becker was trembling with rage as he entered the room, unseen as yet by any of them.

Then he flung himself at Andros Almer, grabbing him clumsily around the throat with one arm and punching at his body with his free fist.

Almer shouted and tried to release himself. Becker was weeping as he punched. Almer's sword fell to the floor as he turned and began to grapple with Becker.

One of the men let go of Fastina and came forward, drawing his sword. Becker managed to swing Almer round so that the vigilante leader formed a shield between himself and the other swordsman, but Almer twisted away and broke free.

For a little while they stood there, panting and glaring at one another. Almer's man seemed uncertain what to do and kept looking to his leader for instructions.

Becker dived for the fallen sword, picked it up and aimed an awkward blow at Almer who skipped aside.

Becker found himself confronting the other swordsman. He had no idea how to use the weapon he had in his hand and knew that he had no chance against the vigilante who was now beginning to edge around him, crouched and feinting. There was a smile on Almer's face now.

THE SHORES OF DEATH

339

"I'll have your blade," he told his man. "This really will be quite dramatic."

Almer took the sword from the vigilante and clashed it lightly against Becker's. He half turned his head, his smile broadening, and spoke to Fastina who was looking on, her expression tragic.

"There's a bargain, Fastina," Almer said. "He who wins this duel shall have your hand. What do you say?"

She said nothing. She knew there was nothing to say which would make Almer stop.

Becker now held his sword out clumsily before him, backing away as Almer advanced.

Almer grinned and lunged, pulling the point of his sword just short of Becker's heart. Becker had made a defensive movement with his sword, but it would have been too late to save him if Almer had been in earnest. He swung the sword out in an arc, slashing at Almer who leapt lightly backwards.

"You haven't the same interest in these romantic old customs, Clovis — if you had, you would stand a better chance."

He thrust again with the sword and again Becker parried it too late. Grinning, Almer moved his sword from side to side as Becker tried to return a lunge. Becker knew that Almer was going to kill him eventually.

He lowered the sword.

"You will have to butcher me as you butchered Narvo," he said quietly. "I still refuse to play your game, Andros."

Almer assumed an expression of mock disappointment.

"Oh, Clovis — where's your sense of fun?"

"When you have killed me, what do you intend to do with Fastina?"

Almer put his masked head on one side, his eyes gleaming from behind the cloth.

"What does a villain always do? He *rapes* and he *humiliates* and then he *slays!*" He chuckled as he saw Becker raise the sword again. "That's better, Clovis. That's better."

Slashing wildly, Becker attacked and then, quite suddenly, the sword was gone from his hand. Almer had twisted it away.

Almer was grinning no longer. Hatred was there now as he drew back his · sword arm to finish Becker.

There was a movement from behind them and a new figure could be seen standing in the gravishute. He held an object in his hand, a bulbous instrument from which extended a tube. Becker thought he recognized it. It was probably a gun. Almer lowered his sword.

"Who are you?" one of the vigilantes said.

"My name is Mr Take. This thing in my hand is a weapon. It fires a poison charge which kills as soon as it touches any part of your body. It will be my pleasure to use it unless you release Clovis Becker and the girl at once."

"A gun! Where did you get a gun?" Almer took a step forward, staring at the object.

"I have had it for a very long time. I am a soldier — or was once. This is one of many guns of all kinds I had."

One of the vigilantes sneered. "He's mad. We haven't made any guns yet ourselves. I'll soon…" He lunged at Take with his sword. Take's hand moved abnormally fast. There was a brief hissing sound, the vigilante groaned, clutched his chest and fell to the floor.

"A gun, as I said," Take continued. "I have no feelings of mercy for you, Andros Almer. I will kill you without reluctance if you do not obey. Throw that sword thing down."

The sword clattered to the floor. Becker and Fastina moved to join Take at the gravishute entrance.

Almer shouted: "I'll find you! Where are you from?"

"Titan," Take replied as he followed Becker and Fastina up towards the roof.

CHAPTER FIVE

MEN OF VISION

Take took them away in Fastina's golden bird-shaped air car, heading east.

All were silent; Take because he was concentrating on the instruments and Becker and Fastina because they were too stunned by recent events.

Gradually, the light began to change in quality as they crossed the Bay of Bengal and left the sun behind.

Below, the water darkened to deep blue, reflecting the red rays of the sun. The air car cast a long, black shadow ahead and the sky was full of rich, hazy yellows, reds and purples.

Becker spoke, eventually, in a low voice. "Where are we going?"

"Home, Clovis Becker." Take's own tone was as vibrant and deep as it had been when they had first confronted each other in the house at Lake Tanganyika.

Land was ahead; the coastline of Burma. The dark jungles of the twilight were soon beneath them and from time to time they passed over the ruins of cities, mysterious in the perpetual half-light. Sometimes, too, they saw a tower standing alone in a clearing. The towers looked as if they had been formed of molten rock that had cooled so that it was impossible to tell if they were natural or man-made. They were familiar to Becker, for he had been born in one.

Take changed course slightly and began to drop lower. Becker now recognized the land area as the region where once the borders of Burma, China and Thailand had met. Now Take was heading north, towards the country that had once been Mongolia, and Becker realized what Take had meant.

"We're going to my father's house, is that it?"

"Yes."

"Why?"

"You will be safe there. You know the house."

"Of course!" Becker said. "The defenses."

"Exactly."

All the old towers had defenses, though there had never been any use for them. It was just one effect of the introverted character of the twilight people who had hidden themselves in their towers and taken every possible precaution to see that they were never disturbed.

It was quite true that they would be safe there, even if Almer followed them, for the armaments of the tower would still be in working condition and could be used to repel any attack Almer could make.

Soon the landscape below changed from forests to mountains and then to desert.

Red dust and brown lichen were now all that could be seen for miles. A light, cool wind blew over the desert, rustling the lichen, stirring the dust; and then a tower came into sight.

The tower was tall and bulky, and though its materials were primarily of steel and a kind of fibreglass, it, like the other towers they had passed, had the appearance of a strange volcanic rock formation. Darkly shining greens and yellows merged with gulleys of orange and blue and thin frozen bubbles of pink covered the openings of windows. There were no straight lines or angles in the building. Everything flowed and spread and curved like living matter that had suddenly petrified. There was no symmetry to the tower. Even the main doorway was an irregular shape, rather like a crudely drawn letter G on its side, resembling the entrance to some undersea grotto.

Take landed the air car. Fastina shivered as she looked around at the dead landscape and the looming, twisted tower that was illuminated by the mellow sunlight.

"Only you can open the tower, I believe," said Take.

"How do you know that?" Becker asked as they trod across the soft, sighing dust towards the entrance.

"I know a great deal about you," Take said.

Becker had begun to notice that Take's voice was always deep and vibrant and that the basic tone never changed so that while the voice was pleasant, it was also almost expressionless.

They reached the entrance. It was protected by a sheet of smooth material that looked like a thin membrane but was actually impervious to anything that tried to destroy it. Only Becker's touch on it could make it ripple downwards to the ground.

Becker touched the warm membrane and it responded at once. The entrance was open.

They walked through.

Becker put his arm around Fastina's shoulders and stretched out his free hand to touch the stud to re-awake the tower's heating and lighting system.

Faint, yellow light now filled a passage walled by dark, veined crystal. The light actually emanated from the walls, floors and ceiling. They stepped from the passage into an oddly shaped room with a roof that slanted close to the floor at the far end.

Two low, oval passages led from this room. The passages had walls of a soft, pinkish colour. The furniture of the whitish room was as asymmetrical as the rest of the tower and took odd forms. Here a chair was designed to look like a crouching gargoyle with open arms, there a table resembled a kneeling, grinning beast with a broad flat back.

The grotesque, half-barbaric ornamentation of the tower so contrasted with the simplicity of the daylight houses, that Fastina was obviously finding it hard to get used to the place. The design everywhere as they wandered through the upper parts of the tower was like the brilliant imaginings of a certain kind of surrealist painter; morbid, yet moving, fantastic, but inspired. Not one room looked the same. All were contorted to resemble nothing so much as the innards of an animal, save that every room had its particular colour, though all the walls resembled silicon or crystal.

In a top room Becker found the controls for the tower's armament. In keeping with the rest of the place, the control panel was ornate, in beaten brass and heavily worked gold and silver. Each individual control was in the form of a fierce fantastic beast's head and the instruments were arranged to look like eyes and open mouths, with dials, meters and indicators inset.

He found a book beside the panel, written in his father's hand. It was a manual for operating the force-screens, laser cannon, energy-guns and other armament both offensive and defensive.

He worked the controls and saw the panel registering activation all over the tower. The defenses were in good order.

Take and Fastina were watching him from near the doorway.

"All the towers in the twilight region are similarly equipped," Take said, his voice reverberating through the place. "If anyone wished to oppose Almer they would have a great arsenal at their disposal. Almer could not match it. It would take too long to redevelop weapons on this scale."

"Are you suggesting I use this stuff to carry a war into the daylight region?" Becker asked.

"Not at all, Clovis Becker. My comment was merely a comment, nothing more."

"What was your purpose in rescuing us, then?" Fastina asked. She looked a little less pale now.

"None, other than that I knew how much Clovis Becker valued life. I have been watching you in Anuradhapura, you know, for some time. I saw the black-cloaked ones arrive, I saw Clovis Becker arrive. It occurred to me that you would be in danger, so I came to help."

"Why have you been watching?" Becker asked. There was no anger in his question, only curiosity now.

"I was not sure that you had given up your earlier quest."

"The one for Orlando Sharvis?" Fastina said.

Take nodded. His head still lolled slightly, as if kept up by an effort.

"What would you have done if I had taken up the search again? Becker asked.

"If you had got close to him, I should have killed you," Take replied.

"And yet you saved our lives...?" Fastina began.

"So Orlando Sharvis does still exist!" Becker's tone was eager.

"I saved your lives," Take agreed, "but I would have killed Clovis Becker to save him from something else — from Sharvis."

"Where is Sharvis?" Becker left the control panel and approached Take. "On Titan? You said you were from Titan..."

"I am, in a sense," Take answered, "but I told Almer that partly to confuse him. I am the only survivor of Sharvis's colony."

"Other than Sharvis, himself," Becker said. "Where is he, Take?"

"At this moment? I don't know."

"Where does he live? On the night side? That's where Alodios went and I know that Alodios was looking for him, too."

"Alodios was following an old trail."

"He didn't find Sharvis, after all?" Becker moved to look through the window that faced the night. The red sunlight poured in from the window opposite, throwing dark shadows on the twisted walls of the room. All their faces were tinted by it.

Take seemed to be deep in thought.

"Alodios did find Sharvis eventually," he said.

"Did he give him what he wanted?"

"Sharvis gave him what he thought he wanted, just as her gave me what I thought I wanted once. That is Sharvis's sense of humour, you see. He always gives people what they think they want."

"Did you and Alodios want what I wanted?" Becker faced Take. "Did you?"

"More or less, yes. We both wanted immortality, as you did. But Alodios and I did not escape. Luckily, I gather, you saw reason in time."

"So immortality is possible!" Becker exclaimed.

Fastina looked up at Take. "Then why can't Sharvis be found? If the world knew this, the things that have been happening would stop soon enough. If everyone were immortal..."

"Sharvis is not idealistic," Take said with a slight, ironic smile. "He would not go to the world with the offer off immortality. If anyone went to him, he would give it to them willingly, but his gift would not be appreciated by many."

"I don't understand," Fastina said. "Why won't you tell us where Sharvis is — so that we can tell others?"

Take laughed humourlessly. The sound was a frightening one and Fastina moved closer to Becker.

"I hate no-one sufficiently to send them to Orlando Sharvis and I would advise you, very strongly, never to think of Sharvis again, to assume that he is dead. If I underestimated his power, I would show you things that he had done to warn you away from him, but I know from experience that even these sights are not enough to overcome the fascination Sharvis can exert on the strongest of wills. Listen to my advice — particularly you, Clovis Becker. Stay here where you are safe. You are in love — you can live here together for the rest of your lives. Be as happy as you can be — enjoy each other's love and the life you have." Take's voice was still rich and vibrant, still essentially without expression. He was trying to give his words urgency, trying to use his eyes to emphasize his words, but, strangely, he could not. He spoke emotional words without emotion.

He obviously realized this, for he added: "Consider my words. Take them seriously. Do not become like me."

He began to walk back down the passage, his pace quickening until his movements were a blur of speed.

Becker knew that this time Take could not escape him. Only he could open the membrane at the entrance to the tower.

He followed the man, shouting after him. The tower and its associations, his conversation with Take, his experiences at the house in Sri Lanka, all had combined to revive the old, dark thoughts that he had managed to submerge in Fastina's company.

As Becker ran after Take, Fastina ran behind him, calling: "Clovis! Clovis! I'm sure he's right. We'll stay here. Let him go."

Becker caught up with Take at the entrance. The man was trying to force his way through the membrane but it would not yield.

Becker said: "Tell me where Sharvis is, Take! I am my own man — I won't be deceived by him or whatever it is you fear will happen to me. I don't even want what I wanted before when I searched Earth and space for him. But he is a brilliant biologist and physicist. Can't you see that there is a chance he can help the race somehow? He might know of a way to revive the poisoned sperm and ova, to…"

Take leapt forward so quickly that Becker did not realize anything had happened until he felt Take's hand gripping his wrist in a hold that could not be broken.

"Do as I told you," Take said. "Stay here. Forget everything but that girl behind you. Make her happy and let her make you happy. Stay in the tower!"

"And go mad as my father and sister went mad?"

"If it happens, it will be a human madness. Accept it!"

Take hauled Becker forward. Becker tried to resist but Take's strength was incredible. He forced Becker's hand towards the entrance and pushed it flat against the barrier. The membrane dropped down. Take dropped Becker's wrist and sped towards the air car.

"You have stocks of food here," he shouted as he took the car upwards. "I will bring you more when I can. I will visit you when I can. I am your friend, Clovis Becker!"

They stood together in the twilight, watching the air car disappear.

"We haven't any gravstraps," Becker murmured as Fastina put her hand in his. "And he's taken the car. We couldn't go back if we wanted to — except by walking and the journey is almost impossible as I well know. He has marooned us!"

"He means well, Clovis. Take his advice, please."

"Whether he means well or not, what I said to him I meant, Fastina. I am my own man. I will not be given orders by Take or anyone else."

"You are proud, Clovis. You are proud, after all."

He sighed as they went back into the tower. "I suppose so. Arrogant, Almer said — more arrogant than himself. Does it matter to you, Fastina?"

"Does it to you?" she said.

"It would have done just a little while ago," he told her. "But I'm not so sure now."

"Then I don't mind," she smiled. "I don't mind what you are, Clovis. We are together, we are secure, we have each other for all our lives. Isn't that enough for you?"

He drew a deep breath. "You're right," he said. "I can do nothing in the world Almer has created. I should appreciate my exile. Yes, it's enough."

BOOK THREE

THE ROADS BETWEEN THE WORLDS

CHAPTER ONE

THE TOWER

But it was not enough. Not eventually.

For over two years they lived together in the tower. They never went out, for there was nowhere to go on that red, barren plain. They were in love; that did not change. If anything, their love became fiercer, though their love-making became a shade stranger. They spent the greater part of their time in the huge bed in the deep yellow room. In that bed Clovis's father had been born; in it his wife had conceived and borne a daughter; in it father and daughter had coupled and conceived a son. Now the son sported there, but this time there would be no issue.

True to his word, Take visited them from time to time, bringing them food and other things they needed. He came fairly regularly, about once every three months. Becker gave up trying to discover from Take where Sharvis was.

Take was reticent, also, about the state of affairs in the daylight world. He mentioned that Andros Almer was now in complete power and that the Brotherhood of Guilt was all but extinguished. On a more personal note he told them that Almer had blamed them not only for the destruction of Narvo's transmitter, but also for Velusi's murder. According to Almer, they had perished by crashing deliberately into the sea.

When not in bed, Becker would read his father's books, or look through tapes of his family history since his ancestors had settled in the twilight region. There was a strong resemblance between all the men and many of the women towards the end. Valta Becker and his daughter Betild might have been twins as far as appearance was concerned, and for that matter Clovis Becker could have been a twin to either. They all had the same tall, delicate-boned bodies, the large eyes and heavy brows and broad cheekbones. Becker began to identify with them again and think that he was a fool to have left the tower for the daylight region and that there was only one good thing that had resulted from that boyhood decision — Fastina.

He would wander back through the twisting, crystal corridors that were bathed in dim, shifting light, and seek her out.

Their need for each other was almost always so strong that they could not bear to be apart for more than an hour at a time.

Sometimes they quarreled, but not often and never for long. Sometimes, more frequently, they would lie side by side hating each other with such an intensity that they would have to make love or kill the other person, and the love-making then was brutal and selfish.

Becker devised a trap for Take. It was modeled on something his father had made for slaughtering animals. There was no game in this part of the twilight region, so it had never been used. It was one of many such useless inventions of his father, who had turned his attention to such things after Betild's death.

It was a couch now. It had been a bench. The couch was broad, but could curl up on itself rather like a Venus flytrap and crush or stifle whatever lay in it. It would not be strong enough to kill a man like Take, but it would hold him and give Becker a chance to question him.

Becker's desire to question Take was no longer based on any particular wish to act on the information he might get; he had lost sight of that. His single obsession now was somehow to get his jailer at a disadvantage — get him in his power if only for a short time.

The couch could be controlled by a little device that Becker kept in his pocket when dressed.

He had tried to get Take to sit on the couch the last time the man had visited them, but Take had not stayed long enough.

Fastina did not know about the couch. He kept it in his father's room, where he kept the books and the tapes.

Time passed, though they had no record of its passing and there were no signs outside until the rains came.

The rains came infrequently to this part of the world, but when they came it was for days at a time. They welcomed the change in the climate and would sit by the windows watching the water mingle with the dust and turn it to mud. It fell without pause in a great, pounding sheet.

It was during this rainfall that the vigilante found the tower.

C H A P T E R   T W O

T H E   P U R S U I T

The vigilante landed his small, one-man air car close to the entrance of the tower. The rain fell on the force-bubble protecting him and washed over it.

They watched from a small window as the man drew his cloak about him, switched off his force-screen and dashed for the entrance.

"What shall we do?" Fastina said to Becker who was thoughtfully rubbing his lips with his fingers.

Becker had suddenly thought of a new plan.

"We must let him in," he told her, getting up and making for the entrance. "Perhaps Almer found a record of this place as my family home and sent him to investigate."

"We can't let him in. He's armed. He might kill us."

"An assassin would have come more cautiously. I'll let him in." He paused for a moment. "You stay out of sight, Fastina. I'll take him to my father's room. If you think I'm in trouble, you'll be able to help better if he doesn't know you're here."

She nodded mutely, her large eyes full of anxiety.

Becker went along the passage and saw the outline of the vigilante as the man tried to push his way through the protecting membrane.

Becker stared through at the black masked, hooded face. The mask was edged with light blue.

The vigilante spread his hands, making gestures to show that he came in peace.

Becker put his palm against the membrane and it folded down to the floor.

The vigilante recovered himself and swaggered through, one gloved hand on his sword-hilt. There was another weapon at his belt. Becker recognized it as a gun of some kind.

There was a damp, musty smell from the vigilante's cloak as he entered and watched as the membrane shimmered back into place.

THE SHORES OF DEATH   351

"A peculiar sort of device," the stranger said, indicating the membrane. "I've seen nothing like it before."

Becker said, with a trace of humour, "It was an invention of my father's. Only members of my family can make it open or close. Since I'm the last surviving member of my family, you would do well to remember that only my *living* hand can open it and let you out."

The stranger shrugged.

"I haven't come to offer you any harm, Clovis Becker. On the contrary. I have come…"

"Tell me in my study," Becker said. He led the way up the winding, sloping crystal passage until they reached his father's room.

"A strange, bizarre sort of place," the stranger said as Becker poured him a drink. He sat on the couch, lounging back and raising a hand to refuse the drink. "No thanks — old habit — never trust an offer of food or drink in my job."

Becker drank the wine himself. "What is your job?"

"I am Security Scout 008, especially commissioned to find you by our leader himself."

"Almer knew where I was? How long has he known?"

"Our leader suspected you could be here. Since you did not seem to offer him much immediate harm, he did not bother to check his suspicion. He has more important things on his mind."

"What kind of things? What has been happening back there?"

"I'm coming to that, Clovis Becker. The Control has succeeded in establishing order and peace throughout the daylight world. It is a tribute to Chief Control, our leader, that the old Brotherhood of Guilt has been virtually stamped out or driven underground and now offers no threat to the security of the people. The birth struggles, perhaps, were what you witnessed and, looking back, we can see that these might well have horrified you…"

Becker interrupted suspiciously. "The Control? Is this the term you now use to describe the vigilantes?"

"It is. Having established the Rule of Law, we decided the old term was no longer functional." The man's pale lips smiled. "We were forced to do certain things at the beginning, but they enabled us to bring peace and security to a disordered society. You would not recognize it now, Clovis Becker…"

"I'm sure I wouldn't." The terms and phrasing were familiar to Becker from his reading. He could imagine the repression that must now exist throughout the daylight world.

"Instead of the old, hard to administer, system of living, we now have all houses grouped in strictly-defined areas. This enables us to deal with the needs of the people with greater efficiency and also makes it more difficult for violent elements to threaten…"

"Don't go on," Becker told him. "Just explain why you're here."

The security scout looked down at his hands and cleared his throat gently. "Your old friend needs your help," he said.

"My old friend? You mean Almer?" Becker laughed.

"I am told to say that he realizes he did you harm in the past, but that he thinks you will now recognize the difficulty he was in, establishing order in the world. Some people have to suffer in order that the majority…"

"He killed my closest friend," Becker said. "He killed Brand Calax, too. He killed people working on Velusi's transmitter — idealistic, innocent people. He murdered scores…"

"Hundreds," said the scout, with a touch of pride. "But it was necessary for the common good."

"And now he has mellowed, has he?" Becker said sardonically. "He only kills a few every so often. Soon only Andros Almer will be left…"

"He appreciates the anger you must feel," the scout continued imperturbably. "But he thinks your sense of duty — always marked in the past — will make you understand that now he needs your help in order to control the ordered society he has created…"

"He has created nothing but ignorance and misery. The race will peter out of existence in fear and despair. That is all he has done for the world."

"It is a matter of opinion. Please let me finish, Clovis Becker."

"Very well."

"Chief Control has discovered recalcitrant elements amongst his upper echelon officers…"

"Only to be expected. He knew this would happen, surely?"

"… and the officers have managed to get a great deal of support in the more naïve sections of the community. They have used your name…"

"My name?"

"… your name to convince the people that they are guided only by idealism and wish to return the world to what they call the paradise it was before our leader restored order. They tell the people that you have returned and are secretly in charge of this splinter-group."

"So they plan to overthrow Almer and set themselves up in his place — and continue in the same way as Almer."

"They have not our leader's principles and strength of mind. Society will collapse as they war among themselves…"

"I know the pattern. What does Almer want of me?"

"He offers you joint command with him as Chief Control if you will return and give your support to him."

Becker did not reply immediately. He had the feeling that the story was just a little too glib. If Almer had already blackened his name as Velusi's murderer, why did that name now carry weight amongst the ordinary people? He was almost certain that this was a trap of Almer's to get him out of his tower and into a position where he could be killed easily. He must still represent a threat to Almer — and Almer must still want Fastina Cahmin.

"So Almer needs my help," he smiled. "I can't believe that. What are you to do if I refuse?"

"Take your message back to our leader."

"And what then?"

"He has another plan — to tell the people where you are hiding and then launch a heavily publicized attack on this place and destroy you — thus checking his officers' plans. You would do better to accept his offer. If you accept he will send a carriage to collect you."

"This tower is invulnerable. He would waste his time attacking it."

"That's as may be — but we are developing strong weapons nowadays. You are not as secure as you think."

"You said Almer was not sure I was here?"

"I did." The scout placed a hand on the butt of his gun. "I have a commission to try here and then try the other towers in the region. If I do not return in a month or so, he will check to see what has happened to me."

"A month?"

The scout tightened his grip on the gun butt, looking into Becker's eyes, obviously guessing why Becker was asking these questions.

"And if I am offered violence, Clovis Becker, I am instructed to kill you."

"You forget that you cannot get out of here unless I am alive."

The man hesitated, glancing instinctively towards the door.

Becker reached into his pocket and pressed the single stud on the little device he had there.

The sides of the couch curled in on the scout well before he could drag the gun from its holster. Slowly, they began to squeeze in on the frightened man.

The couch had been designed to have enough force to hold but not harm a man of outstanding strength like Take.

The black-masked scout had only ordinary strength. The couch began to crush him and he began to scream.

Becker turned away. This was the first creature he had ever knowingly killed.

He covered his ears as the man's screams changed to a panting gurgle and bones crunched as the couch slowly squeezed him to death.

Becker shuddered. Tears ran down his face, but he knew he could not stop what he was doing. The man was as good as dead already.

In a short while the man stopped making any noise at all.

Becker looked back at the couch. It was folded neatly in on itself.

A little blood seeped out of it, but that was the only sign of what had happened.

Then he looked towards the entrance of the room and saw Fastina leaning there, her face covered by her hands. She must have heard the screams and come to the room, thinking Becker was in trouble. She must have seen the scout's death.

Becker crossed the room and guided her out of it, up the sloping, winding passage to the yellow room. He made her lie down on the disordered bed. He went to the window and, for the first time since he had been here, opened it.

The rain swept in to the room, and the cold air came with it. The water washed over the floor and Becker stood by the window, the rain beating at his face, running down hands and body, soaking his clothing.

Fastina began to sob from where she lay with her face buried in the bedclothes, but Becker did not hear her, and eventually Fastina fell asleep while Becker continued to stand stock still by the window, letting the rain lash his face.

After a long while, he turned, closed the window, covered Fastina with dry blankets from a cupboard, and went to dispose of the couch and what it contained.

The couch went into the incinerator easily enough. The last corpse Becker had put in it had been his father's.

He wrapped a heavy cloak about him and went to the entrance of the tower, opening it and slopping through the thin, red mud to the air car. He reached into it and activated its controls so that it drifted just above the ground. Then he began to drag it towards the tower.

The rain made it difficult to see, and twice he slipped in the mud, but eventually he got the air car into the tower and began guiding it through the passages to his father's room where he put it where the couch had been and covered it with a large cloth.

Now he was ready for Take's next visit. He went to bed.

Take came a week later, with his car full of provisions.

The rain had stopped and the mud had hardened to earth which would soon become dust again. It was already cracking as Take, his shadow long and black behind him, hauled the sack of foodstuffs from the landed air car and stumbled towards the tower.

Becker greeted him with apparent cheerfulness. Fastina was still in bed, where she had been since Becker had murdered the scout. She had recovered a little and evidently did not blame him for what he had done, since she believed the scout had tried to kill Becker, but she had not been willing to talk much and this had suited him as he had waited impatiently for Take's arrival.

Take noticed the difference in Becker's manner as he entered the tower. "You seem in better spirits," he said.

Together they dragged the provisions into the nearest room and Take sat down in one of the grotesque chairs.

"I don't feel too badly, for a prisoner," Becker replied. "Perhaps the rain washed my depression away. Have you seen Orlando Sharvis recently?"

"Not recently — only the effects of his work. You are well off here, my friend."

"I wish you would let me decide that," Becker replied equably.

"How is Fastina Cahmin?"

"In bed. She's sleeping."

"Sleeping? She's lucky. Do you sleep often?"

It was a strange question. "Frequently," smiled Becker. He sat down opposite Take. "Why do you ask?"

"I envy you, that's all." Take's head began to sink forward in the familiar, lopsided way, and he straightened it slowly. It was almost as if his neck were broken, Becker thought.

"You don't sleep well, Mr Take?"

"I don't sleep at all, Clovis Becker. You are a very lucky man. I wish I were the 'prisoner' and someone else the 'jailer', as you put it..."

"I would be the first to agree," Becker smiled. "Can I offer you something to eat? A drink?"

"No. Is there anything you particularly want me to bring on my next visit?"

"Nothing."

"Then I will get back." Take raised himself to his feet.

Becker escorted him to the door and opened it for Take. He did not close it again, but said hurriedly, "I think I heard Fastina call. Goodbye, Mr Take."

"Goodbye." Take began to trudge towards the golden air car he was still using.

Becker ran rapidly through the corridors to his father's room, tore off the coverings from the small one-man air car and jumped into it.

At a crazy speed, he drove it through the passages, twisting down and down until he reached the entrance. He slowed the car. There was a glint of gold in the dark sky.

The air car was equipped with a fixing device. Becker adjusted his speed, homed the air car on the one above, and began to climb into the air, leaving the tower, and Fastina, behind him.

This had been his reason for murdering the scout. Now he could follow Take to wherever the man came from.

He suspected that Take would lead him to Orlando Sharvis.

CHAPTER THREE

THE CAGE

Take's air car was heading deeper and deeper into the night.

Becker had suspected that it would, which was partly why he had not relied on keeping the golden car in sight but had made sure his own car's instruments would follow it. As the light got fainter, the shadows lengthened until they merged into a general darkness and the air became cold.

The car, built only to be used in the daylight and twilight, had no heater and Becker huddled in his cloak wishing he had brought more clothing.

At last it became pitch black and Becker could see nothing of the land below and above him were only massive clouds and the occasional stars. The moon had been dragged down into the sea by the space-dwellers when they had brought the Earth to a gradual stop. It now lay in the North Pacific somewhere, with much of its bulk below the surface.

The air became damper and even colder. Unable to see his instruments. Becker had no clear idea where he was now, although, judging by the air, he was probably over one of the many ice fields that covered both land and sea on the night side of Earth.

As he traveled his perceptions became dulled and his contact with reality so tenuous that it did not occur to him to protect himself by means of the car's force-screen.

Much later, when his body was numb with cold and he was half-certain he was going to die, the car began to fall in a gradual dive.

Looking over the side of the craft, he just made out the glint of ice reflecting the sparse starlight, and ahead was a dark outline that seemed to be a great mountain range, though it was peculiarly rounded. The car was heading straight for this. Becker wondered if Take had led him into a trap and if he was going to crash into the side of the curved mountain that protruded from the ice-flats. The air car sped nearer. It was only then that Becker switched on his force-screen to help cushion the impact he anticipated.

No impact came. Instead the car reached the cliff and kept going. It had entered a great cave in the face of the cliff.

The air car continued to sweep downward through the utter darkness of the gigantic tunnel and Becker's air became foul in time so that he was forced to switch off the force-screen.

To Becker's relief, it was much warmer in the tunnel.

Deeper and deeper down the tunnel went the air car, banking occasionally to take turns, until a faint light could be seen ahead.

As the light increased, Becker could see the walls of the tunnel, far away on both sides of him. The tunnel was obviously artificial and could take a large spaceship.

The air car began to slow as it reached the source of light and eventually stopped altogether, moving in to the side of the tunnel. There, in a niche, Becker saw the golden air car that had once belonged to Fastina. Take seemed to have hidden it there.

Running his hand over the rock, Becker gradually realized where he was.

He was in the moon itself, now far below the surface of the Pacific.

He searched through the little air car until he found a gravstrap in a locker. He fitted it under his arms and left the air car, drifting cautiously forward towards the blaze of light ahead.

The light hurt his eyes for a while, as the tunnel opened out into a vast, artificial cavern.

Shielding his eyes, Becker looked upwards into the "sky" and saw the source of both the heat and the light. It was a globe of energy, pulsating slightly, a man-made sun.

Below was a rolling landscape of what appeared to be scarlet and black moss that was relieved in the distance by slim, jagged crags of brown rock. The "sky" itself was a lurid orange colour, fading to pink near the horizon.

It was a world of rudimentary and primordial colours, like a planet half-created and then abandoned. But this place had been created by a man — or at least some intelligent agency. Becker guessed who the man had been. He thought he had found where Orlando Sharvis lived.

How long had it taken to hollow out the moon and make this tiny world within it? Why had Sharvis made the world in the first place?

Becker began to feel afraid. He could see nothing of Take, and the rest of the place seemed deserted. Ahead of him now was a tall mass of rock, a plateau rising suddenly out of the scarlet and black moss surrounding it.

Through the warm, utterly still air, Becker drifted along on his gravstrap, heading towards the bluff.

*

THE SHORES OF DEATH 359

As he rose above the level of the cliff top, the first thing he saw was the metal. In the distance it looked like a great, static mobile, only momentarily at rest. Multi-angled surfaces flashed and glared.

The thing lay in a depression on the plateau, ringed by rocks that all leaned inwards so that the object seemed to lie in the gullet of some sharp-toothed beast. The rocks were long, black fangs, casting a network of shadows into the depression. Sometimes the individual surfaces would merge as he turned his head, and then the whole would combine — a blaze of bright metal — and as suddenly disintegrate again.

Only as he got closer did Becker realize that this was a settlement of some kind; a peculiar shanty-town with shacks of gold, silver, ruby, emerald and diamond, built from sheets of harder-than-steel plastic and metal. They all seemed to lean against one another for support; were placed at random, forming a cluttered jungle of artificial materials on the barren rock.

Soon Becker could make out individual buildings. All were single-storeyed. There too were patches of cultivated land, small, deep reservoirs, featureless cabinets of machinery, and thin cables.

There seemed to have been no design to this strange village. It appeared to have grown little by little and it was quite plain that whoever lived there existed in conditions far more primitive than anyone else on the planet. Why? Surely they had a choice? They did not need to live in an artificial world, artificially maintained.

Becker dropped to the ground, within the circle of black rocks but beyond the limits of the village.

Now he could see one or two figures moving slowly between the shanties.

From the ground, the place did not look quite so makeshift, though it was also evident that the shanties were not made of prefabricated parts but constructed from the plates of spaceships and other large machines.

Becker walked cautiously forward.

And then a tall old man, with curling white hair, a cream-coloured cloak, yellow tights and a huge box strapped to his naked chest, appeared from behind the nearest building and greeted him.

"Stranger, you are welcome," he said gravely, dropping his chin to his chest and staring hard at Becker. "You enter a holy place, the Seat of the Centre, Influencer of the Spheres — come, pilgrim!" With a great show of dignity he swept his arm to indicate a low, narrow doorway.

Becker did not move. He recognized the jargon. The man was a member of the new Deistic Church of the Zodiac, a cult that had flourished before the raid but which had died out after it.

"Who are you?" he said. "How long have you been here?"

"I have no name. I am the guardian of the Seat of the Centre and I have been here for eternity."

The man was mad.

"What's that box fixed to your chest?" Becker peered at it. Wires seemed to leave the box and enter the man's body. "What is it?"

"Box? There is no 'box'!" The demented old man bent and disappeared into the doorway.

Becker continued to move through the village. From the shanties he heard stirrings and soft voices, low moans and whines that were either human or mechanical, heard a scraping noise once or twice, but saw no-one until he entered a small clearing.

There, to one side, in the shade of a building, sat a man. Becker went up to him. The man stared out at him but his eyes did not move as Becker knelt beside him.

"Can you tell me what this place is?" Becker asked.

"Heaven," said the man tonelessly, without looking at Becker. He began to laugh in a dry, hopeless voice. Becker straightened up.

Further on he saw something that appeared at first to be nothing but a tangle of coils and thin cables, a dark, static web standing nearly two metres high and some sixty centimetres in diameter, of a dull, red colour with threads of blue, gold and silver closer to its centre. As he got closer Becker saw the outlines of a human figure inside the web. A clear, pleasant voice came from it.

"Good morning, newcomer. I saw you approaching across the fields. What a warm day it is."

"Fields?" Becker said. "There are no fields. You mean the moss?"

The voice chuckled. "You must have been in a daze. You have only just left them. You came past the farm and walked along the lane and came through the gate there and now you are here. I like visitors."

Becker began to realize that the man was living an illusion, just as the other old man he had first met. Was this the function of the village? Did people come here to have their illusions made into some sort of reality? He recognized the basic design of the machine in which the man sat. It was one of many invented in an effort to defeat the effects of the space ache. Every function of a man's mind and body was controlled by the machine which completely simulated an earthly environment for him. The thing had worked quite well, except it left a man all but useless for anything but piloting a spaceship and, it was discovered later, it spread a peculiar kind of cancer through the spinal fluid and the resulting death was worse than the space ache. Also once the thing was connected, it had to stay connected, for disconnection generally resulted in an acute psychic shock that brought death instantly.

The cage of metal moved jerkily forward. From inside it an emaciated hand reached out and touched Becker's arm. "You," said the clear voice. "You. You. You." It paused. "Me," it said at length. Then the encaged figure turned and went back to its original position.

Becker moved on. The man he had questioned had called the place heaven, but it seemed more like hell. This was like somewhere that might have existed in pre-raid days. The village seemed populated only by the insane.

He knocked on the wall of the nearest shack. He called: "Is anyone in?" He bent his head and entered the room. The smell was terrible. Inside the room, on a big, square mattress, a young man sat up suddenly. Beside him lay a young woman.

But were they young? Looking closer, Becker could see that they had the appearance of old people whose flesh had somehow been artificially padded and whose skin had been worked to remove all signs of age.

"Get out!" said the man.

Outside, Becker sighed and looked around him. He began to feel that it would be wiser to leave the village and return to his air car and then make his way back to the tower and Fastina.

Why had these people come here? Why had they subjected themselves to such a dreadful existence?

He found another man. This one's skull was open to reveal his brain. Electrodes poked out of it and were fixed to a box on his back. The brain was protected by some kind of force-screen. The man himself looked quite normal.

"Why are you here?" Becker asked him.

The man's smile was melancholy. "Because I wanted to be."

"Did Orlando Sharvis do this to you?"

"Yes."

"As punishment?"

The man's smile broadened. "Of course not. I asked him to do it. Do you realize that I am probably the most intelligent man in the world thanks to all this?" He pointed a thumb at the box on his back. Then an expression of fear came over his face.

"You mustn't delay me, I must hurry."

"Why?"

"The power-pack uses an enormous amount of energy. It must be recharged every twenty minutes, or I die." The man stumbled away between the shanties.

"Sharvis giveth and Sharvis taketh away," said a maliciously amused voice behind Becker. Becker did not recognize the quotation, but he recognized the face as he turned.

The man was pale-faced and thin-lipped and he had bitter eyes. He was dressed in a loose black toga and on his hands were a great many rings. The jewels in the rings were Ganymedian dream-gems. By concentrating on them, one could rapidly hypnotize oneself.

The man's name was Philas Damiago who had once had the reputation of being the world's last murderer, though his victim had been revived in time and lived to die of old age. Damiago had disappeared a hundred and fifty years before, but his face was familiar to Becker from the history Vs. Becker thought ironically that Damiago would now be merely one among many if he returned to the daylight.

"Philas Damiago?"

"I am, indeed. Do you recognize the origin of the quotation?"

"I'm afraid not."

"You are not a literary man?"

"I think I'm well-read, but..."

"It comes from the old Christian Bible — the English translation. I used to read that a lot, as well as more or less contemporary works — Shakespeare, Milton, Tolstoy, Hëdsen. You know them?"

"I know of them. I have read a little of them all, I think."

"I was a scholar, you know. Ancient literature was my speciality. I became too absorbed in it, I suppose..."

"You murdered your brother..."

"Exactly. All that blood and death, my friend. It went to my head."

"You've been here ever since?"

Damiago shook his head. "No. Originally I went to the twilight region. I was there for some time. Then I came here."

"Looking for Orlando Sharvis, I suppose."

"Yes. As these others had done before me — and since."

"You do not seem as affected as they are."

Damiago smiled. "Not externally."

"What did you want from Sharvis?"

"Time. I wanted time to study every work of literature that had ever been written and time in which to write my history of literature."

"Sharvis gave you time?"

"Oh, yes. He operated on me. I can now live for at least another five hundred years."

"Surely that is enough time to do what you want to do."

"Certainly." Damiago's mouth moved as if to add something thing.

"Then what's the trouble?" Becker felt impatient. He wanted to find Take.

"The operation affected my brain — my eyes. I am word blind."

Becker felt sorry for Damiago. "In the circumstances you have kept remarkably sane. You must be very strong minded, Damiago."

Damiago shrugged. "I have ways of staying sane. I have my work — new work. Would you like to see it?"

Damiago strode towards a hut and entered it. Becker followed him. The place was well lit and bigger than he expected. In the centre, on a plinth, surrounded by tools and furniture, stood a great half-finished sculpture. It was a crude thing, yet powerful. The whole thing was constructed from human bones.

Becker changed his opinion of Damiago. The man was only apparently sane.

"Do you hunt for your materials…?" Becker asked harshly, trying to humour the man.

"Oh, no. They come to me eventually. I'm the most valuable member of the community, really. They want to die — I need their bones. Perhaps, in time, you, too, will come to me?"

"I don't think so."

"You never know. You are looking for Orlando Sharvis. are you not? You will not go away, having seen what will happen to you?"

"I might well go away."

"Sensible." Damiago sat on the edge of the plinth. "Go away, then. Goodbye."

"First I want to find out more about this place. I think Alodios, the artist, came here. And a man called Take…"

"You're hesitating already. I advised Alodios against going to see Orlando Sharvis, and I advise you, likewise. But it will do no good."

"Does Sharvis resent visitors?"

"On the contrary, he welcomes them. He will welcome you, particularly when you tell him what you want. You do want something from him, of course?"

"I suppose so. But I did not really come to see Sharvis. I'm not even sure now why I came at all. But now I'm here, I'd like to see Alodios, at least. I knew him well…"

"If you did, then don't go to see him."

"Where is he?"

Damiago spread his hands and then pointed. "He lives about a hundred kilometres to the right over there. You'll see a cluster of high rocks. Alodios lives there. Sharvis lives in the mountains to the north-east of there — you will see the mountains from the cliff. His laboratories extend throughout the mountains. You will see a tall shaft of polished stone. That will show you where the entrance to the laboratories lies."

"I told you — I didn't think I wanted to see Sharvis now."

Damiago nodded. "If you say so."

Clovis Becker stood on the edge of the cliff beneath the artificial sun. Next to him was a high-backed chair in which sat a silent man.

For the second time, Becker said politely: "Alodios? Am I disturbing you?" But the seated figure did not reply or move.

Nervously, Becker stepped closer.

"Alodios. It is Clovis Becker."

He moved around the chair. He was careful where he put his feet for he was very close to the edge. It was a long, sheer drop to the red and black moss below.

Alodios continued to stare fixedly outwards. The sun in his eyes did not seem to bother him. Becker wondered if he were dead.

"Alodios?"

There was great character written in the old man's face and hands, in the very shape of his body. He was a big man, with great hard muscles, a broad chest and huge arms and hands. His head was of similar proportions, strong and massive, with thick dark hair framing it. Heavy black eyebrows bristled on his jutting brow, heavily lidded eyes were half-closed, but the black eyes could be seen. The nose was aquiline and the mouth seemed the mouth of a bird of prey, also. The full lips were turned downwards in a way that was at once cruel, sensitive and sardonic. But it was all frozen, as if Alodios were a living statue. Only the eyes lived. Suddenly, they looked at him.

In his horror Becker almost lost his footing on the cliff. There was absolute torment in the eyes. From that frozen face they stared out at him, without self-pity, without any true intelligence. It was as if some mute, uncomprehending beast were trapped in the skull, for it was not the look of a man at all. It was the look of a tortured animal.

Alodios plainly did not think now. He felt, only. Sense was gone, leaving only sensibility. Becker could not bear to look into the eyes for long. He turned away.

Alodios had been a genius. His intellect and sensitivity, his creative powers, had been unmatched in history. He had created great novels — combinations of poetry, prose, pictures, sculpture, music and acted drama that had reached the peak of artistic expression. Now it was as if something had destroyed the intelligence but left the sensitive core unsullied. He was still receptive, still aware — but with no mind to rationalize the impressions.

Becker thought that there could be no worse experience than this. For Alodios's sake, he began to push the chair towards the very edge of the cliff. Alodios would crash to the bottom and die.

A voice came from behind him, then. "I doubt if that will do any good, Clovis Becker." It was Take's rich voice.

Becker turned. Take stood there with his head on one side, dressed in his dark clothes, with his white hands clasped before him.

"Why won't it do any good?"

"He has what you wanted."

"This? This isn't what I wanted!"

"He has immortality. Alodios went to Orlando Sharvis and Orlando Sharvis played a joke on him. Alodios found immortality, but he lost the sense of passing time."

"A *joke?*" Becker could hardly speak. "Alodios was the greatest…"

"Yes, Sharvis knew what he was. That, you see, was the joke."

After a moment, Becker said: "Isn't there any way of killing Alodios?"

"I think you would find him invulnerable, as I am."

"You are immortal, Mr Take? I thought so."

Take laughed flatly. "I am immortal. I am a superman. My reflexes are ten times faster, my strength ten times greater, my reasoning powers ten times better than they were. I cannot be destroyed — I cannot destroy myself, even! Only Sharvis, who made me, can destroy me. And he refuses. I was his first immortal. I was a soldier, originally, who escaped with him after the Last War. I was his chief lieutenant when he had gathered his Titan expedition together. By that time he had experimented on myself and two others. They had died, but I had survived. I wanted immortality at the time. It may sound strange, but I was prepared to risk dying for it. We went to Titan after he had operated on himself in the same way. It was because of these operations that we were able to survive Titan."

"The others?"

"In spite of more and more experiments on their bodies, they died one by one. Sharvis and I returned to Earth — to the night side and the moon."

"How did you create this world?"

"We had begun work on it before we left. This was where the Titan ship was built. He has machines — they can do anything. He gets his raw materials either from the moon itself, or else from the sea-beds."

"And you found immortality unbearable. Why was that?"

"He gave me immortality, but took my life."

"Sharvis giveth and Sharvis taketh away," murmured Becker. "That's what Damiago said. You know Damiago?"

"I know them all. It is I who look after them. Sharvis does not."

Becker looked towards the mountains far away. "That's where Sharvis has his laboratories, Damiago said. Surely, Take, he has the means to do anything — to revive our diseased cells — make the world well again… If I paid Sharvis a visit…"

Take lunged forward, arms outstretched, and, before Becker realized it, the man had hurled him over the cliff.

Becker, as he fell, almost welcomed the fact that he was going to die. In killing him, Take had absolved him from all responsibility. Then, automatically, he had squeezed his gravstrap and began to float gently downward. More pressure on the strap and he was rising again.

Take was waiting for him, arms folded.

"As you see, Clovis Becker, I am in earnest. I would kill you rather than let you go to Sharvis. You do not understand the fascination that he can exert."

Becker sank back to the ground. Nearby he saw a piece of loose rock. He stooped and picked it up.

"The only point you have made, Take, is to prove yourself as irrational as anyone. How do I know that your judgment of Sharvis is the correct one? You hate him because he gave you something you wanted. Is he to blame for that?"

"You see," Take said. "Your mind is already twisting. If you persist, if you will not return to the tower with me, I must kill you. It will be an act of mercy."

"I still wish to decide for myself."

"I will not let you."

Becker flung the jagged rock at Take.

Take reached out and caught it. Then he moved towards Becker, his arm raised.

Becker pressed his gravstrap and began to rise into the air, but Take seized his ankle and hauled him to the ground. He swung the rock and smashed it down on Becker's head. Becker felt nothing, but he knew he was dead.

CHAPTER FOUR
THE RESURRECTION

In his last moment of life, Clovis Becker had realized how much he wanted to live and had at the same time been reconciled to the fact that he was dead; yet now he was conscious again and full of infinite relief.

He opened his eyes and saw nothing but a milky whiteness. He became frightened suddenly and shut his eyes tightly. Was he dead, after all? He seemed to be drifting weightlessly, unable to feel the presence of his own body.

It seemed that he remained with his eyes shut for hours before he opened them again, curiosity overcoming his fear.

Now in front of him something crystalline winked and shimmered. Beyond the crystal a shape moved, but he could not define what it was. He turned his head and saw more crystal, with dim outlines behind it. He tried to move a leg, but could feel nothing. Something happened, however. His body began to turn slowly and he could see that he was completely surrounded by the crystal. Attached to his mouth was a muzzle and leading away from it were several slender tubes which seemed imbedded in the crystal. He could look down and see the rest of his body.

With some difficulty he stretched out his hand and touched the irregular surface of the crystal. It tingled and made him feel less intangible. He tried to make some sound with his mouth The muzzle stopped him from speaking, but he managed a muffled murmur. The awareness that at least he retained his senses of sight, touch and hearing reassured him.

He closed his eyes again and lifted his hand to his head, but could feel nothing.

Far away, a voice said softly, "Ah, good. You will be out of there soon, now." Then Becker fell asleep.

He woke up and he was lying on a couch in a small, featureless room. It was warm and he felt very comfortable. He looked around, but could not see a door in the room. He looked up. There were indications that the room's entrance was in the roof directly above the couch. He could make out fine indentations forming a square.

He swung himself off the couch. He felt very fit and relaxed, but there was the slight feeling of being watched. Perhaps the walls of his room could be seen through from the other side.

He saw that he was dressed in a one-piece garment of soft, blue material.

He touched his head. It had been partly shaven where Take's rock had struck it and there was an indication of an old, healed scar, but nothing more.

He had been dead and someone had revived him. Had this been a second warning from Take? His brain must have been damaged, he was sure, and only a few surgeons in the world were capable of the operation necessary to revive a man with a bad head injury of that kind.

Orlando Sharvis? It could only have been the mysterious immortal.

A voice whispered and hissed through the room. At first it sounded like a wind sighing through trees, but then Becker recognized words.

"Yes, Clovis Becker. It is Sharvis who has saved you. Sit back — sleep — and soon, I assure you, Sharvis will be at your service…"

Becker returned to the couch, aware, but somehow not surprised, that Sharvis could read his thoughts. He lay down and slept again.

The next time he awoke he was still on the couch but it was rising towards the ceiling and the ceiling was opening upward to let him pass. He entered a far larger room, adorned with fluorescent walls of a constantly changing variety of colours. The walls moved like flames and dimly lighted the room.

"Forgive the rather gloomy appearance," said a voice only slightly less sibilant than the one he had first heard, "but I find it hard to bear too much direct light these days. As you guessed, I am Orlando Sharvis. You have been seeking me a long time, I gather, then you gave up, but now you are here. Your unconscious mind was taking you towards me all the time. You realize that now, of course."

"Of course," Becker agreed.

"Then it is a mutual pleasure that we are able to meet at last. As I said, I am at your service…"

Becker turned and looked up at Orlando Sharvis.

He had expected to see a man, but he saw a monster; albeit a beautiful monster.

Orlando Sharvis's head resembled a snake's. He had a long tapering face of mottled red and pink. He had faceted eyes like a fly, a flat, well-shaped nose and a shrunken, toothless mouth.

His body was not at all snakelike. It was almost square and very heavy. His legs were short and firm. His arms and hands, when he moved them, seemed sinuously boneless.

Becker's first impression, however, was one of height, for Orlando Sharvis was nearly ten feet tall.

Bizarre as he was, there was something attractive about him; something, as Take had said, completely fascinating. He could not always have looked like this...

"You are right," whispered Sharvis, "my body is the result of extended experiments over a great many years. I have made alterations not merely for convenience, but also to satisfy my own aesthetic tastes and curiosity."

Sharvis was casually reading his mind.

"Another of my experiments that succeeded quite well," Sharvis told him. "Although I must admit that my ability is not perfect. Your mind is, in fact, something of a mystery to me — it harbours so many paradoxical thoughts..."

"How did you find me?" Becker asked. His speech was slightly slurred.

"A minor invention of mine to bring me information from not only everywhere in the moon, but everywhere in the world. It is a device a little larger than a poppy seed. Call it a micro-eye. I use many thousands of them. I saw what the ungrateful Take did to you and I sent one of my machines to pick you up and bring you here."

"How long have I been here?"

"About a month, I'm afraid. The initial operation failed. I nearly lost you. You need not worry, incidentally, that I have tampered with your mind or body in any way. If you find you are a little numb or that speaking is at first difficult, be assured that the effects will soon disappear. I pride myself that I have done a perfect repair. Your hair growth has been accelerated as you will discover."

Becker touched the top of his head. The bald part of his scalp was now covered in hair again.

"How do you feel generally?" Sharvis asked.

"Very well." But now memories were returning — the colony outside, Alodios, what Take had told him about Sharvis.

"Again, I must be candid," Sharvis said. "Perhaps I will lose your trust, but I must tell you the truth. I did perform an operation on your artist friend, although I warned him of the consequences. Yet he still insisted. Every one of those others you saw were also warned that there would probably be side effects to their operations — and every one begged me to continue." The tiny mouth smiled. "I am an equable soul, Clovis Becker. I only do for people what they ask. I use no coercion. If you are thinking of my Last War days, please realize that I was young and headstrong then. I knew no humility. Now I know much. The Titan expedition and its failure taught me that."

"You could give me immortality, then?"

"If you wanted it."

"And what's the price?"

Sharvis laughed softly. "Price? Not your 'soul', if that's what you mean —
and I see you have some such thought in your mind. You mean your individuality
— something like that? I assure you it would remain intact. I am here only to
serve you, as I said; to give you your heart's desire."

"Take seemed to think you were guided more by malice than by idealism…"

"Take and I have known each other too long for me to regard him with
complete objectivity, and the same is true of him. Perhaps we hate each other
— but it is an old, sentimental hatred, you understand. I gave Take his freedom.
I gave him immortality. Are those the actions of a malicious man?"

Sharvis had a power that was almost hypnotic. Becker found himself unable
to think with anything like his old clarity. It was probably the after-effects of
the operation.

"You have been guilty of many crimes in the past…" Becker began heavily.

"Crimes? No. I serve no abstract Good or Evil. I have no time for mysticism.
I am entirely neutral — a scientist. When called upon, I do only what is asked
of me. It is the truth."

Becker frowned. "But good and evil are not abstract — ethics are necessary,
there are fundamental things which…"

"I have no ethic other than my will to serve. Do you believe me?"

"Yes, I believe that."

"Well, then?"

"I see your point of view…"

"Good. I am not pressing you to accept any gift of mine, Clovis Becker. I
have revived you, you are well, you may leave here whenever you wish…"

Becker said uncertainly: "Could I possibly stay for a while — to make up
my mind?"

"You are free to go wherever you like in my laboratories. You are my guest."

"And if I decided to ask you for immortality…?"

Orlando Sharvis raised a sinuous hand. "To tell you the truth, I lack all the
materials to give you an absolutely perfect chance of immortality."

"So even if I asked you, you could not do it?"

"Oh, yes. I could make you immortal after a fashion, but I would not
guarantee you a normal life."

"Could you get the materials you need?"

"There is a chance, yes." Orlando Sharvis seemed to consider carefully. "I
see from your thoughts that you are torn between seeking immortality for
yourself and asking me to 'cure' humanity in general. I doubt my ability to do
the latter. I am not omnipotent, Clovis Becker. Besides, what if most of the
human race dies eventually? There are others who will never die living here,
inside the moon."

"Freaks," said Becker without thinking.

"You fear the end of the 'normal' human race, is that it?"

"Yes."

"I can't appreciate your fears, I'm afraid. However, I will think about this. Meanwhile I should tell you that enemies of yours seem to be everywhere at the moment, both within the moon and on its surface."

"What enemies?"

"Take for one. He is your enemy, though he thought himself your friend..."

"I have always known that much."

"And Andros Almer and his gang are currently running about all over the surface trying to find you. They have your woman — Fastina — with them."

"Is she safe?"

"Extremely. I take it that Almer regards the girl as his chief piece in the game he is playing with you..."

"Not a game I have any willing part in. How did he get to the moon? Why hasn't he discovered your tunnel?"

"I gather that his men's air cars all have tracer devices planted in them. This is to guard against them making any move that is contrary to what Almer wants them to do. Almer became suspicious after his scout had been gone longer than he expected. He traced the air car to your tower. He found Fastina there and you gone. He seized her and discovered that his air car had disappeared into the night region. It did not take him long to equip an expedition and come in search of you. The air car was traced to the moon, but now they are puzzled. I have sealed off and disguised my tunnel. Almer's instruments show that your air car is deep within the moon — but he cannot discover how it got there." Sharvis laughed softly. "He is extremely perplexed. They have begun boring into the moon, but I have managed to damage their instruments in one way or another. I shall have to think of a way of dealing with them soon. They are threatening my privacy."

"You'll make sure Fastina's safe. She's innocent..."

"There was never a woman so innocent, I agree. Yes, I will make sure she is safe. I was not planning any sort of spectacular destruction of Almer and his crew, Clovis Becker. No, I am subtler than that, I hope."

"And what of Take?"

"Actually he is outside my laboratories now. He has been trying to get in for ten days without my noticing. I don't know what he wants here. He knows that he is free to come and go as he pleases, but he is a narrow, suspicious man. I expect we shall see him soon."

Sharvis turned gracefully. "I will leave you now, if you will excuse me. I

have more than your particular problem on my mind. Go where you will —
you may find my home interesting."

Apparently without the aid of any mechanical device, Sharvis began to
drift towards the flickering wall and sink into it until he disappeared.

Becker began to see that Take had been wrong, after all, in attributing malice
to Sharvis's actions. The scientist's actions were neither good nor bad as he had
said. It was what one made of them that counted.

CHAPTER FIVE

THE TRUTH

Orlando Sharvis's vast network of laboratories impressed Clovis Becker as he wandered around them in the days that followed. Becker had seen similar places on daylight Earth, but none so spectacular. Orlando Sharvis's laboratories had been designed not simply for function, but also for beauty. The complex building, carved from the interior of mountains Sharvis had himself created, had been built by Sharvis alone. It was difficult to realize this as he explored room after room, passage after passage.

The laboratories were only part of the system. Some rooms seemed to have been designed merely as rooms, with no other purpose than to exist for their own sake. The building was, in fact, a palace of incredible beauty. There were galleries and chambers in it which, in their sweeping architecture and colours, were unmatched by anything in the history of the world. Clovis Becker was moved profoundly, and he felt that no-one capable of such work could be evil.

In one very large chamber he found several works that were not by Sharvis. They were unmistakably by Alodios.

Becker went to look for Sharvis and found the self-deformed giant at last, sitting thoughtfully in a chair in a room that twirled with soft, dark colours. He asked Sharvis about Alodios's work.

"Normally," Sharvis told him, "I ask no price for my gifts — but Alodios insisted. He was the only modern artist I admired, so I was pleased to accept them. I hope you enjoy them. I hope that someday others will come to see them."

"You would welcome visitors, then?"

"Particularly men and women of taste and intellect, yes. Alodios was with me for some time here. I enjoyed our talks very much."

374   THE ROADS BETWEEN THE WORLDS

with me for some time here. I enjoyed our talks very much."

Memory of Alodios's trapped, tormented eyes returned to Becker, and he felt troubled.

Sharvis's shriveled mouth smiled as if in sadness. "I can refuse no-one, Clovis. In many ways I would have enjoyed Alodios's company, but, in the end, I had to do what he demanded of me. I fear that you will not stay long, for one reason or another."

Still confused, Becker left the room.

Sharvis's palace was timeless. There were no clocks or chronometers to tell Becker how long he had been there, but it was probably a day or two later that the scientist sought Becker out as he listened to the singing words of the mobiles in the Alodios chamber.

"You must hate me for interrupting," whispered Sharvis, "but our friend Take has arrived at last. He finally took the simple way in and entered by the main door. I am glad he has arrived, for I wanted to speak to you both together. I will leave you to finish the novel if you like..."

Becker glanced up at the red and pink mottled face that seemed to look at him anxiously, although it was impossible to tell from the faceted eyes what Sharvis's feelings were.

"No. I'll come," said Becker getting up.

Leaving the novel, Becker went with Orlando Sharvis to the room of flame where they had first confronted each other.

Take was there, standing in the middle of the room, the coloured shadows playing across his face. He had his hands clasped behind his back and there was a defeated look about him.

He raised his strange head and nodded to Becker.

"I should have battered your skull to pulp and taken your corpse with me," he said. "I'm sorry, Clovis Becker."

Becker felt disturbed and hostile as he confronted the man who had twice tried to murder him. "I think you're misguided, Take. I've been talking to Orlando Sharvis and..."

"And you are as gullible as all the others. I told you that you would be. He has deadened your brain. What have you said to him, Orlando?"

The giant spread his sinuous hands. "I have only answered his questions truthfully, Ezek."

"Glibly, you mean. Your truth and mine are very different!"

Becker began to feel sorry for Take. "What Sharvis says is correct," he said. "He has been fair with me. He hasn't lied. He hasn't tried to encourage me to do anything I do not want to do. In fact, to some degree, he has tried to discourage me."

"To some degree?" Take's deep voice rose until it bore a hint of despair. "You fool, Clovis Becker. I wasted my time when I tried to protect you."

"I told you — I am my own man. I need no protection."

"You are no longer your own man, whether you realize it now or not. Already you are Sharvis's — you cretin!"

"Please, Ezek, this is unworthy of you," Sharvis interrupted, gliding forward. "When have I ever tried to exert my will on others — at least since the Titan failure? Have I ever tricked you, Ezek? I have always been straightforward with you."

"You devious man — you destroyed me!"

"In those early days I was still learning. You wanted what I could give you. Why blame me for my ignorance? These outbursts only do you discredit."

"You were never ignorant. You were born with knowledge — and it made you the evil monstrosity..."

"Take!" Becker put his hand on the man's arm. "He has a point."

"You know nothing of all this, of all he has done. Not only to me, but to all who have ever had any dealings with him. He is subtle, persuasive and malevolent. Do not believe anything he tells you. He gave me immortality, but he robbed me of any ability to appreciate life. Happiness and love are denied me. There is only one thing that moves me now — and that is suffering. I am dead, but he won't give me proper death. All his 'gifts' are like that — all are flawed. He pretends to exert no power over you — and you find yourself a creation of his warped need to make others like himself!"

"You want me to kill you, Ezek?" Sharvis said. "Is that it? You must understand what that implies. Death. It is final. I could not revive you."

"Now you are trying to raise my hope," Take said, turning away. "Then you will say you have not the conscience to kill me."

"It depends..." Sharvis mused. "It depends on Clovis Becker's decision." Before Becker could ask what he meant, he continued, "Almer and your woman, Fastina, are here."

"Here? How did they get here!"

"Almer had Fastina Cahmin with him in his air car as he went on yet another circuit of the area of the moon above the ice. I had waited for this to happen, as it had to eventually. I opened the tunnel a little way. Almer entered it to investigate. I closed the tunnel. Almer came here. It was the only way he could go. After that, my robots escorted them to my laboratories. They are at the entrance now."

"And his men are still outside?"

"Yes. I was forced to remove all sources of heat from the area. They are not dead — merely in suspended animation of sorts."

"Frozen?" Becker asked.

"In a way. Now, you must tell me what you want me to do with Almer and the girl. Do you want to see them?"

"Almer might try something violent…"

Sharvis chuckled "He could try all he wanted, but I doubt if he could do much damage here."

"I would like to see Fastina. I would like to ask what she thinks of my accepting immortality from you. And there's one other thing I would like to ask you…"

"What's that?"

"Could you give her immortality as well?"

"I could give you both immortality, yes — with the materials I have at hand now."

"You have got hold of them."

"I might have done, yes."

Becker could not puzzle out exactly what Sharvis meant. He turned to Take. "You've spoken very melodramatically just recently, Take. Do you really want death?"

Take still had his back to them. "Ask Sharvis how many times I have begged him to destroy me properly," he said.

Sharvis pursed his shriveled lips. "Who knows?" he said. "Perhaps everyone's wish can be made to come true today. I will go and fetch the new arrivals."

Sharvis glided into the wall and disappeared. Take turned back to face Becker. "Come to your senses while you have time," he said urgently. "Leave with Fastina. I will deal with Almer, if Sharvis does not. You will be free."

Becker shook his head impatiently. "Sharvis is obviously not normal in any way," he said, "but I am sure your judgment of him is biased…"

"Of course it is — by all I've seen. He is wiser than any man has ever been. He knows how to trick someone of your intelligence. He means you nothing but harm. If he gives you immortality as he gave it to me, you will feel nothing except despair — *eternally*. Don't you realize that?"

"Surely your emotions are only dead because you have refused to awaken them?" Becker said. "Have you never thought that the fault lies with you and not with Sharvis?"

"Your mind has already been turned by his logic," Take said. "I have tried to save you from an eternity of misery. You will not listen. I'll say no more."

"Misery for you? It need not be for me. Besides, I have not decided yet."

"You decided the first day you heard of Orlando Sharvis. Don't deceive yourself, Clovis Becker."

Sharvis came back through the walls of flame. Behind him, looking about him warily, stepped Almer and behind Almer came a pale-faced Fastina.

Almer still wore his heavy black hooded cloak and mask. There was still a sword at his side. He was still arrogant in his manner, though his arrogance was now plainly inspired by fear.

"What is this place?" he asked as soon as he saw Becker. "Who is this creature?"

Fastina moved uncertainly towards Becker, her expression changing from despair to relief. "Oh, Clovis!"

He took her in his arms and kissed her as she trembled there.

"Whatever happens, we are safe together now," he assured her. "I'm sorry I left you as I did — but I had to. And it was for the best, as you'll find out."

She looked up at him. There were tears in her deep blue eyes. "Are you sure?"

"I'm sure."

Almer pointed a gloved finger at Sharvis. "I warn you, whoever you are — I rule Earth, even the night side. I have an army at my command…"

Sharvis smiled. "I have offered you no harm, I believe, Andros Almer. I see from your mind that you are afraid; that you are afraid of your own weakness more than anything else. I will do nothing to you. All who visit me are welcome. All who ask something of me are granted it. Take off your armour and relax."

Almer dropped his hand to his sword-hilt and turned to Becker.

"Is he some ally of yours, Becker?"

"He's no-one's ally," Becker told him. "Do as he says. Relax."

"That world out there," Almer said, walking to a couch and ostentatiously leaning back on it. "How was it created? I never heard…"

"Orlando Sharvis created it," Becker told him.

Almer looked at the giant with the pink and red mottled skin and the expressionless, faceted eyes. "You are Orlando Sharvis? The scientist? I thought you were dead. What happened to you? How did you become like that?"

Sharvis shrugged. "Clovis Becker will answer your questions. I must leave for a while."

When Sharvis had gone, Becker explained everything to Almer and Fastina. As he finished, Almer said: "He's neutral, you say. He'll do anything for anyone who asks?"

"Anything within his power."

In the shadows Take stirred. "You deserve a gift from Sharvis, Almer," he said.

"What does he mean?" Almer asked.

"He's demented — he has an old grudge against Sharvis," Becker told him. He now realized that Sharvis was indeed neutral. If he granted a request from Almer, what would the consequences be?

Sharvis returned to the room of flame.

"Well, Ezek," he said to Take, "here is what I can do. I can use certain elements in your body to give Clovis Becker immortality. It will mean, of course, that I shall have to destroy you. So there it is — his immortality for your life, and everyone gets what they want."

"I haven't yet said I want immortality," Becker said, "unless Fastina can have it too."

"I promised you both immortality," Sharvis reminded him.

"What do you say, Fastina?" Becker asked her.

"Would you want me for all that time?"

"Shall we accept Sharvis's gift and become immortal?"

She hesitated. Then she whispered: "Yes."

Sharvis looked at Take. "What do you say, Ezek? Becker's immortality for your life?"

Take shook his head. "Another of your jokes, Orlando. You know I would not do that…"

Becker broke in. "I thought so. You have talked about the horror of immortality, but, now it comes to it, you want to keep your life, after all. Very well."

Take moved into the centre of the room and grasped Becker by the shoulder. "You were once admired for your intelligence, Clovis Becker — look what you have become. Selfish and stupid! My desire for death probably far outweighs your desire for immortality. You have missed the subtlety of Orlando's bargain."

"And what would that be?"

"He knows that I have tried to prevent you from doing something that will cause you terrible misery, that I would have no other human being suffer what I suffer. I sought only to prevent that suffering in you. Now he offers me peace at the price of letting you become what I am. Do you see now?"

"I think you are over-complicating the matter," Becker said, coolly. "I will have immortality. I will make use of it, if you dare not!"

Take moved away again, towards the shifting wall. The dancing shadows seemed to give his face an expression of anguish.

"Very well," he said quietly. "Take it and hope that one day Orlando Sharvis makes you the offer he has made me!"

Concentrating on this argument, no-one had noticed Andros Almer draw his sword and stalk towards Orlando Sharvis to press the tip against the scientist's great chest.

Sharvis was not surprised. It was evident that he had read Almer's mind before the man crossed the room.

He reached forward, displaying the same rapid reflexes as Take, and snatched the sword from Almer's hand. He snapped the sword in two and then into four and dropped the pieces casually in front of the astonished man.

"What did you intend to do?" Sharvis asked gently.

"I intended to force you to release me."

"Why?"

"Because you are in league with Becker."

"I have told you, and he has told you, that I am in league with no-one, I merely do what I am asked, if I can."

"Could you turn the world again?" Almer asked suddenly.

Sharvis smiled thoughtfully. "Is that what you want me to do? I see from your mind that you could claim credit for the action, that you think it would give you an advantage to seem some sort of miracle worker. You are full of superstition, aren't you?"

"Could you turn the world? Have you that power?"

"You think if I did it would give you mastery over it all, don't you?"

"I think it would. I would be able to control it all, then. I would leave you in peace. It would not be in my interest to reveal your presence in the world."

Orlando Sharvis looked down at Almer and smiled again.

"Would you interfere with Clovis Becker and Fastina Cahmin?"

"No, I swear. Give me the opportunity — and I will do the rest."

"I have had a project ready for some time," Sharvis said. "It is as yet untested. Since the raid I have been fascinated by the space-dwellers and the forces they commanded. I have discovered something of their secret. I might be able to do it."

"Try!" Almer said eagerly. "I will give you anything in return."

Sharvis shook his head. "I ask no price for my gifts and services. We shall see what we can do when we have settled Clovis Becker's problem." He glanced at Becker, Fastina and Take.

"You are sure you are willing to make this sacrifice, Ezek?"

"It is no sacrifice. Becker will be the sufferer, not I."

"And you two — Becker? Fastina?"

"I'm ready," Becker said.

Fastina nodded hesitantly.

"Then we can begin at once," said Sharvis, with a trace of eagerness. "You will wait here, Almer, and we will discuss your request later. Go where you like in my laboratories. I will seek you out when I have finished."

Take, Becker and Fastina followed him through the wall of flame and into an arched corridor.

"I have already prepared my equipment," he told them. "The operation itself will not take too long."

Fastina gripped Becker's hand and trembled, but she said nothing.

CHAPTER SIX

THE TURN

When Becker eventually awoke it was with a feeling of increased numbness through his body, as if he were paralyzed. But when he tried to move his limbs, he found that they responded perfectly. He smiled up at Orlando Sharvis who was looking down at him. Behind Sharvis were the blank cabinets in which his equipment was housed.

"Thank you," Becker said. "Is it done?"

"It is. Poor Ezek's few remains were flushed away a couple of hours ago. It was a pity that that was the only way."

"And Fastina?"

"She, too, has been operated on, With her it was an altogether easier job. She is perfectly well as you will see when you join her."

"Were there any difficulties in my operation?"

"There could be some side effects. We shall have to see. Come, we'll go to find Fastina."

Fastina was in the Alodios room. The novel was in progress, with abstract colours and delicate music mingling with the voice of Alodios himself narrating the prose sequences. She turned it off and ran towards him, her face alight with pleasure. She looked now as she had first looked when they had met on his return to daylight Earth. He felt something like pleasure, himself, as he reached out with his insensitive fingers and took her hands.

"Oh," she said, "you *are* all right. I wasn't sure…" She glanced at the scientist. "Did Orlando Sharvis tell you the good news? He didn't tell me until after the operation!"

"What's that?"

"I can have children. My ovaries weren't badly affected by the omega radiation. He was able to make them healthy again. That's what he meant by immortality. He is a good man, after all!"

Becker was puzzled. "But you alone being able to bear children isn't enough…"

"You, too, are now capable of fathering children," Sharvis told him. "I hope you call your first son Orlando."

Becker did not feel the emotion he expected. He tried to smile at Fastina, but it was difficult. He had to make his lips move in a smile. She looked at him in alarm. "What's wrong, Clovis?"

"I don't know." His voice now sounded just a little flat.

Behind them there was a rustle of cloth as Sharvis folded his strange arms.

"I'm feeling numb, that's all," he said. "The operation did it. It will wear off soon, won't it, Sharvis?"

Sharvis shook his mottled head. "I'm afraid not. That was the side effect I mentioned. In using various glands and organs extracted from Take, I somehow made the same mistake I made on him. You will not be able to feel anything very strongly, Clovis Becker. I'm sorry."

"You knew this would happen!" He turned on the scientist. "You knew! Take was right!"

"Nonsense. You will get used to it. I have."

"You are like this all the time?"

"Exactly. I have been for centuries. Mental sensations soon replace the physical kind. I find much that is stimulating still." Sharvis smiled. "What you have lost will be made up for by what you have gained."

"Damiago was right. You give and take away at the same time. I should have listened to Take." Becker struck at his body and felt nothing. He bit his tongue and there was only a little pain.

"I must live forever like this?" he said. "It defeats the whole thing."

"You knew the dangers. Take told you of them. But Take was weak. You are strong. Besides, you can now have children."

"How, when I feel nothing?"

"I have done my best. I have seen to it that certain stimuli will still have certain effects."

Becker nodded despairingly and looked at Fastina.

"I still love you, Clovis," she said. "I'll stay with you."

"It would be wise," Sharvis agreed, "if you wish to continue your race. Clovis Becker, I have given you both the things you asked of me."

"I suppose so," said Becker. "It is a sacrifice I should be proud to make. But I wish I had known I was to sacrifice something…"

"An unknowing martyr is no martyr at all," Sharvis agreed. "For your own sake, I would not make you that."

"Are you so neutral?" Becker said. "Are you not simply a complicated mixture of good and evil?"

Sharvis laughed. "You describe me as if I were an ordinary man. I assure you, I am entirely neutral."

"You have forced this girl to live with a man who cannot respond to her, cannot love her except in a strange way — a way he cannot demonstrate…"

"I have forced her to do no such thing. She is free to do as she wishes. She will bear your children — that is her immortality. You will live on. Her life will be short enough…"

"Am I invulnerable — like Take?"

"That happened, yes, in the transference of Take's parts to your body."

"I see." Becker sighed. "What do we do now?"

"You are free to leave. However, if you wish to stay and see me try to answer Almer's request…"

"You can do it? You can make the world turn?"

"I think so. Do you want to come with me, back to the flame room?"

They went with him to the flame room and found Almer there. He looked as if he had not moved since they left him.

"Why didn't you do as I suggested?" Sharvis asked him. "You could have seen everything there is to see in my laboratories."

"I didn't trust you," Almer mumbled. "Are those two immortal now? They don't look any different."

"He's sulking, Clovis," said Fastina with a smile. In spite of what had happened to her lover, she seemed elated still.

"They are," Sharvis told Almer.

"I'm hungry," Almer said.

"I've been a poor host. Let's go and have something to eat."

After they had eaten, Sharvis led them through a door and down to a hall which was empty save for two bronze air cars covered in baroque decoration. They climbed in to one.

They began to descend through a tunnel narrower than the one which led into the hollow world of the moon, but which wound downwards at a much greater incline. The air became thick and salty. The tunnel was lit by dim strips in its sides and they felt the blood pound in their ears as the pressure increased.

"We are just about to reach the level of the ocean bottom," Sharvis told them. "This tunnel leads from the moon to the rock below it." He continued to talk, but Becker could hear very little but the booming in his eardrums. Sharvis seemed to be explaining how he had managed to build the tunnel.

At last they left the tunnel and entered a huge, dark cavern. Sharvis guided the air car to the side and turned on the lights.

Water seeped down all the walls of the great grotto. The place seemed of natural origin. On its floor stood a machine.

The machine was large and had been coated in some kind of yellow protective plastic. In its centre was a gigantic power unit. From this led a structure of rigid pipes and cables attached to a grid which encircled the whole apparatus.

"As you can imagine," Sharvis's voice said over the pounding heartbeats that filled Becker's ears, "I have had no chance to test this device. The model seemed to work successfully enough, but I was never sure that the power was sufficient to do the job. The thing is, in effect, an engine which will push in a given direction. It will, with luck, begin to turn the world sufficiently rapidly to restore the planet's momentum."

Sharvis took the air car down to the slimy floor of the cavern and stepped out of it, gliding across to the machine. "The only control is on the machine itself. I thought it unwise to risk connecting another control that could be operated from my laboratories. I only invent, as I told you. I never use my inventions for any specific purpose unless asked to do so. I am grateful for the opportunity you have given me, Andros Almer."

Dimly, Becker saw Almer huddled in his cloak, his hood drawn about his face. The man seemed to be watching Sharvis intently as the scientist stepped over to the machine and, after hesitating for a moment, depressed a stud on the small control panel.

Nothing happened.

Sharvis came back to the air car and clambered in, his huge bulk dominating them.

"It has a timing mechanism so that we can return without undue haste to my laboratories." He turned the air car back into the tunnel.

Later, they sat looking up at the huge screen which showed a view of the Earth from above, evidently transmitted from an old weather control satellite.

Sharvis swung a chronometer from a hidden panel below the screen, watching closely as the seconds indicator swept around it.

A faint tremor began to be sensed in the room.

"It will be gradual," Sharvis told them. "It will take quite a few hours. This is to ensure that no major upheavals take place on the planet. The whole operation should be quite smooth, if I have judged correctly."

The laboratory shook violently for a few seconds and then subsided.

The picture on the screen showed the day side of Earth. They could see no indication of movement as yet.

"Of course," Sharvis said casually, "there is just a chance that the engine will begin to push in another direction and carry the Earth out of her normal orbit. I hope it is not towards the sun." He chuckled.

"It's moving," whispered Fastina.

It was moving. A shadow was beginning to inch across the outline of Asia.

The laboratory trembled, but this time the vibration was steady.

They watched in silence as the shadow lengthened over Asia and touched Africa. The coastline of South America came into view.

As the hours passed and the vibration in the laboratory became familiar, the shadow reached Europe and spread into the Atlantic.

Later they saw the whole of the American continent appear. The vibrations increased, as if the engine were labouring.

Sharvis looked calmly at the instruments below the screen.

They could now see the blinding whiteness of the ice-covered Pacific and then they could make out the visible surface of the moon rising from the ice in clear daylight.

The vibrations increased. The laboratory rocked. They were flung to the floor and the picture above them wavered and then became steady again.

From far below them they heard a deep, echoing sound and again the laboratory shook.

Then everything was still.

They looked at one another and at the screen.

The world had stopped turning.

Almer turned to Sharvis. "What's happened? Start the thing up again."

Sharvis chuckled. "Well, well. I've turned the world for you, Andros Almer. But the engine must have reversed its thrust…"

"Keep it turning!" Almer bellowed.

"I'm not sure that I can. Come, we'll investigate."

They followed him as he glided from the laboratory and back to the place where the air cars were.

Again they flew down the tunnel, through the moon and beneath it through the ocean floor until they entered the cave.

The air was scorching hot and there was no longer any moisture on the grotto walls.

They saw the machine. It was now merely a fused tangle of blackened metal.

"Overloaded," Sharvis shouted, and began to laugh.

"You expected this?" Almer called over the roar of his own heartbeats. "Did you?"

Sharvis looked around. "We'd better leave immediately. The section joining the tunnel from the moon to the bed of the sea has been weakened. You can imagine the pressure outside it. If we don't go, we'll be crushed or drowned."

Almer stood up in the air car. "You did this deliberately! You knew the machine was incapable of turning the Earth!"

Sharvis swung the air car into the tunnel. Water was already running in a steady river down its sides.

Almer beat at Sharvis's heavy body, but the scientist continued to chuckle while he guided the air car upwards.

Becker and Fastina clung together as Sharvis increased the speed. There was a strange creaking noise filling the tunnel now.

Eventually they returned to the chamber below the laboratories and Sharvis hurried to the door, with Almer still clinging to him and repeating again and again, "Did you? Did you? Did you?"

Sharvis ignored Almer and entered another room. The wall slid back at his touch and he began to run his seemingly boneless fingers over a console, his eyes on the indicators above. Again the room trembled slightly.

A little later he stepped back.

"I've sealed off the tunnel," he said. "There'll be no trouble there."

Sharvis seemed to be relieved. He turned his pink and red mottled face towards Becker and Fastina and regarded them with his expressionless, faceted eyes.

Almer appeared to have exhausted himself. He lay against a wall mumbling.

"Did you know the engine could not work properly?" Fastina asked Sharvis innocently.

"I have given Almer what he really wanted, I'm sure," Sharvis replied enigmatically. "He wanted the world turned. I turned it. Now his empire lies in the night. Could that be where it belongs?"

"The people," Fastina said. "The ordinary people…"

"Those who wish to escape him may now do so. But few will, I think. The darkness is safe. They can huddle in it until death comes. Isn't that what they want? Haven't I given everyone what they really wish?"

Becker looked at him unemotionally. "Certainly the darkness mirrors the darkness in their minds," he said. "But do they deserve it?"

"Who is to say?" shrugged Sharvis.

Almer stepped forward. "I wish to go home," he said levelly. Apparently he had recovered and had accepted what had happened. It seemed strange to Becker that he should do so with such apparent equanimity.

"You may do as you please," said Sharvis with a trace of malicious humour. It was almost as if he felt he had paid Almer back for the pitiful attempt the man had made on his life. "Will you find your own way out?"

Almer marched from the room. "I have found it, thanks to you," he called as he left.

"And what of you, Clovis Becker?" asked Sharvis. "What will you do now?"

"We will return to my father's tower," Becker said stiffly.

"And raise your children?" Sharvis said. "I trust you will think in time that your sacrifice was worthwhile."

"Maybe." Becker glanced sadly at Fastina. "But will you think the same, Fastina?"

She shook her head. "I don't know, Clovis."

Becker looked suddenly up at Sharvis. "I have just realized," he said. "You have played another joke on us, I believe."

"No," said Sharvis, reading his mind. "The radiation still exists, certainly. But your children's life cycle will be shorter since you will now lack the means to induce longevity. They will have time to adapt and reproduce. And I have made sure that you will never be affected by the radiation. Doubtless you will help father your children's children. It appears to be an established tradition in your family already."

Fastina took Becker's arm. "Let's go, Clovis," she said. "Back to the tower."

"If it means anything," Sharvis told them as they left, "something has changed which might give you encouragement. It is a sentimental thing to say, I know…"

"What's that?" said Fastina, looking back at him.

"You once faced the evening. Now you face the morning. I wish you and your offspring well. Perhaps I will come to see them sometime, or you will send them to see me?"

Even then, as he walked away from the strange scientist, Becker was still unsure if Sharvis was moved by malice or charity, or whether the neutrality he claimed was founded on some deep understanding of life which was available only to him.

E P I L O G U E

The tower now existed in the dawn, but the quality of the light had not altered. The red dust continued to blow and the brown lichen grew around the base of the tower.

The tower's shadow lay behind it now, and the shadow never moved, but one day Fastina told Clovis Becker that she was pregnant.

"Good," he said as he sat immobile by the window watching the distant sun on the horizon, and Fastina put her arms around his neck and kissed his cold face and stroked his unresponsive body, and loved him with a love that now had pity in it.

Mechanically, he reached up with one of his numb hands and touched her arm and continued to stare out at the sun and thought about Orlando Sharvis, wondering still whether the scientist had acted from good intentions or evil, or neither; wondering about himself and what he was; wondering why his wife cried so silently; wondering vaguely why he could not and never would cry with her. He wanted nothing, regretted nothing; feared nothing.

RENARK VON BEK, *Count of the Rim, turns from where the tail of the Chaos ship vanishes down-scale. He eases the strap of his Purdy on his shoulder, takes off his hat and runs his hands through his pale hair. Then he prepares to continue his long walk along the moonbeam roads, to pursue his eternal quest for that lost treasure of antiquity, the stewardship of which his family had undertaken in its earliest centuries; that Grail which he has sworn to restore to Bek. And, as he walks, all his descendants, all his ancestors, walk with him, an eternal champion, eternally reincarnated, eternally destined to destroy all that comforts him, to restore justice and virtue to the multiverse, to seek the peace of fabled Tanelorn, to walk the roads between the worlds.*